Praise for Emily Barr's novels:

'A great read from start to finish . . . believable characters that are variously biting, insightful and sympathetic'
The Times

'This dark, but funny, tale is full of shocking twists, making it a terrific page-turner' *Cosmopolitan*

'We can't praise Emily Barr's novels enough; they're fresh, original and hugely readable' *Glamour*

'Mixing girly infighting with insightful travellers' observations and the joys of motherhood, Barr certainly knows how to spin a yarn' *Guardian*

'A blast of fresh air' *Sunday Express*

'She has a nice line in black humour and the travel details seem absolutely authentic' *Daily Mail*

'Has all the emotional ups and downs of a Marian Keyes novel and none of the annoying travellers of Alex Garland's *The Beach*' *Company*

'Honest, sharply observed, funny and sad' *List*

emily barr
plan B

headline
review

First published in 2005
by REVIEW

First published in paperback in 2006
by REVIEW

An imprint of Headline Book Publishing

1

Cataloguing in Publication Data is available from the British Library

ISBN 0 7553 2542 7

Typeset in Garamond Light by Palimpsest Book Production Limited,
Polmont, Stirlingshire

Printed and bound in Great Britain by
Mackays of Chatham plc, Chatham, Kent

Headline's policy is to use papers that are natural, renewable
and recyclable products and made from wood grown in
sustainable forests. The logging and manufacturing
processes are expected to conform to the environmental
regulations of the country of origin.

HEADLINE BOOK PUBLISHING
A division of Hodder Headline
338 Euston Road
London NW1 3BH

www.reviewbooks.co.uk
www.hodderheadline.com

For James, Gabriel and Sebastien

Thanks to Griselda Muir for bidding at Free Tibet's auction and deciding to have the name Glad Muir included in this book. Thanks also to Kate Ireland, Tim and Heidi Marvin, Jonny Geller, Jane Morpeth and everyone at Headline. And thanks, as ever, to James, Gabe and Seb.

chapter one

February

It was a terrible day to emigrate. The sun was shining. The sky was a deep spring blue. My breath came in clouds all around me.

Clifton Street was beautiful. The tall white houses opposite were bleached by the light. I could smell the sea in the air, hear the distant seagulls. Anne, who lived across the road, was looking at me from inside her bay window. She waved when I looked at her, and motioned to me to come in and see her before we left. I had lived opposite Anne for seven years. I prided myself on knowing all my neighbours. I didn't know any of them very well, but I was on friendly terms with just about everybody at our end of the street. For the past seven years, this house had been my home, my place of safety. I had lived here with lodgers, then with Matt, then with Matt and Alice. I brought my daughter to this house two days after she was born. It was the only home she had ever known, yet she was going to grow up with no memories of it at all.

When I finally accepted that the move was going to

happen, I hoped that we would go in the rain. I wanted all the bad things about the life I was leaving to be spread before me, as reassurance. I wanted spiky rain blown at me by a driving wind, a blanket of black cloud, the street full of uncollected rubbish bags pecked open by seagulls. I wanted to hear drunk stag parties arriving at the station. Ideally, there would have been a Labour Party conference blocking off the seafront with barriers and covered walkways, which always irritated me as I believed that people had a right to see their leaders walking along the street. I hoped that it was going to take us three hours to drive to the ferry port at Newhaven.

Instead, the day was perfect. The rubbish had been collected two days earlier. The seagulls circled far overhead, up in the blueness, screeching in the distance. I knew that we would leave soon. It was all out of my hands, now. We were only going because I had been weak, and because I hated confrontation, and because I always did what Matt suggested, and he knew that.

I was heartbroken. This was an enormous mistake, a massive misjudgement. I imagined myself trying to rectify the situation. I wondered what would happen if I touched the arm of one of the removals men. 'I'm sorry,' I might say. 'I've changed my mind. Would you put all the furniture back, please?'

I was not sure that these removals men would look at me even if I spoke to them. By a strange quirk of science, my physical form appeared to be invisible to their eyes. Soon after they had arrived, at nine in the morning, I had put a tray bearing a cafetière of coffee, four cups, a jug of milk, a bowl of sugar and a plate of biscuits, neatly arranged, on the front wall. Even then, they had ignored me, but for a collective grunt that might have been 'cheers'. They were more than happy to chat to Matt, to accept his questionable help and his diffident instructions. They looked straight through me when I tried to catch their eyes with my polished, cheerful smile.

I sat on the next-door neighbours' low wall and watched the exodus of the boxes, each one marked by me with thick black pen and labelled by the removals men with a yellow sticker. I saw a box marked 'Alice's toys' pass by, followed by 'Matt's books' and 'Emma's shoes'. My life was in those boxes. My life, Matt's life, Alice's life. Nothing I said or did was going to stop the move from happening. I had sold my house. It had never been Matt's house, always mine. I was proud of it. It was a city centre cottage, with small rooms and low ceilings. It felt homely. I had painted all the walls, picked up cheap furniture wherever I could, and I had made it my own. Mine, and Matt's, and Alice's.

I was trying to be proud of myself now, for the obscene amount of money I had made from it. I had bought it for almost nothing and had sold it for a third of a million pounds. Now it belonged to a pleasant professional couple who were moving down from London. If I had asked them, if they had heard me, the removals men would not have been able to replace everything. It was too late to cancel. I had a new house, and it was in Gascony.

Matt and Alice and I were moving to France. We had known it for months. Until last week, the idea had meant little more to me than it had to Alice, who had parroted

'Moob-a-Pance', meaninglessly, at anyone within earshot. For months, I had efficiently blocked out reality, and made the whole insane adventure into an interesting talking point. I had assured myself that it could not really be going to happen, that everything would inevitably fall through at some point in the long and complicated process. It had seemed phenomenally unlikely that such an outlandish scheme could work out; it was, I knew, just another of Matt's wild ideas.

Before Alice had come along, he had proposed a move to South Africa, where we would buy a vineyard near Cape Town, and sell our wines directly to Oddbins. 'I have a good contact at Oddbins,' he had assured me, as if this made the plan foolproof.

After that, he had posited that I might care to take my newborn daughter to Thailand, where the three of us would buy a beach hut and make some kind of idealised living from catching fish and picking fruit.

It was currently extremely fashionable to pine loudly for a house in rural France and, although Matt had seemed serious when he started on about it, I had assumed that he was simply repeating conversations he had had with his colleagues. I had played along to humour him. 'Yes,' I had agreed blithely. 'A big house in the French countryside would be just the thing. Good schools, cheap property, bilingual children. Mmmm. It would be perfect.'

It had been stupid of me to encourage him, but I'd had no idea that he was serious. Everybody watched documentaries about people making that move. Everybody said they wanted to do it. Nobody actually went through with it.

Plan B

Nobody that I knew had ever seriously considered it. As far as I was aware, a few of Matt's colleagues had darling little farmhouses in Provence or the Dordogne, but they stood empty for most of the year, then hosted crowds of squabbling families through the summer. Nobody actually spent the winter in the south of France. Nobody but us.

I had put my house on the market in the sincere hope that no one would want to buy it. At that price, I didn't expect the offers to flood in. I had agreed with Matt that we would make an offer for a big stone house in the Gascon countryside, on the assumption that the offer wouldn't be accepted, that we wouldn't get a mortgage, and that something in French law would prevent us from buying it. It had all been a game. Then a couple of barristers had loved my house and exclaimed over how reasonably priced it was, compared with London. They offered the asking price after the estate agent told them that a fictitious 'cash buyer' was on the verge of snapping it up. A week ago, we had exchanged contracts. My house, my home, was no longer mine. The silly plan had suddenly become real. I realised how stupid I had been.

I never behaved rashly. I did not make brave moves or step into the unknown. It was not in my character to do anything that had not been thoroughly thought through and declared to be safe. Left to myself, I would not have left Clifton Street. I would not have seen any reason to go to a different part of Brighton, let alone abroad. Alice would have gone to the primary school on the next street and when she got older I would have found her the best comprehensive in town. I had never lived in the country, and I had never wanted to. I liked cities. I liked knowing that there were people all around me. I felt safety in numbers, and I liked being an anonymous member of a crowd.

In fact, I had lived in the country once. My mother and I had lived in a village in Hampshire until I was three. Then she had died. That was when I had been taken to London and reshaped as a city girl. The country was another world to me now. I had grown up in a big house in Holloway, with my cousins and my aunt and uncle. Geoff and Christa still lived there, so I had my childhood home. Christa and Geoff were the only parents I had ever known, since I had almost no memories of my mother. Their three children were, to all intents and purposes, my siblings. Bella, my eldest sister, was married, and I was as good as married, but Bella and I both retained our old bedrooms, replete with single beds and pink and purple decor, in Holloway. We all went back there at Christmas, with husbands, partners and offspring in tow, and we always had a magical time. I made sure of it. Magical times were important.

I forced a smile as a neighbour, a young mother from halfway down the street, walked by and beamed at me.

'Off today, then?' she asked. Paula was always full of energy. She was pushing a double pushchair, which contained her twins Tallulah and Nemo, and she was heavily pregnant.

'Hey, wow!' she exclaimed, without waiting for my reply. 'Nobody told me you were having another! When's it due?'

I looked down at my stomach. I was wearing a jumper that was tight around my stomach, and as I looked, I saw that she was right. I did look pregnant.

'That'll be a French baby!' she continued, and I searched for the right words to let her know about her mortifying mistake. 'Congratulations.'

I gave up. 'Thanks,' I said, and stood up to pretend I was needed back in the house. As soon as she had gone indoors, I sat back down on the wall. I had been meaning to lose weight but I could never quite be bothered.

The sound of the phone ringing made me leap back to my feet. I rushed inside to answer it, aware that I was almost certainly answering my telephone for the last time. I was surprised it hadn't already been cut off.

'Hello?' I asked breathlessly. My voice seemed to echo in the unfurnished house.

'So you're still there! That's good.' It was my aunt. 'How's it going?'

'You know.' I looked around the bare hallway, and flattened myself against a wall to make way for two men carrying a large cupboard. I pulled the phone into the sitting room and stood in the bay window watching the last pieces of furniture and boxes going into the van. 'Looking pretty bare.' A lump rose to my throat. I wanted to stay so much that it hurt. Christa knew that. She thought the move was a mistake. She was angry, in her buttoned-up, tight-lipped way, that Matt had forced me into it. She was angry with me for capitulating.

'We're just ringing to say good luck. You take care of yourself. Let Matt do everything that needs doing. Just look after yourself and ring any time you want. *Any* time, OK?'

I nodded. 'Mmmm,' I said, not trusting myself to speak.

'Have a good journey. Ring us when you're there.'

'OK.'

'And give Alice a big kiss. Here's Geoff.'

I smiled as Christa handed over to my uncle. Christa couldn't get off the phone quickly enough, and I knew it was because she was uncomfortable saying things like 'ring *any* time'. Everyone thought she was prickly and difficult. Matt found her impossible. I thought I understood her, and I knew that this call was her way of saying she loved me.

Geoff, on the other hand, was perpetually jolly but spent as much time as possible shut away in his study. He left all the decisions to his wife and provided a benevolent presence when required.

'*Bon voyage*,' he said now. 'Look, Emma. If this doesn't work out, you can always come back. *You* bought that pile out there, so that means someone else would too. There's always a place for you and Alice here in sunny Holloway.' I heard Christa say something in the background. 'Matt, too,' he added.

None of my family would ever have said they didn't like Matt. Matt was charming and chatty, and everyone in the world got on with him. But three months earlier, Matt and I had invited Christa and Geoff and my cousins Bella and Charlotte to Brighton for the weekend, and had told them about our plans.

'Wow,' said Bella. 'France. Fantastic! Lucky you. Living the dream, hey?'

'Will you have a pool?' Charlotte had demanded. 'Lots of spare rooms? Hey, will you have one of those brilliant Frenchwomen as a cleaner – the ones in the print overalls?'

She, Bella and Matt had all roared with laughter. I had noticed Christa and Geoff both staring at me.

Plan B

'Emma?' Geoff had said. 'You don't seem excited.'

I assured Geoff that I would come back to Holloway any time I needed to, though I knew I wouldn't. I hung up the phone and looked around. With the furniture gone, every mark on the cream walls was noticeable. There were rectangles where pictures had hung, and a surprising number of pencilled scribbles at Alice's height. I wondered how she had made them without my noticing.

If things didn't work out for us all in France, I knew we would come straight back to Brighton. I could not have lived in London again. I didn't even like visiting any more. It unnerved me. It was bad for me.

I had left London when I was twenty-four. I was scared there. Something strange had started happening to me. My anxiety was spinning out of control. I had a reasonably well-paid job working for a charity, and I enjoyed what I did – essentially, creating order from chaos – but away from my desk, I could barely function. On the way to work I worried that the tube might break down and make me late, or that I would get stuck in a tunnel in the dark, squashed up against invisible strangers. If I was out after dark, as I inevitably was when I left work in the winter, I was perpetually on guard against being mugged. It had never happened. If I passed a man or a group of men on the street, I crossed the road as a precautionary measure. However, if any of them were black, I was terrified that crossing the road made me racist, so instead I would walk past, trying to look confident, while my heart pounded and my muscles tensed, ready to run.

Every day, I would get home from work and bolt the door

behind me. I shared a flat with my cousin, Charlotte, who had the opposite attitude to life to my own. Charlotte and I had never been best friends. I had adored Bella from an early age, but Charlotte thought I was dull and I thought she was reckless to the point of stupidity. During those London years, I lay awake in bed until three in the morning, waiting for the sound of her key in the lock. Often she had company. I waited until the footsteps, the giggling, and often the sex noises had died away, and then I would pad out of my room to double lock the door and put the chain on. Occasionally I would bump into a conquest outside the bathroom and would exchange embarrassed greetings. Charlotte's conquests seemed extremely random.

Charlotte had long, platinum-blonde hair and a skinny body, and she hated being seen with me and Bella because, as she used to say, 'One look at you two and they know I'm not a natural blonde.'

'Most of them probably find out soon enough,' Bella would reply, and they would laugh while I struggled to get the joke.

London had been too much for me. I hated seeing so many homeless people. I could not give money to all of them, but I felt I ought to. I particularly hated seeing homeless women; I *had* given money to all of them, and I still did, because it turned out that the homelessness problem was nearly as bad in Brighton. I continued to worry about Charlotte. She was single and I knew she still enjoyed indiscriminate sex. These days she was a struggling actress, so I worried, as well, about her precarious financial situation. I worried about my younger cousin, Greg. He was away travelling. The fact that I could not imagine the dangers he was facing in Cambodia made it easier, in a way, but the nagging fear never went away. Greg was the baby of our family, and all of us felt protective of him. I thought this might have been a factor in the development of his habit of boarding a long-haul flight whenever he had the chance.

In London, I began to be scared by my own neuroses. The fears spiralled: I became scared of being scared, and my world started to close in on me. I realised that I was not rational, that I was infuriating Charlotte and worrying Christa.

Brighton was the perfect compromise. As soon as I arrived here, I calmed down. I came to Brighton shortly before everyone else in London decided to do the same, and I managed to buy my little house for £90,000. It had seemed like a lot, but I'd had a deposit saved up and the mortgage was relatively small. I still commuted up, until I had Alice, but my office was near Farringdon station, so I could take the Thameslink train almost to the door. I never had to go on the tube or fight through the crowds. I felt safe again. After my maternity leave, I resigned and took a part-time job with a small charity here. I walked to work and dropped Alice at nursery on the way.

Life in the middle of Brighton was easy. It was conven-ient. I knew that everything I needed was within walking distance. There was a Marks and Spencer's food store at the station, two minutes' walk away, and it was open for all my waking hours. I could always nip out to buy milk, or a pizza for dinner, or chocolate. I bought my paper from a newsagent up the hill. Two minutes away, in the North Laine, there was a fine array of cafés and restaurants, and friendly, non-chain shops. There were parks and playgrounds, children's music, painting and yoga groups. Walking along the seafront made me happy, whatever the weather. In many ways I preferred it out of season, when the sky was slaty grey and the sea its mirror. Alice would rush up and down the esplanade and I would watch her. She threw stones into the sea while I held her hand. Matt and I took her to the pier and indulged her obsession with one particular ride where she rode a Barbie motorbike. There were very few people around on a Sunday morning in winter. I liked that.

I stepped outside and sat back down on the wall. It was getting colder, and I hugged myself to keep warm. I watched Matt emerging from the house bearing one end of a box of books. I knew we had packed some of them too full, so they would be really heavy. Matt was smiling under the pressure.

That was the main reason I liked Brighton. I liked it because I had met Matt here, four years ago. Meeting him had demonstrated to me that my decision to move here had been absolutely the right one. We were introduced in a café by a university acquaintance I had never imagined I would see again, and from that day on he had been the centre of my life. I imagined the way I would be now had I stayed in London. A life without Matt, a world without Alice. It was impossible. Matt still worked in London, and usually stayed overnight for at least half of the week, but when he was with us, we were a perfect unit, and when he was away, we looked forward to his return. I never took him for granted. On days when he managed to work at home, I loved listening to him on the phone, or typing on his laptop, in the little study at the back of the house. 'Smith here,' he would always say on the phone. It was one of his idiosyncrasies.

And today, I was leaving. In France, our nearest shop was going to be ten kilometres away. Everything would shut down for lunch. Every café would be smoky. Even though I had once spoken fluent French, I would struggle to communicate. I would be acutely and constantly aware of being an outsider. Matt would still be working in London for most of the week, so now he would be five hundred miles away from me, rather than fifty. I liked France for holidays. I would never have considered it as a potential home. Not even after watching umpteen thousand documentaries about people moving there.

Matt sat down next to me, on the wall. His eyes were shining and his face was flushed.

'All done,' he announced.

'All done?' I echoed. I looked up. One of the men closed the back of the lorry while the engine revved impatiently. Then he leapt into the front passenger seat and slammed the door behind him. We watched the truck pulling out and driving down the street.

I looked at Matt. He was happy in a genuine, straightforward way. Everything about him was glowing. I realised that he really was delighted to be making this move. I had assumed that his enthusiasm was exaggerated to counter my reluctance, but now I saw that it was not. Even now, sitting on a low wall next to the empty shell that had been the home we had shared, even now, when we could barely imagine the day-to-day reality of the life that lay before us, Matt had no doubts.

'Christa on the phone?' he asked. I nodded. 'Am I still the bogeyman?'

'Of course you're not.'

'Dragging their poor helpless little girl across the sea, away from them?'

'It's not like that,' I said weakly. 'Not at all.'

Matt was going to stand out in France. He looked English. I didn't; I could easily pass for French and so could Alice. We were short and dark. Matt was tall and thin. His hair was dirty blond, like straw that has been in a barn for a while, and in the sun he turned a deep pink even when he was wearing factor fifty. Matt had a kind face; an open face. I always knew what he was thinking. He was charismatic, larger than life. I often wondered what he was doing with me. I knew I was no great catch; and yet he cherished me. I knew that he was selfish, but I never criticised him for it, never mentioned it, because I was so grateful that he had decided to spend his life with me. I was annoyed that Christa and Geoff had made their feelings plain to Matt. I didn't want him to hold that against me.

'You're happy,' I observed.

He draped an arm over my shoulders. 'Emma,' he said. 'Of course I am.' His blue eyes crinkled as he smiled down. 'We're embarking on an enormous adventure. I know you're not excited about it, but you will be.'

I leaned on him and tried to imagine it. I was desolate. I searched for something positive to say. I did not want Matt to see the depths of my desolation. No one saw my depths. I didn't want to see them myself.

Plan B

'It's a leap of faith,' I told him, eventually, with a small smile. He grinned back.

'Something like this is always a leap of faith.'

'It doesn't appear to be for you.'

He kissed the top of my head. 'I do know that it's different for me,' he conceded. 'I'm going to be commuting every week. Half my life will still be in London. Much easier to deal with.' He pulled back and looked into my eyes, and I caught my breath at the effect he had on me.

'That,' I told him, 'is the first time you've admitted it.'

'I know. Sorry. I admit it now. I keep my job, I go on planes twice a week, I have the best of all possible worlds.'

'I'll work in London,' I told him suddenly, desperately, and I meant it. I could live in London again if I had to. I could stay with Christa and Geoff. 'You stay in the middle of nowhere with Alice every day, and I'll work to support us all.' I looked into his smiling eyes. He did not even consider that I might be serious. He knew I would hate to be back in London, that I didn't enjoy flying, that I had never spent a night of my daughter's life away from her. And I would have hated it, but it was infinitely more appealing than the alternative.

'I had a dream that we had dinner with Bill and Hillary Clinton,' he said, changing the subject suddenly with transparent desperation. 'That has to be a good omen, doesn't it?'

'Was Hillary going to run for president?'

'Yes. That was why we were having dinner with them.'

'If she was seeking our campaign advice, that's probably a good omen.'

15

We were interrupted by Anne. She strolled across the road and sat on my other side.

'So you're off?' she asked, looking at the lorry, which had paused at the Give Way sign at the end of the street, and was indicating right. Anne was a lovely woman, an artist who seemed to do ceaseless voluntary work. She was small and blonde and the corners of her mouth were always twitching into a smile.

'Looks that way,' Matt agreed.

I assumed my best cheerful look, for her benefit. 'You will come and see us, won't you?' This had become my mantra, lately. I was desperate for friends to visit. The thought of familiar people coming to see us, of our life in France being a kind of extended holiday for friends and family, made it all seem bearable. I could imagine myself as a useful hostess.

'Of course we will,' she said warmly. 'You lucky things. We adore France. We'll be thinking of you out there in the sunshine.'

'I'm sure you'll have plenty of sun here, too,' I told her, looking up at the deep blue of the sky. 'You'll have to let us know what the new people are like,' I added. I was slightly jealous of the people who had bought my house. I didn't want Anne and the other neighbours to like them better than they had liked us.

I kissed her goodbye.

'Oooh, two cheeks,' she said. '*Très français!*'

Matt shepherded me into our car, which he had filled to the brim with stuff, leaving only Alice's car seat empty. I was grateful that he had done it all, that I did not have to go back into the empty house. He dropped the keys through the letter box. I slammed the passenger door. Matt started the engine and looked at me. He raised his eyebrows, smiled, leaned over and kissed me. I did my best to look brave. I had no other option.

A few other neighbours came out as we pulled away, and we opened our windows and waved until we had turned the corner. We were going to stop at the nursery and pick Alice up, and then we were driving to Newhaven.

I swallowed hard and concentrated on thinking about the journey. I did my best not to consider what might await me at the end of it.

chapter two

A solitary tractor was sitting forlornly in the corner of a field, under a looming sky. It was the first vehicle we had seen in ten miles.

'Look, Alice,' I said, dully. 'Tractor.'

Matt looked across at me as he changed gear, and smiled bravely. 'Not quite the way we imagined it,' he said. His laugh was short and forced. I sensed him watching me, anxious about my state of mind. He looked at the road, in the mirror, then quickly back to me. He wanted me to pull myself together and to tell him that this was a temporary blip, that everything would be fine.

I could not smile back. For once, I didn't even pretend to be happy.

'No,' I told him. 'It's not.'

We were nearly at our house. Alice was demanding to see the tractor, but it was already far behind us. It was four o'clock in the afternoon, and it was almost dark. The clouds had been building during our mammoth drive. Now they were black. The headlights were on. The storm was going to break at any moment.

We were driving past field after field. There didn't seem to be anything growing in any of them, and the marooned tractor was the only sign of farming life. The clouds were descending. The landscape looked forlorn, barren, dead. There were no other cars on the roads. There were no leaves on the trees. Matt had promised me spring in the south of France. He had mentioned cherry blossom and sunshine and rosé on the terrace. The terrace did not exist, yet. Neither did the blossom. I would have preferred a cup of tea to a bottle of rosé, though I had little appetite for anything.

This was the road that led to our house. Our nearest town, St Paul, was behind us now. We were heading into deepest countryside, towards the tiny hamlet that was, somehow, our home.

'Mummeeeeeee!' called Alice from the back. 'Mumm-EEEEE! Where's the tractor?'

I turned round and looked at my little girl. She was frowning, bored and cross. Her brown hair was matted with the chocolate we had been giving her for the past two hours to keep her quiet. She was sitting next to boxes and bags filled with everything that was going to keep us going until the lorry arrived, sometime within the next week. Her books and toys were strewn on top of the bags. Alice fixed me with an intense stare, and restated her demands. 'I want to see the tractor,' she said forcefully. 'Let's go back to the boat. I want milk.' She thought for a moment. 'More choco-late,' she added, for good measure.

Her hair had been cut before we left, so she had a perfectly straight bob with a blunt fringe. I had dressed her for the journey in my favourite of her outfits: a blue corduroy pinafore over a red top, with red tights and blue shoes. I had wanted her to look like an immaculate French child, but she was smeared with chocolate and covered in biscuit crumbs. I was going to have to wrap her in sweaters and a blanket to carry her into the house. I had bought into the idea of spring so completely that I hadn't even brought her winter coat with us. It would arrive later, in the removal lorry.

'Let's look out for another tractor,' I suggested. 'Anyway, we're nearly there.' I tried to sound as if this were a good thing. 'Nearly at our new house. When we get there we can explore.'

'I want milk.'

'Daddy will go to the shop and get some milk.'

'Want milk now.'

Matt half turned. I could see from his face that he was feeling the strain of being the person solely responsible for this move. Although he had contributed nothing financially to the whole adventure, beyond paying for the removal, he still managed to be the Head of the Family, and he was very much in charge.

'You can't have milk now because you've drunk it all already,' he said slowly and clearly. 'Look, this is our road. First person to see our house gets a chocolate button.'

We turned a corner. Suddenly, it was before us: a stone house set apart from the rest of the hamlet. It was huge and closed, uninhabited for years. It loomed above us. In the steely half-light, it was forbidding and unwelcoming. The façade was peeling. The shutters were closed. The creeper was dead.

Matt looked at me. I said nothing. He turned to Alice.

'Well?' he asked. 'Can you see our house?'

She shook her head, confidently. 'No.'

He stopped the car, turned the engine off, and pointed. 'This one here. This is our house,' he announced. Then he took a new packet of chocolate buttons from the ashtray, ripped it open, and poured its contents into his mouth. Brown saliva dribbled down his chin. As he chewed, he held his head in his hands.

I was steeling myself to leave the car, to take the first footsteps over the threshold of our new life, when the clouds burst. One moment the car, the house, the road were dry. Then, instantly, they were soaked. Matt opened his door, closed it again and looked at me, grinning nervously with his mouth but not his eyes. He knew I would smile back, because that was what I always did. I always put a brave face on things and made sure everyone else was all right.

I fell into line, and forced out a laugh.

'OK,' I said, affixing a smile. 'It's raining. Rain happens. It doesn't matter.'

'I want to get out of mine car seat!' called Alice imperiously. I reached back and unclipped her straps, and she clambered across the handbrake onto Matt's lap. Alice was unambiguously a daddy's girl. It pained me, sometimes. They would go off into their own little world, share their own jokes, stroke each other's faces. Matt spent so much time working, so many nights away from us, that his presence was the cause of endless excitement. I did everything for Alice every day, and so I was as dull as wallpaper. I knew that it was my very constancy that made me less exciting. That was what I wanted, really. I wanted to be the kind of mother who could be taken for granted, who could instil a sense of security that would only be appreciated in retrospect. I would have been quite pleased, however, if I had been able, even occasionally, to provoke a fraction of the excitement and affection that Matt did.

Alice took the steering wheel and pretended to drive. Matt and I watched rain coursing down the windscreen. Everything outside was distorted. The water was coming down so heavily that the short run up the garden path was going to leave all three of us soaked. This didn't matter. It was a detail. What mattered was that we would soon be in our new home, that we would make it warm and cosy, despite the lack of furniture, and that we would all get a hot bath. What mattered was that nobody was allowed to acknowledge that, so far, it was shaping up to be a disaster.

I took charge.

'Right,' I said, dredging up some brightness. 'Right' was a word I often used. It signalled no-nonsense, optimistic enthusiasm. A fresh start. I saw Matt's features relaxing slightly. Emma was making everything all right, as usual.

The rain on the windscreen turned to hail. It bounced onto the glass and up again. The stones were large. This was not polite British hail. It was its more dramatic continental cousin.

'Right,' I said again. 'We're going to run for it. I'll go first and unlock the door. You bring Alice. I'll take a couple of bags. We can sort the rest out later.'

Plan B

Matt looked at me. He was sheepish. He was, I knew, hoping that I wasn't going to mention his fulsome promises of sunshine. No one is in a position to make promises about the weather, particularly not in February. I had allowed myself to believe that the sunshine was guaranteed because I had wanted to believe it.

'It may be hailing,' I told Matt and Alice stoically, 'but it's still the south of France. We're still going to have more sunshine than England. Later in the year.'

'I suppose this is Europe,' Matt agreed glumly. 'It's not the Caribbean.'

'And thank goodness it's not,' I told him. I hated sounding like a Girl Guide. It was, however, my default position. 'All that sand getting everywhere. Having to watch Alice with the sea all day long. It would be terrible.'

We both looked out at the road and our overgrown front garden, both of which were covered with stones of ice.

'Awful,' Matt agreed. We looked at each other and laughed. 'Come on then,' he said, opening his door a crack. 'Race you.'

We rushed to the front door. Hailstones pricked my cheeks and stung my eyes. I saw Alice burying her face in Matt's shoulder. His arms enveloped her. She burrowed into him. As we ran into the wind, I felt a rush of love for them both. I shifted from one foot to the other while I struggled with the door. There were three huge wrought-iron keys on the ring, as well as seven smaller ones. The first big key I tried didn't fit. The second fitted into the lock, but didn't turn. As I fumbled with the third, a gust of wind almost lifted me off my feet. It blew a faceful of hail directly at me. Alice began to wail.

'I don't like it!' she said. 'I don't like it I don't like it I don't like it. I WANT TO GO HOME.'

The key turned in the lock. I gave the door a hard shove with my shoulder, and Matt and I stepped inside. Matt pulled the door shut behind him.

It was colder indoors than out. It smelt musty, and the whole house was pitch black. I fumbled for a light switch. Nothing happened when I pressed it. The wind blew the front door wide open, and a pile of hailstones hit the cold tiled floor.

'Um, this *is* home, darling,' said Matt, stroking Alice's hair.

In the gloomy half-light, our eyes met over her head. I looked away.

There was no electricity and the heating wasn't working. The interior of the house was icy and it was impossible to stand still. We had corresponded with Electricité de France, and we had been told, by Marie, that there was plenty of fuel left in the heating tank. We opened a few sets of shutters, and rushed in and out of the house, unloading the car, while Alice stood in the hallway looking stunned. She was red-eyed and puffy-faced, and she was sobbing with intermittent, shocked gasps. The hail turned back into rain, but it showed no sign of abating.

We had brought with us everything we had imagined that we might be going to need before the lorry arrived. Thus we had a big blow-up mattress for the three of us, sleeping bags for us all, and a blanket. We had tea bags, and a few utensils. I checked that the gas rings were working – they were, by some oversight – and boiled water to make black tea. We had a torch, but no candles, so I tried to do everything that needed to be done while there was still a small amount of what passed for daylight. Matt left Alice and me huddled together on the lilo, and set off for supplies. I made a nervous call to Electricité de France and hoped that I had succeeded in getting our power restored at some point in the future.

'Come on,' I said to a very confused Alice, forcing myself to keep up the jollity. The last thing I wanted was to face reality at that particular moment. 'This is exciting, isn't it? We're camping inside a house.'

She frowned at me, cross and suspicious. 'Why camping inside a house?'

'Because we haven't got our furniture yet, but it will come.'

'Why haven't got our furniture yet?'

'Because it's coming on the lorry. It should be here next week.'

'Why should be here next week?'

'Because that's when the lorry will get here.'

'Why that's when the lorry will get here?'

'It just is.' All my conversations with Alice seemed to end with a firm 'It just is' on my part. Unfortunately, Alice did not always recognise it as final.

'Why it just is?' she continued.

'Because. It. Just. Is. Now, shall we . . .' I cast around quickly for an activity. 'Shall we explore the house? This is our new house.'

She shook her head. 'I want to go home to our real house. I want mine nursery rhyme CD.'

'We haven't got our CD player yet,' I reminded her. 'It's coming on the lorry.'

'Why it's coming on the lorry?'

'Come on, let's have a look around.'

Alice and I held hands, and walked round our new home, opening it up. I opened so many shutters that my hair was soon drenched again. It hadn't dried from the last time. I felt myself freezing to the bones.

We had first seen this house in October. It had been an Indian summer, and even to me, reluctant as I was to find a new home, it had been seductive. It was a big old farmhouse, and it had stayed wonderfully cool in the hot autumn. The floors were covered with old tiles. The plaster was crumbling from the walls. The house had belonged to an old woman who had died ten years before. Her children had finally agreed that they would sell it, and they had been delighted to find foreign buyers who were going to renovate it.

Matt had been in heaven from the moment we drove around that corner and laid eyes on the white house, with its terracotta tiled roof and the fig tree in the front garden. We had pulled up outside, with Ella, the estate agent. The fig tree was laden with fruit. Every window was open. The small front garden had been carefully tended, and the bushes, flowers and trees were tidy and pruned, with the odd late bloom. The air had smelt of pollen and warmth. The house was still partly furnished and, crucially, it had not looked as if it was going to need very much attention.

'This is it,' Ella had said, smiling at Matt's rapt reaction. She was a sensible Swiss woman who knew exactly what Matt was looking for, and had led us directly to it. This was only the second house we had seen.

We stepped into the hall, which smelt old and atmospheric, as old houses do, particularly in France. Alice looked to the end of the corridor, where the French windows had been open onto the back garden. She ran straight out to play on the grass before we had even said hello to Marie, the old lady's daughter-in-law. Marie followed her out, and told us firmly that she was going to take care of Alice while we looked around.

'*Vous êtes chez vous*,' she called back to us, cheerfully.

'We are, you know,' Matt said softly. 'We really could be.'

It had been lovely when the outside temperature was thirty-five degrees. Both of us had pictured Alice and future children running in and out of the house in bare feet and cotton dresses, brown legs exposed. I had seen myself tending the fruit trees, making jam, perhaps painting the odd watercolour while my brood were at school. I had imagined Matt sauntering in from the airport, changing directly into shorts and a T-shirt, and the two of us sharing some cold wine on the terrace we would lay outside, while Alice and her younger brothers and sisters climbed trees and played happily together, calling to each other in a mixture of French and English. I had, in October, compared that vision with our terraced house and handkerchief of garden in Brighton, and I had realised that I was not able to say no.

Now it was freezing outside, and below freezing indoors. A house that was cool in summer due to its thick stone walls, cold tiled floors and charmingly ill-fitting windows was, by definition, going to be arctic in winter. My breath appeared in front of me in clouds. What I could see of the garden outside through the sheets of rain was dead and grim. It had all been folly. We had bought into an escapist dream that had been cunningly sold to us by television documentaries and glossy magazine features, and cemented by the fact that this area looked pretty in sunlight. Matt had bought into it and I had failed to resist in the face of his enthusiasm. Of course that dream had been based on nothing. Nobody could really leave their home and expect to step into Utopia. Life was not like that. If it had really been possible to find an idyllic new life just a few hundred miles from Britain, everyone would have been doing it. They were not. They were just watching it on telly and getting on with their lives. Everybody else was more sensible than us. We had been ridiculous. We were stupid. I knew that Matt would agree with me and hoped that within a month or so we would be able to reverse this ludicrous move and return home to Brighton, poor but wiser.

We went upstairs carefully, one step at a time, and shone the torch around. I didn't bother to open the shutters up there because I knew I would only have to shut them all again when it got fully dark, and I knew that the view of the dead foliage outside would not have lightened the mood. There were relatively few shutters upstairs anyway, as there were no windows at all in the back of the house. The whole of the back façade was closed but for a single door, apparently because the wind and rain came from the west, and in the days before central heating, people liked to shut it all out. I could sympathise.

Alice ran ahead of me, and I angled the torch anxiously to light her way.

Plan B

'Mummy!' she exclaimed in amazed delight. 'It's raining inside the house!'

She was jumping in a puddle that covered most of the upstairs landing. I forced a laugh. This was the first time she had sounded happy since we had driven off the ferry.

'So it is, darling,' I said with an enthusiasm whose irony was lost on my daughter. 'It's raining through a hole in the roof *and* a hole in the attic floor! We'd better see if we can find some pans to collect the water.'

It had obviously been 'raining inside the house' all winter. The beautiful oak floorboards in the upstairs hallway were discoloured and beginning to warp. The water had passed through the attic to get there. I dreaded to think what state the attic was in, above our heads. I vowed not to go up there. Matt could check the state of it. I ran downstairs, forbidding Alice to move, and grabbed all the old pots and pans that I could locate in the cupboard. When every drip I could find was landing sonorously in metal, I searched around for something to mop up the puddles with. All I could find was a dusty pink bedspread that was under the stairs. It didn't soak up all the water, but it was better than nothing.

I hoped that the water was not going to come through the floorboards and make the hall ceiling collapse. There wasn't very much I could do except attempt to tone Alice's behaviour down.

'Alice!' I said sharply. 'Please stop jumping. It's dangerous.'

Alice glared at me, but she stopped without even asking why.

'It's mine turn,' she said sullenly, and she took the torch and strode ahead of me into the main bedroom.

'Careful!' I cautioned her.

'Mummy?' she called a moment later, her voice serious. 'What's that?'

She was pointing the torch into a corner of our future bedroom, and looking intently at something. I rushed to her side. My heart sank.

'It's a mouse,' I told her. It was, to be more accurate, the rotting corpse of a former mouse. It looked as if it had been there for some time. Parts of its entrails were on the floor next to it. Its glassy eyes stared at something past our heads.

Alice was transfixed. 'Why's it not squeaking? Eeee, eee,' she said, encouragingly, to the body.

'It's . . .' I hesitated. As usual, I could not bring myself to say the word.

I had long dreaded the day when Alice would become aware of the concept of death. I dreaded the string of whys that would have followed any truthful explanation of the state of the mouse. I wanted to protect her from the fear, from the creeping realisation that one day I would die, that Matt would die, that even she would die. I felt vehemently about protecting her. When I was barely older than she was, death had come into my life abruptly. My daughter was never going to suffer anything remotely similar. I wanted her childhood to be different from mine. I wanted her to be protected and cosseted by two adoring parents, for ever. I wanted hers to be a world without the possibility of abandonment. I wanted to preserve her assumption of universal immortality for as long as I possibly could.

I had always looked with curiosity upon those who had it easy. There had been plenty of them at school, girls and boys who thought they were victims of cruelty because their parents would not let them go clubbing on school nights. They got 'depressed' about homework, were 'traumatised' by the break-up of silly teenage flings. Their world fell apart if they could not afford the right shoes for the party. I never considered myself depressed or traumatised, but I knew that these children were spoilt, secure, unbelievably lucky. I envied them, even without knowing exactly what was wrong with my own life. I never had a real boyfriend until I met Matt, just in case relationships really were as catastrophic and consuming as my classmates, and my sisters, made them appear. I had short-lived, half-hearted affairs instead. I never got involved.

Alice was going to be one of the lucky ones. Alice would never have to worry about anything worse than clothes. She would be 'stressed' over the choice between the Sorbonne and Oxford. She would go out with a spotty boy for a month and be devastated when they broke up.

She was never going to have to explain her family situation. She would never utter the wretched words 'my dad's girlfriend' or 'my mum's new bloke'. I had always pitied the people who'd had to force their mouths round those phrases. In a way that would have been even worse than the explanation I had always had to give: 'They're not actually my parents, they're my aunt and uncle. My mum died and I never had a dad.' In the end I used to say that he was dead too. People respected me, as an orphan. It gave me cachet at school, and then, later on, it had somehow made me desirable. My father could be dead, for all I knew.

I knew that Alice would be even more secure if Matt and

31

I were married. He had hinted that he might find himself ready to bend his principles on that point once we were settled in France. I would love it. I would be properly happy if I had a ring on my finger and the promise of security for ever. Alice would love it.

'This mouse is ill,' I told her firmly. 'We have to leave it alone. When it gets better it will run away.'

In the reflected light of the torch, I could not catch the exact look my daughter gave me, but I thought it could roughly be interpreted as, 'yeah, right'. Thankfully, she did not press the point, although I knew she would come back to the subject later. We carried on exploring, to the point where we discovered that Marie had removed the entire contents of the ensuite bathroom: everything but the bidet was gone.

When Matt returned, we were playing with Alice's dinosaurs. The living room was as cosy as an empty room with a tiled floor and no heating could be on a February evening. I had thought about building a fire in the grate but had been unable to face going to the garden to gather up wet wood that would only have smouldered and made everything smell smoky.

Alice and I were huddled together on the lilo, wrapped in a sleeping bag, and the dinosaurs were having a party. The mummy and daddy dinosaurs were drinking from my mug of black tea, and the Alice dinosaurs (all of the smaller ones were named Alice) were sharing their namesake's glass of water.

A gust of cold air came in with Matt. I could smell the rain. He stood on the threshold and smiled broadly.

'Hello, girls!' he said loudly.

I looked at him. His hair was hanging down in rat's tails. He looked different with it plastered to the sides of his face. It was darker like that. His coat looked heavy with water. Still, he was smiling.

'Hello!' I replied with self-conscious jollity.

'Daddy!' Alice ran over to him. 'There's a funny mouse. There isn't a loo.'

Matt looked amused. 'Is that the latest bulletin? There isn't a loo? Please tell me you're joking.'

'There is downstairs,' I told him. 'But not upstairs. It seems to have vanished somewhere in the purchase proceedings. Along with the bath and the basin.'

'And the bidet?'

'No, they left the bidet.'

'So we can wash our bums. That's a relief.'

'Isn't it just?'

'Just as well, then, that I stocked up on a sizeable quantity of local wine and a bottle of brandy.'

Matt hung his coat on the door and, in the absence of a towel, rubbed his hair with his hands. He gave off a spray of water, like a dog. We sat down on the lilo. It sank down so far that I could feel the cold of the floor against my buttocks. He unpacked his plastic bags with pride.

'Dried pasta,' he announced. 'A jar of pesto sauce, beloved by the ladies in my life. A bag of grated Emmental. Six yogurts. Six small cartons of apple juice, with straws. Three bottles of hearty red wine. One bottle of rosé in case the sun ever comes out. A large amount of UHT milk, sadly all that was available. *Voilà!*'

He looked inordinately pleased. As ever, I joined in with his hearty appreciation of himself.

'Well done!' I said and leaned over to kiss his lips.

'Well done, Daddy,' echoed Alice. She put her arms round his neck and pulled him away from me, towards her. I left them to their hugs, and went to the gloomy, brown-tiled kitchen to prepare the pasta. I soon discovered that the worktop was at a height that would have suited a four-foot tall person, and the wall cupboards were high enough for a seven-foot basketball player. Their doors swung open at precisely the right height for me to bang my forehead on the corners.

An hour later, we got a fire going with the magazines I had brought with me as my going-away luxury. I crumpled up yesterday's newspaper, which I had planned to keep as a historic memento of our last day as British residents, and added it to the pathetic flames. We had found two rickety chairs in the back of the house, so we burned the chairs and sat on the floor. Suddenly the fire was roaring. It might have been the varnish, or the glossy magazines.

Matt and I sat up and stared into the leaping flames, while Alice slept, curled in her sleeping bag at the head of the lilo. Every time I took a gulp of wine, he refilled my plastic cup. I had no idea how much I was drinking. Usually I knew exactly how much I had had, because getting drunk was one of the things I did not do. Today, even with a stomach full of pasta and pesto, I felt dangerously light-headed.

The fire had finally warmed the room. I looked around, at the plaster which had fallen off the walls and was lying in heaps on the cracked tiles. At the floor tiles themselves, which were brown, cream and yellow checks. We were going to replace them with terracotta. We needed a new heating system, new electrics, new plumbing. This, I realised with a sinking heart, was an enormous project. When we had made the offer on the house, we had imagined ourselves cleaning it up, replastering some walls, and painting it all bright white. We had thought we might do it all for about ten thousand pounds. We were wrong.

I knocked back the contents of my cup, and Matt instantly leaned over with the wine bottle.

'Are you getting me drunk?' I asked him. We had been talking about everything except the huge truth that was staring at us. We chatted about details: about what we would do in the morning, whether Alice would get a place at the nursery class of the village school, when our furniture might arrive. We were both relentlessly and falsely optimistic; neither of us mentioned the fact that the house needed tearing down and rebuilding, nor that we had clearly made a gargantuan mistake. If I spoke about it, I felt that everything might tumble down.

'It's the least I can do,' said Matt, downing his own wine. 'You need it. We both do. Come on, drink up.'

I drunk up.

'What's the difference between having a drinking problem and being an alcoholic?' I asked, for something to talk about. 'I've always wondered. Is there a difference or is it a presentational thing?'

'I think it goes like this,' he said. '*I* have a drinking problem. *You* are an alcoholic.'

35

'Or maybe I like a drink, you have a drinking problem, he is an alcoholic.'

Matt nodded. '*I* like a drink. *You* have a drinking problem. *He* is an alcoholic. *We* know how to party. You guys should give it a break. *They* are a bunch of no-hoper loser pissheads.'

I laughed. 'That's why English is a difficult language to learn. All those irregular conjugations.'

'But sweetheart,' he said, suddenly serious, 'you don't have a drinking problem. You are not an alcoholic. I realise I am stating the obvious. Getting a teeny bit pissed under these circumstances –' he looked around with wide eyes – 'is not going to make the sky come crashing down.' We both looked anxiously at the ceiling. This seemed to be tempting fate most unwisely. I snuggled into his shoulder for protection. 'I love you the way you are,' he continued, once we had established that this particular disaster was not imminent, 'but you can join me for more than two glasses of wine occasionally, specially now we're out here. Christ, you probably wouldn't even get drunk at your own wedding.'

I looked at him, trying not to smile. 'What did you just say?'

He blushed slightly. 'Nothing. Just a figure of speech.'

I let it go. His words, and the wine, had given me a warm glow. Matt and Alice were my entire world, and that was what mattered wherever we were. I decided that I could be fairly certain that Matt was coming round to the idea of marriage. He owed it to me. He owed it to Alice, who would be exquisite as a bridesmaid.

Matt, like me, had an unconventional background. He

had never said much to me about his parents. Although, as far as he knew, they were both still alive, he had not spoken to either of them for fourteen years. He did not like to talk about what had caused the rift between them and him, but he had told me that he had vowed long ago that he would never get married, both because of their disastrous union and because he would hate his absolute lack of a family to be as apparent as it would have been, at the ceremony. He had always told me that we did not need a piece of paper when we had each other, and that Alice was far more of a bond than a marriage certificate could ever be.

I knew that was true. Nonetheless, my family was unconventional as well, and I knew that he had enough friends to fill a few seats at a registry office. I had suggested a tiny ceremony with witnesses off the street, but he had turned me down.

Our strange family situations had bonded us in the first place, when we met in Brighton. We had recognised something in each other. Matt had never told me exactly what had happened between him and his parents and I had never told him more than the barest details about my mother.

'Have you phoned Christa?' he asked suddenly. 'She'll be frantic if you haven't.'

'She won't be frantic.'

'Ring her. She'll blame me if you don't.'

'OK.' I looked at him and smiled. 'I'll tell her it's brilliant.'

chapter three

Hugh tried to work out exactly when he had started hating himself, and when he had stopped. With reflection, he could pinpoint the precise moment when it had started. Just over three years ago, two women had sat him down, separately, within the space of six weeks, and each one had told him that she was pregnant with his child. Both of them had been delighted. Both had looked at him expectantly, watching eagerly for his reaction. Both times he had composed himself quickly, made his mouth smile a little. Each time he had said the same thing:

'But I thought we said we weren't thinking about children yet?'

The first time it had been a terrible shock. He had hoped it might be a joke; then, when it wasn't, he had prayed for a miscarriage. If Emma's pregnancy had ended naturally, he would have taken the divine hint and sorted his life out. That had not happened. The second time had been worse. He had been psyching himself up to leave Jo, to regularise his affairs and settle down to his new responsibilities. When

Jo had made her announcement, he had hoped that perhaps she might have been lying, testing him. Jo liked games. But she wasn't. Eight months later, his son had been born.

He had hated himself for a year or so. He had called himself weak, pathetic, unkind, unfair. He had known he was a bastard. His brother had been so horrified that he almost admired him. Nobody else knew. He acknowledged he was going to be found out one day, but after a year of waiting for it to happen, he had decided, unilaterally, to forgive himself. This was the way his life had turned out, and so, while it lasted, he was going to play along with it. He knew he was a coward, but he had told himself so many times that this was the only way to keep everybody happy that he almost believed he was doing the right thing.

There had been several scares. A few times he had been so close to being found out that he could still barely believe he was getting away with it. Once he had been walking on Hampstead Heath with two-month-old Olly in the sling when he had spotted Emma's battleaxe of an aunt out walking with her moronic husband. He had ducked out of the way and, astonishingly, they hadn't seen him. At least, he assumed they hadn't. Several times Jo had offered to meet him 'at the airport', when, in fact, he had only come up from Brighton. A couple of times he had got off the train at Gatwick and rushed into the airport, picked up some perfume and chocolate, and milled around looking for her. The worst of all, however, had been Jo's sudden announcement that they had to move to Brighton. That was what had prompted the shift to France. She had set her heart on leaving London and opening a second gallery on the south coast. Hugh had almost instantly got Emma to put her house on the market. Then one of Jo's artists had given Jo the house listings magazine, and she had, inevitably, honed in on Emma's place. She had drawn a firm ring round it, and asked him to go and look at it with her. He had wriggled out of it by pretending to phone the estate agent and pretending that he'd been told it was under offer, but that had been the moment when he had known he was on borrowed time.

His unusual situation no longer shocked him. From time to time he saw cover lines on women's magazines, and sometimes he smiled to himself. 'My love-rat husband had secret family.' He sometimes picked up a magazine and flicked through the article in question, finding some perverse solidarity with a fellow bastard. Those magazines would have loved his story. At least he knew that, if he ever did get found out, neither woman would ever consider making his behaviour public. They had more dignity than that.

As he kissed his girlfriend and his daughter goodbye, he wondered whether he had made things better or worse by forcing them to move to France. Tearing Emma away from her home in Brighton had been painful. She had been so settled there that he had never imagined he would succeed in doing it, but he had had no choice, and so his will had prevailed. Jo was stronger than he was, and he was stronger than Emma, so it made sense that Emma was the one who had to be shifted. Once he had started his campaign, it had been surprisingly easy. He refused to let himself analyse this. He knew that Emma had come to France for no other reason than because she loved him. She would literally have done anything for him and Alice.

Now he was leaving her there. It was time for him to pay his dues back on the other side of the Channel.

Emma pulled herself in, close to him, into his treacherous shoulder where she imagined she was safe. She clung for a few seconds, then released him.

'You look after each other,' he told them both solemnly. 'Be good. Be careful. Lock the door at night. It's not long till Wednesday.' Then he gave Alice a last kiss, disentangled her arms from around his neck, got in the car and slammed the door.

'They will be all right here,' he muttered as he started the engine and waved to them both. There was a light drizzle in the air. They stood by the gate, getting wet, and he drove away.

'They will be fine,' he repeated. Emma was always going to be fine. She was one of life's copers. He was pleased, now, that they had had the baby. He was glad that Emma had a focus other than him. Whatever happened in the future, Emma would be all right. She was a natural mother, and she would always have Alice. If things went well in France, he thought, they might even have another child. Perhaps they would do it properly, this time.

Hugh drove out of the hamlet, waving cheerfully to the lady who lived by the church. Martine. She stared intently at him for a full five seconds before her face cleared with recognition, and she returned his wave enthusiastically. Hugh smiled to himself. How many other people drive around Pounchet in British-registered cars in February? he wondered. The woman, Martine, had already been over to the house to welcome them to the village. She would make sure Emma and Alice were all right during his many absences.

As he left the tiny hamlet, and then their local town, St Paul, behind him, his excitement began to mount. He often surfed from one life to the other on a wave of adrenaline. He felt his guts bubbling with anticipation, thrilled that nobody involved had any idea about his secret. It was going to be much more clear cut now that he was taking a plane between his two lives. He would step onto the aeroplane as Matt, and step off it as Hugh.

Hugh was genuinely excited that half his life would now be in France. He had wanted this. He had wanted something different, had come to be exhausted by dashing from one part of the south of England to another. He was not going to keep this up for long because of the fucking money, but he reckoned he could manage a year. That was his deadline. He could live this double life for a year, and then he was going to have to decide. A year was optimistic. A year meant calling various credit cards into play and cutting down on extravagances, but he could do it. Thinking of it as a year meant that the decision, the showdown, was a comfortingly long way off.

He was tentatively assuming that when his year was up he would leave Jo and make the France thing permanent. Admittedly, the new life had not got off to a good start. Hugh smiled to himself as he sped away from it, in relief at the certain knowledge that he was not going to spend that night pretending to be comfortable on a lilo that, even when fully inflated, plunged down to meet the stone-tiled floor as soon as he lay on it. At least his weight see-sawed Emma and Alice high into the air. They had genuinely slept. He had been sure of it. Alice, at least, was incapable of pretending.

Tonight, he would sleep in an obscenely comfortable queen-sized bed, under a thick duvet, with his beautiful wife next to him. He switched the radio on and sang along with Otis Redding. 'Sitting on the dock of the bay.' He was a bastard, and he got away with it because his behaviour was out of character. He was not one of life's natural bastards. He was an accidental bastard. He hummed as he drove through miles and miles of pine forests, towards Bordeaux.

He parked in the medium-stay car park, locked his car, and headed for the terminal. Once there, he used the phone card he had already bought to call Emma and Alice.

'Darling!' he said to Emma. 'How are you two? OK so far?'

'Oh Matt!' she exclaimed. 'We're a bit lost without you. It's Daddy,' she added as an aside. 'How was the drive? Is the flight on time?'

He reassured her on both fronts, although he hadn't checked about the flight.

She chatted, barely pausing for breath, eager to keep him on the phone for as long as she could. She went over her plans for the next few days. She would try to enrol Alice in the local school. She would chase up the builders and the architect. Matt loved the fact that she had refrained from pointing out to him that their much-fanfared emigration was, so far, utterly miserable. That the house was terrible, the weather was terrible, that she was already horribly lonely because he had removed her from everything that had always held her together. She should have been screaming at him. Luckily, Emma did not do screaming. She would go to any lengths to avoid confrontation, and this was what made his lifestyle possible. He castigated himself, again, for taking advantage of her sweet nature.

Then he made a second call.

'Darling!' he said, with exactly the same inflection he had used when he called Emma. 'It's me. Not too bad at all. I'll be home around seven, with any luck. I'll call from Gatwick. Love you both.'

Hugh was surprised at how pleased he was to be back in London. Everything was familiar and easy, here. He took the Gatwick Express to Victoria, marvelling at the rush-hour crowds on the station. He bought a paper and a coffee and forced his way onto a packed tube train. He changed onto the High Barnet branch of the northern line at King's Cross, and got off the train at Highgate. From Highgate station, he walked through the rain for ten minutes, swinging his carrier bag of guilt-stricken airport presents, and turned left into Highcroft Road. He stood outside a tall brick house and gave himself his customary pep talk.

He inhaled slowly, and marched up the steps, pushed a hand through his wet hair, and put his key in the door marked 24A.

'Hello?' he called. 'Anyone here? I'm back!'

Oliver's footsteps thundered towards him from the direction of the kitchen.

'Daddy!' shouted the boy, and he ran headlong into

Hugh's arms. Hugh caught him, kissed his creamy cheek, and tousled his blond hair. He was glad, once again, that Alice looked like her mother. Oliver was the image of himself. Hugh derived some perverse sense of security from the fact that his children did not look like brother and sister.

'Olly!' he said. 'What have you been up to?'

The boy ignored the question. 'You got a present?' he demanded.

Hugh looked at his wife, who had followed their son out of the kitchen, and raised his eyebrows. 'Nice to see you, too, Ol,' he said. 'Surely he's too young to be Thatcher's child? Shouldn't he be pleased to see me for my own sake?'

'It's got nothing to do with Thatcher,' Jo told him crisply, pushing her blonde hair back from her face. 'It's your own fault. You always bring a present. You made him associate you coming home with him making some material gain. You instilled the covetousness.' Jo, Hugh reflected, did do confrontation. He liked the fact that she took no crap from him. He also liked the fact that Emma always wanted to make everything smooth and, as she constantly said, magical. He loved them both, although they were so different, and felt comfortable with them both, and they both made him happy. And he was weak and could barely believe his luck. That was the trouble.

'True,' he told Jo, dumping his things and rummaging through a tax-free plastic bag. It didn't mention Bordeaux on it. He had checked very carefully.

'And as it happens I do have a little something for each of you,' he told them. 'But can't a man take his coat off and get a drink when he comes back from supporting his family, before he has to start handing out the knick-knacks?'

Jo patted his cheek. She was looking beautiful in jeans and a crisp white shirt. He knew she didn't do it for his benefit. 'Don't play the martyr. Don't pretend you don't love the travelling. Spending half the week lounging in Novotels on expenses. Watching the porn channels and eating lukewarm chips from room service.' She kissed him on the lips and he returned her kiss, placing a hand on her waist and pulling her tall, slender body close to his.

Hugh muttered into her ear, 'You haven't mentioned that I don't particularly support the family yet.'

'You partly support the family,' Jo told him, generously, as she pulled away from him. She was a confident woman with short, sharply styled blonde hair. Jo worked full time, running a successful art gallery. She made more than enough money to keep the three of them comfortably. Hugh had been in infatuated awe of Jo from the moment they met, and he still was. He thought she was far out of his league.

Jo was slightly disconcerted by the fact that she did not mind Hugh's regular absences at all. He was away for at least half of every week, and although she would never have told him, she enjoyed not having to worry about another adult. She and Olly had their routine down to a fine art. The nanny would arrive at eight, Jo left for work at ten past, and arrived at the gallery between nine and nine fifteen. This gave her enough time to catch up on urgent paper-work before her two employees arrived at nine forty-five and the gallery opened at ten.

Plan B

When Hugh was around, she found him in the shower at her allocated time, and ended up drying her hair after Jenny had arrived. Then her whole day was out of sync. She did miss him at weekends, but even then, she and Olly enjoyed the intimacy of their lazy mornings. They ate their toast together, cuddled on the sofa, watching Dick and Dom. It was cosy and it still felt slightly naughty.

Jo frowned as she poured Hugh and herself a large glass each of Cloudy Bay. She reminded herself that she did love having him around, when he was around. He had worked away for years, but she still looked forward to his return. A friend whose husband worked in New York for three weeks every month had told her that he often took her by surprise by coming home. He didn't turn up out of the blue; she just forgot to expect him. She had told this to Jo conspiratorially, expecting her to make the same confession. She hadn't been able to. She spoke to Hugh every day, she knew when to expect the sound of his key in the door. She was pleased to see him. She really was.

And when he was home, she could relax. She had trusted Hugh implicitly, until recently. Now, as she put the wine back in the fridge, she tried to remember when, exactly, she had started to suspect that something was awry. Eighteen months ago, she thought. Little things did not make sense. She tried not to think about it, as a rule. She loved him, and he adored her. They had been married for eight years and she couldn't imagine being without him. Everyone had been surprised when she married him. He had not been smooth or suave, but he had been real. They had thought he wasn't her type, but he was. Something about him had immediately made her feel comfortable. She could say anything to him, do anything with him.

He had been in Paris for a whole week, and she had missed him. She wondered why, exactly, he had needed to be in Paris for a whole week. Whether he had been alone in Paris, all week.

She and Oliver coped remarkably well without him.

It must be the case, she thought, that their relationship simply worked better that way. They were both capable, both strong and independent, and they trusted each other. People sometimes mistook them for brother and sister, not just because they were both tall and fair, but because they had been together so long they had a common set of mannerisms, a full complement of catchphrases. They were each other's other halves.

She held out a glass, and Hugh took it.

'Cheers,' he said. 'I missed you.'

She clinked her glass against his. They were drinking from the enormous glasses that Hugh's brother Peter had given them for Christmas. He had always complained that their wine glasses were too small. In fact Jo had liked the old ones, which had, she felt, implied a pleasing degree of moderation and maturity. Still, these new ones were fabulous. They were also deceptive.

'I did an experiment with these glasses while you were away,' she told Hugh. 'They take a third of a bottle each.'

Hugh smirked at her. 'Sounds like a good experiment.'

'Your brother's trying to get us drunk.'

'He's a pisshead. He wants to bring everyone else down to his level.' Hugh put his glass down on the table and produced two carrier bags. 'Here you are, Olly,' he said, handing one over. 'One for you and one for Mummy.'

Oliver reached straight into his bag and produced a toy aeroplane. 'A plane!' he exclaimed. 'I wanted an orange one,' he added, frowning at his father.

'I know you did,' Hugh admitted. 'They didn't have an orange one. They only had blue ones.'

'And blue ones are very nice,' said Jo. 'Olly, what do you say to Daddy?'

'Fanks, Dad,' said Olly, who was already flying his plane around the room.

'Hey,' Hugh remarked to Jo. 'I had a dream last night that we were having dinner with Bill and Hillary Clinton.'

She looked at him and roared with laughter. 'You had a dream that Bill Clinton was coming on to me, you mean, don't you?'

'Maybe.'

'You're obsessed with that man's sex life, Hugh. I will never shag Bill Clinton, OK? I never would. I'm sure he's very adept, but not my type.' Jo peered inside her bag and sighed. 'And Hugh,' she added. 'For Christ's sake. Stop buying me perfume. I've got stacks of the stuff and I only wear Calvin Klein. What would I want with J-Lo? Am I that vulgar? Stop spending your money on it. I know you only get it because it's in the airport shop.'

Hugh looked at her anxiously. 'Sorry. I thought one was expected to buy one's wife perfume at duty free. Clinton does, I'm sure. Chocolates better?'

Olly looked up from his elaborate aeroplane game. 'Chocolate?' he echoed, hopefully.

Jo smiled. 'Chocolates would be better. Nothing would be fine. And whatever Clinton does to make his wife happy, he does it because he's always got something to hide.'

Hugh nodded and kicked his shoes into the corner. 'I won't get you anything then,' he said lightly. 'It's nice to be back.'

chapter four

It was pitch black and extraordinarily cold when I went to bed. I could hear the noises of the night outside. Owls screeched. Trees rustled in the wind. Creatures I could not imagine made other-worldly sounds. The building creaked and a shutter blew back and forth, crashing into the front of the house. For a moment I considered going outside to fasten it closed, but the idea was unbearable.

I was used to sleeping alone, since Matt had always travelled with his work. I was used to sharing a bed with Alice, from time to time. I was not, however, accustomed to sleeping on a blow-up bed in a foreign country, particularly not while trying to compute the fact that I was at 'home'. I could not close my mind. Sleep seemed further away than it had ever seemed before.

It was one in the morning. I was dreading the day ahead. I wanted to keep the doors locked, the shutters closed, until Wednesday. I wanted to hide away with Alice and do nothing. Alice, of course, was two. She did not countenance the concept of inactivity. We had immense amounts to do. I did not want to do any of it. I cringed at the thought of going into St Paul, the local town five minutes' drive away, because I knew that everybody would look on me as a strange foreigner, an interloper. I did not know anybody and I could not bear the idea of being the object of scrutiny. I lay in our bare sitting room, watching the embers of the fire glowing gently in the blackness, and repeated my mantra under my breath.

'I want to go home,' I murmured to myself. 'I want to go home. I want to go home. I want to go home.' I must have drifted off to sleep muttering this phrase, and I woke up, at half past four, still whispering it. This project was far too big for me. Matt was only going to be with me for half of the time. I had to be able to live here on my own.

I ran through the tasks I needed to accomplish later that day. I needed to buy a cheap, second-hand car. A Renault, Citroën or Peugeot. For now I was driving a hire car, at vast expense, because Matt had taken our English car to the airport. I needed to go to the school and explain who we were, and ask whether they were willing and able to take in a displaced English toddler and teach her French. I needed to find the local supermarket and do a proper shop, not just a bitty one. The electricity was working now, but the heating was not. I thought the fuel tank was empty. I needed to call the people to sort it out, but first I needed to find a way of making myself intelligible on the phone. Someone had rung up the previous day and I had been unable to understand a word he was saying. Matt and Alice had been out looking for swings and slides and other children. I'd had no idea what to do. I was mortified. I ended up gently placing the receiver down on the floor and walking away from it, blinking back tears of frustration. Half an hour later, I went back to it. It was emitting a shrill shriek. I hung it up.

I was going to have to conquer my stultifying reluctance and do all these things. I knew I had no other option.

Part of me wanted to become a two-year-old again, to stamp my feet and refuse to do anything. I don't want to do it. So I won't do it. That was how it worked for Alice. I longed to pack a bag and take her home. But I couldn't.

I dozed and fretted for hours, then fell into a deep sleep at around half past six. Suddenly Alice pulled my nose with one hand and flung the other arm round my neck.

'Mummy, I'm awake,' she announced unnecessarily.

I was heavy and uncoordinated. I removed her fingers from my nostrils and closed my eyes again, but Alice put a finger on each eyelid and pulled them open.

'Me too,' I told her, reluctantly.

'Please fetch mine milk. Read a book with me. Where's Daddy? I want Daddy.'

I stood up, drenched with exhaustion. I could not wait to sleep in a real bed, my own bed. 'I want Daddy, too,' I agreed wearily. 'He's in London, at work. We'll ring him in a bit, shall we?' I looked at my watch once again. 'Christ, Alice, it's five to seven.' I managed a small laugh. I hoped my sleep had been deep, because it certainly had not been long. 'That means it's five to six where Daddy is. We'll give him a chance to wake up before we call him.' I had never envied Matt's job before. Even though I had yet to work out what a project manager actually did, I would have done anything to have swapped places with him now, to have been slumbering peacefully in a bed in a quiet flat, with clean sheets, central heating, and shops on my doorstep. I was certain I could manage a project or two. My own project was surely more complicated than whatever it was that Matt was working on.

I stumbled into the kitchen, opened a carton of UHT milk, and poured it into Alice's beaker. I set a pan of water on the stove, yawned, and instructed myself to rally.

The café was a small, busy establishment. The air was thick with smoke, but I refused to allow myself to find this objectionable, because I had known it would be like that before I moved here. I had no right to be sanctimonious. France, I thought, would surely be the very last country to ban smoking. Everyone seemed to have a cigarette in their hand.

The tables were battered, with rickety metal legs and formica tops. Alice and I were sitting opposite each other. She drank apple juice from a small glass bottle, through a straw. I was on my third cup of coffee, and was contemplating a fourth. Gradually, I was beginning to feel human again, if in a slightly jittery way. The table top was covered with croissant crumbs.

Every other customer but one was a man. They sat at the bar and drank what looked like alcohol. Some of it was bright red and I was curious as to what, exactly, it could be. At ten o'clock in the morning, it could not possibly be a liqueur. The men had looked at Alice and me with unabashed curiosity when we came in, and every time anyone new came through the door, he looked at us too.

I smiled. After a few seconds' delay, they would smile back. They said, 'Bonjour.' I felt a small but unmistakable glow of satisfaction every time this happened.

Alice was the only child there. This was a huge contrast to the cafés of Brighton, which were jammed with three-wheeler pushchairs and NCT group outings. In Brighton cafés, there were often baby-changing rooms and boxes of toys. I decided that I had to find out, when I dared, where the mothers went. There had to be a child-friendly café somewhere in this town. If I couldn't find it, I would have to try Villeneuve, the regional centre, which was further away.

I looked at Alice. Her hair was in desperate need of a wash. She was swinging her legs and gazing around. I licked my finger and reached forward to wipe a pain au chocolat smear from her cheek.

'This is fun, isn't it?' I asked her cheerfully, and firmly. She looked at me sceptically. She realised that she was not allowed to say no, so she said nothing. I was relaxed with Alice. If Matt had been there, I would have put on more of a show, but since he wasn't, I was allowing myself to linger in the café with my daughter, gathering my strength. Soon I would become brisk and businesslike and capable.

'Do you do this with your mummy?' Alice asked.

'You mean Christa?' I asked her.

'Christa's your mummy?'

'No. Not really. She's my aunt.'

'Who's your mummy is?'

I sighed. 'I haven't really got a mummy.' She frowned and I hesitated. 'She's not . . .' I stopped. I wished I did have memories of sitting in cafés with my mother, but I barely recalled anything about her. I never tried. In fact, I tried not to. 'No,' I said firmly. 'I did not do this with my mummy. So you're a very lucky girl to be taken out to a café like this. Sit up properly.'

I knew I could switch into capable mode whenever I needed to, with a bit of willpower. People thought that was just the way I was, but it wasn't. I could project efficiency however I was feeling. Today I was feeling utterly lost, but I knew I was going to rally myself. I would have made a brilliant Girl Guide. I never joined because both my sisters laughed at the idea.

Suddenly, I longed to speak to Bella. I was desperate to hear her voice. Bella was three years older than me and, though she hadn't realised it, she had been my rock and my idol since I was three. She would laugh at that if I ever told her. When I had gone to live with Christa and Geoff, it had been Bella who looked after me. Christa had no doubt been dealing with her own grief for her sister, plus she had three of her own children, and although she looked after me, was kind to me, and attended to my material needs, it was Bella, aged five, who took over the maternal role. Geoff, I imagine, had done his best, but small children had never been his thing and I had few recollections of him during that period. He was distant with all of us, I thought, until we were old enough to hold a conversation, and then the barriers all seemed to come down. Charlotte was not much older than I was, and Greg had been a baby.

Bella had been one of those five-year-old girls who were already casting around for people to nurture. She had been the sort who would put her arm round the child who fell over in the playground, even if it was the fat girl who no one liked, and would march her to the teacher, saying importantly, 'Miss, Pearl's crying.' She would then be dispatched to take Pearl to the sickroom and stay with her till the nurse sent her back. Having her own orphaned – as good as orphaned – cousin moving into the bedroom down the corridor had been Bella's idea of heaven. She made sure I sat next to her for every meal. She gave me toys. When she discovered that I didn't have a special toy to take to bed with me, she had given me her second-best teddy, Gavin. I still had him.

Bella had grown up into a flamboyant fashion editor with six-year-old twin boys and a penchant for expensive, tightly fitting clothing. She was my sister and my best friend. I did not doubt that she would have dropped everything for me had I needed her to. I had never needed her to, and I did not intend to start now. I just missed her.

The only other woman in the room was sitting three tables away, with a man. She had been smiling at Alice. Alice was ostensibly ignoring her, but she was sucking on her straw with studied cuteness. She knew exactly what she was doing. Finally, the woman came over.

'*Que tu es mignonne,*' she cooed. Alice looked at her briefly, and looked away, beaming but shy. '*Que tu es belle. Comment t'appelle tu?*'

I looked at my daughter. 'What's your name?' I translated.

It came out in a near whisper. 'Alice.'

'Alice!' exclaimed the woman. She turned to me. '*Elle es jolie, votre fille.*'

I thanked her, and we conversed in French as best I could manage. Despite my French degree, I was desperately self-conscious about speaking the language. She told me about her two-year-old grandson. I explained that we had just moved here from England.

'I know,' she assured me. 'You've bought the Leclerc house in Pounchet. You're the English who've come without the television people. How are you finding it? The weather's terrible, isn't it? Did you bring this rain from England?'

I looked at her. She was, I guessed, in her late fifties. She was expertly made up, and elegantly dressed in black and white, with a pair of black stilettos. I was acutely aware of my crumpled shirt, my muddy jeans and my scuffed boots. I hadn't had a shower for four days, and my hair was pulled into a tight ponytail to try to hide its lank and greasy state. I was wearing no make-up and I was certain that my face was red and shiny, and that the bags under my eyes were as black as bruises. I vowed to buy some cosmetics, to wash my hair in cold water that evening, maybe even to purchase some new clothes. I recalled Paula asking about my due date in Clifton Street, and pulled my stomach in.

I was overcome with embarrassment, to the point where I could barely say another word. The woman looked at me kindly. I felt compelled to explain.

'I am sorry,' I told her, haltingly. 'You are very chic. We are waiting for our things to arrive on the lorry.' For some reason, I found myself miming a steering wheel. 'From England. We have no . . .' I tailed away, unsure of the word. 'No hot. No hot water. We are not chic.' I tugged my life-less ponytail to emphasise my point.

She laughed. 'You are both so pretty. You have no hot water? No heating? That is terrible. Have you spoken to the company?'

I shook my head and reached into the handbag to show her the letter with the address and phone number on it. The woman instantly took out her mobile phone and dialled. She looked at it and tutted. No reception. 'One moment,' she told me, and went outside. I saw her talking animatedly, indignantly, gesturing with her free hand.

'OK,' she announced, when she came back in. 'It's done. They're coming to refill your tank this afternoon, about three o'clock.'

I gaped at her. 'You're very kind.'

'It's nothing. Welcome to the region.'

I smiled. A genuine smile felt novel and pleasant. By the time I had composed a suitably grateful sentence in my head, the woman had gone. I watched her talking to her companion, and saw him turning to look at us. He smiled and gave a little wave. I waved back. My breath escaped in a big rush. I remembered her mentioning television people and tried to catch her eye to ask what she had meant, but she was looking the other way.

Buoyed by the kindness of the woman, I paid our bill, buttoned Alice into her raincoat, pulled her hat down almost over her eyes, and took her out into the gloom. The tourist office, our first official stop of the day, was in the main square.

I knew, theoretically, that St Paul was a lovely town. I knew because we had sat outside one of the other cafés in the autumn, and shared a beer and looked at the long shadows the late-afternoon sunlight cast on the stone buildings. The church here dated from the tenth century. The buildings around it were tall, and stone, with wrought-iron grilles and balconies. There were bakeries, a fishmonger, a little cinema and a couple of grocers. It was a classic small French town and I had almost been able to imagine us settling here happily, back in October. I had imagined Matt and Alice and me, with an entourage of happy, envious house guests, sitting outside cafés laughing and whiling away summer afternoons.

Today, the black clouds were piled above us. It had stopped raining but the clouds clearly had no intention of moving. I stepped into a puddle and felt the water seeping into my trainers. Sometimes I thought I saw a chink of clear sky, but it never was. It was just a grey cloud, standing out amongst its black colleagues. The square looked bleak and dull. The tourist office was on the corner near the car park, and we tumbled in, out of breath and dishevelled.

'*Oui?*' asked a bored-looking woman with blonde hair in an immaculate chignon. She barely looked up.

I stumbled through my little speech, about being new in the area and needing help with a few things. She looked at me closely, smiled a little and cut me off mid-sentence.

'You want your local school?' she asked.

'And a car,' I added.

She marked St Paul's *école maternelle* on a map. There was a car dealer on the way.

'Good luck,' she said, with a small smile, and we left.

'It's still raining?' Bella asked incredulously. 'Sweetie, are you sure you're in the right place? You did go to the *south* of France? You're not in Calais?'

'It's fine,' I told her, firmly. 'It is still raining, and we are in the right place, but I don't mind the rain. Alice has got a place at the village school which is brilliant. I've got to go to see the mayor and get her a certificate, and she's got to have a TB jab, but once that's done they're happy to have her in the *tous petits*. It's the sweetest place and she loved it. And at least we're warm, now. I've had a shower. I can't tell you what a luxury it was. I just wish I had a hairdryer.'

I shifted closer to the radiator, and looked out of the window at the small front garden. The trees were bare. Water was coursing down the path, into the ditch. At least the front garden was manageable. The water drained away and the plants were small and bare. The fig tree didn't look, to my inexpert eyes, as if it needed pruning. The whole of the back garden seemed to be a swamp. A hectare had sounded just right. Half of it was completely wild. All of it was boggy. I stretched the phone lead and pulled the cable through the hall, so I could look at the back garden through the windows in the door. It was a wasteland. I tried to imagine the trees in bud, the lawn soft and not muddy, the flowers pushing up.

'All this water must be good for the garden,' I added brightly.

'Emma!' Bella was almost shouting at me. 'Emma, for fuck's sake. Let me get this straight. You're in the arse-end of nowhere with wet hair. You know nobody. Your central heating has just been fixed after five days and that's only because a random woman in a café took pity on you. It's rained every single moment since you arrived. You're sharing a camp bed with a two-year-old. Water is pouring into your attic and you have to empty twenty containers every hour or so. Matt's in London, merrily working away without a care in the world. He's taking nice long lunches and sleeping in a bed under clean sheets. OK, he has a bachelor pad, doesn't he, so maybe they're not that clean, but still, it's a bed. And you're still pretending that this does not constitute a disaster of the first magnitude? I know you've half convinced Mum that it's great, but I'm not that gullible. Don't you dare try to tell me you wouldn't rather be in Brighton.'

'I would rather be in Brighton,' I admitted, putting on my bravest voice, 'but it's all fine. All this is temporary. And it's an air bed, not a camp bed. How are you? How's Jon and the boys?'

'We're all right. You know, working. Boys are on good form. Do you want me to come out?'

I bit back my 'Yes!' I did want her to come out – I wanted to see her, desperately – but I couldn't have borne it had she felt sorry for me. She would have been angry with Matt for ever. She would have seen that the house was a shell, that everything needed replacing. I wanted to present my friends and family with the finished product, not with the present mess. I wanted to show them success. I wanted them to admire me. I needed to sort everything out before anyone was allowed to see it.

'Oh God!' I exclaimed, suddenly. 'Bel, can I call you back? I haven't rung the builders.'

By Wednesday, I was almost proud of myself. It had always been me, rather than Matt, who had made arrangements, but I had never sorted out a whole new life before, and particularly not in a foreign language, even if it was one that I used to speak well and which was coming back quickly. One by one, I was getting things done. It was a steep learning curve. The school was delightful. It was a welcoming place, built around a central playground. The window frames were painted blue. There were coat pegs with the children's photos next to them, there was a canteen with its own chef, and there was a row of little toothbrushes for after-lunch brushing. I had been overcome with delight when the teacher said they had a place for Alice. I wanted to go there myself.

Alice was bored out of her mind and was desperate to go. She had already had the skin test for her BCG, and had an appointment for the injection on Friday. She was due at school on Monday. Monday, however, seemed a long way off. I felt that I might as well have been telling her she could start school in twelve years' time.

'I want to go *now*,' she kept sobbing.

'You can go on Monday,' I told her, yet again.

'NOT MONDAY,' she shouted. 'I tell you already. NOW. I want to play with the fire engine and the kitchen and the scooter and the books!' She had retained, it seemed, a photographic mental record of every toy in the classroom.

The school was the best thing about our new life, so far. I hoped that Alice was going to like it as much when she got there as she had done on our two visits. It was a long day, from nine fifteen till half past four, and the school provided a three-course lunch and an afternoon nap. I worried about whether she would cope, alone among children who would not understand her. I told myself again and again that children pick up languages quickly, that she was going to be bilingual in no time.

I knew that my own French was fine, but I still felt self-conscious. I hated approaching people, making my foreignness known. If Alice and I walked down the street speaking to each other, heads turned, people clocked us as *les anglaises*. Every time I made a phone call, or approached anybody for any reason, I had to steel myself. It was an effort for me to push open the door of a shop, any shop. I was constantly overcoming my nerves, my reluctance, my fear of looking stupid.

I had bought my own car. It was a small Peugeot, a silver 206 automatic and I was surprised at how easy it had been to buy it. I did not think the salesman had ripped me off. It had come in just under what we had budgeted and I actively liked driving it. I had never had my own car before, and I had always hated driving in Britain. The roads here were empty and I was still getting used to the novelty of not having to change gears. I had found a radio station called Nostalgi which played French chanson and the Beatles, and if I was on a clear stretch of road and it wasn't raining, I could get Radio Four on long wave.

On Wednesday morning, Martine popped round, just as I had finished washing up the breakfast dishes. I had vowed that when the builders came round that afternoon, I was going to make sure that the kitchen was a priority. I had had enough of bending double to wash the dishes. A normal-height sink would be good. A dishwasher would be better.

Plan B

I went outside to meet her. She looked at the house and declined my invitation to come in.

'Would you like some eggs?' she asked, smiling broadly. Martine was in charge of Pounchet, I had come to realise. She was small and wiry with her hair in a bun, and, as Charlotte had prophesied, she wore a blue printed overall under her thick coat. Martine monitored all the comings and goings in the hamlet.

'Matthieu will be back today?' she asked, as she handed over a plastic bag containing ten eggs, freshly laid by her chickens.

'He will,' I agreed. I wanted to sort things out a bit before he arrived. But almost as soon as she had gone, some other neighbours turned up. These ones were a couple, about ten years older than Matt and me. He had a shock of jet-black hair, and she was small and soft and well dressed. They were farmers, and they lived a little way up the hill. From the end of the garden, I could see their farmhouse, across a couple of bare fields. They smiled constantly, and congratulated me, repeatedly, on my French.

'You speak like a Frenchwoman!' they kept marvelling. I knew this was not true. Either they were being kind, or the reputation of the English as monolinguists was so well established that French people were amazed and impressed that I spoke any French whatsoever.

I invited them into the house, without thinking. We stepped into the living room. Then I saw their faces as they took it all in. They saw that we were living in a single room, sleeping on a blow-up bed. Clothes and toys were strewn around the floor, and Alice was playing an elaborate game with her dinosaurs in the grate. Her face was smeared with ash and her hands were covered with it.

I had noticed over the few days we had been here that French children were immaculately turned out at all times. I had no idea how their parents contrived it, but I had yet to see a child in public with a single stain or mark on his or her clothing. All Alice's clean clothes were drying on radiators after my marathon hand-washing session the previous night, so she was wearing her pyjamas, at eleven in the morning. I saw the scene through their eyes, and put my face in my hands.

'Would you like a drink?' I managed to ask politely.

They looked at each other. 'No thank you,' said the woman quickly.

'Would you like to come and stay with us?' asked the man, kindly. 'We have plenty of rooms now our children have left home. And a hot shower.'

'And a washing machine.'

I managed to decline. As I tried to say goodbye, I realised I had irretrievably forgotten their names.

In the afternoon, Alice played with old pans on the kitchen floor while I went through the architect's plans for the new windows in the back of the house. Monsieur Dumas, the head of the builders' cooperative, was laughing at the mess in which we were living.

'It can only get better,' he marvelled, as the rain dripped into a bucket at our feet. I had tidied up for their visit, but they would never have believed that if I had tried to tell them.

All the forms were apparently in order, and we were ready

to apply for planning permission for the windows. Both Monsieur Dumas and the architect were convivial, and we understood each other with a mixture of languages and a dictionary. I knew no French building terms, and most of the key words that were being bandied about were not in the dictionary, but mime seemed to be doing the trick. I was looking forward to the new windows. Suddenly, half the house would be usable; and life might become a little bit more bearable. At least there would be plenty of space for visitors.

Monsieur Dumas handed me a sheaf of forms to sign. After purchasing the car, I knew exactly what was going to come next. He peered at my first signature.

'Em-ma Meadows?' he asked, looking at me, puzzled. He frowned slightly. Like all the other Frenchmen I had seen in the past week, he was clean-shaven and well turned out. 'But we have here Monsieur et Madame Smith.' He pronounced it 'Schmidt'. They both stared at me, waiting for an explanation. I sighed.

'We're not married,' I told him, and watched both men's surprise registering on their faces. 'In England it's not at all rare. There are many families where the parents aren't married. We will get married soon.'

There were raised eyebrows and uncertain nods. 'Perhaps it's best if Monsieur Schmidt signs the forms?' suggested the architect.

I smiled. 'OK. Leave them with me. He'll be back soon.'

'MummEEEEEE,' said Alice, tugging at my jumper. 'Mummy. I'm bored. I want to go to school. I want to go back to our house. I want to go play with Lily. Mummy. Play with me. I want Daddy.'

There was a crunch of tyres on the gravel outside. I rushed to the window, but it was not Matt arriving home on cue. It was a lorry. A lorry bearing all our possessions. I picked Alice up and rushed out into the rain to look.

Five minutes later, I was standing in the hall, directing the British removals men, who were thankfully not the same people who packed it all up in England. These ones were willing to speak to me. After initially addressing themselves to Monsieur Dumas, they quickly decided that a British woman was better conversationally than a foreign man. I stationed myself inside the front door, and made sure that every piece of furniture, every box, was taken straight to the correct room, even though it would all be shifted around for the total renovation of the house.

My heart lifted when I saw our double bed coming off the lorry, in pieces. Alice's low single came soon after. I vowed to puncture the lilo and throw it on someone's bonfire, to be sure that I would never have to attempt to sleep on it again. At the thought of sleeping in my old bed that night, I suddenly became weary. I had barely slept for four nights. I hated the sitting room, hated the tiles, hated the mice that scurried perilously close while we slept. I was going to have sheets and a mattress. It felt like an enormous luxury.

I offered a cup of tea and ended up making five. The builder and architect were horrified at the addition of UHT milk. They asked for a slice of lemon, and when I couldn't oblige, ended up accepting a glass of wine each instead.

I looked at the lorry to check progress, and suddenly saw Matt, standing in the front garden, getting wet, surveying the scene. He was wearing his work clothes, with his top button undone and his tie sticking out of his jacket pocket. He looked tall, handsome, and a little confused.

'Well, well,' he said, catching my eye. Alice noticed him seconds after I did, and rushed out of doors and into his arms. I followed her. 'So you're coping with all this?' he asked, pulling back and looking anxiously into my eyes. He picked up a strand of my hair and examined it. 'Not torn out yet. Hair intact. Not white. Still brown. That has to be good.'

'Of course I am,' I told him, suddenly relaxing. 'It's been a huge learning curve. Come on. Out of the rain. Have a glass of wine with the guys. Sign some forms.' I pointed to the side of the road. 'Do you like my car?'

'Look, Daddy!' yelled Alice, pointing to the treasures being unloaded. 'Mine bike! Mine doll's house! Mine garage!'

'Monsieur Schmidt!' said Monsieur Dumas warmly. 'You must marry your wife.'

'Now if you're offering, we wouldn't say no to a drop of the old vino,' observed a passing removal man, eyeing Monsieur Dumas' glass.

I kissed Matt's lips.

'Welcome home,' I told him.

He looked at me sharply. 'You said home.'

I shrugged and looked away.

chapter five

Jo grinned with anticipation as she opened the envelope. It was her Eurostar ticket. She checked the dates and times carefully, to make sure they hadn't made any mistakes. Everything was perfect.

'Mum!' shouted Olly. 'I *need* you!'

She walked back into the open-plan kitchen and dining room, barely glancing at the rest of the post in her hand. She put the tickets carefully on the sideboard and resolved to ask Hugh why he always flew. The Eurostar was not much more expensive. So much more civilised to sit on a train all the way, she thought. And better for the environment, too. She couldn't wait to hand Olly over to her mother – nervous but willing – and to curl up in her seat, with a book.

She was going to Paris for the weekend, in three weeks' time. It felt good. Her friend Lara had had the idea.

'Have a weekend away,' she had suggested, when Jo had divulged a little of her unease about Hugh's behaviour. 'He's working in Paris every weekend for six months? Well, hello?

Plan B

Go to Paris for a weekend with him. It's the only thing to do, surely?'

Jo had been horrified to discover that her initial reaction to the suggestion was, 'I can't.' When she thought about it for a split second, she'd realised she could and she must. They hadn't had any time together without Olly since he'd been born. She had been away working fairly often, and Hugh had been away almost all the time. At the moment they were both so busy that they barely saw each other from one week to the next. She would be able to put her niggling worries aside, she was sure, after some proper quality time with her husband. Their problem stemmed from the fact that their lives were so separate. Paris would sort that out.

'Why do you need me?' she asked Olly, smiling indulgently and making sure the tickets were out of his reach.

'Because,' he said imperiously, 'I drop my spoon.'

chapter six

On Alice's first day of school, I was determined to be early and make a good impression. I was far more nervous than she was. I put on a token lick of make-up. My one lipstick was brown and slightly fluffy, but I smeared it round my mouth as delicately as I could. Unfortunately I couldn't find any foundation or powder. I used an old mascara on my eyelashes and hoped no one would notice my shiny face. I pulled my hair back into a ponytail because it was so greasy, and put on the least worst clothes I could find, which meant not wearing my faded old jeans.

Alice looked much better than I did. She was dressed simply, in a skirt and jumper, tights and sturdy shoes. Her hair was glossy, and she shrugged her new school bag – her *cartable* – onto her shoulders proudly.

'I'm ready for school,' she announced, looking at me with eager brown eyes. It was quarter past eight. She had been up, raring to go, since six. It would take me four minutes to drive her to school. I knew because I had timed it. She had to be there in an hour.

'Too early,' I told her. 'You play. I'll wash up the breakfast. We'll phone Daddy.'

Matt's phone was switched off. I knew he was still asleep. At ten to nine, he called us back.

'Am I too late?' he said instantly, anxiously.

'Not at all,' I assured him. 'We're going in ten minutes.' I looked at Alice. 'We have one impatient little girl.'

'So my timing's perfect.' He sighed. 'Excellent. Oh, I do wish I could be there. It's a milestone, isn't it, taking our child into the classroom for her first day. And what am I doing instead? Going to a meeting about some cost benefit analysis that I won't bore you with.'

'Don't give yourself a hard time,' I told him, watching Alice standing by the door, shifting her weight from one foot to the other. 'It's not your fault. And she's only staying till lunchtime, so it's not her first full day. You can take her on Friday.'

It had been an extremely cold night, though I hadn't realised it as I had yet to work out how to regulate the heating system. Its only setting, so far as I was aware, was extremely hot. We both slept on top of our duvets, and I was surprised, that morning, to discover my car so iced over that I had to use all my strength to yank the doors open.

'Oh dear,' I said as casually as I could.

'Why oh dear?' asked Alice, climbing into her car seat, putting her school bag down by her side, and threading her arms through her straps. I scraped some ice off the windscreen with my fingernails. It was dispiriting work. The ice was so tightly attached to the glass that I could barely make scratch marks in it. I wished I had a scraper or a can of de-icer. Matt had both in his car, sitting useless at the airport.

'Oh dear because I can't drive the car,' I told her, beginning to panic slightly. Two cars drove past in quick succession, both containing children on their way to school, both with ice-free windscreens and happy-looking mothers who waved to me. For a split second I considered flagging them down, but I could not get past the fact that I didn't dare. 'I'm going to boil the kettle,' I told Alice, snapping her straps into place. 'You stay there,' I added unnecessarily.

We did not, of course, have a kettle. I put a lot of water in a pan, stuck a lid on it, and waited, and waited and waited.

We arrived at school four minutes late. I knew, logically, that this was not the worst crime in the world, but I felt terrible. I thought I had failed my daughter. I imagined the teacher, who was kind, calm, and younger than me, rolling her eyes and complaining behind my back about the slapdash English.

Alice looked around the large classroom. Twenty-four children looked back at her. She smiled. Some of them smiled back. I watched her looking at the art on the walls, the little tables with four children sitting at each one. She looked up at me.

'Where are we going to sit, Mummy?'

'The teacher will find you a place,' I told her quietly. 'I'll come back and collect you later.'

She held my hand tightly. 'No, you stay here.'

I squeezed her hand. 'No, I have to come back later. Look, these boys and girls haven't got their mummies here, have they? You're a big girl. The teacher will look after you.' I bent down to kiss her, and she attached herself to me. I pulled her fingers off my coat and tried to yank her arms from around my neck. She began sobbing. The teacher came and held her, and tried to comfort her. Alice's arms waved like tentacles, trying to find me through her tears.

I disappeared as quickly as I could. As I walked across the courtyard, back to the car, I heard shrieks of '*Mummeeeeeeeeeee!*' I glanced at the classroom windows, and saw Alice staring out at me, desolate. Her eyes were full of my betrayal. I looked away.

I waited by the phone for an hour, awaiting a call asking me to come and fetch her. While I waited, I busied myself with the list I had been given. Alice needed a napkin for her school lunches. 'Please sew elastic onto two corners,' read the note. I was hoping that she could start having lunch at school the following week, so I began to sew elastic onto the corners of the pink linen napkin that she had chosen.

I sat by the window and sewed, wondering why the school hadn't called yet, and also speculating on when the daffodils would begin to grow, and wishing that Matt was with me.

'There we are,' I said, eventually, and held up the napkin. I was pleased with the loop of elastic on each corner. She would now be able to hang it on her peg. I cast around for another activity to fill the void. In the end, I left the phone behind and went out for a walk through the icy lanes.

I wrapped up warmly, and stomped up the hill. The road was just wide enough for two cars to pass, though it was rarely necessary. The ditches on either side were dotted with icy puddles, and the black and white cows in the field next door were clustered together. I wondered whether they were sharing body heat. A tractor chugged past me, and I recognised the neighbour whose name I had forgotten. I waved to him and he slowed down.

'*Ça va?*' he asked. I assured him that I was fine, and we exchanged pleasantries. This mainly involved me assuring him that we had furniture and thus that we were fine. I trudged on.

How strange it was, I thought, that my life had brought me here, to the depths of the French countryside, to a place where I had no roots at all. I had never imagined myself emigrating. I was lost. I looked across to the next hill, and eyed a huge old stone house enviously. That house must have stunning views. But it was far bigger than ours, and our house was already too big. Besides, I told myself, if you lived on a hill everyone would look at your house all the time. I liked being insignificant. I thought, with a pang, of my insignificant terraced house in Brighton.

As I passed some hunters, dressed incongruously in camouflage gear and orange caps, I wondered whether this boring life was going to suit me. The men smiled and said hello, and I returned their greetings and carried on walking, hoping they weren't going to shoot the deer I had seen in the garden earlier. I knew that there was someone spirited hiding inside me, but I did not intend to let her out. Nobody knew I had an alter ego who popped into my head from time to time, making bitchy comments and suggesting rash courses of action. Nobody appeared to have noticed that I was normal to the point of parody, that, like an abstaining alcoholic or a newly naturalised citizen, I was too zealous, too keen, because I had made myself into something that, essentially, I was not. Of course nobody noticed; the only social interaction I had was small talk that invariably involved Alice, the weather, or both.

Ever since I had moved into the box room in Holloway, which had been decorated in pink by my cousins in honour of my arrival, I had shut off my true nature and concentrated on being good. Being good at the age of three and a bit had involved not having tantrums, always saying sorry even when whatever had happened had not been my fault, and allowing Bella to dress me up and use me as a prop in her games. Being good when I was fourteen had involved doing my homework, laying the table without being asked, and staying well away from boys.

I had gone to university, like a good girl. I studied French, on a campus a couple of miles outside a small city. I spent the third year in Paris, but I let the experience pass me by. I spent the year sitting in my hall of residence, doing my homework and reading books. I looked at art on my own, and sat in cafés on my own pretending to be engrossed in English and French newspapers, and I waited for it all to finish. Everyone else had the time of their lives, which, according to received wisdom, was the correct course of action. I kept to myself. After a while the other students stopped asking me to their parties, and I was relieved.

For four years, I did my work on time. I got a first, and almost sang with relief when it was all over. I never got drunk. I never had mindless sex. Occasionally, I would become slightly tipsy, and then I would panic because I hated the loss of control. A couple of times, I slept with someone, but only when I had planned it in advance. For six months I had a closet relationship with one of my tutors. I broke it off because, although he was thirty-seven and single, it was technically not allowed. I did not like feeling that I was doing something that was forbidden. Although my relationship with Stephen was harmless in the extreme, I did not want to become accustomed to breaking the rules.

I suppressed my inner rebel, and concentrated on being boring. I cleaned red wine stains out of carpets to avoid the loss of a deposit, even when it wasn't my house. I pushed people into taxis and handed money to the driver. The following day, I would often hear the person in question marvelling, 'I have no idea how I got home!' I would smile to myself, and keep quiet.

My fellow students liked to sit up late, drinking cheap alcohol and swapping confidences. Sometimes I would go to the bar and sit at the corner of a table, but I never joined the conversations. I remained aloof and largely ignored.

I looked at my watch. I had to be at school on the dot of twelve fifteen to collect Alice. It was time to turn back. The sky had cleared, and it had become much warmer. The ice was melting, and I was hot in my big coat. As I walked back down the hill, I noticed that the trees on either side of the road had the very beginnings of buds on them.

My dullness at university had not saved me from drama altogether. The fact that I was, essentially, an orphan made me strangely attractive to a particular type of young man. They would corner me and ask me questions. I normally managed to shake them off by being unfriendly. Only one persisted. He was a self-consciously troubled art student, who called himself Po.

'What happened?' he would ask, cornering me in a bar. 'Do you want to talk about it?' My answer was unequivocal. I never knew my father. My mother died when I was three. No, thank you, I do not wish to talk about it; least of all to you.

This seemed to make me more attractive to him. The primmer I was, the more determined he became.

Po followed me around for years. He revelled in being riven with angst, and tutted despairingly over the trivia that preoccupied our colleagues.

'Like I'm supposed to give a fuck about her hair!' he muttered to me one summer evening, with a complicit smile. 'Some people have no sense of perspective, do they, Ems?'

He made my skin cold with distaste. The bar was crowded and smoky, and on the pretext of letting someone else in at the table, he moved his chair cosily up to mine. 'I mean, who cares about their hair when there's so much that really matters going on in the world, hey, Emma? I mean, I don't hear you demanding that the whole bar gives you an opinion on the perm versus bob conundrum. You have beautiful hair, and that's that.' He lifted his hands defensively. 'I know, I know, I shouldn't even notice. But you know what's what. I can see that, because you've suffered a terrible loss at an early age. You're self-reliant and I respect that. So, what actually happened to your mother? Was she ill? Or do you not feel ready to talk about it?'

I looked at him. He ostentatiously made no effort over

his appearance. His hair was dyed orange and stood up on end. His face had, in the past, been ravaged by acne. He wore tie-dyed trousers, Doc Martens, and an enormous granddad shirt. I suspected that it took him quite some time to perfect his look, not least since the degree of dishevelment did not vary from one day to the next.

Po apparently had a much better looking older brother and tried to extract some angst from the fact that he was constantly living in his shadow. I had no sympathy, and I was sure my face said as much.

'My mother died,' I said, in answer to his question. 'What happened to *your* mother?'

He was surprised. 'Mine?' I could see him casting around for something to say. 'Oh, she was a bit ill last year, as it happens.'

'But she's better now?'

'Yes. Well, as far as I know she's OK.'

'What was wrong?'

'Um.' He looked down, as if seeking some genuine trauma on the fag-burned carpet. 'Women's problems, I believe.'

'The menopause?'

'Something like that.'

I looked at him. 'Poor Po,' I said softly. He looked into my eyes, and smiled winsomely. 'You would actually like to trade your menopausal mother for my dead one, wouldn't you?' I continued. 'You have no idea.'

That was a gross confrontation as far as I was concerned. As I got up to leave, he pulled the edge of my T-shirt.

'My parents had a trial separation,' he pleaded. 'It's not my fault they got back together.'

Plan B

Po almost stalked me. He left me notes, wrote me poems, painted my portrait (from memory: nothing would have induced me to sit for him). For a while, he left a single red rose in my pigeonhole every Friday. Often, I would discover it when I plunged my hand in and was pricked by the thorn; I was sure he infuriated everyone else whose surname began with 'M'. For two years, he laboured under the misapprehension that I was not interested in him because he could not produce an emotional scar from his past. He thought that I would tear off my clothes and pour out my feelings if only he could match me, trouble for trouble. I was scared of him. I came to dread the sight of him. I ignored him. I pretended, unconvincingly, to be someone else when he rang.

Then, during the summer after we graduated, he turned up on the doorstep in Holloway.

'Emma!' Geoff called up the stairs. 'There's someone here for you! A young man!'

I walked down gingerly. I did not have unexpected visitors, least of all young men. I didn't really have visitors at all. I tagged along with Bella and Charlotte and their friends.

My heart plummeted when I saw him standing there. His trousers were torn cotton. His shirt was crumpled. Everything about him was distasteful.

Geoff had rushed back to his study, no doubt to give me 'some privacy', and everyone else was out. If Bella had been around, she would have seen him off for me.

'Hello, Po,' I said stonily. 'Come in.'

He followed me into the kitchen. 'Do you want a drink?'

I asked, in a voice that I knew conveyed that the desired answer was no.

'Mmmm. I could murder a cup of tea,' he said enthusiastically, and sat at the table. 'You look lovely. I like your trousers. So, what have you been up to?'

'These are my pyjama trousers,' I told him. 'I've been applying for jobs. What can I do for you, Po?'

I put the kettle on. I calculated that it would take me five minutes to make the tea, ten minutes to drink it. I would get him out of the house before twenty minutes had passed.

He looked at me intently, and laughed, a hollow laugh. His manner was suddenly confrontational, hostile.

'What can you do for me?' he echoed. 'Do you have any idea? I've loved you from the day I met you, Emma Meadows. You've made it plain that you don't feel anything for me. I need you. I can see your soul. You need me, too. One day you'll realise it. But by then it will be too late.'

He sounded self-conscious, and I knew that these weren't his words, that he was parroting lines from films and songs and trashy books. I tried not to laugh.

'Po,' I told him, 'I like you, but I'll never, ever be in love with you.'

'You will. But like I said it will be too late.' He stood up and started walking towards me.

'What are you talking about?' I asked, a kettle half full of just boiled water in my hand.

'I'm talking about this,' he said. He reached behind me, took a knife from the block, and swiftly pulled it across his wrists. He did it the right way, cutting downwards rather than across. Blood spurted out. It splattered my clothes, my face, my hair. I dropped the kettle and scalded our feet. Po placed the knife on the worktop, and held his wrists out.

'Now do you believe I love you?' he asked, triumphantly, as blood poured out.

I must have screamed, because suddenly Geoff was there, pulling me away from Po, and phoning an ambulance.

Po left me alone after that. He had, I supposed, achieved his ambition. He had given himself some literal scars and an excellent anecdote to recount secretively to vulnerable girls. My feet were scalded by the hot water, and I had the marks for life. I thought he probably did, too.

I kept away from anyone who was interested in me after that. I kept my feet covered. I closed myself off further, stayed at home, and only spoke to men who were evidently sane and well balanced. I learned to call Christa and Geoff 'my parents'. I kept my mother a secret. For a long time I was sure I was destined to be alone for ever.

Yet I do not have bad memories of Po. He reappeared in my life in Brighton, where we ran into each other from time to time. By then he had wisely reverted to the name Peter; and, four years ago, he turned my scared little life upside down by introducing me to Matt, one sunny day in Brighton.

When I walked into the classroom to fetch Alice, I could see the tear stains on her face. She ran straight at me and clung to my knees. I picked her up. She buried her face in my shoulder.

'How was it?' I asked the teacher. She put her head on one side.

'I nearly rang you,' she said. 'It was hard because I tried to comfort her but she didn't understand what I was saying.'

I felt soiled with guilt, and left as quickly as I could. I tried to drop the planning application in at the *Mairie* on the way past, but it was closed for lunch.

chapter seven

A week later

The garden needed an immense amount of work, and I suddenly realised that I could do it. When Matt was away, when Alice was at school, I had little to do except for my daily nagging phone call to the builders. I did not dare make these calls without a full transcript of the way the conversation might go in front of me. I would go for walks and wait for the post, which yielded official communications of various daunting sorts or, occasionally, a postcard from my cousin Greg in south-east Asia. I treasured the postcards, but I needed a project. On Alice's first full school day, I started to negotiate my way around a hectare of abandoned, boggy land.

That morning, I dropped Alice off, with her napkin in her bag and a lunch ticket tucked into her book. She didn't scream and yell and cry because she had realised that did no good. She just looked at me with miserable reproach, and stalked off to play by herself in the toy kitchen.

I drove home feeling guilty, as usual, but looking forward to a day by myself. I changed into my worst jeans and my wellies, and took my coffee outside to examine the garden. It had been a wonderful weekend with Matt, and because he had commented about the terrible state of the garden, I had decided to tidy it up a little as a surprise for him on Thursday.

The garden had looked thoroughly dead when we had arrived. In fact it was so muddy and overgrown that I had barely walked around it. Now that I did, however, I noticed that, everywhere, there were signs of life. Leaves were about to bud on many of the trees. There were weeds everywhere, but as I stood on a flower bed to get a better view of the lower branches of a cherry tree, I noticed something strange. In between the weeds and nettles and self-seeded beginnings of new, unwanted trees, there were green shoots. Strong, green shoots pushed up everywhere I looked. I thought they might be daffodils, though my horticultural knowledge was limited. But they were there. The garden was still alive.

I rushed out and bought myself three pairs of gardening gloves and a random selection of trowels and spades, and a scythe. I spent the rest of the morning pulling weeds out of the soil, digging up those tiny trees, which were surprisingly tenacious, and patting the soil carefully into place around the shoots. At half past one, I stopped for lunch, and wolfed down a baguette, a chunk of cheese, two tomatoes, a bag of crisps, seven chocolate biscuits and two cups of tea. Then I carried on hacking until four twenty-five, scything away as much of the bramble as I dared, and piling it all up into a future bonfire.

It was only when I parked in the gravelly square next to

the school that I remembered that the other mothers always looked smart, or at least tidy, and that today I had forgotten to make myself in the least bit presentable. This was the first time I had joined the parents at the gate for the afternoon collection, and there was already a sizeable gaggle of smart mothers and a few fathers standing there. I scanned my face in the rear-view mirror. I had a streak of soil across my nose, which I wiped off with my sleeve. There was a livid red gash down one cheek, the result of a bramble jumping up at me. My hair was sweaty, but the sweat had turned cold as soon as I had stopped working. Now it just looked greasy. I looked as if I had stepped straight out of the shower, but for the fact that I was dirty. I was wearing my oldest jeans and a fleece I'd bought Matt a few years ago, which he had rarely worn because fleeces weren't his style.

I shrugged and got out of the car. I was letting Alice down again, but there was nothing I could do about it.

There were a few hellos at the gate, a few sidelong glances that I may have imagined. Then the children appeared on the other side of the courtyard. The teacher kept them all beside her, and called their names one by one as she spotted their parents. Each child ran across the playground to his or her parent. I screwed up my eyes and tried to gauge Alice's mood, but it was impossible to see at this distance.

The teacher kept her back, then called me over. Of course she did. Because I was wearing my gardening clothes I naturally had to have a discussion with the teacher.

'How was it?' I asked, as Alice jumped in front of me, arms held up for a carry. I picked her up.

'It was all right,' the teacher said, guardedly. 'She didn't eat any lunch. She cried a lot at siesta time. She didn't want to sleep at all. I had to take her out to see the bigger children so she wouldn't disturb the others.' I stroked Alice's hair. 'But then she fell asleep in my arms, and I was able to lay her down.'

I nodded. I had wondered how she was going to cope with the post-lunch nap, when she no longer had one at home.

'We'll try again tomorrow,' the teacher continued. 'But if it doesn't work, maybe she could go back to half days for a while. Oh,' she added, looking embarrassed. 'The napkin. The elastic. It's not important, but it goes like this.' She took her scarf from round her neck and mimed a piece of elastic leading from one corner to the corner next to it. 'So they put it on like this.' She mimed the elastic going over her head, holding the scarf to her chest like a bib.

I was mortified. I could barely meet her eyes.

'I'm so sorry,' I muttered.

She laughed. I looked up. 'It's not serious,' she said, giggling. 'It's a common mistake. We should put a diagram on the note. Alice will bring the napkin home on Friday.'

In the car, Alice refused to speak to me. I asked gentle questions about her day at school, but she folded her arms round herself and looked out of the window.

'What was for lunch?' I asked brightly as we arrived at the house. She said nothing.

'What sort of food?' I persisted.

'Funny food,' she said grumpily. 'I want chocolate.'

Under the circumstances, it seemed only fair to concede.

chapter eight

Jo smiled as Hugh walked through the gallery doors. It so rarely happened that they managed to meet for lunch; and he had virtually never made the trip from east London to Mayfair. She knew he must have taken almost the whole afternoon off work to come over here. It would take forty minutes to get here, forty minutes to get back, and he was taking her to Wiltons, so lunch would not be speedy. She was touched that he was making such an effort.

'Darling,' he said, walking over and kissing her on the lips. Jo was pleased, though she thought she heard Sylvie, her assistant, sniggering. As usual, Hugh made a point of looking at the canvases on the wall and the sculptures that dotted the floor.

'You know I'm a dunce when it comes to this,' he said apologetically, staring at an austere white and grey abstract on the wall.

'I know, I know,' she said impatiently. 'Please, don't even begin to go there. Come on.' She put on her camel cashmere coat. 'Let's go. You'll be all right, Sylvie?'

Sylvie nodded, her mouth full of cheese and pickle sandwich. 'Have fun,' she said through her food. Jo was pleased to usher Hugh out of her gallery. She hated to admit it, even to herself, but she was embarrassed by his comments on modern art. He sounded so . . . parochial.

She was grinning by the time their starters arrived. She had ordered smoked salmon, and Hugh was having crab. They were sharing a bottle of white Burgundy.

'I've got a little surprise,' she said, looking him in the eye and beaming.

'Oh fuck,' he said. 'You're pregnant, aren't you?'

'No! Christ, no. Nothing like that.'

'Good. So?'

'I know you're having to do all these weekends in Paris.'

'Mmm.'

'So I thought I'd come and visit. In fact I've planned it all. I know you'll be working, but I also know you won't be working all the time. I mean, Christ, they can't really expect you to put in a seven-day week and it's not as if anyone's going to be checking up on you on Sunday. So Jenny's going to drop Olly with my parents on Friday night, and he'll spend the weekend with them, and I'll catch the train out straight after work, at six forty-two. Then I'll come back on Sunday afternoon. Seven minutes past four. In fact you might want to come with me. It's so much nicer on the train.' She looked at him, waiting for a reaction. 'And I've taken the liberty of upgrading the accommodation,' she added. 'There's a room reserved for us at the George V.'

Hugh raised his eyebrows. Then he lowered them. He

shifted a little in his seat and took a sip of wine, followed by another. He smiled, and then frowned.

'That might be a little bit tricky,' he said.

Everything he told her sounded reasonable. He had been frantic at weekends on his project. Busier than he'd told her because he hadn't wanted to complain. This coming weekend he was going to be spending all day visiting some important people who were crucial to the project, which was to do with the euro. Yes, it was strange to work on Sundays, yes, he should be being paid a huge amount of money for it. He would contribute more to the household in future. It was a lovely idea, and perhaps some other weekend they could do it. He was terribly sorry.

Jo stared at him, not quite believing what she was hearing. 'You mean I have to cancel my tickets, and our reservation? I have to stay home with Olly after all? You don't want to see me there, even after all your important meetings?'

Hugh swallowed hard. 'No. Of course I want you there. Don't cancel. I'll see what I can do.'

Neither of them enjoyed their food. Jo was annoyed that she had had to force him to agree to what should have been a delightful and irresistible proposition. Hugh felt sick. He was committed, now, to spending next weekend in Paris, with Jo. He was going to have to concoct the pretend frame-work of a life there, or he would be found out. He would be expected to pay for the George V and at least two Michelin-starred restaurants. And he would not be able to spend the weekend with Emma and Alice.

There was still nearly a year left before his self-imposed deadline. Perhaps, he thought, he should sort his life out sooner than that.

chapter nine

I was not happy when Matt stayed in London for an entire weekend. We did not see him from one Sunday afternoon until the Thursday eleven days later. I knew he had to work, and he promised to buy a load of antique furniture to fill in some of the gaps in the house as a penance, but none of that leavened my loneliness. Alice was bitterly disappointed.

I put a brave face on it. 'Don't worry,' I told him, as he almost cried in frustration down the phone. 'It's a one-off. It doesn't matter. Just take care of yourself.'

Then I put Alice on. 'Daddy,' she said crossly. 'You come back. Just right now. Or I'm going to be very angry.'

She had the right idea. But we hung on, and eventually Thursday came and Matt was home.

On Friday, we took Alice to school. She hung her coat on her peg, held out each foot in turn for me to take off her outdoor shoes and put on her red slippers, and walked off.

'Bye then,' Matt called after her.

Alice looked casually over her shoulder. '*Au revoir,*' she said, and ran to a group of children sitting cross-legged on a mat. The teacher gave me a nod and a smile.

'She settled quickly, in the end,' she said.

Matt laughed. He had barely seen her unsettled, had never been the parent who broke her heart by abandoning her. 'She's a good girl,' he said in careful French.

We drove on into town, and parked behind the central square. From there we strolled through the drizzle to the café and ordered large white coffees. I looked around. The woman who had sorted out our gas tank was in there again, with a young woman and a little boy. As soon as I caught her eye, she came over.

'Hello!' she said warmly, and she introduced herself to Matt as Celine. 'How's the house? Is it warm?'

'Yes it is,' I told her. 'Thank you very much. It's fine. The builders should be arriving soon. Then we'll see some differences. They're going to take the heating out, for one thing. But for now it's just fine. We have some furniture. We have beds.'

'And the little one? She's not with you?'

'No,' I told her, looking at the little boy who was returning my gaze with frank curiosity. 'She's at school. Is this your grandson?'

'Yes. And my daughter.'

We were all introduced to each other. The lady's daughter was called Coco, and she was frighteningly chic. She was probably younger than me, and she was dressed in the same way that Bella dressed, in classic, clean, ironed clothes. Her long blonde hair hung to the middle of her back, and was obviously blow-dried every morning and cut every month. She wore make-up and she knew how to apply it. Her white shirt emphasised her tiny waist. Her black trousers hung down from her hips, as if she had no thighs. I envied everything about her. I was particularly jealous of the fact that she managed to keep herself beautiful while simultaneously being the mother of a two-year-old.

Not only was she beautiful and intimidating, she was also friendly.

'Come to see me,' she told me. 'Come for coffee. With your daughter.'

'OK,' I agreed nervously. 'Wednesday? When Alice is off school?'

She nodded and told me where she lived. I wondered whether I had made a friend. It could not, surely, have been that easy.

Matt and I passed an idyllic day together. At lunchtime, we sat in the crêperie in the centre of town. We took the window table, and looked out at the square, leaden under the looming sky.

'This is something,' Matt said, grinning at me. 'Yesterday I was at work, in Canary Wharf, the epitome of London capitalism. Today I'm sitting in a French crêperie, watching men in berets amble past with baguettes under their arms.'

I followed his gaze. An old man was, indeed, doing exactly that. I looked around the square. Next to the ancient church, the bakery had a sign in ornate lettering, reading 'Pâtisserie'. Next to that was the butcher's shop. On the other side was a stone arcade over the pavement, with picture windows in the building above it. The windows had wrought-iron grilles across the bottom of them. Even though this was, by all accounts, the wettest and most miserable spring anyone could remember, St Paul was a stunning little town.

'It is wonderful,' I told him. 'But you know I'd go back to Brighton like a shot.'

Matt looked at me, eyebrows raised. 'I know you would. Why, though? What can Brighton offer that St Paul can't?'

I laughed, but without meaning it. 'Friends, mainly. Family not too far away. Handy for times when you have to stay away for eleven days.'

'Sorry. I've said sorry. I wasn't having any fun, you know that.'

'I know. I shouldn't harp on about it. And I miss being able to walk to the shops. Brighton's familiar. I know where things are and how they work. I can communicate without worrying that the nuances of what I'm saying are making me seem rude or stupid. I can walk into the post office without having to say hello to everybody in the queue. I'm not foreign, not on show all the time and representing a nation. I could relax there. But we're doing OK here, aren't we?' I added this hastily, because my job was to look on the bright side.

'We're doing brilliantly. You are. Look how you made friends with that woman back there. And you know what? One day, when we're all settled, I'll sort out my job so I can do it from home most of the time, and after that . . .' he smiled at me. 'We'll get married. Promise.' He leaned forward. 'I'll tell you something. When we got here I gave myself a deadline for sorting it all out. A year. I knew I couldn't hack this commute indefinitely. So I promise to have it all in order by next January.'

'Next January,' I echoed. I pictured my life with Matt here full time, and a ring on my finger.

I knew that I would be able, and happy, to stick it out, if he meant it.

We found the nearest Friday market and bought fruit and vegetables, cheese and bread. We chatted to the stallholders, explained our situation and held the usual conversations about why we had come here, what we liked about it. We went home and walked hand in hand around the garden.

I knelt down and stroked some of the green shoots.

'Look,' I told Matt. 'The daffodils are doing brilliantly. They're really shooting up since I took the weeds away. I hope there's no more frost.' I pulled out small regrowths of weeds as I spoke. Then I noticed the roses. 'Oh Christ,' I exclaimed. 'Those roses have gone wild! Hang on a minute.' I made a run for the old chicken coop that had become my garden shed, and came back with my secateurs. My pruning was slightly random, but I thought that as long as I was cutting the growth back, I was doing approximately the right thing. 'I might need you to help me with the trees, actually,' I told him, 'when we've got a minute. I'm pretty sure they all need pruning, and it's going to be tough actually getting up there and doing it.' I looked at Matt.

'Sure,' he said. He looked somewhat bemused.

'The grass is growing quite fast now,' I told him. 'Did I tell you about my lawnmower?'

He frowned. 'That old lawnmower in the shed?'

'No! That's rubbish. It takes me eight hours to cut the grass with it, and I'd never get it over those brambles.' I gestured to the wilderness area. I was slightly affronted that

Matt had not mentioned the progress I had made in cutting back the jungle while he had been away. The brambles, nettles and thick grass were now less than a foot high, and I thought that the red tractor mower I had ordered would be able to cope with them. 'I ordered a proper mower and I'd like to get a strimmer too. Save a lot of time and stress with the scythe.'

Matt nodded. 'You're barmy,' he said mildly. 'But I love you. You're doing a strangely great job with this garden. Have you been possessed by the spirit of garden obsession? Am I going to have to get you exorcised?'

'Is it a benign spirit?'

He put his arms round me and pulled me in close. We fitted together perfectly, my head against his shoulder. 'As benign as can be,' he whispered.

'No need for exorcism then, is there?' I whispered back. He said nothing; just shook his head.

In the evening we put Alice to bed in her own bedroom, with Gavin the bear whom she had requisitioned. Matt read her far more stories than I usually did. I cooked onion soup and listened to his voice drifting down through the floorboards. I could make out the cadences but not the individual words.

Then he came down. I got the fire going, while Matt opened a bottle of red wine. We sat in our chairs, looked at each other, and sighed simultaneously.

'OK?' asked Matt.

'Yes,' I told him. 'Tired, but fine.'

'The trouble with you,' Matt said lazily, 'is that you're always fine. Nothing troubles you for long, does it?'

I laughed. I was pleased that Matt saw me like this. He was wrong, but this was the way I had always wanted people to see me. 'I suppose not,' I said, playing along.

'Equable, that's what you are, Emma. So, what don't you like?'

I looked at him. 'What do you mean, what don't I like?'

'Name some things you don't like.'

I raised my eyebrows. 'I don't like war. Or famine. Or other things like that. I don't like inequality or racism or sexism. There's lots I don't like.'

Matt laughed and drained his wine. 'Let's move away from Miss World territory. I want to hear you being nasty. What don't *you*, Emma Meadows, like? What do you hate? What drives you mad?'

I hesitated. 'I don't like Margaret Thatcher.'

'Passé. And unoriginal.'

'George Bush?'

'Ditto. What don't you like in your own little world?' He gestured around our living room. 'You have to be microcosmic. And specific.'

I was uncomfortable, because I was not quite sure what Matt was trying to make me say. 'I don't like the fact that the builders haven't shown up yet even though we've got planning permission. I don't like that stone cladding around the fireplace. I don't like feeling stupid. I don't like uncertainty. You know that. I don't like too much change. I don't like drinking and I don't like being out of control. I certainly don't like giving birth, although I wouldn't mind giving it another go.'

He sighed. 'Emma. I'm trying to make you be mean. I'm

trying to make you wicked. Try harder. Say something bitchy. What do you see around you that makes you think nasty thoughts?'

A surprising number of things that I could never have admitted to. Mentally, I ran through a list of things that brought out my nasty side and settled on the most innocuous. 'I hate wet-look hair gel,' I told him triumphantly. 'One of the checkout women in Intermarché wears it.' I did not mention the fact that, as well as hair gel, I could easily hate a large number of people. I hated people who had it easy. I hated lazy people, thin people, successful people. I hated Charlotte and the way she lived her life. I hated Matt for not telling me what had happened between him and his parents; I hated him for holding so much of himself back from me. I hated Alice, sometimes, for her constant demands. I hated my aunt for not being my mother, and for not being maternal enough towards me, and I hated my uncle Geoff for not being my father, although I quite liked him in every other way. Above all, I despised my mother for leaving me.

I looked at Matt, smiling. He had his head in his hands. 'Everyone hates bloody wet-look gel.'

'Perms, too,' I added brightly. 'Specially corkscrew ones. What about you?'

Matt stood up and walked to the window. He opened it and closed the shutters. 'Me? I hate everything. I hate beggars even though it's not their fault. I really hate those charity mugger twats who stop you everywhere in London to try and get your bank details off you. I hate people who don't know how to order properly in restaurants. I hate people who drink during the day and get rowdy and obnoxious. I hate pushchairs in busy shops even though we have a pushchair and we have been known to take it into busy shops. I hate people who use the automatic doors or the lift when they haven't got a pushchair and are perfectly able bodied, thus clogging it up for those who actually need it. I hate things that make me feel guilty. I hate cheating and dishonesty. I hate people with hard skin on their feet who wear sandals, forcing me to look at their ugly heels.' He sat back down with a smile. 'I could go on.'

I laughed, and frowned at him. 'So how ought one to order in restaurants?' I asked. 'Do I do it properly, or do you hate me?' I put some fingers inside my sock and stroked the sole of my foot. There was some hard skin there. But I had my scarring, so I never wore open sandals anyway. I did not want my future husband – my fiancé – to hate my feet.

'I'm talking about smart restaurants. If you're in a smart restaurant, then the person who's paying should ask everyone what they want before the waiter comes, then place the order for the whole group.'

I laughed. 'You're joking! I never knew that. You actually care about that? Is it some obscure form of etiquette?'

'It's the way it should be done. And while we're at it the loo roll should hang with the sheets in front, not behind.'

I shrugged. 'OK.'

'Right. Now you're making me feel I'm a petty misanthrope. I was trying to make you admit that you're not sweetness and light through and through, but it hasn't worked. Four years after meeting you, I'm still searching

101

for the chink in your armour. My partner, the perfect human being.'

I smiled at him. 'You have no idea.'

On Sunday night, I opened Matt's bag, which was already packed for his early flight in the morning, and I slipped in a picture that Alice had done for him. It was exuberant and splodgy, with lumps of glitter glue in it. I had written underneath exactly what she had said after she painted it: *A picture of Alice and Mummy and Daddy and our new house in France*. Then I had written, *We miss you x x x x x*

I imagined him opening his bag in his dark, gloomy flat and finding it in there. I pictured the smile that would spread across his face. I saw him propping it up on a dusty mantelpiece, and decided that I was going to hide a surprise for him every week. That way he could brighten up his flat, and it would mean that we would always be with him.

chapter ten

Hugh was feeling the pressure. He was uneasy almost all the time. The weekend in Paris had been excruciating. The most excruciating thing, if he was honest, was the fact that he had enjoyed it so much. He had presented the façade of a life to Jo and he was fairly sure that she had had no suspicions. He had bought her champagne at every opportunity, to distract her from the vague way he talked about his life here, and the convenient cancellation of those vital meetings. They had strolled around the Musée D'Orsay, guiltily taken in a few of the *Da Vinci Code* sites (pretending to each other that St Sulpice was simply one of the architectural splendours of the city, and that this was the sole reason for their visit), and they had surveyed the city from the top of the Eiffel Tower. It had been fun. Jo was always good company.

All the same, it had thrown him off kilter. He was massively poor now. He could not keep this up until January if Jo was going to throw surprises like that at him. As he had predicted, he had ended up paying for everything. He had felt horrible when he had spoken to Emma, and he had missed Alice like crazy. He was angry with Jo now and couldn't help snapping at her when, normally, he was amenable and agreeable. For fuck's sake. She had given him no choice. He felt, unreasonably, that she had had no right to do it. She had had no right to make him have a wonderful weekend in Paris when he was meant to be with Emma.

Emma had not questioned him staying away that weekend. She had always been easy to dupe because she had a far more pliant personality. Hugh felt worse about deceiving Emma than he did about Jo. Jo was a powerful, confident woman, where Emma was vulnerable. He knew that he could have told anything to Emma and she would have believed him. Now she thought they were getting married. He had talked about it because he had wanted to see her smile. He thought that procrastination was the only way to play that one. In January, he half intended to divorce Jo and marry Emma instead. He wondered whether he could get his divorce without Emma knowing anything about it. There was, of course, that line about a man marrying his mistress and creating a vacancy, but it wouldn't be like that. It wasn't his nature to be like that. This was an exceptional situation.

Hugh was reading a bedtime story to Olly. They were reading about the Elephant and the Bad Baby. Hugh could have read this in his sleep. Jo had bought it for Olly because she remembered it from her childhood. When Olly had become attached to it, Hugh had bought a copy for Alice. Both children were intermittently obsessed with the naughty elephant.

Plan B

Olly slumped onto Hugh's chest, and twisted round to see the book. Hugh had his arm round Oliver's narrow shoulders. Olly was much taller than Alice, even though she was older than he was. She had been born, a week late, five and a half weeks before Olly had arrived on his due date. It had been typically efficient of Jo to give birth on the correct day, Hugh had thought at the time. He cringed at the memory. That had been a hairy time for him. He had fully expected to be found out and to be forced to abandon one of his children, or, more likely, both of them.

Then he had discovered that new mothers turned inwards, that their every second was spent concentrating on the milky bundles of baby. He came and went. Whichever house he went to, he was greeted with joy, and was told every detail about the relevant baby's day. He had realised that, in a way, fathering these children had been a masterstroke. Now the women weren't focused on him any more. They were obsessed with their offspring instead.

Before it had all happened, he had been a married man behaving badly, enjoying himself, stringing Emma along because he was taken with her. He felt comfortable with her, he had been touched by the way she had looked up to him and loved him. He had never intended much to come of it.

When he met her in Brighton, he had been feeling playful. He had walked over to her for no other reason than out of curiosity, because she was the woman who had broken Pete's heart. He had used his middle name on a whim. Emma had looked at him with trusting brown eyes and had stupidly judged him to be safe. He had liked the way she

105

smiled at him, and he'd sensed that she would be unquestioningly loyal and devoted. He had also been engaged in an unkind game with Peter. He had been overjoyed, in the meanest sense possible, by his effortless seduction of the famous Emma, the woman who had rejected Pete on a daily basis for years, to the point where he had cut his wrists and bled all over her ('Mmm,' Hugh had told him, just after the event. 'Good strategy. She'll come round now.' She had, in fact, responded by pouring boiling water on Pete's feet, and Hugh had not blamed her.)

He had known from the start that, unlike most of his temporary conquests, she would not have come near him if she had known he was married, so he had never mentioned it. He had been experimenting, seeing how great his powers of attraction could be. He had also been trying to piss Pete off. In that, he had succeeded with honours.

It had been fun, having two women on the go. Pete had been shocked at the way he was deceiving Emma, but although he could have stopped Hugh's games at any time by telling her the truth, he had held back. In a way, Hugh knew, Pete had been pleased to see Emma being duped into a relationship that was bound to end with her being terribly hurt. Pete had been horrified and delighted to gain that sort of revenge on her. He said he was over her now, but Matt knew that he was angrily in love with her, in spite of everything.

Hugh had found himself spending half the week in Brighton, at Emma's house, and the other half in London in his marital home. He liked waking up twisted around Emma, and looking at the light coming through her blinds onto the ceiling, and hearing the seagulls screeching. He also liked waking with Jo in their bedroom, which at Jo's behest, was entirely white. She had sanded the floorboards and painted them white with some special sort of paint, and there were white curtains and white bedlinen. He had laughed at the idea, but in fact it was lovely. He had been happy with both of them.

Then it had happened. He must have been going through a particularly fertile time.

'Strong swimmers,' Pete had said. He had not approved, had not wanted Emma to be hurt to this extent. Hugh could not possibly have left Emma when she was pregnant and happy, and there was no way he was going to leave Jo and have her hate him for ever. He wanted to know his children. He wanted to be in both their lives. There was nothing he could do but attempt to cover his tracks and see what happened. He still pretended to himself that there was no other option.

He had watched the two women he loved going through childbirth within six weeks of each other, and he had realised why monogamy was a cultural norm. It had almost been too much for him. Jo thought her labour had been hard, because it had taken twenty-four hours and had needed a ventouse and stitches. But she had had an epidural as soon as she had taken her coat off and had been laughing with him and chatting on the phone for most of the birth. Emma's labour with Alice still haunted him. She had struggled for forty hours, using just gas and air and a birthing pool, until the baby's heartbeat had started accelerating then slowing, and suddenly the room had filled up with doctors and a resuscitation table and all sorts of implements. They cut Emma's perineum, and yanked Alice out with forceps. She was blue. As they whisked her away, Hugh had been petrified. Emma was gripping his hand, and he had decided, in that second, that he was going to leave Jo and lead an honest life. But the baby was fine, he had a daughter, and he left things as they were.

For the next few weeks, before Oliver was born, Jo had overflowed with excited anticipation.

'Let's go to the cinema,' she would suggest. 'Let's go to dinner. Let's do all the things we won't be able to do any more once the baby's here.'

He had acquiesced. When he wasn't sitting in front of films with a hand on Jo's bump, feeling his unborn son kicking and squirming inside her, he was looking after Emma, taking Alice for walks to give Emma a break, walking around the sitting room with Alice half asleep on his shoulder. He woke up when the baby squeaked at midnight, three o'clock, half past five and seven; he stroked her soft hair as she lay on the duvet between her parents. He pined for Alice. She was the innocent in his life, and he had already let her down.

Hugh sighed mentally, still reading to Olly. It had started as a normal infidelity. Now he had two toddlers to contend with, and he couldn't ever put them in a room together and tell them to play.

Olly squirmed. 'Why didn't the baby say please?'

Bloody two-year-olds. 'He just didn't.'

'The bad baby was *very naughty*.'

'Yes he was. That's the elephant's point, in a nutshell.'

'What's a nutshell? What means point in a nutshell?'

It had been Jo's fault, to begin with. Before he met her he had been geeky and boring. Jo had told him that he was lovely; genuine, sweet, unthreatening. He had, she insisted, a warm and tender smile. He was the antithesis of a bastard. He made her feel safe and happy and loved. Hugh had been amazed, and he had worked on his good points.

He thought of the shameful string of extra-curricular liaisons he had had before he met Emma. His present situation was, he imagined, karma. He wondered what would happen if he told Olly, right now, that he had a sister.

'Why? Why's she got a different mummy? Why's she live in France?' There would be hundreds of whys, and the answer to every single one of them would have been: because I'm crap. Followed by: no. No, you can't meet her. No, Mummy doesn't know her. No, you mustn't tell anyone. No, no, no, no, no. This had all started off as a celebration of his unexpected ability to attract women, and it had ended up, he admitted to himself, as a complete fucking nightmare. He was deeply impressed with himself for the fact that he had carried it off so far.

There was no obvious way out. He knew that, when his year was up, or sooner, he would have to leave one of them. The thought of actually leaving Jo was gut-wrenching. In Paris he had been surprised by how much he still loved her, by how funny she was, by how much he relaxed in her company. He had a creeping, unanalysed feeling that he might be swinging towards choosing Jo, after all. Then, at other times, it was Emma he wanted. It was all very confusing.

He pictured Oliver growing up scarred by his father's behaviour and emulating him by turning into a grade A bastard. He imagined Alice, scared of life and anxious not to offend, like her mother. He knew that his behaviour was potentially blighting the future happiness of his children, and yet he did not know how to make everything better.

Jo listened to the comforting hum of Hugh's voice through the wall as she tidied their bedroom and filled the white laundry basket with dirty washing. She unzipped his bag, ready to add his clothes to the laundry heap, and to put a load in the washing machine. Pants, socks, a spare shirt. He never took much away with him and most of it still seemed to be clean. She rolled her eyes. Men.

As she tipped it all out, a piece of paper fluttered down from the side of the bag. Jo picked it up from the white floorboards, and studied it.

'Hugh?' she called. 'When you're finished, can you come in here?'

chapter eleven

One Wednesday morning, Alice and I called round to Coco's flat, which was in the middle of St Paul. It was large and airy, with huge front windows looking down onto the street. The sky was pale blue and the sun was out, shining into her sitting room and dazzling us.

Coco grinned as we came up the narrow stairs. 'Come in!' she called. 'Alice, Louis wants to do some painting with you.'

Alice nodded, understanding, and looked around for Louis. We had been to Coco's flat a few times now, and we were both still shy there. Coco was friendly and Alice liked Louis, but I still held back, and Alice sensed that. I had always found it difficult to make friends. I was polite with Coco, but I could not relax with her.

'Coffee,' she said, and handed me a tiny glass espresso cup.

'Could I have a tiny bit of milk?' I asked.

'Of course you could. I forgot again. You are so English, drinking milk in your coffee.'

'Don't the French? You must do or the English wouldn't always call it a *café au lait*. Every English person knows that phrase.'

'Which is funny since the French are much more likely to call it *café crème*.'

'But the English can't say *crème*. It's too throaty for us.'

'You just said it.'

'It took years of practice.'

'The French might drink a *café crème* in the morning. Afterwards, a coffee is just to wake you up and give some focus. To have milk in it would be to make it into something else. It's like food then.'

'Anglo-Saxons like a snack. That's why we're so fat.'

The children were soon deeply involved in their painting. Coco chatted away and I answered as best I could. I watched her while she talked. She was impossibly chic. I thought my waist must be twice the circumference of hers, and her clothes were far, far out of my league. I wondered why she wanted me for a friend.

'She just turns up!' she was saying, huffing in annoyance. 'Any time she feels like seeing us! Last night she brought food. I tell her that I don't want it but she insists. It's so annoying.'

I laughed. 'My aunt would never do that. She's the opposite. Quite distant.' I decided to try to open up and to tell her about my mother. 'Hey,' I said. 'At least you've got a mother.'

Coco raised her eyebrows: 'At least you've got a partner.'

I stared. 'You haven't got a partner?'

She looked around. 'Do you see him?'

'I just thought he was at work.'

She shook her head. 'Louis' father and I split up when Louis was seven months old. It was horrible. He's Swiss. He lives in Geneva now.'

'Does he see Louis?'

She put her head on one side. 'Mmm-hmm. Not regularly. When he can fit him in. I refuse to go all the way to Switzerland so he has to come here to see him. He's coming this summer. He always makes it into some big event as if he's the best father in the world for travelling for a few hours to see the son he deserted. Arsehole.' She said the word in English. 'We manage. That's why my mother's in my hair all the time.'

'God, Coco. I couldn't do that.' As I said it, I knew that it was literally true. 'I don't have the mental strength to be a single mother. All that responsibility.'

She laughed at me, not unkindly. 'Emma? You are almost a single mother as it is. Whenever I see you you're on your own. OK, sometimes I see you and Matt at the market on Saturday, but mainly it's just you and Alice. Isn't it? You'd be fine.'

'It's not the physical presence. You're right, I am fine, and that's because I know that Matt's going to be back tomorrow. I know that he's always with us on Thursday evening and he always stays till Sunday. Nearly always. That's why I can manage three days on my own. I need that kind of support. When he stayed away for the weekend it was horrible. I couldn't manage on my own at all.' I looked at her and smiled. 'Of course I'm pretty sure it's not going to happen.'

Coco smiled. 'Of course not. But if it did you would surprise yourself. I stayed with André far longer than I should have because I had the same fears. He left me in the end. I regret that. If I could go back in time, I would leave him as soon as I was pregnant.'

Alice and Louis stampeded into the room. Alice was holding a toy ladybird that lit up. Louis was starting to cry.

'*C'est à moi!*' he shouted. Alice hugged it tightly, her brows knitted into a tight frown.

'Share your toys!' Coco told Louis.

'It's Louis'. Give it back,' I told Alice.

They both glared.

'Shall we take them for a walk?' I asked hesitantly.

We walked towards the café. The sun was bright, now. I thought of my flowers coming into bud. The daffodils and other, surprise flowers that I could not yet identify were going to flower soon. There were lots of birds in the garden. Even the boggy ground was almost dry now.

I looked up. 'How long will it last this time?' I asked. There had been intervals of good weather, but the rain and clouds always came back.

'How long will it last?' Coco echoed with a smile. 'This is spring. Finally! I've never known a spring as bad as this one has been. You must have brought the weather from England.'

'Sorry. Everyone says that.'

I looked around. The trees had leaves on them. All the blossom had been washed away by the rain, but now the greenery was strong and blooming. The paving stones beneath our feet reflected the sunlight, almost dazzling me.

Plan B

All the cafés had their chairs out. I decided to send Matt a text later to announce the delayed arrival of our French summer. I felt silly for not having noticed it before.

Coco suddenly burst out laughing. I followed her gaze. A man and a woman were strolling towards us, deep in conversation. A man walked backwards in front of them, with a camera trained on them, and a platinum-blonde woman dressed in black was next to the cameraman. The camera crew looked sorely out of place in this tiny town, and passing shoppers were turning to stare.

The couple looked as if they were in their mid-thirties. The man saw Coco and raised a hand in greeting. He had a small goatee beard. The woman was rosy-cheeked, with short, curly hair and a broad smile.

'*Bonjour*, Coco,' the man called. She laughed under her breath and took me by the hand.

'You might like this,' she said quietly. 'Or you might hate it.'

Coco approached the couple and kissed them on each cheek. She nodded to the woman in black. The cameraman stepped back and turned his camera off.

'This is Emma,' Coco said, in English. 'Emma – Andy and Fiona.'

Andy and Fiona both laughed warmly.

'Oh, *hello*!' said Fiona. 'Are you the other English people? The ones who live in Pounchet?'

'I am. We are. I take it that you're the ones with the television people?'

They shrugged their shoulders, uniformly sheepish. 'That'll be us,' the man admitted. 'This is Rosie.' The woman smiled politely, and went back to conferring with her cameraman. 'Rosie is in charge of our lives. So tell me, Emma, how did you manage to move to France *without* featuring in your own documentary?' We all laughed. I turned to Coco, suddenly embarrassed about Andy and Fiona hearing my French when I had no idea how good theirs was.

'In England,' I told her hesitantly, 'there are too many programmes on the television about people who move to France, Italy, Australia, Spain . . .'

Coco raised her eyebrows and nodded brightly, not really interested. She was watching Louis and Alice, who were holding hands and jumping off a step together, screaming with fear and laughter.

'Louis!' she called. 'Shhh! *Doucement!*'

I felt obliged to tell Alice to stop screaming too, although I could not really see who they were disturbing. I supposed that this was why French children had beautiful manners and their British counterparts ran wild.

'Do you always have an entourage?' I asked. 'Isn't it horribly intrusive? I'd feel self-conscious all the time.'

Fiona cocked her head to one side. 'You get used to it,' she said. 'I'm actually surprised at how quickly you do get used to it. They're nice people. When they're filming we just pretend they're not there. When they're not filming, we have a laugh with them. It's been good to have the company, to be perfectly honest with you.' She looked at the children. 'Is that your little girl? She's a *treasure*.'

I called Alice over to say hello and, as she approached, I saw Rosie looking speculatively at the children. Coco took

Louis by the hand, and bade us all goodbye. I could understand her not wanting her little boy in a British documentary.
I did not particularly want Alice or me in it, either.

'Come next Wednesday,' Coco called back over her
shoulder.

Andy and Fiona were friendly. Andy suggested going for
a coffee, and Rosie immediately asked if she could come
with us and film us. I thought about it, assessed my scruffy
appearance, ran my fingers through my hair, and agreed.
Before anyone pointed a camera at me, however, I
announced that I was not pregnant.

'The last thing I want,' I explained to Fiona, 'is you making
that mistake and me having to correct you on camera.'

'I didn't think for a moment you were!' she said, patting
my shoulder. The cameraman checked with the café owner,
and we went in and sat down.

'What does your husband do?' Andy asked. 'That's always
the first question, isn't it? I can't count the number of friends
at home who've said, we'd love to do what you're doing,
but what would we do for money? How have you worked
it?'

I decided not to correct his use of the word 'husband'.

'He's a project manager,' I said, feeling awkward in front
of the camera. I fiddled with my hands and twisted my hair
around my finger. 'I've never entirely understood what projects he manages, or what he exactly does on a day-to-day
basis. But he still works in London three or four days a
week. He works from home most Thursdays and every
Friday, and of course he's here for weekends.' I noticed
Fiona pulling a sympathetic face. 'It's not ideal,' I conceded.

'Alice and I knock around the house a bit when he's not here, but we do OK. And when he is here, it's just brilliant.'

'Ahhh,' said Andy. 'Look at the way her face lights up. You can't do a thing like this without sacrifices, can you?'

'No,' I agreed. 'To be honest, it was Matt who wanted to move here, not me, and when he's with us, he's so happy. He loses all that tension he used to have when we lived in Brighton. It makes it all worthwhile. He's absolutely in his element, and that fires me up as well. And he's looking into ways to work from home almost all the time, so that'll change everything for the better.' I smiled, feeling braver than usual. 'It's all good,' I said.

'You'll be getting ADSL soon, won't you?' Fiona said. 'I know we will. That'll make it all easier, I'm sure.'

'What about you? How have you managed it?'

Andy smiled proudly. 'Property,' he said grandly. 'I've speculated and accumulated, my dear. Managed to buy years ago in areas that are now highly desirable. I've got houses rented out all over Leeds, and a couple in London. The proceeds keep us in the style to which my wife has become accustomed.'

She nudged him. 'You!'

'It's true. There's everything on tap for the ladies in France, isn't there? I mean, how big is this town? Five thousand people? And yet it's got more hairdressers than bloody bakeries. Plus beauticians on top of that. Eyebrow waxing, manicures, pedicures, you name it, it's all essential. I'm scared to stand still in some parts of this town in case someone jumps out and waxes me. And don't get me started on clothes.' He rolled his eyes. I imagined Andy performing monologues for the cameras. I knew he must love it. I looked at Fiona's eyebrows, which were barely there, and her hands, which were soft and flawless. I hid my own nails – bitten, and ingrained with dirt from the garden. I rarely bothered to wear my gardening gloves because they made me feel clumsy. I noticed that Fiona's rosy cheeks were delicately made up with blusher, and that her clothes were floaty designer offerings rather than the baggy casual wear I had first taken them for.

She saw me assessing her. 'Don't worry, lovie,' she said kindly. 'I do it for the telly. Plus, I've nothing else to do. You've got your kiddy to think about. And,' she added hastily, 'you look lovely anyway.'

I snorted. 'Right.'

Alice was playing under the table. She popped up next to me. 'Can I eat your sugar?' she asked Andy conversationally.

'No you can't,' I said, but tailed off as he handed her two cubes. Alice looked at me, triumphant, and stuffed them both into her mouth before I could take them away. I checked to see if the exchange had been captured on film. It had.

I was relieved to walk away from the camera. I dreaded to think how I would come across and hoped that I had been so awkward and inept that the footage of me could not appear in the finished product.

We were all invited to Sunday lunch with Andy and Fiona at the weekend. I felt odd about making friends with people purely because they were British.

'Will we be filmed?' I asked anxiously. I knew I would not be able to eat with a camera trained upon me.

'Not a chance,' Andy replied immediately. 'They're all off to the beach for the weekend, the slack buggers.'

And so I accepted. Andy and Fiona lived, I realised, in the huge hilltop house I had admired every time I was out walking. It was seven or eight kilometres away from our house, but it still seemed to loom. I had driven through their village several times, and always slowed in front of the château. Close up, it was immaculate. They had a cleaner and a gardener, and when they bought the house six months earlier, it had needed no work at all. This made me extremely jealous.

My secret bitch was dying to butt in with acidic observations about my new friends, but I restrained her. All I would admit to myself was that I was intrigued to find out what the interior of the fabulous house was like.

chapter twelve

Matt arrived home on Friday afternoon. He stood in the front door frame, with the late afternoon sun behind him, making his shadow extend halfway down the hall. I could barely make out his features but I knew something was wrong. Normally he rushed in and gathered us both up and squeezed us close to him.

'Sweetie!' I said. I was concerned because I was in a buoyant mood at the prospect of his return, and could not bear to see him hanging back. I ran up and hugged him. 'What is it?'

He shrugged and kissed my mouth. He smiled, but it was a feeble effort. Normally his face shone when he came back to us. Today he looked pale and tired.

'Sorry,' he said. 'Work. There's too much of it. You know I'd promised to do a short week next week, to go back Monday night and be back here for Thursday? It's not going to happen. I'm sorry, darling.'

'When are you going back, then?'

'Sunday night. Last flight. I've got a six thirty breakfast meeting on Monday.'

I smiled. 'That's OK then because we have a Sunday lunch engagement with some expats. They live in that huge house.' I took his overnight bag from his shoulder and his briefcase from his hand, and led him into the kitchen. 'Alice!' I shouted. 'Daddy's home!'

I heard her footsteps overhead.

'She's playing upstairs?' Matt asked, surprised. Alice generally liked to be as close as possible to one or the other of us.

'Watching a DVD,' I admitted. 'I needed to get on with the dinner, and she was doing my head in. Plus she's been at school and she's knackered. She wasn't interested in anything except the telly.' I felt terrible, because I had always resisted TV. I had vowed that my child was not going to be pacified by moving dots on the screen. I had held out for over two years, turning down Bella's offer of a complete set of Postman Pat, various Teletubby adventures, and *Pingu*.

'You have to have *Pingu*,' Bella had told me, incredulous. 'It's hilarious. Now the boys have grown out of it, I watch it on my own sometimes.'

'I just don't want children's videos in the house,' I explained. 'I don't want her to be aware of telly at all. And if I had them, I know I'd end up sitting her down with them. If I had any strength of mind I'd get rid of our own telly.'

'Suit yourself.'

Yesterday, I had found myself buying DVDs in Intermarché. Alice adored the entire experience. I had tried to buy only quality films, but I still felt as if I had failed her.

Matt squeezed my shoulder. 'Don't feel you have to explain. Kids like telly. If I was here more, I'm well aware

I'd be able to entertain her at such moments. But I'm not, so I'm hardly going to judge you if you occasionally park her in front of the box. God knows, I would. Every parent does. What's on?'

'*Toy Story.*'

'Well, there you go. It's a classic. I might watch it with her.'

I looked at him closely. 'You're down, aren't you? You're down because you think you're missing out on Alice.'

He snorted. 'It's more of an accumulation of factors. Where's the wine? And who are these expats and where the fuck did you find them?'

We spent Saturday at the beach. It took just over an hour to drive there – a largely silent journey with Matt frowning and huffing in the driving seat. He was oblivious to the morning sunshine lighting up the pine trees that lined the route. He didn't notice the blue sky, didn't seem to realise that, in a flush of optimism, I hadn't even brought our coats with us.

When we saw the sandy beach stretching away into the distance in both directions, I was sure that he was going to start to be happy. I stepped out into the sunshine and felt the warm breeze on my face. I pulled my cardigan off and wondered whether I dared wear a swimming costume. It would be good to let my skin see the sun.

'Come on!' I called to him and Alice, and I set off down the steps to the beach.

'All right, all right. Doing my best,' he said crossly.

The beach looked endless. I felt happily insignificant as I chose a spot and put down our plastic-backed rug and a couple of towels. The sand was sprinkled with groups of people. I took a deep breath. This was beautiful. The sea was big, the sky was clear, the beach extraordinarily long. The sand dunes behind us cut us off from the real world, so for a while our universe seemed to consist only of sand, clear water, and sky. The nearest group of people was about twenty metres from us, and they were surfers. I watched them for a second, forcing limbs into wetsuits and fastening leashes round their ankles.

'Lots of surfers,' I said to Matt, with a smile, when he came and sat next to me. He never stayed grumpy for long. 'I've always loved to see surfers. I might try it one day. Do you think I could?' I laughed out loud at the idea of standing on a board, on the sea.

He looked at me and looked away. He pushed a hand through his hair and slicked it back. 'Right,' he said, with a little snort. 'You're going to surf. Now I've heard everything.'

'I'm serious. I could have some lessons. I'd love to give it a go.'

'Emma, you couldn't surf. And you won't. You're just saying it to get me to speak to you.'

I stared at him.

'Alice!' I called. 'Hat back on, please!'

Alice smiled wickedly. 'Don't want to.' She ran away. I chased her, hat in hand, pleased to escape from Matt. She collapsed, giggling, onto the sand. I fell down next to her. Her nose crinkled as she laughed. Her cheeks were perfectly round. She was so gorgeous that she was edible. I told myself to forget about Matt snapping, and to be nice until I wore him down.

Plan B

'Come on,' I told her, pushing the hat down over her hair. 'Let's go and make Daddy happy.'

He relaxed, slowly, as the day wore on. The three of us went down to the sea, and Matt and I held Alice's hand as she jumped over waves. She was almost hysterical with excitement. On a whim, I walked away from her and Matt, out into the waves. I wanted to experience this wild ocean, to see whether I could imagine myself on a surfboard. I jumped over the white, breaking water, and paddled out to the calm sea, where I lay on my back and let myself be heaved up and down by the waves. I looked up at the sky. A few birds flew overhead. The waves picked me up and dropped me as if I were a piece of driftwood. I closed my eyes.

I never felt myself being carried in to shore, but that is what happens to driftwood, and that is what happened to me. Suddenly, I was pulled back, and when I opened my eyes, the wave was just about to break on me. It crashed into my face, onto my body. I spun around, forced down to the sand. I struggled to stand up. My eyes and mouth were full of salty water and I lost all control. It was over in a few seconds. I got up, knee deep in water, and rubbed my face.

'Jesus, Emma,' said Matt, running through the shallows with Alice in his arms. 'What were you *doing*?'

I laughed. 'I was just experimenting. I'm fine.'

'God. You scared me. Christ.'

I was shaken but strangely pleased by my experience. I liked wild oceans.

We carried buckets of sea water back to our camp to pour over sand and make it sticky enough for sandcastles. We built a huge fort with a moat that steadfastly refused to fill with water because we were sitting at the top of a steep slope that was several metres above sea level. To our right, the beach stretched halfway up France. To our left, it reached Spain. I was still tingling from my encounter with the water. I wanted to do that again.

'Who wants an ice cream?' Matt asked, after a couple of hours.

'Me!' shouted Alice. 'Chocolate one.'

'Me too,' I added, with a few reservations. I had to have one, since it was a perfect day on a sunny beach in the south of France, but I still hadn't lost the weight I had gained having Alice, and the women on this beach were making me feel woefully inadequate. In a swimming costume, even a one-piece, I could not escape my flabby stomach and thunderous thighs. The tops of my arms disgusted me. I knew I had a double chin.

A little way down the beach, there was a woman who was probably ten years older than me but who was lying back wearing a tiny pair of black bikini bottoms. Her body was impeccable. She was toned and slender, with pert breasts that pointed straight upwards and did not slide into her armpits. She was tanned but not overly so. Three teenage boys were getting ready to surf next to her, and I watched her speaking to them, unable to hear, but knowing that she was telling them to be careful. I could not believe that it was possible to give birth three times and still have a body like that. Nor could I believe it was possible to be so unselfconscious in front of one's teenage sons.

I had let myself off the hook on the body front, entirely

excusing my flab on the grounds that everyone got a little podgy in between babies. Now I saw that if I were to carry on living in France, I was going to have to raise my standards.

'Actually, just a bottle of water, thanks, nice and cold,' I said loudly, as Matt started to walk away. Alice leapt up.

'I'm coming too, Daddy,' she shouted, and I watched Matt stop and wait for her, smiling indulgently.

While they were away I gazed at all the figures in the water. They were black and glistening, like seals. I could not take my eyes off them. Matt was right: I would probably never surf, but I could still watch. I could empathise. I picked a figure, randomly, and watched him until he got a wave. I was frustrated with him as he jumped up a little too late and missed his ride. A few waves later, he tried again. He jumped up and caught the crest of the wave. I saw him slowly rise to his feet. The wave carried him along. He stood triumphantly. I felt a vicarious exhilaration as he prolonged his ride by executing a turn and gliding back with the wave arching over his head. It broke over him. I relived what that had felt like, pleased to be able to involve myself to a tiny degree. He bobbed to the surface a moment later. He paused for a couple of seconds before turning back towards the horizon, throwing himself on his board, and paddling out again. I shook my head. I could never have done that.

'I'm sorry,' Matt said, later, in the back garden. Alice had just gone to bed and we were watching the sun set behind the house. 'I'm hopeless, aren't I?'

'Of course you're not hopeless,' I told him, relieved that he had admitted it.

'But I am. I let work and exhaustion get on top of me, and I've ruined half our weekend. You can't tell me that's not crap.'

I stroked his hand. 'It's completely understandable. Commuting by plane can't be easy. It is not, on the face of it, a sane way to live your life. And I know how busy you are with work. You're being pulled in half.'

He smiled, a funny little smile. 'I certainly am. You have no idea how right you are. I miss you girls when I'm not with you. I hate being away from you all the time. So, obviously, I deal with it by getting depressed and taking it out on the pair of you and making you both miserable. Because I'm a modern man and that's what we do.' He put his head in his hands so his hair fell forward, then looked at me with a comical hangdog expression. As soon as I laughed, he crinkled his eyes and chuckled along with me, and we were officially friends again.

'Getting a bit cold now,' I observed. 'But it's so lovely. I think I can stick it out a bit longer.'

'More wine,' Matt prescribed. 'It'll warm you up, and anaesthetise you.' I held out my glass and he topped it up with local Sauvignon. I looked again at the back lawn. I was pleased with the short grass. I had cut it specially for Matt's return, though he hadn't commented. I had tied the listening end of the baby monitor onto the front of the lawnmower, where I could see the flashing lights, and cut it after Alice was in bed. The longer evenings were a blessing. I had loved driving up and down, making stripes on the grass and thinking of the future.

I sipped my wine and tried to judge Matt's mood. I was pretty sure that this was not a good moment to discuss the timing of our next child. I took a gulp and wondered whether I could steel myself to mention it. If I got pregnant right now, there would be three and a half years between Alice and the new baby. I would have preferred a smaller gap. I was anxious that, because we had not planned to have Alice, Matt might be assuming that she was an only child. I knew I needed to discuss it with him. Communication was everything.

The wine seemed to be slipping down a lot easier these days, I reflected. I even, occasionally, poured myself a glass when I was on my own. I would never have done that in England. I opened my mouth to speak, then decided not to mention the putative baby just yet. It would have alienated him all over again; and I could not bear the prospect of Matt slipping back into his black mood.

'Lunch with your new friends tomorrow, then,' he said, stretching his legs out and gazing across the tame grass at the sun disappearing into the maize field behind the house. The maize, I noticed, was beginning to put up its green shoots, in perfectly straight lines. 'What are they like, then, really?'

I considered a few adjectives. Brash would be one. Crass, another. Not really my sort of people, would have been kinder. 'They're lovely,' I said blandly.

'You're far too nice, Em,' Matt replied laconically. 'That pause said it all. You don't like them. I'll look forward to seeing why tomorrow. There is absolutely no chance whatsoever that they'll have these bloody filming people hanging around, is there?'

'No chance at all,' I told him confidently.

I was excited to park outside the house I had admired for so long, and to walk through the wrought-iron gates and into the front courtyard. There were pots of flowers against the walls of the house, and a small fountain in the centre of the yard.

'Why didn't we buy something that was already renovated?' I asked Matt as we walked to the door, which was ajar.

'Money,' he replied. 'Obviously.'

I pushed the door and called, 'Hello?' Then I turned round to fetch Alice, who was kneeling beside a flower pot arranging her dinosaurs around a geranium. I knelt down next to her to gather them up.

'You can come and play out here afterwards,' I said. 'First we have to go in and see Andy and Fiona.' I took her hand to pull her up.

Suddenly, there was a commotion.

Matt was shouting. He ran back towards me and Alice, with his back turned forcefully towards the door and his arms protecting his head. 'Don't film me!' he shouted, 'Don't film me!'

Alice was startled. She looked at her father, who had nearly reached the gate, and started to laugh. Then she copied him. Her little hands were on her head, and she shouted, 'Don't film me! Don't film me!' I saw Matt looking at her. Her face was crumpled with delighted laughter. For an instant Matt's face had a look of abject horror. Suddenly he did not look like my Matt at all.

He straightened and ran out to the street, and away down the middle of the quiet road. An old man cycled by, and turned on his saddle to stare back at Matt.

I watched him running off, as baffled as the old man, then looked at the house. Alice was still giggling.

'Can I go with Daddy?' she asked. 'Is it a chasing game?'

'It will probably have to turn into a chasing game,' I told her. 'Daddy has suffered an extreme overreaction.' I frowned. 'Daddy is under a lot of pressure.'

Alice nodded knowledgeably. 'I under lot of pressure too,' she informed me.

The film crew, as well as Andy and Fiona, were standing around on the paving stones. I looked at them, shook my head and spread my hands.

'Sorry,' I said, walking closer. 'I'm afraid I have no idea what that was about.'

Andy chuckled. 'I don't think your husband was overly enamoured of the prospect of being beamed into the nation's living rooms,' he suggested. 'Just a wild guess.'

'He's never liked having his photo taken,' I told them, 'but that was a little extreme. I'm sorry.' I looked at Rosie, who was clearly in charge. 'You won't show that bit, will you? He'll look stupid and everyone will laugh at him.'

She shook her head, efficiently. Rosie wore tight black trousers and a black Lycra top. Once again, she had a pair of sunglasses balanced on her blonde head. I had thought she was in her late thirties, but, close up, she looked closer to thirty-three or so. How could someone my own age be so pushy? I wondered. And so successful. 'Of course not,' she said briskly. 'We can't show him without his permission anyway. When Andy invited you to lunch we thought it would be a nice scene to shoot, but obviously it's not appropriate so we won't.'

Fiona stepped forward. 'I would have called you to run it by you, but of course we didn't exchange numbers. I

131

would have dropped by to see you, only I've been up to my eyeballs.' She looked to the director. 'Rosie, what would you say to this idea? Emma and I will go out next week, get our hair done and her eyebrows sorted out, maybe a manicure.' She picked up my hand. I had scrubbed my nails that morning, but they were still ringed with earth.

I winced and pulled it away. 'Gardening,' I explained. 'A manicure sounds good. I don't think I'd mind Rosie coming along. Alice is in school every day except Wednesday.'

Rosie nodded. 'Tuesday morning? We'll go with you into town. Do you want me to make the appointment, Fi?'

Fiona laughed. 'So says the only woman who speaks worse French than I do! Go on then, I dare you.'

Andy swaggered to the gate and made a show of looking right and left.

'Guys?' he asked. 'Shall we get Matt back? Shall we promise not to disturb his peace of mind? Shall we swear a solemn oath not, under any circs, to capture his image on celluloid? Why don't you guys all bugger off to the beach, after all?'

The house was immaculate. Every detail had been taken care of. The dining room was huge, with a vast ceiling, a wooden mezzanine floor, and a table that would comfortably seat twelve. A vase of dried flowers lurked in the fireplace. There were ornaments of shepherdesses and china cats on the mantelpiece, and there was not a speck of dust, as far as I could see, anywhere. The terracotta floor tiles were shining. There was something incongruous about the house. The building itself was spectacular, and its decoration rather . . . I tailed off, mentally. It was becoming harder to force myself not to be judgemental. I told myself not to be a snob. It was not to my taste. That was all.

I knew that we would have to return Andy and Fiona's hospitality, and I knew they would be shocked by our peeling walls and heaps of rubble. I hated entertaining at the best of times. I would never do it with the film crew around. Our house was furnished, but it was messy and dirty and had an aura of being held together with sticky tape. Water still coursed through the roof whenever it rained. We had stripped some walls in preparation for the builders, and it looked thoroughly tatty and shameful.

Once the awkwardness had been dissipated by alcohol, lunch was not too bad. Fiona had cooked roast beef, complete with roast potatoes, bits of bacon, and two dishes overflowing with green vegetables. Andy had red and white wine ready, decanted and chilled respectively. They had bought a bottle of the ubiquitous *sirop* for Alice, and didn't seem bothered when she decided on a whim that she wouldn't eat anything except bread. Fiona delighted her by producing a jar of Marmite and happily boiled an egg when it was requested.

'Aren't you a good little girl for saying please?' she cooed, and I watched my daughter squirming in her chair and simpering. I tried to catch Matt's eye to laugh at Alice's behaviour, but he was involved in an animated discussion with Andy about London house prices. I knew he was not interested. He had never owned a house or even a flat. He had rented in London, and then, when he had moved into my house in Brighton, he had kept his rental flat on and usually stayed overnight on work nights. He must have been feigning an interest. I had a feeling he was keen to talk about anything except his earlier behaviour. Nobody mentioned it until we reached pudding.

Fiona made a grand entrance from the kitchen. She was carrying an enormous cut-glass bowl. Matt sat up and panted comically, like a dog. Alice stood on her chair to peer into the dish.

'Is it custard?' she asked hopefully.

'It certainly is,' said Andy, 'and I'll tell you a secret. It's custard, but it's better than custard. It's called trifle.' He poured dessert wine into new glasses, and handed them to Matt and me. 'Cheers, m'dears,' he said, and we clinked glasses. I was glad to see Matt half-drunk. It meant he would not be able to drive to the airport. He would have to stay with us overnight now, catch the early flight on Monday and give the six thirty breakfast meeting a miss. He was relaxed at last, and I decided that he had to apologise.

'How's the documentary going?' I asked Andy. Matt took his cue.

'I do apologise for earlier,' he said, looking at the white tablecloth. 'I just can't bear to be filmed. I suppose it's something of a phobia, though I never realised that before. I don't quite know what came over me.'

'He has got a phobia.' I felt bound to offer my support. 'When Alice was born, it was all I could do to get him to have his photo taken holding her. I think I had to cry before he agreed. The photo is so meaningful that Alice has it framed in her bedroom, as a trophy.'

'Don't worry about it.' Andy patted Matt's forearm. 'Must

be a bit of a shock, to go to someone's house and there's a bloody great camera pointing in your face.'

'I suppose so. I knew you were doing this show, you nutters, but Emma told me they wouldn't be here today.'

'Should have checked with you first, mate. Our fault. We solemnly swear never to do that to you again. OK?'

Matt smiled tightly. 'Deal.'

chapter thirteen

Jo sat and looked at the picture. She had refused to give it back to Hugh, and kept it in a drawer at her gallery, where he would never find it. He had explained, smoothly, where it had come from. A colleague in Paris had taken it out to show him. This man had just moved his family to France and settled in the countryside within commuting distance of the city. He had been proud of his daughter's picture and had shown it around. It had stayed on a table and Hugh had accidentally picked it up with his papers and shoved it in his bag.

She knew he was lying. What frightened her was that he was doing it so well. As soon as he had come into the bedroom, looked at her face, looked at what she was holding, he had raised his eyebrows casually.

'Oh, that,' he said. 'Can you put it in my briefcase? I'll give it back next week.'

He had given his explanation, and she had grilled him. 'What's the man's name?' she had asked, feeling sick.

'Matt.'

Plan B

'What's his daughter called?'

'Alice.'

'What's his wife's name?'

He had frowned. 'His wife? I'm not sure. Emma, I think. Or Anna. Something like that. Why?'

She had asked why, if he had gathered it up with his papers, it was not in his briefcase with everything else. He had an answer: 'Because I found it in there and left it out to give back. Then I missed him so I just shoved it in my overnight bag.'

His story hung together, but she knew it wasn't true. When she let herself think about what this might mean, her knees trembled and she felt sick. Their weekend in Paris had been great, but his reaction to the idea had made her deeply uneasy, particularly since he seemed to have next to nothing to do when they were there. Alarm bells were ringing loudly.

Her assistant, Sylvie, knocked on the office door with a banal question about the new burglar alarm. Jo threw her the manual. Then Sylvie reminded her about her three o'clock appointment with a rich collector she needed to woo. It was quarter to three now. Jo put some coffee on, checked her make-up, smoothed down her dress, and put the picture back into the drawer. She wondered if it was ironic that she, Joanna Smith, queen of the contemporary art scene, had become obsessed with a child's scribble. She was fairly sure that if she framed it and hung it in her window, someone would pay good money for it.

She forced herself to concentrate on her business. Matt had stayed away the previous night, unexpectedly. He said it was because he'd had so much to catch up on after taking time off to spend with her. She didn't believe him.

He was going back to Paris on Thursday. While he was gone, she was going to do an enormous amount of snooping.

chapter fourteen

August

Coco, Matt and I stood next to the roundabout and watched Louis and Alice laughing as they spun round and round in their fire engine. The local fête was in full swing. Everybody who lived in St Paul appeared to be here. The evening was stickily hot, and men and women stood in groups around the carousel and the amusements which had been shipped in on the backs of lorries and put up in the car park next to Alice's school. Matt had a can of beer in his hand. I was drinking water, because I was driving.

Alice was in her element: overtired, overstimulated, and surrounded by her friends. She knew them all from school, and they were all as pleased to see her as she was happy to see them. I knew that her French was reasonably fluent now but I was astonished to hear her chattering. Matt could not believe it.

'She's not three till October,' he said, staring, 'and she speaks bloody better French than I do. How did that happen?'

'It's one of the reasons we came here,' I reminded him.

Coco nodded. She was insisting that we spoke English

this evening because she had decided to improve her language skills and try to get a job where English would be a bonus. At the moment she was doing part-time administrative work, and she was bored.

'It is very good,' she said carefully. 'Alice speaks French.'

'Does she have an English accent?' I asked. 'Even a little one?'

Coco shook her head vehemently. 'No.' She switched into French. 'What she does have, though, is a local twang. Louis has it too. She sounds exactly like a Gascon.'

People stopped to talk to us, and I enjoyed the interaction. Things that terrified me when I was alone were absolutely fine when Matt and Coco were by my side. The kind farmers from Pounchet came over, and, finally, I managed to discover that they were called Patrick and Mathilde. It had been bothering me for months.

'Alice is sweet,' said Mathilde, as Alice and Louis descended from the roundabout and ran over to demand sweets. Matt picked Alice up and Mathilde stroked her cheek. 'We miss children,' she said. 'If you ever need help, I would always be happy to look after her.'

'How old are your children?' I asked.

'Twenty-two and twenty-three.'

I shook my head. 'That can't be true.'

She nodded. 'We were married when we were seventeen.' Patrick put his arm round her waist. Mathilde leant back on him happily. 'The boys came along soon afterwards,' she added.

When they wandered off, Matt finished his beer purposefully.

'Right,' he said. 'Better get this little one to bed.'

Alice was playing with three other girls, running round the carousel.

'No hurry, is there?' I said. 'She's fine. She can sleep in tomorrow. We all can.'

A band was setting up on a makeshift stage at one end of the car park. The ground was gravelly and dusty underfoot. Suddenly, possibly for the first time in my life, I felt like dancing. I looked at Matt.

'We've got to stay so we can dance.'

He laughed. 'You want to dance?'

'Why not?'

'Because you don't. You don't dance and nor do I. Any more than you surf. Come on. We've shown our faces for a highly respectable length of time now. Let's head off. OK?'

I looked to Coco for back-up. Then I saw Andy and Fiona heading towards us.

'*Les anglais!*' boomed Andy, causing people nearby to turn and stare. I was embarrassed and stared at the stones by my feet.

'Andy! Fiona!' said Matt, perking up. 'Another beer?'

I danced with Fiona and Coco while the men drank and, nominally, kept an eye on Alice and Louis. The older couples danced properly, holding each other as if they were in a ballroom rather than under the stars in a French car park. Even Patrick and Mathilde, barely into their forties, were waltzing and quickstepping. I danced randomly, losing inhibitions, enjoying the hot, late-August night.

We stumbled in at quarter to one. When the builders had finally started work at the end of June, we had toasted them with champagne. I had been ecstatic, imagining that they would work nonstop until the renovation was complete. I had reckoned without the summer holidays. At the end of July, tools had been downed. During their brief burst of activity, they had produced so much dust that it still coated everything, almost invisibly. However much I vacuumed, it never quite went away. Internal walls had come down, others had been replastered, and many of the upstairs floors had been replaced with local pine floorboards. Our two bedrooms were much more habitable, though the house was unmistakably a building site. Next month, I hoped, the back windows would appear.

'Bloody building stuff,' said Matt, as he walked into a pile of floorboards which were piled in the hall.

'Better to have building stuff around than not,' I said.

'Yeah. I know. Come on, Alice. Bed.'

Matt was not happy. He was different from the Matt I had always known. He was grumpy and short-tempered. I was desperately looking forward to him changing his working patterns. I was pretty sure he could work freelance. He wouldn't make much money but we didn't need much, and without the flights to and from London he was going to be richer anyway. I wasn't sure, however, that his ambition would allow him to do the minimal amount of work, from home. Whenever I had suggested it, he had snapped at me. I was trying to keep quiet. I trusted him to sort it out.

I went to the kitchen to fetch some milk for Alice and glasses of water for us. The strange old kitchen had been ripped out, and it was much easier to cook in the makeshift one that took its place. Instead of worktops, we had sheets of plasterboard on trestles, and instead of a rusty old cooker, we had a camping stove and a microwave. I had liked it instantly. The days were almost unbearably hot, so I never felt like cooking anything anyway. The most useful thing in the kitchen was the fridge. I took out the jug of water and poured it, deliciously cold, into glasses. The old tiles were pleasantly cold beneath my feet.

All we needed now were visitors. I wanted Alice to see her cousins, Bella's boys, and I wanted adult company. For six months I had been desperately waiting for summer and the guests I had assumed it would bring. Christa and Geoff were coming out in two weeks' time. Bella, Jon and the boys were not quite committed to coming at the same time, though Bella had started saying they might make it half-term instead. At the beginning of July, I had, in desperation, emailed Anne in Brighton and invited her out for a couple of weeks. She had written back the same day, saying: 'so sweet of you to invite us. have just booked yoga hols in greece – v good karma! – and don't have any other spare time. would love to come and see you sometime. xxx PS paula told me your happy news! congratulations! must be due soon . . .'

Sometime did not interest me. I wanted company. In the middle of July, Charlotte had arranged to come for a long weekend, but cancelled at the last minute because she got an audition for a play in the West End. My inner bitch almost told her not to bother going, since she wouldn't get it, but I stopped myself in time. I was upset not to see her because I had geared myself up for her company, and had even made up her bed and put fresh flowers in her room. Greg was not due back from Asia until September. All I had to look forward to was Christa and Geoff's visit. It felt strange for my lack of friends to be so apparent.

The following Thursday, company arrived unexpectedly. It was a stifling day and Alice and I were sweltering in the garden. I was pruning some roses and Alice was lying in the shade, on the grass, playing an involved game with her toy cars, talking under her breath. I thought she was arranging them into families. Bigger cars were paired off and given two or three little cars to look after. When I heard the car pulling up, I put down my secateurs, took off the gardening gloves I had felt obliged to wear since becoming Fiona's occasional manicure buddy, and ambled round the side of the house to see who was there. I was wearing my coolest clothes, which was to say, a baggy T-shirt I had picked up for four euros in the supermarket, and a pair of faded pink shorts. I half hoped Matt had come home early, but I knew it could not be him because he had phoned an hour earlier from his office.

I could not walk quickly, because it was so hot. Any kind of activity was impossible in this weather. I had only been doing the roses because I could do them with very little movement. The house glared at me, reflecting the strong sun and giving me a headache. The rotten figs that had fallen off the tree were giving off an overpowering stench. Bees, wasps and hornets hummed around them.

There was a French car outside the house, with its engine running. It was not familiar; I knew all the neighbours' cars and tractors. This one had a Parisian number plate, which meant it was probably a hire car. I saw a woman standing by my front door and a small boy still strapped into a car seat.

'*Bonjour?*' I said, smiling tentatively, wiping the sweat off my forehead. We rarely had unexpected visitors, and I was pleased to see even a stranger.

The woman turned to me. She was tall and skinny, with short blonde hair. Although she was probably older than me, I instantly felt middle-aged and dowdy. She was wearing a gleaming white dress that finished halfway down her thighs, displaying long, tanned legs. She was wearing just enough make-up to make her glow, and not so much that it looked silly and shiny in the heat. Her cream flip-flops were beaded. Her hair was carelessly perfect. How, I wondered again, did people manage to look like this when they had toddlers? Coco laughed every time I asked her and reminded me that when Louis was not at school, her mother often had him. She devoted her ample child-free time to grooming herself; I devoted mine to the garden. I was not chic because I could not be bothered.

I watched the woman assessing me for a couple of seconds, and I was acutely aware of my stained old shorts and my cheap T-shirt. I knew that I had put no thought whatsoever into my appearance. I hadn't even bothered to wash my hair for a few days, and despite Fiona's best efforts, I rarely bothered to have it cut.

She smiled a dazzling and apologetic smile.

'*Bonjour,*' she said, speaking carefully. '*Nous sommes un peu perdus. Est-ce que vous pouvez m'aider s'il vous plaît?*'

'Are you English?' I asked.

She grinned, surprised. 'Yes! You are, too. Clearly.'

'Yes, I am. Are you on holiday?'

She sighed and laughed. 'We are. Only I've gone and got myself hopelessly lost. My husband's stayed at Mimizan for the day and Olly and I came to explore the countryside, but I fear we have explored rather too enthusiastically. I've got a map but I'm afraid it leaves me none the wiser. Where are we?'

'I'll show you. Do you want to come round the back?' I addressed the boy. 'My little girl's about the same age as you. She's playing with her cars in the garden. Do you want to play, too? We can fill the paddling pool, if you like.'

He hid behind his mother's legs. He was a nice looking child, blond like his mother, and beautifully turned out in shorts that were still creased from the iron, and a bright white T-shirt.

'Go on, you,' said his mother, giving him a little push. 'Don't be shy.'

The woman and I sat on the chairs, on the patch of brown grass that would, one day, be reinvented as the terrace. She opened her map and I quickly located Pounchet for her.

'Here,' I said, pleased that I could at least point to my village on the map without being ashamed of my nails. They were having a good day today. 'This is us. So if you're going to Mimizan, you need to follow this road here.' I traced it with my finger. 'That takes you right up to the main road to the coast. You'll be on the D38 for the last bit. Once you're on there, Mimizan will be signed and you won't be able to miss it.'

She smiled at me, a warm and open smile. 'You're a lifesaver. Thanks so much. I'm Jo, by the way.'

'Hi, Jo. I'm Emma. And that's Alice. How about a cold drink?'

Jo and Olly stayed in the garden for the rest of the afternoon. I got on with her immediately. I was delighted to have someone to chat to in English, who was neither Fiona nor a member of a film crew. We whiled away a few hours, splashing with the children in the paddling pool, drinking cold water, picking at a bowl of cherries, and chatting about our lives. I realised that I was more confident than I used to be. I had never had close friends other than my sisters, and a year earlier a woman like Jo would have terrified me. Now, perhaps because I counted Coco among my friends, I felt I could talk to Jo on equal terms.

Jo was vocal in admiring me for making this move, particularly when I told her that Matt was away for half the week.

'So he's away, what, Monday to Friday?' she asked, lining up her cherry stones on the edge of the plastic table.

'Usually. It's meant to be Monday to Thursday but he's been snowed under at work lately. But he'll be back tonight. We'll be honoured with his presence even though it's Thursday. He keeps saying he's going to arrange it so he works from home, but it hasn't been feasible. Maybe in the autumn.' I looked at her and smiled. 'It would make the most enormous difference, having him here. I'm always counting down till he comes back. I'd love to have another baby but, frankly, I'm on my own for more than half the week at the moment, and I don't actually think I could manage that if I had two.'

'You're very wise,' she said immediately. 'Hang on till you know where you stand. I'd been thinking about another baby, too, but I'm the same as you. I don't spend enough time with my husband. We don't have much time together as a family. I work full time and have done since Olly was six months, and I run my own art gallery in Jermyn Street, so it's hard to cut my hours back. Hugh's away a lot with his work. He's on a six-month contract now which means he has to work in Paris every weekend, so it seems like we're in the same boat. I feel like a single mother, too, and I don't think I could slot a new baby into our lives.' She stretched her long legs out, and I tried hard not to stare at them. 'It feels strange, though, doesn't it, when all your friends from your first pregnancy are having their second and you're not?'

I thought about it. 'I didn't really make any friends while I was pregnant,' I admitted. 'Everyone else seems to, but I didn't. I chatted to a few people at pregnancy yoga but we never kept in touch. I just used to meet mothers in the park. Matt was away in London all the time so it was a bit lonely. I've never been that good with people.'

'Did you plan to have Alice?' Jo clapped a hand to her mouth. 'Sorry, what a personal question! I only ask because Olly came along as a bit of a mistake, a happy one of course, but I wonder whether that's delaying our second. I mean, I'm not like those women who drop everything to have children and then pop one out every couple of years through their thirties.'

I smiled at her. 'Alice was a mistake, too. I'd never tell her that. Matt and I hadn't even been together that long, but I knew it was the right relationship. He got a bit of a shock, but he came round to the idea pretty quickly. He and Alice are devoted to each other. In fact when he's around I often feel a bit redundant. The phrase "daddy's girl" could have been invented for Alice.'

Jo looked round. 'What are they up to?'

The children had disappeared from view. We got up to look for them, walking slowly at first, trying to be casual, but soon breaking into a jog.

'The garden's enclosed,' I reassured her. 'They can't go anywhere.'

We found Alice and Oliver attempting to climb the fig tree in the front garden. Alice was crouching on a low branch, pulling Olly up after her. They made a beautiful picture.

'Alice,' I said reluctantly. 'Come on. I know you're having fun but you'd better get down from there.' I looked to Jo. 'What about if we put on a DVD for them, and have a glass of wine? It's nice and cool indoors. Matt will be back soon and I'm sure he'd like to meet you. Do you want to ring your husband and let him know where you are? Will he be worried?'

Jo shook her head. 'He's a big boy. I'll text him. He'll be fine.'

We sat down with drinks and crisps, the children happily occupied by *Toy Story*.

'The house is going to be fab,' said Jo, looking around at the wallpaper hanging off the walls and the dusty floor, marked by hardened patches of glue where we had pulled up the limp old carpet.

'*Going to be* being the operative phrase.'

'Yes, sure, it must be a pain right now, but anyone can

see the potential. Next summer it will be absolutely wonderful.' She smiled at me. 'You obviously have great vision. And you seem well suited to this sort of rural life. I couldn't do it. I'd miss England far too much. I'd miss the city. Admittedly London can be a bit much, but I'd miss city life in general.'

I laughed. 'I can't stand London. But I loved Brighton, and I do miss it. None of it has been easy. It's been unbelievably difficult.'

'I'm sure. I've been wanting to move to Brighton actually. Whereabouts were you?'

'Clifton Street. Right by the station.'

'I know it.' She looked thoughtful. 'There was a house I wanted to look at there. It was probably yours. So this move here is very drastic. Was it your idea?'

'Not at all. Far from it. Matt talked me into it, and it took him a while. I thought it would never happen. That's probably why I agreed to it in the end. I assumed it would all fall through, like his other schemes.'

'He's had other schemes?'

I laughed and sipped my juice. 'Oh yes. Too many to remember. There was Cape Town, for a while. Then there was Thailand, closely followed by Nepal. We were going to move to all these places and make a simple living from growing grapes, or fishing, that kind of thing.'

'Not too much fishing in Nepal.'

'No, Nepal was tour guides, I think. Leading treks through the Himalayas.'

'So he's a bit of a romantic, your husband?'

'He is.' I remembered to correct her. 'But he's not my

husband. We're planning to get married.' I felt good as I said it. 'In the autumn. He's going to work from home and then we'll get married, perhaps have that second baby after that.'

'Sounds great.' There was a pause. Just as I was about to speak, to ask an innocuous question about Olly, she spoke again. 'You're staying here, then, you and Matt and Alice?' she asked, looking serious.

'For now,' I told her. 'When we've got the house done, we'll have to live in it for at least ten years to get our money's worth. Alice is happy. She loves school and it's doing her the world of good. She and I are both longing for the holidays to end. I've made good friends.' I tried to think what else I liked. 'We had no garden in Brighton,' I added. 'This garden is my other baby at the moment. I'm proud of the way that I look after it all by myself. I mow the grass, pull up the weeds, do all the pruning. I'd kind of assumed that Matt would take charge, but if it was up to him it would still be a jungle out there. The garden's my job. I don't think I'd like to go back now.' I thought about what I was saying, and marvelled. This was the first time I had realised it. I liked living in France, and I would no longer choose to go back to England, particularly not when Matt changed his work pattern.

'Well, Matt is very lucky to have you,' said Jo, with a wide smile. I looked into her sparkling blue eyes and detected a hint of sadness and jealousy.

'Hey,' I said kindly. 'London's good too.'

'You think?' She looked at me, and away.

Matt called from Gatwick. He had had a crisis at work, and would not be back until late. I told him we had guests, but he was only mildly interested.

'I hate to impose,' Jo said, when I put the phone down, 'but I think I've had too much to drink. If I texted Hugh to let him know, do you think it would be possible for Olly and me to stay over?'

I was extremely pleased. 'Of course! You're more than welcome! We now have a spare room that's halfway presentable, and you'll be the first to use it. Can you believe that? None of my family have come out. My aunt and uncle are coming in a couple of weeks.'

'What about Matt's family?'

'Oh, he hasn't got any. Or rather, he has but he doesn't see them. I've never met any of them.'

I put a pillow for Olly at the other end of Alice's bed. They jumped in together, one at each end. I read them a story, with one of them leaning on each side of me. It felt good to have two. As I was putting the book away, Olly laughed and pointed. 'Daddy and baby!' he exclaimed.

I looked round and saw him pointing to the framed photograph of Matt holding a newborn Alice.

'That's right,' I told him. 'That's Alice's daddy and Alice when she was a baby.'

'Mine daddy,' Alice told him officiously.

'My daddy,' Olly said.

'Mine daddy,' Alice asserted.

'My daddy,' Olly said again. I switched the light out and left them discussing it.

We opened a second bottle of wine, but I did not feel particularly drunk. I thought Jo was drinking a lot more than I was.

'I'll cook, shall I?' I asked, at half past eight.

'Sure,' she said, distracted. Then she jerked herself back to full consciousness. 'Of course. I'll help. Nothing too big, though? When Hugh's away I exist on soup and salad.'

'Me, too. We don't have an oven at the moment anyway. I just have sandwiches and fruit unless Matt's around. Specially in this weather.'

'Has it been like this all summer? It's wild, isn't it?'

'Since June.' I looked out of the open window at the parched garden. 'I know life must be good, because when there's the occasional grey, drizzly day, I love it. It's good for the garden. And I have the luxury of knowing that it won't last.'

I handed Jo a chopping board and knife, and a few tomatoes. She started slicing them.

'Emma?' she said, making swift, strong strokes with the knife. 'Can I ask you something?' I nodded. She seemed to be about to speak, then stopped. After a while, she started again.

'What was it about Matt that made you realise you'd found your life partner?' she asked. 'Again, I'm sorry to be intrusive, but I'm not sure any more whether Hugh and I have a future together. Once you start to analyse things like that, it all begins to unravel. Was it love at first sight for you? Have you ever doubted Matt?'

I hugged her. 'I'm so sorry to hear that,' I told her. 'I'm sure you'll work it out. He'd be crazy to let you and Olly get away.'

She looked sad. 'Do you think so?'

'Of course I think so. You'll be fine. As for Matt and me, we bumped into each other in Brighton, and it just felt right.

I'd never known anything like it. It's hard to explain, but . . .' I looked down at my hands. My right hand was holding a wooden spoon. I stared at it. 'I suddenly felt normal. I'd never felt normal before, never had a real relationship. Suddenly, straightaway, I knew what everyone had been talking about. Matt's very confident and articulate and he has a certain charisma. He's the opposite of me in all those ways. He could have had anyone, but he chose me. I still can't believe it.'

Jo put her elbows on the table and cupped her face in her hands. 'How did you actually meet? I love those sorts of details.'

I looked at her. 'Do you? You must stop me if I'm being boring. OK. I was in a café on the beach with my sister and her little boys, who were toddlers then – now they're nearly seven. Matt was sitting with a guy I used to know, briefly, at uni. There was a whole other story there. What matters is that the man in question was long since over me. He lived in Brighton too, and I used to see him around town from time to time. So I gave this guy a wave, you know. I saw the two of them talking about me and then Matt came over. He asked if he could take a chair, which was the lamest excuse, since he and Pete already had two spare chairs at their table. He admired the boys a bit, and once he'd ascertained that neither of them belonged to me, he asked if he could join us. He was completely focused on me. Nobody had ever been like that with me before.'

'Hadn't they? You really hadn't had a relationship before?'

'Really.' I saw her face. 'Oh, I wasn't a virgin, I'd had flings. But nothing that lasted. Nothing I wanted to last. I'd generally attracted the weirdos, like this guy Pete in fact, who liked me because he felt sorry for me and he thought I was in some way glamorous because I had no parents. I hated him.' I wondered why I was telling all this to a stranger. My nascent friendships with Coco and Fiona had not reached this stage, and here I was, unburdening myself to a woman I had only just met. It must have been the wine. I knew Jo wanted me to keep talking. I sensed that she was genuinely interested in me. I decided to carry on. 'And when Matt started asking me about myself, I felt, this sounds corny I know, but I felt that I was coming home. Meeting him was the most enormous relief. I knew almost instantly that he was the one.' I smiled apologetically. 'Sorry. Our story is full of clichés, I realise that. What about you and Hugh? How did you meet?'

Jo finished her wine in one impressive gulp, and gave a dismissive wave with the knife. 'Oh, Hughie and I have been married for years,' she said. 'Eight, now. Together for ten. Maybe I've just got the seven-year itch, a bit late. It's funny, but my story seems like the opposite of yours. It was Hugh who lacked confidence, and me who brought him out of himself. Sometimes I fear I might have brought him too far out of himself. He's not the man I married any more.' Jo tipped the tomatoes, which were sliced wafer thin and perfect, into the salad bowl. She looked miserable. 'I don't know. I just don't think you can ever really know somebody. Hugh surprises me, and not in a pleasant way.'

'What do you mean?' I asked her. She drew breath, about to say something, and then stopped herself.

'Oh, nothing. It's not worth explaining at the moment. Let's talk about something else.'

In the middle of the night, I heard Matt arriving. I listened to him closing the shutters behind him, and locking us all in. Five minutes later, he appeared in the bedroom. I propped myself on my elbows and presented my mouth to be kissed.

'Sorry to be so late, sweetheart,' he said, kissing me. He pulled his shirt over his head without undoing the buttons. 'Missed the flight. Only just caught the last one of the night, in fact. How's everyone?'

'Great,' I told him happily. 'Jo's sleeping in the spare room. The children are in together. She's lovely. We've been chatting all evening. I think we'll stay in touch. I might see if they all want to meet up at the beach at the weekend. They're staying in Mimizan.'

Matt wasn't really listening. 'Cool. Whatever you like. Might be a nightmare there on a holiday weekend though.'

He climbed in beside me, and pulled me towards him. We were both heavy with heat, but I turned to him anyway. Our bodies were sweaty against each other. I thought of Jo and her unhappy marriage, and made myself take a few seconds to rejoice in my luck.

I half woke up in the middle of the night. Matt was stirring restlessly beside me, taking shallow, wakeful breaths.

'Emma?' he whispered. 'Em, are you awake?'

I was too tired to answer. I rolled over and went back to sleep.

chapter fifteen

Hugh stretched and yawned as Alice climbed on top of him. She was dressed in nothing but a nappy, and he was completely naked. She stuck to him like cheap fake leather.

'Hello, Daddy!' she said loudly, her mouth pressed to his ear. He winced and pulled her down between himself and Emma.

'Hello, Alice,' he told her, rubbing his eyes. 'Good morning. How did you sleep?'

'I had a lovely sleep. Please fetch my milk.'

'OK, OK, give me a chance.' Hugh turned to Emma beside him and sighed. 'She's so demanding! Does she do this to you when I'm not here?'

Emma rubbed her eyes. He looked appraisingly at her. She had no suspicions; he could see that at once. She looked sweet and sleepy. 'Of course,' she said. 'And *of course* you have to do it all when you're here, because you have the novelty factor. I'll have Earl Grey, while you're up.'

He heaved himself out of bed and retrieved last night's

underpants from the floor. Emma laughed. 'We've got company, remember. It's fine if you want to display yourself to a strange woman in your pants, but if not, you might like to put on your dressing gown.'

'Too warm for a dressing gown,' he grumbled, but he took it anyway, and struggled to get his arm into the sleeve.

'Try the other one,' Emma suggested, and suddenly he was in.

Hugh had barely slept. He replayed Emma's voice, yet again.

He was certain she had said Jo. He could hear it. 'Jo's sleeping in the spare room.' He knew his wife, and he knew the games she played. This was exactly what she would do. He had almost got out of bed in the night and opened the spare room door, just to check, but he had stopped himself, because whoever this woman was, she was probably a stranger and he would have looked like a disgusting pervert had he edged into her bedroom in the middle of the night.

He told himself that there were thousands upon thousands of women called Jo, and that this was a cosmic reminder that he needed to get his life in order.

The kitchen was as shitty as ever. Hugh swore as he put the mugs down too heavily on the precarious makeshift worktop and sent the other end of it briefly into the air, sending some teaspoons clattering to the floor. He filled the kettle and waited for it to boil. Above his head, in Alice's room, he heard children's footsteps and voices. He thought Alice was declining to share her toys. The other child had obviously got up too. He could not remember whether

Plan B

Emma had said it was a boy or a girl. He sincerely hoped it was a girl. He did not let himself listen closely to the timbre of the child's voice.

The stairs creaked. Hugh set the tea bags in the mugs and ran his fingers through his hair. He hoped this was Emma coming downstairs. She never followed him downstairs in the morning. She lay back in bed and waited for her tea.

The footsteps came closer, along the corridor. Hugh's heart was pounding. He looked round with a forced smile. The smile turned, very quickly, into horror. He was surprised and displeased to find himself wanting his mummy.

Jo was dressed. She had had a shower. Her hair was still slightly wet. She was wearing lipstick. When she smiled her face was filled with menace.

'Hello!' she said, enunciating every letter. 'You must be Matt. I'm Jo.'

'Christ,' he whispered. He looked around, checking that they were alone, as well as looking for escape routes. 'It is you. I thought it couldn't be. What the fuck are you doing?'

She whispered too. 'What the fuck am *I* doing?'

'Shit.' He spoke louder. 'Cup of tea?' Then whispered again. 'Can we talk about this later?' He listened to the excited chatter coming down from upstairs. 'You mean, that's . . . ?' He pointed to the ceiling.

'That's Oliver, yes,' she said, speaking in a normal voice. 'He and Alice get on like a house on fire. It's lovely to see. You should watch them playing together. They have so much in common. You know what?' she said grimly. 'It turns out that Alice is only a few weeks older than he is!'

Hugh looked down. 'You haven't said anything to Emma yet, have you?'

'No. Hugh, that woman is *Pete's Emma*! She has been part of your family folklore for years. You all talk about her. And you've . . . You are Alice's father, aren't you?'

He didn't answer. He knew he didn't need to.

Jo looked as if she was going to cry. He had never seen her cry before, not even when she was pregnant, not even when she was in labour. 'Does Pete know?' she asked.

He managed to nod.

'I came here to confront her,' she said, swallowing. 'I was all ready to scream and shout and fight her. Then I realised she had no idea. I can't exactly warm to her, but objectively I can see that she's sweet, and she no more deserves this than I do. You should have heard her talking about you last night.'

'How did you . . . ?'

She shook her head. 'Doesn't matter. I'd known there was something up for ages. You're not quite as clever as you think. Here's what's going to happen. We're going to go through this properly before you tell her. You're going upstairs with that tea – and no thanks, I won't have one, I'd rather drink Olly's diarrhoea than take a hospitable drink from you, you fuck – and you're going back to bed with a headache. I'll go up first and take Olly into the spare room so you won't bump into him. Olly and I will leave straight after breakfast. He's not going to see you.' She touched his arm. 'Now, you have a wonderful weekend in this gorgeous house,' she said, in a voice that made him shudder. 'I do envy your lifestyle. You've got the best of both worlds,

160

haven't you?' She lowered her voice again. 'Don't even think about coming home. Come to the gallery Monday morning.'

Hugh held out a cup of tea, then took it back. He left it on the trestle worktop, and left the room without looking back.

chapter sixteen

The new school term was starting at the end of August. Alice was wildly excited. She had missed her friends over the summer. I was excited too. Alice had graduated from the *tous petits* section to the *petits*. My tiny girl was growing up. Moving from very small to small was progress, of a sort. I took her on a shopping trip to Villeneuve, the biggest town for miles around, where we bought new shoes, new slippers, pens and pencils, a new school bag, and a spare napkin.

'I want to show Daddy,' she said, all the way home. 'Mine new bag. Mine new sandals. Mine new slippers. Mine new pens.'

'Daddy will be back this afternoon,' I assured her. I had not heard from Matt during the week, but I knew he was busy with work. He was trying to put the hours in, that week, to impress everyone enough to make them grant his request to work from home all the time, a request he was judiciously going to make the following week. School began the week after next. I hoped Matt would be at home full time by then, so that we could all turn up at school together

162

for the first day of the academic year. I knew, though, that it was unlikely.

We passed the rest of Friday splashing around in the paddling pool. Fiona called round with a Tupperware dish of fairy cakes and a camera crew. I thanked her fulsomely, while secretly vowing not to eat any, and made a pot of tea. Then I realised that I had to eat at least one, to avoid being rude. This was a shame, as I was trying to stick to a half-hearted diet. I didn't want to carry nine extra kilos around for ever, particularly not since I was living in France. My rule was that I ate fatty things only if I really, really liked them.

'How are you, then, Fi?' I asked her. I was only friends with Fiona because we were English but Alice adored her. She was already sitting on her lap and eating her second cake. A third was clutched defensively in her left hand.

'Well,' Fiona said, head on one side. 'Interesting, I suppose is the best word for it.' She winked at me.

'What do you mean?' I was surprised. Fiona normally brushed that question off with the word 'grand'. I looked at her. She was bursting with excitement. I thought she was probably pregnant, and prepared to offer my congratulations.

'Rosie?' Fiona asked, eyebrows raised.

Rosie rolled her eyes. 'OK, OK. Fine. We'll look the other way again. We've got enough of you two together anyway. Come on, lads.' They trooped off.

'Oh, Emma,' said Fiona, sounding relieved. 'I have to tell you. You mustn't tell a single soul, specially not Matt.'

'OK.' I took a bite of fairy cake. Unfortunately, I really, really liked it, so I finished it within seconds and picked up another.

Fiona glanced at Alice. 'Alice, sweetie, could you fetch your very favourite toy to show Auntie Fifi?'

Alice nodded and slipped off Fiona's lap. 'I'll show you my garage,' she said solemnly.

'No darling,' I intervened. 'You can't bring your garage downstairs on your own, can you? Why don't you fetch your dinosaurs?'

'Because I don't even like my dinosaurs any more.'

'Get Buzz Lightyear then.' Buzz had been a gift from Bella. He was high on Alice's list of favourite items.

Alice nodded and stomped off. I turned to Fiona. 'Not easy to be alone, is it? Well?'

She grasped my hand. 'Emma, you mustn't be shocked or anything, but I've been having an affair!' She clasped her hand to her mouth. 'That's the first time I've told anyone, face to face! Oh, Emma, I'm so excited, you can't imagine! I know it's terrible but I can't help myself. I just can't. I do try, but I can't. I'm even wondering whether I might be in love!'

I was astonished. I had only ever had intimate female friendships with my sisters. Neither of them had ever confided anything like this. We had been socialising with Andy and Fiona more and more lately. I was going to have to look Andy in the eye and pretend to be normal.

'Who with?' I asked, wide-eyed.

'Oh, look at you!' shrieked Fiona. 'You are shocked, aren't you? Poor Emma. I think you've led a more sheltered life than we have. Don't worry, lovie. Andy's no angel. Don't feel bad on his account. I swore I'd never stoop to his level, but I have, and here I am. I'm loving it.'

'Wow.' I tried to think of a response. 'So, who's the lucky man?' It sounded forced and clichéd and I wished I knew how to say the right thing.

Fiona giggled. 'The lucky man is none other than Didier, the gardener. Can you imagine? I'm a proper Lady Chatterley, aren't I? Didier's a little bit older, extremely experienced, if you follow me. I feel like I'm seventeen all over again.'

'How long have you been . . . ?' I floundered. I had been about to say 'together', but they were not really together, and for a moment I couldn't think what to say instead. 'Seeing him?' I finished.

'Bonking him? Since May. Three months. I've been watching my step, I can tell you. Every time I turn around there's a bloody telly camera in my face. And what with Andy not working, it's been a bloody nightmare. I've covered my tracks so far. I'm afraid you've been my alibi more than once.'

'Right.' I had no idea how these conversations were meant to go. 'Erm, I'm pleased you're happy. What's going to happen next?'

Fiona leaned back in her chair, stretched out like a cat, and smiled. 'A weekend! Didier's married too, of course – they all are here, aren't they? So we've never managed a whole night together. It's always been a quick fumble in the shed or some such. I'm dying to be in an actual bed with him, and to wake up with him in the morning. He's telling his missus that he's doing a job for some English in the Dordogne, which he got through me and Andy, and I've got my girlfriends lined up to back me up on a shopping weekend in Paris. Of course, we really will go to Paris so I can do the shopping, otherwise Andy would smell a rat instantly.'

I stared at her. 'You're going to Paris for a dirty weekend with the gardener?' I tried to imagine wanting to do that. It was impossible. For me there would only ever be Matt. I could not empathise, but I tried to share in her excitement.

Fiona giggled and blushed and put her hand over her mouth. 'Isn't it brilliant? I've always been a little bit mad, but this takes the biscuit.'

I looked around, and saw Alice standing in the doorway with Buzz cradled in her arms. Fiona saw my face change, and turned to follow my gaze. She was not fazed for an instant.

'Alice, sweetheart,' she said happily. 'Did you fetch your toy?'

Alice walked towards us, holding Buzz Lightyear out for inspection 'I brought my Buzz. Let's play Zurg.' She pressed buttons on Buzz's torso. 'What means a dirty weekend with gardener?' she asked conversationally.

Buzz chipped in. 'Now, *that*'s an impressive attack pack!' he observed.

Matt did not come home.

I went to bed confident that he would creep in after catching the last flight. I dozed, listening for the crunch of his tyres on the stones outside. I woke with a start at three in the morning. His side of the bed was empty. I had been sleeping half under a sheet, hot in the pyjamas I only wore when Matt was away. Normally he pulled the sheet back over me when he got in, and I often took my pyjamas off, still in my sleep, to cuddle up to him. My pyjamas had a photo of a kitten on them. Matt laughed at them because they were so twee, but they had been a present from Christa, and so I liked them.

I walked to the window and opened the shutters. It was a clear night, and for a second I admired the millions of stars and the bright, almost full moon. A moment later, I saw that his car was not outside. I shut the shutters and checked the phone line. It was working. I wondered whether he had left a message on my mobile, or sent a text, whether I could have been out of earshot of the phone any time during the afternoon or evening. I knew I had not been; and Matt knew that we didn't get reception for mobiles at the house. I decided to go up the hill and check the phone in the morning.

I went into the spare room and switched the computer on. I felt gradually sicker. The shutter was open here, and the keyboard was bathed in pale moonlight. I sat in the eerie half-light and thought about death.

Something must have happened. That was what people said when they didn't want to speculate about death. It was much easier to say 'something must have happened' than 'he might be dead'. In the same way, people said, 'I hope she doesn't do something stupid' because it was easier than saying 'I hope she isn't planning to kill herself'. Of course, once she had killed herself, people no longer referred to it as stupidity. They just didn't talk about it at all. I knew that because I had gone out of my way to block out the fact that my mother had ever existed. I was a master of ignoring uncomfortable truths.

I went straight to the BBC news site, which was our home page, and scanned it, petrified, for an aeroplane crash between Gatwick and Bordeaux. There was nothing. Even if he had been on the last flight of the night, a crash would have made it to the news by this point, for sure. Then I checked again for accidents in London. There had clearly not been a massive terrorist attack, which had long been my constant fear. Nothing on the tube. No collapsed office buildings. A fatal accident involving, say, a Gatwick-bound taxi, would not, of course, make it to the BBC news. In search of the most local news I could find, I clicked a button saying 'England'. From there, I chose 'News where you live' and selected London. All the news there seemed to be about footballers on rape charges and children being abused. There was nothing so mundane as a traffic accident.

An hour passed, and I found nothing at all. I pulled myself together, admitted that I was being silly, told myself that there was certainly a perfectly innocent explanation, and assured myself that Matt would stroll in, apologetic but pleased to be home, at some point during the morning. I started padding back to bed, floorboards creaking beneath my feet, when I remembered that French roads were more accident prone than British ones, and that August was the peak month for road deaths in the south of France. I went straight back online to see if I could find news of road accidents south of Bordeaux. Nothing turned up.

Everything outside was silent. The trees and the electricity poles and the buildings cast pronounced shadows in the moonlight. I walked up the hill, still in my kitten pyjamas, with my green espadrilles on my feet, and I looked back at our house. It was grey and forbidding in the moonlight. All the shutters were closed, except for the side door. This was my home, but from time to time it felt more like a prison.

I stared at the phone in my hand. The letters SFR came up, with almost full reception. I watched and watched, willing it to beep into life in my hand with a message explaining why Matt wasn't here. I tried to convince myself that he might have told me he was not coming back till tomorrow, but I knew it wasn't true. I would have remembered. Matt had always come home on Thursday or Friday. My whole life was based around when he was coming back. I waited for a message for fifteen minutes, and then I went back into the house.

By six o'clock I realised I was not going back to sleep, so I opened all the shutters and watched the sun rise over the front garden. The sky was dotted with little wisps of pink cloud. The air was still and crisp. This was the best time of day, and I rarely saw it. I filled the coffee machine with water, spooned ground coffee into the filter, right up to the brim, and listened as it began to splutter and drip. I stood in the French windows that led from the kitchen into the front yard, and waited for Matt. From time to time, I heard a motor approaching, but it was never him. Each time I knew, almost immediately, that it was not Matt's car, because of the sound of the engine, or because the driver was not slowing down, but still, each time I hoped. I gave half-hearted waves to neighbouring farmers on their way to the fields in their tractors. I told myself that he would come back. He had to be all right. If he wasn't, he would have found a way to let me know.

Our relationship had never been tested. It had been balanced and good humoured. It was impossible for me to tell what other people's relationships were like, but I thought we were exceptionally lucky with our equilibrium. That suited me; but it meant that I had no experience of dealing with an upset like this. Matt had come home later than planned many times in the years that I had known him, but each time he had called to let me know. I was on unfamiliar territory, and I didn't know what to do. I tried not to panic. I knew I would hear from him.

I stood outside, looking over the gate, and cradled my coffee in my hands. The morning was filled with the noises of the countryside. I focused on the sounds. A cock crowed up the road. A cow lowed, surprisingly loudly, on the hillside. Tractors were rumbling in the distance. The birds were twittering everywhere. When we moved here I thought that living in the country was going to be deathly dull. It had been, at first. I had only stuck it out because of Alice. I used to lie in bed at night thinking of home and family, and wake up in the morning still thinking of them. I had missed Matt for every second that he was away, even though I had always known that I shared him with his job.

In fact, this life was anything but dull. Country life, it seemed to me, could be more interesting and fulfilling than city life. In Brighton, I used to put Alice to bed, make myself some dinner, and switch the television on. It would stay on all evening, as a matter of course. I would do the ironing in front of it, flick through the paper with half an eye on *EastEnders*, and drink my nightly cup of mint tea while watching a documentary about people moving to France.

Plan B

Now, I tucked Alice up at half past eight and went straight outdoors. I tended my garden with the baby monitor within earshot. I had learned how to prune, how to look after roses, when to pick the cherries. I looked after the house, even though half of it was an abandoned building site. I still missed Matt when he was gone. Our life here was not properly established yet. When Matt managed to work from home, we would be able to settle down properly.

A car came round the corner. I held my breath and waited. It slowed down. I exhaled.

Matt's car was black but this was red. It was Patrick's car. He stopped and waved. *'Ça va?'* he asked, curious.

I tilted my head. *'J'attend mon mari,'* I told him. I realised instantly how bad this sounded. A woman standing at her front gate at half past six in the morning, waiting for a wayward husband who had been out all night. 'He missed his flight from London yesterday evening,' I improvised, praying that this was true.

'When he gets back, you give him a good kick,' Patrick suggested, and drove on, his hand waving back at me through the open window. I smiled. Of course Matt would arrive. But, equally, he was not going to turn up now. The first flight was not until a quarter to nine. He could not land in Bordeaux before eleven fifteen. I was going to have to wait.

I tried his mobile again. It was still turned off.

chapter seventeen

'How long?' Bella demanded.

'Two days,' I admitted. I twiddled my hair. Matt was not back. The heat was unforgiving, and I was possessed. Alice was whingeing for a biscuit and a DVD, and I was ignoring her. I had been ignoring her for two days.

'And what have you been doing? Standing at your gate, looking hopefully at every car that's come past?'

'No. Well, yes, a bit. But I've called all the hospitals in London and Bordeaux, called the airline to see if he was on the flight, which he wasn't. So I know he never left London. I rang Scotland Yard. I tried to get hold of a neighbour at his flat to get them to go and ring the doorbell but I couldn't find anybody because I don't seem to have the address. I know I did have it but it's gone.'

'He's not answering the phone there?'

'The flat hasn't got a landline. He just uses his mobile.'

'And you've left messages on it.'

'A million.'

'Work?'

'I've only got his direct line there. It goes straight to voice-mail. I've been ringing and ringing just to hear his voice. He says, 'Smith here.' He's always said that. It's always made me laugh. Obviously I've left hundreds of messages.'

'The switchboard? Colleagues? That bloke Peter works in his building, doesn't he?'

'Near it. But it's the weekend and I haven't got his home number. In fact I have no numbers for anyone who knows Matt because he keeps them all on his mobile. The switch-board aren't interested. She just told me to try him on Monday.' I tried to quell my panic, again. I knew that Matt was dead, and I was trying to keep myself afloat.

'That's tomorrow,' said Bella. 'Well, if he goes to work tomorrow, we'll catch him.'

'What?' I was surprised. 'Of course he won't go to work tomorrow. That's the whole point, Bella. Something dreadful has happened.'

'You think he's died?'

I took a couple of half hysterical, gasping breaths. 'Yes!' I said. 'I know he's dead. He's lying in his flat all alone and *I don't know what I'm going to do.*'

There was a short pause.

'Not necessarily,' said Bella. 'I have to admit that it's a possibility, and all you've got to do is to find the address and we'll get the police to go round and break in. But he hasn't been in an accident because I know you'll have done a thorough job of calling the hospitals and the police. So we can rule that out. I have to say, I think he's prob-ably fine. He might be having a crisis. It happens all the time.'

I frowned at the phone. 'Don't be stupid. Matt's not like that. He's a family man. He wouldn't have a crisis.'

I wanted this subject firmly closed, because I had run through the other possibilities and I didn't like them. He could have been kidnapped, though by whom and for what reason I could not imagine. He could have walked away from an accident with a head injury and amnesia. Or he could, as Bella said, have had a crisis.

He could have jumped off one of the London bridges, or under a train. There were endless possibilities.

He could not. Matt could not have done that.

'You're probably right,' Bella said quickly. 'Look, I've got no idea, have I, and speculating isn't going to get us very far. I'm coming out. I'll get a flight today and a taxi from the airport.'

'It'll be far too expensive,' I objected.

'It'll be fine. You stay there and keep it together till I arrive. Why did you wait two days to tell me? I'll get Charlotte to go to Matt's office tomorrow and see if they've seen him.'

'If you can tear her away from her West End debut.'

'Mmm. She's very much "resting" at the moment. What about his family? Could you contact them?'

'Matt hasn't got any family,' I reminded her. 'He's estranged from his parents and he's an only child. Alice and I are Matt's family. You know that.'

'I do, I do. There must be a number for his folks somewhere, though. There are degrees of estrangement. He's still got their address. He must have. See if you can dig it out and call them. I'm sure they'd like to know they've got a granddaughter. And I bet they know it already. I bet he sends them Christmas cards on the sly.'

Plan B

I realised that I knew next to nobody in Matt's life. I wondered whether he had had some sort of breakdown. I wondered whether I had failed him.

I grew fed up with pacing around the house pretending that everything was about to be fine. As soon I knew that Bella was coming out, I scooped Alice up and drove to Aurillon, preparing to confide in Andy and Fiona. I dreaded this. I felt as if I was going to see them to announce Matt's death. I had spent two days hesitating to inflict this on anyone.

It was a sweltering day with barely a breeze to relieve the heat. I switched the car's air conditioning on at full blast. My hands shook as I placed my phone on the dashboard. As I drove, as slowly and carefully as I could, I glanced at it every few seconds, checking for reception. As soon as 'SFR' flashed up on the screen, I pulled over and stared at the handset, willing the message icon to appear. When I looked out of the window, I noticed that the maize, now over six feet tall, was beginning to go brown. I wondered briefly why they didn't harvest it when it was green.

I would have embraced a brief text message if it had said that Matt was all right. I did not care where he was or what he had been doing, as long as he was safe. I could no longer imagine any feasible possibilities. 'Abducted by aliens. On Venus. Back tomorrow. Love you.'

There was a voice message, but it was from Fiona. I listened, distracted, as she asked me to back her up. 'I've told Andy we're shopping this afternoon. Is that all right, Emma? Sorry to involve you. If we run into you, all you have to do is agree with whatever I say. Thanks, love. I know I can count on you.'

I noted the view from their courtyard. It was breathtaking. For a moment I scanned the roads around to see if I could spot Matt's car. Both Andy's and Fiona's cars were there. The front door was slightly open. Alice and I stepped out of the intense dry heat and into the cool of the house.

'Hello?' I shouted. My voice sounded too loud. The house was dark, and silent.

'Auntie Fifi?' yelled Alice. 'Are here!' She rushed into the hall, and then into every room on the ground floor. I thought she was desperate to be with someone who wasn't me.

'Come back, Alice,' I instructed her nervously. I did not want her poking about in a house where an infidelity might be in progress. 'We'll have a look in the garden.'

We tiptoed to the back door, and pushed it open. The garden was long and manicured. Even though it had not rained for nearly two months, the grass was green and lush. The flower beds were perfectly neat and tidy and the few trees were pruned and tamed. Andy and Fiona were both leaning back on wooden sun loungers in the full glare of the sun. A bottle of sunscreen lay on its side between them, its contents seeping into the grass. Andy wore a pair of long shorts, and Fiona was trim in a leopard-print bikini. They were both sipping from champagne glasses. Their hair stuck to their foreheads in the heat.

'My two favourite girls!' Andy bellowed. He held up his drink. 'Come and join us. We're on the bubbly.'

'What's the celebration?' I asked, trying to pull myself out of my own misery. I was scared, anticipating sharing my secret. My heart began thumping and my hands clenched into fists of their own accord.

Fiona shrugged. 'Does there have to be one?'

'The occasion,' Andy announced, 'is a property deal. You see, they say the UK housing market's levelled off. Interest rates going up, bubble about to burst, blah blah blah. So it seemed like the right time to offload a couple of my little gems. Item one: an entire house in a recently gentrified part of west London. Purchased six years ago for one hundred and ninety-five thousand pounds, if you can imagine it. Back then, it was in the middle of ganglands, drug deals going off everywhere, shootings, you name it. Nowadays, the trustafarians of Notting Hill are falling over each other to move in there. A lick of paint, sanded floorboards, magnolia walls, and bob's your uncle. Exchanged on it today – total profit, after expenses, an impressive seven hundred and thirty-five grand, give or take.'

Fiona looked at me and yawned ostentatiously. Andy pointed a thumb at her. 'The cheek of the woman! Happy enough to go out spending the proceeds, aren't you, my angel? Emma, I absolutely insist that you join us. I'll fetch you a glass. Then I'll tell you about item two, touch wood. It's not signed and sealed as yet. Where's your old man? Alice, angel, some lemonade? Choccy biccy?'

Alice widened her eyes. I rarely allowed her lemonade, and chocolate biscuits were restricted to the car on the way home from school, because she was always exhausted. She had not had a chocolate biscuit for nearly five weeks. I nodded. 'Go on then,' I told her, and she trotted happily after Andy, back into the house. I sat on Andy's sun lounger. As soon as they were indoors, Fiona leaned forward.

'Got my message?' she asked, in a low voice.

'Yes,' I told her blankly. 'Shopping this afternoon. That's fine.'

She looked at me. 'Ems, what's wrong?' I sighed, and shook my head. I couldn't bear to tell her. 'What is it? Something's up, I can see it in your face. Tell me.'

'Oh, Fi,' I said, quietly. 'I'm sorry to do this to you. It's Matt. He's gone missing.'

I was about to explain when Andy came back. He handed me my drink and stood back. When I looked at his face, I saw that his mood had changed. His face was tight and suspicious.

'Ladies?' he said, in a small voice. 'Ladies, could I put a question to you both?' We stared at him. I nodded. 'Why,' he continued, 'in the kitchen, why did young Alice just ask me the following question? To quote her verbatim: "Uncle Andy, why Auntie Fifi needs dirty weekend with gardener?"' He looked hard at Fiona. 'Would somebody care to enlighten me?'

I jumped into action before she could say anything. 'Oh, Andy,' I said, with a little laugh. 'Did she say that? It was a game we were playing when Fi was over last week. We were talking about the trip to Paris she's planning with the girls. Fi said from the way you'd reacted anyone would think she was off on a dirty weekend with the gardener. And Alice was playing with her Buzz Lightyear, and she picked up on the phrase. That's what small children do.' I started giggling. I had always prided myself on not getting involved in silly lies. But now Matt was missing and I didn't care what I said. I supposed I was half hysterical. 'She got a laugh when she repeated it, so now she says it to anyone who'll listen.'

Andy was smiling sceptically. He looked at Fiona, keen to be convinced.

'Shut up about the bloody gardener,' she snapped. 'Ems just told me that Matt's gone missing.'

'Missing?' echoed Andy. He frowned.

I looked at their puzzled, expectant faces and I shook my head in defeat. 'I've got no idea where in the world he could be,' I told them.

I supposed that I had known that they would rally, but I was still overwhelmed at their kindness and the wave of relief it brought.

Fiona took Alice to the end of the garden to play swing-ball. She took her mobile with her, presumably to cancel her afternoon tryst with Didier. Andy took it upon himself to repeat all my calls to hospitals and police forces, and left a new barrage of messages on Matt's mobile.

The sun was beginning to slide down the sky and the still air became infinitesimally cooler. Andy refilled my glass and squeezed my shoulder. 'I know you don't want to hear this, Emma, and I'm sure you've already thought of it, but is there any chance he could be with a lady friend?'

I turned and stared. 'I don't think so.'

'Can you be quite sure?'

'Yes, I can.' This was an option I had barely considered. I had dismissed it out of hand. Matt would not have an affair, and, besides, if he was leaving me for another woman, he would not have done it like this. Nobody would. 'Why?' I demanded. 'Why do you think he is? Did he ever say anything?' I remembered Fiona describing Andy as 'no angel' and winced at the idea of the two of them swapping stories. 'What did he say?' I needed to know, at once.

Andy looked away. 'Nothing, really.'

'What? You can't get this far and not tell me what he said.' Andy said nothing. I raised my voice. 'Andy! You have to tell me!'

Andy pulled the foil off the champagne bottle. 'I'm sorry, love, I really am,' he said awkwardly. 'You're a super girl. It's a little bit delicate.' He looked around to check that Fiona was out of earshot. 'I've played away a little over the years,' he said quickly. 'Fi might have mentioned it. I'm back on the straight and narrow now, of course, but I mentioned something to Matt and asked him whether he'd ever indulged, what with all those nights in his bachelor pad in London on his own.' I winced. 'I'm so sorry, Emma, I really am. It was just laddish bollocks. He wouldn't say anything, really, but I remember what he did say, because it stuck in my mind. He said, "I might tell you everything one of these days."'

He stopped talking and watched me. I did not know how to react.

'So that's all it is,' I said eventually. 'Matt's traded me in for a younger model.'

'He hasn't,' Andy said at once. 'He's a good guy. If he has messed around, it wouldn't have meant anything. He would never leave you. He bloody adores you and Alice. Not to mention the house, the whole lifestyle thing. I was more thinking, well, if he'd been with a lady, he might not have been in London. We should maybe be casting our net a bit further afield, if you catch my drift.' Andy leaned back in his deckchair and drained his glass. He looked strained.

I drained mine too. I was nearly drunk. I did not know how I was going to get home. Drink and drive, I supposed.

Bella arrived at lunchtime the next day. She swept into the house, ran a hand through her long hair, and threw herself onto a chair.

'This heat!' she exclaimed. 'I don't know how you stand it. I feel like an old tea towel. You look like one. How about a G and T to perk us both up?'

I nodded, and poured two large drinks. 'How much was the taxi?' I asked. I had bought tonic water that morning, specially. Bella had always liked a gin and tonic. Fiona had dosed me up on Valium the night before, and had taken Alice away to stay overnight with Coco and Louis. Alice had barely protested at all. I had, therefore, enjoyed a reasonable night's sleep. I had woken that morning to a rush of terror. This, I was certain, was the day. Today I was going to discover the truth. I was bleak and numb, because after what Andy had reported, I knew that there was a lot about Matt's life that I had never suspected.

'Enough,' said Bella. 'It was fine.'

I looked at Bella. Her thick black hair flowed down her back, and she was wearing a rust-coloured Ghost dress. Her face was thin and shining with sweat.

'Have you lost weight?' I asked.

'Mmm. South Beach,' she confirmed.

181

'Is that low-carb?'

'Yep.'

'Would it be better if he was dead?' I mused. 'If he's fine, he must be with a woman. I suppose amnesia and alien abduction are the best options.'

'Which is a sorry state of affairs,' pointed out my sister. 'Amnesia only happens in the movies. Alien abduction only happens in America.'

I looked at her, desperate for answers. 'What do you think?'

She returned my gaze, levelly, weighing her words. 'I think Charlotte will find out today, one way or another.' She looked around. 'Alice asleep?'

'No. She stayed at a friend's house last night. Being around me all the time wasn't doing her any good. She'd started asking me whether Daddy's plane had crashed. Oh!' I brightened up suddenly and told Bella about Fiona, the gardener, and Alice's innocent query. Bella roared with laughter.

'She asked this woman's husband why his wife was off on a dirty weekend with the gardener?' she bellowed. 'That's fabulous. Good old Alice. I can't wait to see her. When's she back?'

'I said I'd fetch her.' I looked at my drink. 'I hardly used to drink before we moved here. Then I never had more than a glass or two of wine, until this happened. Now I've been half drunk since yesterday afternoon. It's nice. But we'd better go and pick her up sooner rather than later because luckily this is my first drink of the day and I haven't actually drunk it yet. You can meet my friend Coco.' I looked at Bella and tried to smile. 'I think you'll like her.'

'I've never heard you talk about friends before,' Bella remarked as we buckled ourselves into my little car. 'Life here seems to agree with you. Apart from this business with Matt, you seem to be doing pretty well. Mum and Dad can't wait to get out here and see you.'

'I'd almost forgotten about that. They're coming Thursday?'

'Mmmm.' She looked around. 'It's absolutely gorgeous, Ems. The house is going to be wonderful, too.' She looked at me, and seemed to stop herself saying something. I knew what she was hesitating from asking. Would I stay here if Matt had gone? I did not have an answer. The prospect was too baffling and terrifying to contemplate.

'Don't ask,' I said. I knew she understood.

As we stood on Coco's doorstep and pressed the buzzer, Bella looked around. St Paul was quiet, as it always was except on Saturday, because that was market day. The dry-cleaners below the flat was closed, since it was Monday. We looked down the end of the road to the main square and the church. A few people were strolling around, most of them heading in the general direction of the only shop that was open on Monday, the little grocery. The sun was hot and high and the town seemed to have shut its eyes in response. I loved the town. It had come into its own during the summer.

'This is "town"?' Bella asked doubtfully. 'It's not a metropolis, is it? Sweet and everything. Hardly bustling.' She touched my arm. 'Darling, doesn't it make you crave Soho? It would me. I would go insane here.'

I shook my head. '*Bonjour*, Coco,' I said to the intercom.

'*C'est moi*.' She buzzed us in. 'No,' I told Bella, as we started ascending the stairs. 'You know me. I wasn't exactly out clubbing every night in England. I love a quiet life. It suits me here.'

Alice ran into my arms and buried her face in my shoulder. 'Mummy,' she said. 'Mummy Mummy Mummy. I love you too much, Mummy.'

I hugged her tightly. 'I love you too much, too, sweetheart. Have you had a lovely time?'

She pulled back and cupped my cheeks with her hands. 'Yes. Where's Daddy?'

My heart was heavy. I wished I could answer. 'Daddy's not back yet,' I said quickly. 'But look who's come to see us instead!' I pointed to Bella.

'Bella!' Alice yelled. She headed towards her, then looked round. 'Where's Felix and Oscar?'

Bella smiled. 'In London. They're going to come to see you very soon. Do I get a kiss?'

We accepted coffee, and clutching their delicate pink espresso cups, Bella and Coco quickly disappeared into Coco's bedroom, to go through her wardrobe. Bella spoke reasonable French, and Coco and I had spoken English so regularly that Coco had improved enormously since I had known her. I could hear laughter and coos of admiration coming through the walls.

My big sister had long despaired of my fashion sense. I had been through phases, like everyone else. During our teens, Bella had managed to keep me vaguely abreast of fashion by taking me shopping with her and kitting me out with my meagre allowance. Since then, I had been through a period of only wearing black, a phase of jeans and T-shirts, and now I was happily settled into a new system, whereby I would put on anything that came to hand and avoid mirrors. Fiona had led me by the elbow into her favourite boutiques in Villeneuve, but I had walked straight back out again. I could not afford to spend any money on clothes. I was not interested in spending money on clothes. I looked after Alice first, Matt second, the garden third. I had bought some espadrilles and a cotton hat at the beginning of the summer. Matt always told me I looked beautiful and sexy no matter what I was wearing.

As a fashion journalist, Bella spent much of her time sitting by a catwalk, making notes into a little book, before crafting an article for her readers, advising them about what they would need to buy for their autumn wardrobes. She dressed her little boys in shorts and cotton shirts in summer, and cords and duffel coats in winter, and they always looked adorable. Their hair was honey-blond and short on the backs of their necks.

Coco was fascinated by clothes and spent evenings perusing fashion magazines and mentally assembling her autumn wardrobe. She had things dry-cleaned, downstairs. She ironed everything, not just her child's school essentials. She folded her clothes with lavender bags between them. She plucked her eyebrows every other day, styled her hair, and put on her make-up as soon as her feet hit the bedroom floor in the morning. She dressed her little boy in shorts and cotton shirts in summer and cords and a duffel coat in winter. Naturally, Coco and Bella hit it off at once. I felt excluded, but in my haze of terror, I was quite relieved. I tuned out of their conversation and devoted my energies to imagining Matt curled up in sexual bliss with a slender, flawless seventeen-year-old, without stretch marks. This imaginary lover had long auburn curls and creamy skin, and Matt was so infatuated with her that he had abandoned me and Alice, and was never going to see either of us ever again.

I felt as if I had been skewered through the stomach. It had happened. I could invent masochistic fantasies to torture myself, but they were perfectly realistic. If he wasn't with a pre-Raphaelite teenager, then he was with a twenty-five-year-old skinny blonde, or a forty-year-old mother of three. The details were irrelevant.

I forced the images out of my mind, and concentrated on the children. I asked them what they had had for breakfast (croissants and hot chocolate at a café, as a treat) and where they had slept (at opposite ends of Louis' bed). I barely noticed the answers. My stomach was in knots. I prayed that I would shortly find out the truth, however awful it might be. I could not bear myself in this state of limbo.

'Have you packed up your bag ready to come home?' I asked Alice, trying to focus on the details and make the minutes pass.

'Not yet,' she replied happily. A phone started to ring. I jumped nervously at first, before remembering that I was not at home so it would not be for me. Then I realised that it was not Coco's phone that was ringing, but Bella's, and that it was coming from her handbag on the table. I snatched the bag and retrieved the phone from a jumble of receipts, tissues and loose change.

Plan B

I looked at the screen as I was pressing the button.

'Charlotte!' I exclaimed.

'Hi, Bella,' said my other sister. She sounded too languid for my liking. I hoped she had news. 'Just saw him, the bastard. Like we thought. He's at work. Went out for lunch.'

'He's at *work*?'

Charlotte sounded alarmed. 'Emma?'

'Yes, it's me. He went to work? He's gone to lunch?'

I felt blank. I had no idea what I should have been feeling. Was I relieved that he was alive? Or furious? I mentally struck alien abduction and amnesia from the list of possibilities. Matt was neither lying dead in his flat nor unidentified in hospital. In fact there was only one possibility. He had left us, and he hadn't even bothered to tell me.

Charlotte's voice changed. It became softer, sympathetic. 'Ems. How are you bearing up?' she asked.

'Tell me everything. Did you see him this morning?'

'No. I loitered around his office a bit at half eight, but I didn't see him arriving. I decided to try again at lunchtime before striding in and demanding to know where he was, because if he was there I didn't want to frighten him into hiding. So I rolled back up at half twelve and sat in the Starbucks over the road. He came out at ten to one. He did look a bit scared, I have to say. He had a good look up and down the street, but obviously deemed it safe and set off at a brisk pace.'

'Did you follow?'

'Naturally. I had taken the precaution of getting my coffee in a takeaway cup, so I just folded my paper and ambled after him. I was quite the Kay Scarpetta.'

I could imagine exactly how Charlotte had enjoyed herself in that role. 'Where did he go?' I asked.

'To a caff. A greasy spoon type of place. Ali's Diner. It's just round the corner from his office. Full of officey types having fry-ups. He sat there for a bit and then another bloke in a suit came and joined him. Matt looked a bit hunted on his own. But when this bloke came along, he relaxed. They've been laughing. They're still there.'

'Where are you?'

'I'm outside. Looking in.'

'What are you going to do?'

'You tell me. What I would *like* to do is to walk in there, pick up his egg and chips and deposit it on his head, then take his mate's coffee and drench his groin. Or I could hand him the phone so he has to speak to you. What do you want?'

My heart pounded at the idea of talking to him. I panicked. 'Don't do anything right now. Talk to Bella.' I watched Alice and Louis emptying the kitchen drawers, and decided to let them get on with it. As far as I could see there were no knives. 'Bella!' I called. 'Charlotte's found him.'

Bella appeared instantly, a white cotton tunic in her hand. 'Where? At work? Is he OK?'

I nodded and handed her the phone. Coco appeared by my side and touched my shoulder. 'Your sister has found Matt?' she checked, in French.

'Yes. He's at work, just like he always is on Monday.' I turned to her, conscious that I was holding myself together. 'Why hasn't he called me?' I switched into English. 'Why the fuck hasn't he called me? Even if he's leaving me, he has to tell me. He has to leave a note or *something*. What is going on? What about Alice?' Coco pulled me into her shoulder but I stiffened and pulled away. I looked at her. 'Sorry,' I said. 'I can't relax. I need to stay in control.'

She nodded. 'You are very English,' she pointed out, in French. 'A Frenchwoman would be a torrent of emotions. You're keeping it all inside.'

'I have to.' I tried to listen to what Bella was saying, but I couldn't take it in. I did not want to speak to Matt. I could not bear to hear what he might say to me.

chapter eighteen

'Still there,' said Pete. 'She's on the phone.'

'Arse,' said Hugh.

'She's looking at us.' Pete looked away quickly and tried to sip his coffee, which was far too hot. He thought it had been microwaved in the cup, because he could barely touch the handle. He put it down quickly before the scalding liquid got anywhere near his lips.

'Still?' Hugh was pretending to read the tabloid paper that was on the table. His eye drifted over a story about footballers and sex, but his brain didn't process it.

Pete stole a look. He made accidental eye contact with Charlotte, who stared grimly at him until he looked away, which happened quickly. 'Oh yes,' he told Hugh. 'Very much still looking at us. Still on the phone.'

'Christ. She's telling fucking Emma.'

Pete laughed. 'Or she's hiring a hit squad. She must have followed you here.'

'No shit. Fuck it, she's supposed to be the scatty one.'

Pete gathered a large helping of egg, sausage and chips

onto his fork. He dipped it in ketchup, then dipped it in brown sauce, and opened his mouth wide to receive it. He chewed vigorously for a few moments.

'The thing is,' he said, still chewing, 'does it matter? You've left Emma. That was your choice. You're going to have to talk to her sometime. I mean, it's generally considered good manners to let someone know when you dump them. Plus I don't see sexy sis here storming in to confront you.'

'She will. She's an actress. She loves scenes.'

'It's not about her.'

'She never liked me. Nor did Bella. The aunt was the worst. She knew I was a bad 'un the moment she met me. She could see right through me. She was scary.'

Pete shrugged. 'Good thing it's not the aunt out there now, then. Anyway, none of it matters now. You're free of them all. You'll never see them again.'

Hugh picked up his half Guinness. 'Cheers to that,' he said. Pete managed to pick up his coffee, and they toasted Hugh's escape from Emma.

He braved a glance at the window. Charlotte gave him a withering look, put her phone back in her handbag, and walked away.

'I have told her anyway,' said Hugh. 'I sent her a letter.'

chapter nineteen

Jo closed her eyes and took a deep breath. She expelled the air through her mouth as she had been taught to do in her yoga class. She did it again: in, and out. All around her, people were rushing to work. She knew she was blocking the pavement. Men and women in suits, and a few tourists with maps and cameras, were stepping out into Jermyn Street to get past her. There was some huffing and tutting, but nobody addressed her. She tried to keep going. She instructed one foot to step in front of the other. It was no good. She couldn't move.

She had to get to the gallery. She needed to open up. She had meetings all morning and an auction to go to in the afternoon. She was a hundred yards away from the door, but she was paralysed.

A woman stopped next to her. Jo felt her presence, but didn't look.

'Excuse me,' said the woman. 'Are you all right?'

Jo turned her head and looked at her. She had made herself up immaculately that morning, knowing that she needed a mask. Normally a hard look from her could easily frighten off someone like this woman, who was soft, over-weight and kind. The woman put a hand on Jo's shoulder. To her horror, she felt her face crumpling.

As the woman cradled her, Jo sobbed. She cried on the woman's shoulder for two minutes. Then she pulled away and apologised. The woman gave her a cotton handkerchief and walked her to the gallery door.

'If you need anything, I'm a Samaritan. My name's Glad. Glad Muir. Here's my card. Call me if you need to.'

She squeezed Jo's shoulder and watched her open the gallery and turn off the alarm. Jo sat down and stared at the card. Everything had become too strange. She had just been rescued by a stranger whose name was Glad.

chapter twenty

As I drove away from Pounchet I knew that I was leaving half of myself behind. This was the biggest test I had ever faced. I thought about my childhood. It was probably not; but it was the biggest test I could remember. I was Emma Meadows, and I was single. The only reason I was not getting divorced was because he had never wanted to marry me.

Alice was ensconced in our house with her aunt. Bella's husband, Jon, was coming out with the boys the next morning. Christa and Geoff were arriving on Thursday, as planned. It broke my heart that Bella would probably be taking Alice to school for the *rentrée*, on Thursday, and that Christa and Geoff would be there to pick her up.

Matt had left me. It was official.

His letter had arrived the previous morning. Much as I would have liked to have forgotten it, every word was burned on my memory.

Dear Emma,
   I am sorry to be sending you this letter. I am sorry

if I've worried you by disappearing. I suppose you won't get this till at least Tuesday so I hope you haven't been too concerned over the weekend.

I'm afraid that things aren't working out for us in France as I hoped they would. The commute is too much for me and, much as I respect you and love Alice, our relationship isn't working either. I hope you can accept this. Naturally I will continue to support my daughter. Go ahead and put the house on the market. Perhaps we can contact each other by letter or email in a few weeks when feelings have cooled.

I know that you are a strong woman, Emma. You are stronger than you realise and you will get through this without any problems. Believe me, you are better off this way.

With sincere apologies and regret,

Matt

I knew that Matt had not written that letter. I had thought I knew him better than anyone. I had spent four overwhelmingly happy years with him. I could not let this letter mark the end. I desperately hoped that something sinister was going on, that he had, perhaps, been blackmailed, or got himself into a huge financial crisis, and that he was doing this to save me and Alice from his mess. If he needed help, then I was on my way to save him. If he had met someone else, which was, though I hated to acknowledge it, the more likely option, then I was on my way to show him that he had underestimated me. I was travelling to London, on my own, to find him.

Bella had offered to make me 'look fabulous' to win him back, but I had brushed her away. She didn't understand. This was not about outward appearances. A pretty dress and a spot of lipstick was not going to bring him back. Charlotte had insisted on meeting me in London. I had agreed, reluctantly.

I drove north to Villeneuve on the ring road and onwards, to Bordeaux. The countryside, all the way, was flat. Rows of pine trees stretched away on either side of me. There were hundreds of miles of trees. Now that I drove out of our corner of France, I realised how geographically confined we had been for the past seven months. Alice and I had not travelled further than Mimizan. That was an hour from home. We had spent every night under our own roof. Although we had kept in touch with England, it had seemed increasingly remote.

We will have to go back to England now, I reminded myself. It will be a shock, but we will manage. I wondered whether we would look back in the future and see these months as a dreamlike interlude. Alice would barely remember it.

I struggled to maintain my self-possession as I contemplated a future without Matt. I had to find him to see what was going on. Did he really imagine that I would bow out of his life so obediently? He probably did, because I had always done everything I had been told.

I could not remember ever having been angry before. I felt the beginnings of it now. I was possessed, unable to think about anything other than Matt. I was humiliated: abandoned by my supposed life partner, by the man who had said that he would always adore Alice and me. I was devastated that he had downgraded that, in his letter, to adoring Alice and respecting me. We had made Alice together, out of love. She was a combination of our genes. He had left her without saying goodbye.

None of it added up. By the time I arrived at Bordeaux, I had convinced myself, yet again, that Matt needed me to come and rescue him. I could not think about any other possibility. I was on the edge.

I landed at Gatwick at half past three. It felt odd to be making the journey that Matt had made so many times, and to be making it on my own. I thought, in a detached way, that I ought to have enjoyed the journey. It would have been nice to have been in a state of mind to appreciate the pleasures of travelling alone: to have relished sitting by the window for the whole journey and staring blankly at a book, to have appreciated the rare chance to travel unencumbered by crayons, beakers of juice, or emergency biscuits. I found a small plastic dinosaur in my handbag and clutched it in my palm, a kind of talisman. It was a stegosaurus, and its plates pressed sharply into my hand.

I had hand luggage and nothing else, so I walked straight out into the airport. Gatwick was immense and busy. The air smelt stale, as if it had been inhaled and exhaled too many times. People of all ages and nationalities rushed past. Signs showed me the way to places I did not want to go to. Announcements rang out indecipherably. The dull momentum of the place assaulted me, and for a moment I was utterly lost.

I found a cashpoint, and took two hundred pounds from

my British bank account. I checked the balance, which was healthier than I had expected. Then I queued in a newsagents and bought a newspaper, to give me change for the payphone. As I waited to pay, I noticed the huge array of chocolate, crisps and sweets on display. It was obscene. I had got used to the lack of snacking culture in France. It seemed sane. I took a bottle of water from the fridge, and lost my place in the line. When I got to the front, the man at the till said, in a mechanical voice; 'Giant chocolate bar half price with any paper.' He pushed an enormous bar of cheap milk chocolate towards me.

'No thanks,' I said.

He frowned. 'You sure?'

I nodded.

'Suit yourself,' he said, gave me a *takes all sorts* look, and handed me a palm full of change.

I spent ten minutes looking for a payphone. A group of girls, all wearing tight pink T-shirts with 'Amy's hen party – watch out Barcelona!!' printed on them walked around me, shrieking with laughter and drinking Bacardi Breezers. A small Asian man hauled his suitcase behind him, looking around, lost and distressed. Three backpackers were deep in conversation, blocking my path with their bags, and I edged past nervously.

I clutched the phone when I heard Alice's voice. I felt dreadful about abandoning her straight after her father, but I was doing it for the sake of her future.

'You be careful, Mummy,' she said. Then she told me about the games she was playing with Bella, and then the money ran out.

Plan B

I boarded the Gatwick Express. As soon as I sat down, I realised that my head was spinning. For a moment, I felt myself about to faint. I forced a couple of deep breaths, and leaned forward. My mind was full of bright lights and colours and people. I had grown up in London, but now I was dreading everything about it. I had become too rural.

When I regained control, I leaned back in my seat and looked at the people opposite. They were elderly tourists, who were smiling around at everybody and everything. The man caught my eye. He was white-haired, red-faced, and affable in a Hawaiian shirt and Panama hat.

'Vacation?' he asked. I thought he was Canadian.

I shook my head. 'I wish,' I told him. 'I'm English. I live in France. I'm just back briefly.'

'And that doesn't constitute a vacation?'

I forced a small smile. 'It certainly doesn't.' For a moment I considered inflicting my story on this couple, but I decided against it. They looked nice. I didn't want to depress them. Besides, they were in England and everyone knew that British people did not share details about their private lives, least of all with strangers on trains.

'Family problems,' I told him.

I had a terrible fear that this was just the beginning. I had expended an enormous amount of energy over the years in pretending that my mother had never existed. I had never faced up to what had happened when I was a toddler. I had made a point of never thinking about it. I had never asked Christa about my mother. I had shaken my head when she had asked if I wanted a photograph for my room. Instinctively, even as a tiny child, I had decided to make a fresh start.

If Matt had left me, after everything I had done for him, then my whole identity was under threat. I had never uttered a cross word to him. I had done everything he wanted, been sweet when he was grumpy, indulged him when he was tired, comforted him when work was going badly, made him laugh, made his tea, made him come. I had cheered him on when everything was going well. I had borne him a beautiful daughter and had emigrated on his whim. I had done everything in my power to be a perfect partner. He had still rejected me.

'Family problems?' probed the stranger.

'Yes,' I told him. 'I'm on a mission.'

I took out my book and frowned at it, rejecting any further attempts at eye contact. The train rattled through south London. I started staring out of the window. I began to recognise landmarks on the horizon. I saw the Canary Wharf tower pointing skywards in the distance. That marked my destination.

Matt did not work in the tower itself, but in an office block nearby. I easily found the Starbucks that Charlotte had used as the nerve centre of her stakeout. It was perfectly placed. There were a few tables and chairs outside, in honour of it being August, though the afternoon was cool and all the customers were indoors. I sat down at a table near the kerb. I would definitely see him coming or going from there. It was five o'clock. He used to leave just before six. At least, that was what he had always told me.

After five minutes, Charlotte strode down the road. I gave her a small wave, and she accelerated her pace. I stood up as she came close. My sister Charlotte was strikingly pretty. Her bright blonde hair was long and wavy. She wore red lipstick, tight black trousers, and a red top. I saw men in suits watching her. Charlotte loved attention. That was why she was an actress.

We kissed, and she rubbed my shoulder. 'Poor Em,' she said.

'I'm OK,' I lied. 'I just want to know what's going on.'

She shook her head. 'It's low, so low, what he's done to you. I hope you're going to give him hell.'

I shook my head. 'I don't know. It feels like it's happening to someone else. I can't imagine what's gone on.' I stood up to go inside. 'Coffee?' I asked. 'Still on the buckets of latte?'

Charlotte shook her head. 'Not when I discovered how many calories they put in them. Can I have the smallest latte they do, *tall* I think it's called, fair trade, and get them to make it skinny?'

'Tall, skinny fair trade latte,' I said. 'You're just trying to make me look silly. Where I come from, you have coffee, or you have coffee with milk.'

On the way in, I caught sight of myself in the glass of Starbucks' window. For a second, I did not recognise the woman who gaped back at me. In my mind, I looked young and innocent, like a grown-up girl. My mental picture of myself was unobtrusive. I was a little dark person who kept to the sidelines, and whose life was her family. When I was pregnant with Alice, I had studied myself in mirrors and windows at every opportunity, and marvelled at my round belly and the incredible fact that I was making a human being inside it. Since her birth, I had shied away from my appearance. My role as a mother had overshadowed the small amount of vanity I might once have possessed, and as a rule I could not have cared less how I looked.

The woman who looked back at me from the plate-glass window, however, was a farmer's wife after a hard day in the fields. I was wearing a pair of three-quarter-length jeans which had once been my most presentable clothes but which now had unshiftable green gardening stains; a pink T-shirt that had been bleached by the sun; and this summer's green espadrilles. I could have done with a jacket. My hair was sticking to my head, unwashed for several days. I was, naturally, devoid of make-up and shiny of face.

I wondered what Charlotte had thought when she saw me. Her face had given nothing away, but then again, she was an actress. I suddenly deeply regretted turning down Bella's offer of a makeover.

I looked round. Charlotte had lit a cigarette.

'I'll just be a second,' I told her, and I turned and walked quickly towards Canary Wharf itself. I followed a sign for shops, hoping that I had time in hand before Matt left work. I knew that Charlotte would catch him for me if she had to.

The first clothes shop I saw was a branch of Gap. I had long avoided their shops on principle, because of Third World child labour, but today I didn't feel I had the choice.

'Hi,' beamed a young man stationed by the door. He seemed delighted to see me.

'Hello,' I told him, slightly baffled, and I hurried to the

clothes. I saw sales assistants watching me. They probably thought I was a shoplifter, a single mother desperate to clothe herself and her children. With a jolt I realised that I *was* a single mother. It was temporary, I was determined of that, but for the moment I was a lone parent. Coco had assured me that I could do it on my own. She had been wrong.

I walked over to the woman with the nicest face. She was just a girl. She could not have been more than twenty.

'Hi!' she said cheerfully, her face betraying no alarm at my scruffiness.

'Hello. I need your help,' I told her urgently 'My husband's left me and I need to get him to come back. I've just realised what I look like – I've been a bit distracted. Can you make me look half decent in the next ten minutes?'

She grinned. 'Sure we can! What size are you? I'd guess a twelve UK? Or fourteen? What colours do you like?'

I opened my mouth to protest that I was a size ten in British sizes, thank you very much, before realising that it was probably not true any more. The last thing I wanted was to squeeze myself into clothes that were too small. I did not want to pop buttons and strain seams just to attempt to prove a point.

I thought of Coco's chic wardrobe, which was full of white and beige, black and grey. 'Neutral colours,' I suggested. 'Classic and chic, maybe?'

'You got it.'

Twenty minutes later, I sat down opposite Charlotte, feeling much more confident. I was wearing black, wide legged trousers that still felt a little tight despite being so big, a black Lycra top with an absurdly flattering wide neck-line, and a neat little cream raincoat. My feet were already aching in a pair of boots with small stiletto heels.

'Wow,' she said. 'Weird disappearing act. You look great. You should have let me help.'

'Sorry,' I said with a smile. 'I saw myself in the glass. Not pretty.'

'Bought you a latte.'

'Thanks.' I sipped it. It tasted of slightly burnt, coffee-flavoured milk.

Charlotte rummaged in her capacious handbag. 'Got you!' she said, triumphantly. 'Right. Come here.'

I moved my chair closer, and she applied foundation to my face with the expert touch that I recognised from years before.

'You used to do this when we shared the flat,' I remembered.

'Bloody right,' she said, her brow furrowed in concen-tration. 'Only because otherwise you'd go out with nothing on your face at all. Someone had to make you care.' She held up two lipsticks and considered them with her head on one side. 'Dark red,' she said, after a minute. 'Subtle but sexy. And a bit of mascara and eyeliner and we're done.'

Charlotte told me about her life while I kept my eyes firmly on the door to Matt's building. I half listened to her stories about her 'boyfriend', Antonio, who was *divine*, and her 'fuck buddy', Bradley, who was *scrumptious*. Men left the building in a constant stream, but Matt was not among them. They wore suits and talked in loud voices, often into mobile phones. They were busy, impatient to be in transit, keen to get to where they were going.

By six thirty, we were getting cold. The exodus was tailing off, and I knew that Matt was not going to appear.

Charlotte gathered her things together. 'Let's give him half an hour,' she suggested. 'I'm frozen here. Let's go inside and have hot chocolate and cake at that window table.'

I nodded. As I stood up, I looked up and down the street. Instantly I noticed a familiar figure standing on the corner. Without looking at Charlotte, I ran towards him as fast as I could. He saw me, and turned and walked away briskly. I shouted his name. As I rounded the corner, I saw him trying to disappear into the crowds, so I yelled his name again.

'PETER ALISTAIR SMITH!' I roared.

Pete had almost been running in his desperation to escape me. When he heard me shouting, he, and all the other busy commuters in the area, stopped, turned, and stared at me. I trotted up to him, hobbling slightly in my new boots. It was clear, from the expression on his face, that he would rather have been absolutely anywhere else in the world than here, near his office, with me.

'Pete,' I said. 'Where is he?'

Pete groaned. I looked at his brown hair, which was longer than it used to be, touching his collar. I looked at his acne-scarred skin. I felt the old distaste. 'Hello, Emma. I don't know.'

'You fucking do know!' I was surprising myself. 'I know you know. Give me some credit, you twat. Where is he?'

Pete held up a hand. 'Look, don't involve me, all right?

This is nothing to do with me. This is between the two of you.'

'I know. I don't want to involve you either. Christ, you know that. But I've got to find him. Was he at work today? Were the switchboard lying when they said he wasn't?'

Pete sighed. 'No. Switchboards don't lie. I don't think they'd have much truck with the idea of covering some poor sucker's tracks.'

'Where is he?'

Pete was looking around, searching for an escape route. 'Look,' he said quickly. 'I'll tell him he's got to call you. Have you got a mobile? I'll tell him you're here. I agree with you, the two of you need to talk. He owes you that. Where's Ally?'

'*Alice*. She's in France, asking why Daddy hasn't come home.' I thought about it. 'Give me the address of where he's staying, Pete. You may as well. Let me go to him and get it over with. I don't care if she's there, whoever she is – I'm taking a wild guess that there's a she?' Pete's face confirmed it. I felt sick. 'I'm not asking you to tell me anything,' I said. 'I just need to find Matt, so I can go home to my daughter, who needs me more than she's ever done.'

I stared at him. He looked back into my eyes. He looked for so long that it became disconcerting. I did not look away. He didn't either. It was a charged look. For a minute I thought of our shared history, of his inexplicable obsession. Then I pushed it from my mind. That was irrelevant and had been for many years. It would be embarrassing to him even to mention it.

I tried, instead, to read his eyes.

'Just tell me this,' I said quietly, not taking my eyes off him. 'Am I in the right city?'

Pete held my gaze. 'Yes. You'll find him. And when you do, I'm sorry. All right?'

He squeezed my shoulder. I thought he was trying to give me a serious hug, so I pulled back and walked away.

A drop of rain fell on my cheek. The rush of workers walking briskly across the square had finished, abruptly. I walked back to Starbucks, where Charlotte was waiting with hot chocolate, and told her what had happened.

'Go in,' she said. 'See if he's there.'

'He's not.'

'But ask anyway.'

'Why?'

'Nothing to lose.'

The foyer was large and brightly lit. An obese security guard with thick grey hair was sitting at the reception desk, looking bored. I hung back. Charlotte strode up to him.

'Hi!' she said, with a wide smile. He smiled back.

'Hello, love,' he said. 'What can I do you for?'

'Right,' she said, lowering her voice confidentially. 'We need your help. We're after a man.'

He raised his eyebrows and leaned towards her. 'Any man in particular?'

'Yes. Matthew Smith. He works for BB Johnson. Can you tell us if he's here?'

The guard nodded and took out a booklet. He traced his finger down a line of numbers.

'Smith, Smith, Smith,' he said. 'There's a few of them.

Hugo Smith, BB Johnson? No, here we are, Matthew. Same extension. Must be confusing.'

Charlotte nodded, with a bright smile. I watched the man punch in the digits. I could hear the phone ringing through the earpiece. It rang and rang.

'Sorry, love,' he said. 'No doubt you ladies will locate him in the pub.'

Charlotte shot him a dazzling look. 'Thanks. We'll try. Have a good night.'

I did not think the man had even noticed I was there.

Then, suddenly, I was lost. Matt was not at work. He was in London, and I was in London. I could walk around this city for months, for years without stopping, and still not bump into him. Pounchet was a universe away. I tried to picture Alice, and Bella, and Jon and the twins, and Coco and Louis and Andy and Fiona. I wondered what they were doing, in their various places. Wherever they were, whatever they were up to, they were in the countryside, and it was quiet.

I, meanwhile, was feeling foreign. I knew London. I knew it well, yet I felt far removed from all these people.

'Thanks, Charlotte,' I said sadly. 'I'll head off, I think.'

'What do you mean? There's loads we can do. We haven't tried any of the bars.'

'He won't be in a bar. He knows I'm after him. I'm going to go. Thanks.'

'But where are you staying? Come home and stay at mine. There's supposed to be a little party later. It might cheer you up.'

I shook my head and walked away. A gentle drizzle was

barely falling. Drops of water were hanging in the air. I headed towards the river and stared at the workers sitting in bars. Some of them were still sitting at outside tables, anaesthetised to the weather by alcohol. I could smell their drinks as I walked past. Jackets rested on backs of chairs. Men drank pints, while most of the women seemed to have a glass of white wine in front of them. Bags of crisps were torn open and placed democratically in the centres of tables. Everybody was talking. Bursts of laughter reached me. Excited chatter. In-jokes about office life. A woman squealed, 'NO!' in exaggerated disbelief. Men threw back their heads and guffawed in parodies of themselves. I had never felt more of an outsider. I walked past them, down to the water's edge. This was where Matt had been coming for all these months. This was where he had been engineering whatever had just happened. This was his world. It was not mine.

I looked round. Charlotte was not following me.

In front of me, a queue of people was waiting by a sign for river buses. I stood at the back, and got onto the boat. I wanted to be away from Canary Wharf. I was not sure where I was going, so I decided to do whatever everybody else did.

The river was wide and grey. I looked across the water, at the Millennium Dome and at Greenwich. London's topography was curiously familiar, yet utterly alien. I stared down at my hands, which were trembling. Even so, they were the best part of me. I was glad Fiona took me with her for manicures. When I got home I would try to lose a stone and take more effort over my appearance. I thought my new clothes had helped me shout and swear at Pete, for all the good it had done me.

The other people on the boat were commuters. Many of them were young, fresh-faced, puffed up with the importance of their first proper jobs. I wondered how many of them would be burnt out by thirty, clinically depressed by thirty-five, alcoholics incapable of fidelity by forty. I looked around. There were a couple of jaded older people here. I tried to process the fact that Matt had chosen this life above our peaceful community in France.

The boat stopped, but no one got off. More office workers got on. I stayed put.

At the Embankment, I followed a crowd off the boat, smiled wanly at the captain, and trudged along the riverbank with everyone else. Most of them walked into Embankment station, so I did too. Some walked across the concourse and out onto the road that led up to Charing Cross. I followed these people, because I didn't want to get on the tube. It started raining, gently and then harder. The people in front of me diverted into a wine bar, and I went with them, since I didn't know where else to go. I was desperate to sit down.

The wine bar was downstairs. It was dark, cosy and very busy. I found a tiny table in the corner and took out a book to act as a shield. Once, I would have been too self-conscious to drink wine on my own, but now I could not have cared less what anyone thought of me. Nobody was looking at me, anyway. If they did, they would assume that I was waiting for someone. I ordered a glass of New Zealand Sauvignon.

'Large or small?' asked the studenty waiter.

'Large,' I said, forgetting that a small British glass was bigger than a large French one.

It was impossible to buy anything other than French wine in France. I sipped from my bucket of wine, and breathed deeply. I felt the alcohol entering my system, and I welcomed it.

Sitting and thinking was terrifying, but I had to do it. Otherwise I could see myself drifting all evening, following random people around London and existing in a haze. It was half past seven. In France it was half past eight. That was Alice's bedtime.

I took out my phone and made an extremely expensive call to see how she was. I had to put my finger in my other ear to block out the noise of the people around me.

'Night night, Mummy,' she told me, sounding all grown up. 'I miss you, Mummy. I lub you.'

'I love you too, sweetie,' I said. 'I miss you so much.' I gulped as I put the phone down. Suddenly, I realised that I was properly angry. I, sweet, amenable Emma, was furious with my former partner and the destruction he had wrought upon my life, and, far worse, upon Alice's life. Alice was still a baby. He had taken away everything I was trying to give her. She would come from a single parent family now. She would have to explain about her dad's girlfriend and, maybe, one day, her mum's boyfriend, or her stepfather. I could not imagine that I would ever meet anyone else. Matt was the only serious boyfriend I had ever had, and he had left me.

With horror, I mouthed the words that had forced themselves into my brain, the words that I was sure I had not spoken since I was three. I was on frightening, forbidden territory. Suddenly I could not shut it out any longer.

'I want my mummy,' I whispered. I left too much money on the table and ran up the stairs before anybody noticed the tears that were pouring down my face. I stood on the street and sobbed into the rain.

I want my mummy.

chapter twenty-one

Christa opened the door. She looked surprised to see me, then concerned.

'Emma?' she asked, although she knew it was me. 'Geoff!' she called over her shoulder. 'It's Emma.' Geoff shouted something inside the house, but I couldn't hear him. I followed Christa indoors.

The house had a pacifying sameness to it. It was a large house in a street of large houses, not far from Caledonian Road tube station. I stepped into the hall, with its soft blue carpet, and looked up through the banisters, searching for Geoff. He duly appeared, taking the stairs two at a time, rushing down to see me.

I hugged Christa, who was stiff and wiry, and Geoff, who was soft.

'Come in,' said Christa. I noticed that her hair was entirely white now. 'Dry yourself. You're soaked. Geoff, you'd better call Charlotte. She's been worried sick about you.'

'Sorry,' I said, handing my aunt my raincoat. I wished I wasn't always so aware that they were not my parents. I was still not quite able to relax around them in case they decided that they didn't want me any more. The fact that I was not their child had always stood unspoken between us. They would have assured anyone who had asked that I was exactly like a natural child to them; but I wasn't. 'I shouldn't have run off,' I added. 'I got myself into a bit of a state.' I was trying to be brisk and self-deprecating. I could barely force the words out. Christa did not go in for big emotional displays, and neither did I. She looked at me shrewdly.

'I'm sorry about what's happened,' she said. 'Why don't you sit down?'

I followed her into the kitchen and sat on a stool. She threw me a tea towel and I rubbed my hair till it was almost dry. Geoff took three tall glasses from the dishwasher and opened the fridge.

'I see you're looking like a chic French lady these days,' Christa said, admiring my mac as she hung it on the back of the kitchen door, next to her apron.

'Hardly,' I told her. 'I look like a farmer's wife, except that the farmers' wives are all pretty well turned out round where we live. I smartened myself up in an emergency dash to Gap when I was staking out Matt's office. Charlotte did my make-up.'

She shrugged. 'You look kind of well, anyway, under all that exhaustion. Beneath those tear stains.'

I managed to smile. 'Thanks. I think.'

Geoff held out a drink. It was clear, and it fizzed. 'G and T,' he explained, unnecessarily. 'Get that down you. Do you good.'

I took the glass and felt the tonic fizzing.

Christa sat opposite me. 'No sign of the bastard then?'

I smiled genuinely this time, shocked at my uptight aunt saying such a word. 'Christa!' I admonished her. 'I'm surprised at you.'

'You're surprised?' asked Geoff, widening his eyes. 'You should hear her in private.'

'This is in private,' Christa reminded him. 'And if anyone ever deserved it, Matt is that man.'

Nobody spoke for a moment.

'A week ago,' I said, 'I would have sworn that we had the safest and most secure relationship out of everyone I know. Now I've no idea where he is. Charlotte probably told you that we did manage to stalk his friend Pete who said he's in London. He wouldn't tell me anything else except that he's sorry.' I shrugged and forced myself to carry on speaking. 'Apparently, in spite of my fantasies about alien abduction, he is alive and well and not in the least bit innocent.'

Christa nodded. 'Obviously.'

'And to be honest, I'm already sick of it. I'm sick of looking for him, sick of feeling like this, sick of the guilt I feel about Alice. I've just had enough. I don't have much in the way of inner strength to fall back on.' I looked at her, then at Geoff, hesitant to make my request, but knowing that I had to say it. 'Christa. Um, Geoff.' I was hesitant to ask Geoff because I knew he shied away from anything too emotional. 'I realise this is coming out of the blue. It's going to seem like a huge change of subject, but it's not really. Could you tell me about my mother?'

Christa put down her drink. 'In the middle of all this, you develop a sudden interest in your mother?'

Geoff stood up. 'Sorry, girls. I've got a move to make in my online chess game. I'll leave you two to it, if that's OK. Better you talk about this together than have me hanging around.'

Christa nodded and waved him out of the room. She looked at me expectantly.

'I've never wanted to know,' I said, 'but now I don't know who I am or where I came from. Everything's fallen down around me. Everything that I thought I had is gone, and I want my mum.' I paused and collected myself. A large gulp of gin helped me. 'You're my mother, I know you are, and you've been brilliant at it. I've always felt like one of the family. But I can't stop thinking about my first three years.' I was almost talking to myself. 'I barely remember her. I haven't tried before, but now, when I do, there are just fleeting impressions. I'm walking along a pavement, holding her hand, seeing everything from a low level. My arm's raised right up, stretching to meet hers. I'm wearing a purple anorak.'

Christa nodded. 'I remember you in that purple coat.'

I forced myself to breathe calmly. 'And her hand feels safe. I can't remember her at all. Just what it was like to hold her hand and know I was safe.'

'Anything else?'

'Her saying goodnight and putting me to bed. I remember leaning up against her while she was reading me a story. I remember that it was a book called *The Great Blueness*. I can remember the story. It was about a king in a black and white world and a scientist discovering colours, one by one. I can remember what the pictures in the book looked like. But I can't remember what she looked like. And I can't remember her voice.'

Christa swallowed hard. 'Funny to think that it was twenty-eight years ago. I remember it as if it was yesterday. I used to long to get this far away from it all.'

'Why did she do it?' I realised as I said it that this question had haunted me. Everything I had done since the age of three had been directed by this great, unanswerable question. I looked to Christa hopelessly, knowing that neither of us could possibly know the answer. All we could do was guess.

'She was ill,' Christa said at once. 'It wasn't her fault.'

I put my drink down, hard. It slammed onto the table, which I hadn't intended. 'Of course it was her fault! If she was ill she could have got treatment. That's not so hard. Everyone's depressed. Most people manage to get through a bit of depression. Particularly if they've got a child!'

I was outraged. My fury with Matt was nothing compared to this. I suddenly wondered whether all my life I had been seething below the surface. My mother had taken the decision to leave me. She walked out of my life, for ever. She knew that she was all I had, and she killed herself. I avoided Christa's eyes. I had always thought that, with enough will power, I would be able to live happily without ever having to deal with any of this. I probably could have done, if Matt hadn't left me. I felt myself beginning to unravel. 'It looks like I'm going to be a single mother too,' I added. 'And I would put Alice before anything and everything.'

'Of course,' said my aunt. 'But Sarah was ill, Emma. You say everyone's depressed, but that's not true. The word has been devalued to the point where it's practically meaningless. Real depression, serious depression, is a very different matter. Sarah had bipolar disorder – manic depression – and she suffered the most almighty delusions. It was horrendous to see because we all feared this outcome. And there wasn't really much we could do.' Her voice was brittle and tight. 'Of course with hindsight there is a lot we could have done. Needless to say I'm haunted by that knowledge to this day. We should have taken you in sooner. We should have had Sarah sectioned. It was one of those things that was constantly under discussion. All she had to do was to take her medication. But she craved the highs so she often pretended to be taking it. I think that even when I was standing over her watching her take a pill, she'd sometimes hide it in her cheek and spit it out later. What could I do? Should I have pulled her mouth open and checked? With hindsight, yes, I should. The highs were wild. She'd disappear with you for days on end, and you'd come back with your hair dyed purple, both of you, with glittery stars glued all over your bodies. That sort of thing. She had a predilection, when she was in that state, for dancing naked, out of doors, with flowers in her hair. You lived in a tiny village, very staid and conservative, and they weren't used to that kind of thing. There were women there who were always calling the police. Sarah was desperate to move to Cornwall with you, and Hampshire was a compromise between London and St Ives.'

'What about her lows?'

She shook her head. 'Everybody dreaded them. Blacker than black. She would become hopeless and we would desperately try to get her to hospital. We would come to take you home with us, but that made her bleaker than ever. Emma, it was horrific.'

I looked down. There was a gaping hole at the centre of my life. 'Can you tell me about that last time?' I asked.

Christa drained her glass. 'If you want. I still relive it. I'd spoken to her the day before. I knew as soon as she answered that she was low. It was heartbreaking to hear it. Sarah wasn't herself. She was taken over by hopelessness. I said we would drive down. She knew what I meant. She knew we were coming to collect you until she was better.' She looked at me closely. 'Are you sure you want to hear the detail?'

I nodded.

'I drove down with Greg, because he was still a baby. I arrived and let myself in. Straightaway I heard little footsteps. You came running up to me. You have no memories of any of this?' I shook my head. 'I'm not surprised, I suppose. You came running up and as soon as I saw the look on your face I knew that it was different this time. You were wearing a little blue velvet dress with purple shapes sewn haphazardly onto it with green thread. Sarah had embellished it for you. I put Greg's carrycot down, and you ran into my arms. You kept saying "Mummy, Mummy". I walked around, carrying you. You were clinging onto me, burying your face in my shoulder. I found her in the bedroom.'

'Her bedroom?'

'You slept in the same room. The same bed. She was lying on the bed. It's an image I will never forget.' She paused and swallowed. 'Her eyes were open but it only took a glance to see that she wasn't there. She had taken pills. They said afterwards that what she had taken would have killed her four times over. They estimated that you had been there, with her body, for at least an hour before I arrived.'

I was numb. 'I can't remember it at all.'

'You forgot it instantly. I'm sorry, Emma. I couldn't deal with you very well. You're so like she was – obviously you don't suffer from her illness which is a tremendous blessing. You reminded me of her all the time, but almost as soon as she died, you blanked her. You wouldn't talk about her, wouldn't have pictures of her. Sometimes, when you were three or four, you'd ask where your mummy was, but after that you stopped. You wanted to be like Bella so you just fitted yourself into the family. You were the most amenable child anyone had ever met.'

I smiled, but without any joy. 'Still am. That's why Matt thought he'd get away with buggering off and sending me a crappy letter.'

'You know, every year I'd ask you if you wanted a photo of your mother and you'd always say no.'

'Is that an offer?'

'If you want.'

'I think so.' I was ashamed of the fact that I had no idea what my mother had looked like. I was even more ashamed of the fact that until an hour ago I'd had no interest in knowing.

'There's something else, too.' Christa got up. 'I think we

could both do with another drink, don't you? Make it a strong one.' She left the room. I half filled our glasses with gin, and topped them up with tonic. Then I added ice and lemon, and opened the snacks cupboard. This was always filled with crisps, biscuits and nuts. Now that we had all left home, it was Geoff's domain. I smiled at the idea of Geoff's online chess. I opened two packets of crisps and tipped them into bowls. Christa's story went round and round my head. I pictured myself, Alice's age, circling my mother's body. Somewhere inside, I had already known that. Although I had no memories of it, the image was somehow familiar. I recognised it. And although it was devastating to face it, facing it was essential. Something inside me had just come back to life.

When Christa came back in, I was circling the room, thinking about nothing, unable to keep still. She motioned me to sit down, and handed me a photograph in a frame.

'I got this done for you twenty-seven years ago,' she said with a little smile. 'I put it in your room when you were three. Geoff found it half buried in the garden a week later. Here you are. Better late than never.'

I stared at the woman in the picture. This was my mother. My dead mother. I was looking at my past, at Alice's grandmother. She was smiling broadly. She looked like me, and like Alice, and a bit like Christa. The picture was of her head and shoulders. She was outside, with trees behind her, and her eyes were slightly screwed up against the sun. I propped it up in front of me.

'What was the other thing?' I asked, without taking my eyes off it.

221

'Here.' Christa looked worried as she passed me an envelope. 'Sarah gave me this a couple of months before she died. She was very rational at the time, very stable, and her condition was scaring her. She asked me to look after you if anything happened to her, and to give you this when you asked about her.' Christa looked at me. 'I expected to be giving it to you when you were about thirteen, not thirty. I have no idea what it says. I hope it's helpful.'

I took the envelope, my hand shaking. Christa's hand, I noticed, was shaking too. The last thing I had ever expected was a letter from my mother. I looked at my name. *Emma*. The handwriting was unfamiliar.

'God,' I said, inadequately. I took a large gulp of gin before opening it. Inside the envelope was a folded sheet of A4. I spread it out and read it.

Darling Emma,

I am writing this longing that you will never read it. If you are reading it, it means I have done something unforgivable. Please try to forgive me all the same. You are the most precious thing in the world, the best thing that has ever happened, the most adorable baby girl. You deserve far better than me as a mother. I know that Christa and Geoff will look after you better than I would have done. Oh Christ, I hope you never read this. I hope I keep myself together. I pray every day that you won't have this affliction.

All I need to say is that I love you more than you can possibly imagine, and that I am sorrier than you can imagine for doing this to you. I am in floods of

tears writing this. Be brave. Be strong, and be sane.
Go to Cornwall and dance on the cliff tops with flowers
in your hair, but keep your feet on the ground. Forgive
me if you can. Forget me if you like.

All my love to you, my little girl. All my love for ever.

Make Christa tell you about your daddy. She will say
she doesn't know, but she does. Make her tell you.

Bye bye, my darling.

Your loving and stupid, mad, crazy mother

xxxxxxxxxxxxxxxxxxxxxxxxxxxxxxxxxxxxxxxxxxxxxxxxxxx

xxxxxxxxxxxxxxxxxxxxxxxxxxxxxxxxxxxxxxxxxxxxxxxx

I swallowed hard. I was aware of Christa looking anxiously
at my reactions.

'You never read it?' I asked her.

'No. It wasn't for me.'

'Christa? Who's my father?'

She frowned. 'I don't know, darling. You've always known
that your father was a great unknown.'

I turned the letter round and pushed it towards her. 'I
suppose you're going to say she was deluded.' I studied my
aunt as she read it. 'But you just said she wrote this when
she was sane.' Christa twitched a little, and things flickered
over her face briefly.

'I really don't know,' she said flatly.

'Well, if you do, I'd really like it if you'd tell me one day,'
I told her. 'Just something that might help me find him. Not
now. There's too much else going on now. But one day,
when things are settled down. I think a parent might be a
good thing to have, however absent.'

223

She said nothing for a while. Then she stood up.

'Come on, Emma,' she said. 'I'm taking you to Shillibeers.' She stood at the foot of the stairs and shouted for Geoff. He bounced down, looking at us both anxiously. Shillibeers was the family's favourite local bar. It had always served as a destination when anyone felt they had to leave the house.

I took my coat and followed Christa and Geoff out of the door. We had a lot to talk about.

chapter twenty-two

Hugh crept out of the marital bed. It had taken Jo ages to fall asleep, but her breathing had been regular for fifteen minutes now. He had timed it on the bedside clock radio. Now it was probably safe for him to tiptoe downstairs. He had nothing particular to do downstairs. He just wanted to be by himself. He had been by himself today, supposedly working from home, avoiding Emma's family. He would be by himself tomorrow for the same reason.

As his foot touched the wooden floor, he held his breath. He stood up, hearing the mattress creak as his weight left it. He reached for his pyjamas.

'You didn't think I was asleep?' she said in a clear, high voice.

'I hoped you were getting some sleep,' he told her evenly. 'You need some rest.'

'We all do.'

Hugh sat down beside her. 'Jo, I can't tell you enough how sorry I am that the situation developed. I don't know what I can do. I never meant it to happen.'

She turned away. 'I know you didn't. You were weak. I can't get over how weak you were.'

'But,' he said, 'you're going to have to get over it if we're going to have a chance.'

'I know.'

He sat down on the side of the bed and reached out to stroke her hair. She pulled back and rolled over.

chapter twenty-three

I didn't try to sleep. I sat at the kitchen table with my mother's photograph standing in front of me, and her letter spread out before it. I picked a couple of flowers from the garden and put them on either side of her image, making a little altar. I looked at her. She had been younger, when she died, than I was now. And I had been just slightly older, when she died, than Alice was now. I had been grieving for her all this time without realising it. I had been bitterly angry with her. I had thought I was getting on with my life, when I wasn't. I had always felt rejected. I had always known that my position was fourth, after Bella, Charlotte and Greg. I had always wanted to be somebody's most beloved person. I had stupidly assumed I had achieved that with Matt. Now I knew that the only bond you could be sure of was the bond between a mother and her child.

I had been Sarah's most beloved person for three years and two months. And I decided that, despite the abrupt ending, that meant something. I was Alice's most beloved person and she was mine. I missed her so much that it hurt.

I was not sure how I would be able to function if the worst had happened with Matt. I wanted to curl up and be a little girl again. I wanted to move back into my old bedroom in Holloway. I wanted to find the cottage in Hampshire and dance on the Cornish cliffs with flowers in my hair. I did not want to be a responsible adult and make the kind of decisions that I knew were facing me.

I needed to track Matt down. Together we would be able to work out what had gone wrong and I could explain everything that I had discovered about Sarah. He would understand. He, in turn, would tell me about his family and we would start again with no secrets. I supposed I must have been irritating with all that eager sweetness. I knew that Matt was the one for me and that, whatever had gone wrong, we could fix our relationship and make it stronger and better. Matt and Alice were my future. I would do whatever it took to sort that out. That was what I thought when I was feeling optimistic. At other times, I looked deep into the chasm that had opened up before me.

I made a pot of coffee. The smell mingled with the indecipherable smells of the house, the smells I had grown up with. I had no idea what it was that made this house smell like home. Perhaps it was some laundry, some food, Christa's handcream. I walked from room to room, disconcerted by the light that shone round the curtains all night long. The orange of the street light outside made a stripe on the sitting-room floor. It was odd to be away from Alice, but comforting to be in the house where I had grown up. If it hadn't been for Alice, I would have stayed in that house until I felt ready to leave. I would have curled up there for months. But I didn't live there any more. My life and my daughter were in France. I needed to keep going.

As the sun rose, I put on Christa's boots and walked into the garden to look at the dirty smudge of pink in the dark grey sky. I was worn out and confused and strangely elated. I expected to wake up, at any moment, in Pounchet, with Alice climbing on top of me and Matt beside me.

I considered my options for the day ahead. I was certainly not going to mess around any more. I could go back to Matt's office and get the receptionist to tell me whether he was in the building. I could wait in the foyer until he arrived. But he would never arrive. Christa and Geoff were supposed to be flying to France today, to see me. I had asked them to go, without me. They had refused.

At quarter to seven in the morning, I had a breakthrough. I was remembering the humiliation of walking into his building, and skulking while Charlotte breezily asked the security guard to phone his extension. I remembered looking around, marvelling at surroundings that must have been familiar to Matt, and which were completely strange to me. I recalled once suggesting that I could bring Alice into the office to see him, when she and I had been visiting Christa and Geoff. Matt put me off, saying he was too busy. I wondered what his real reasons had been, and how long whatever it was had been going on.

I remembered the admiring look the man had given Charlotte. Even tarted up, he had not noticed me. Then I remembered him mentioning that there was a Hugo Smith on the same extension number.

People don't share telephone extensions. Not at a company like BB Johnson.

Peter's surname was Smith, too, and I had never thought anything of it. Matt had joked about their shared name, said they must have been related generations ago. But it was not Pete who was listed on that same phone number. Pete did not work there. It was someone called Hugo.

I remembered the woman, Jo, who had called by, lost, in France. Her husband had been called Hugh. She said she had sent him texts from my house, but we had no reception there.

I tried to remember whether I had ever seen Matt's passport. The house and everything else were in my name. He had never registered with the French health service. I had never seen an official document of his. This had never struck me as strange, because I had never realised it before. Matt had never made a big deal out of not showing me his passport. On the few occasions we had travelled together, he would simply take mine and Alice's, and give them to passport control together. I had never been the type of person who makes a big issue out of seeing passport photos.

I had owned my house in Brighton, and he had insisted that I should buy the house in France, as sole purchaser. He had said it was simpler that way. He was left out of the buying and selling process entirely.

Things had become very strange the morning after Jo had stayed with us. Matt had retired back to bed. I thought he was being rude, except that he really did look ill. Jo had rushed off with Olly without even staying for breakfast.

Plan B

The thing that really stuck in my brain was Oliver. He had had that competitive little exchange with Alice over whose daddy was in the picture. I remembered his voice saying, 'My daddy!' On the one hand, that is the kind of nonsensical thing that toddlers say.

On the other hand.

I was not sure what was happening, but things were adding up in an unexpected way. I kept thinking things through, trying to find something that would prove that my thoughts were the ramblings of a shocked and sleep-deprived brain. I could not find the conclusive proof that I was wrong.

I must already have had the suspicion. That was why it was rushing to the fore now. It was as good an explanation as any. I slipped upstairs, to my childhood bedroom, and switched on my mobile phone. Jo's number was in there.

I did not phone her. I would have had no idea what to say to her.

Hello, remember me? Is your husband called Hugo? My husband shares a telephone at work with someone of that name. Did you ever hear of anyone sharing a work phone?

She would have thought I was mad, and she would have been right.

Instead, I switched on Geoff's computer and searched around on the internet until I found a site which offered what I wanted. I had to pay for the service, which I did, happily, with my Visa card. I typed in the telephone number. An address came up. I copied it carefully onto a piece of paper, sent it as a text message to myself, and looked it up in Geoff's London A-Z and circled it with a pen. I did not want to take any chances. Then I lay on my single bed, with its ancient pink duvet, and drifted off to sleep.

I woke at half past ten. Weak sunlight was edging round the magenta curtains. I turned my head and was surprised to see the photograph of my mother beside my bed. I almost felt that she was a new friend. She was not older than me, not in any meaningful sense. I was older than my mother. If she were alive today, she would have been fifty-four. As it was, she would always be twenty-six.

I lay still in my little bed and listened. The house was silent. Christa and Geoff should be on their way to France by now. I wondered where they were, instead. I wondered what Charlotte was up to. I should not have run away from her. I got up slowly, feeling hungover, tired and heavy. There was too much to think about, so I pushed it all from my head and had a long, hot shower. I dressed in my Gap clothes again, which were only slightly crumpled, and left the house with Geoff's A-Z in my bag. My raincoat was still damp. I could have walked the route to Caledonian Road tube station in my sleep. The trees were the same, the dog shit was the same, the adverts were the same. Some things didn't change at all.

Highcroft Road existed. Although I had found it on the A-Z, I had half expected it to have vanished, and I expected 24a to be a garage. In fact it was part of a well-maintained terrace of grey brick houses. It had blue window boxes bursting with geraniums. The window frames had been painted recently: the white gloss was dazzling.

I walked up a short flight of stairs to the front door and pressed the bell. It was half past eleven, and I was not

expecting Jo to be home. She was sure to be at her gallery.
I planned to head for Jermyn Street after this, and to walk
into every gallery and ask for Jo until I found her. If she did
happen to be at home, or if there was a nanny or lodger
there, I was going to be blasé and talk about happening to
be in the area and dropping in on impulse. I had no plan
at all, beyond proving my wild surmising to be wrong.

Heavy footsteps approached the front door, and it swung
inwards. I attached a bland smile to my face and waited, my
story on my lips.

Our eyes locked.

He was tall and handsome, and his eyes had the same
laughter lines they had always had. His hair needed a cut.
It was falling close to his eyes. He was wearing tracksuit
trousers I had never seen before, and a white T-shirt.

He kept staring at me. His eyes were wide. His mouth
gaped for a second before he closed it. He looked panic-
stricken. He looked weak.

'Hugh?' I asked him. I watched him wondering whether
to close the door and put the chain on. It was one thing to
desert me and Alice in France. I think he lacked the guts
to slam a real door in my face.

He slumped. 'Emma,' he said. 'Shit. I suppose you're
going to come in.'

'I suppose I am,' I agreed, and pushed the door wider.
He stood back and I walked past him. I walked into an
entrance hall with a scratchy beige carpet, white walls
adorned with frames displaying swirls of abstract art, and
a neat row of shoes next to the skirting board. The shoes
came in three sizes. Some of them I recognised as Matt's.

Others must have been Jo's. Then there were the little ones.

Everything seemed hyperreal. I knew I was in Matt's home, that this, rather than a grotty studio apartment, was his other home. I could not, however, process the information. All I knew was that I needed him back.

Matt was still standing by the door, so I walked past a staircase, into a kitchen. I heard slow footsteps following me. The kitchen was light and white and reasonably tidy. The chrome-fronted dishwasher was swinging open. A pot of coffee was the only thing on the sideboard. My hand shook as I took two white mugs from a shelf and filled them with coffee from the cafetière. I tried a few cupboard doors, looking for the fridge. When I found it, I added some milk to the mugs. I tried to steady my hand as I handed Matt his drink. He took it wordlessly.

I needed to be strong. This was unfortunate, but it did not change the way I felt about Matt and about our family. I still loved him. I needed him. I wanted to start again now that I knew about my mother. Matt was going to need to start again for his own reasons. I did not hate him. I wanted to make him understand.

'So.' I said it as a conversation opener, nudging him to say something. He was not meeting my eyes. 'Matt,' I said, in a firmer voice. 'I can kind of see what's going on here. I do realise that you are the father of Jo's son. Aren't you?' He nodded. I knew that I had to be straightforward. I had never forced a confrontation in my life. I had always defused arguments, mollified, consoled, compromised. Now I had to be different. I had to make him think he had no choice.

'But that's OK,' I continued. 'I mean, admittedly it's not ideal. We'll go into the details later. But I still love you.' I looked him in the eye. He met my gaze.

'Do you?' His voice was expressionless.

'Yes. I love you totally. I can't think about anything other than us being all right. I can forgive you for anything.'

He smiled. 'That's my Emma. Em, it's not that simple. I have fucked up big time.'

'I noticed.'

'Jo's my wife.'

'I worked that out. She was talking about Hugh all the time she was with me. Is that your real name?'

'Yes. Matthew's my middle name.'

'Jo said she didn't think she and Hugh – she and you – had a future together. I know that we have. So leave here and come home with me. Matt, think of Alice. You can't abandon your daughter with that crappy letter which I know you didn't write. Come to France with me and we can work things out. She keeps asking when you're coming home and I say it will be soon. Because it will be. We can't manage without you. Please, Matt. Look, I've been talking to Christa, and I've found out lots of things about my mother, and that's really making me feel quite strange, and so I kind of need you. I know I've been silly, being so fucking amenable all the time, but it won't be like that any more. I'll be different. It'll be better.'

I turned away so he couldn't see my tears. I had said my piece. I was holding myself together, pleading with him to say yes. Once I had him back, we could work on everything else.

'I'm sorry,' he said.

'Don't be sorry. We can make it OK. We can start again and rebuild our lives, better.'

'You and Alice don't deserve this. You're better off without me.'

'We are not. We're *so* not. Come on, Matt. Loads of women would be mad with you. I'm giving you a chance, here, to make it all better.'

He put his head in his hands. 'But I can't make it all better, can I? If I went back with you, what would happen to Olly? Either way, I lose contact with a child. I can't pick which one it is.'

'I wouldn't make you lose contact with Olly. You could see him as much as you wanted.'

'And my job in London? You'd never trust me. You think you would now, because you don't like the prospect of being on your own. But you wouldn't. How would you feel while I was still away working half the week?'

'I'd feel bad. But I'm going to feel a lot, lot worse if you're never with me.'

'Emma. This is not going to be easy to tell you, but I have to. As I said, Jo is my wife. She has agreed to have me back, to see if we can work it out between us. I am committed to her. I'm going to give my marriage every-thing I possibly can and I'm going to make it work out. I'm sorry. I know this isn't what you want to hear. I've messed you around and you deserve someone better, and you'll meet someone better.'

I could not control my voice, which came out in a high-pitched shriek. 'I WILL NOT.' My words were scrambled together, incoherent. 'You can't say that. You are the only person I've ever loved. I can't believe you've done this to me. Jo will leave you. She already told me so. She won't be able to forgive you and she'll end up throwing you out because she's strong and she's got dignity. I'm not strong! I haven't got any dignity! Your place is with me. I'm begging you to come back with me. I don't know what I'll do if you don't.' I was hiccuping and half hysterical.

Matt put a hand on my shoulder. 'Emma,' he said kindly. 'You are strong. Come on. I'm glad you're talking about your mother. That's great. You'll have a great future, without me. You need to get a grip. I'm sorry I tried to fob you off with that awful letter. Jo wrote it. She'd be furious with me if she knew you were here.'

'See? You're already going behind her back.'

'I'm not because I didn't invite you. How did you find me?'

'Woman's intuition,' I said, with a bitter smirk. 'Things just fell into place. I think I'd half known for a while. I just hadn't let myself think about it. Christ, Matt. You were married when you met me. You were married when Alice was born. You were married when you suggested that *we* get married.'

'I didn't mean it to happen like that.'

I shook my head. 'I don't care. That's the bit you don't understand. It's all a detail. I don't care. The best thing for everyone –' I broke off to blow my nose. 'Is. If. You come back. To. France.'

We sat in silence for a few moments, as I waited for him to agree with me. After a while I realised I had to say something, to keep the conversation going, to prevent him from telling me to leave. I collected myself.

'Jo knew about me, then, when she turned up in Pounchet?'

He nodded. 'Because you put that picture in my suitcase. Mummy and Daddy and Alice at our house in France. Miss you. Kiss kiss kiss. That one. I tried to explain it away. I told her that a colleague in Paris had shown it to me and I'd gathered it up with my papers, and she let it drop but she didn't believe me for a second. I had a receipt from the removals people in a trouser pocket, and I stuck it in a load of paperwork to shred and forgot about it. She went through every single thing and found it. So she decided that rather than asking me about it, like most people would, she would pitch up with some half-baked story about being a lost tourist.'

'She was convincing. Self-possessed.' I tried not to think back to the evening I had spent with her. I did not want to remember what I had said.

'Jo's good like that.'

'I wouldn't be.'

The silence descended again. After a minute or so, Matt put his hands on the table. 'I'm sorry!' he said suddenly. 'I'm really sorry. When we got to France I gave myself a year to sort it all out. I was going to decide and I wasn't going to keep you both in the dark any more. I thought you'd both kick me out on my arse. I never imagined you'd both be up for giving it a go. I never thought I'd have to pick one or the other.'

'But you're making the wrong choice. Alice and I, we're the one. Jo is the other.'

'No, Emma. That's not true. You're the other. I've been married to Jo for years longer than I've even known you. I'm afraid you're not the one. You've always been the other.'

I was stunned. 'That's not true.'

'I'm sorry to be harsh, but it is.'

I was outraged. 'Matt. Hugh. Whoever you are. You do not talk about me and Alice like that. You are the man I love, but you're acting like – like scum. I'm offering you a second chance when I shouldn't be. Alice is a jewel, she's perfect, she adores her daddy. You don't deserve a daughter like that. You fuckwit.' I was consumed not with fury but with the passionate desire to stop Matt doing the wrong thing. My mother had left a little girl behind because she was ill. Matt could not reject Alice. He had no excuse. I looked at the cup in my hand, and decided that I probably had little else to lose. In a detached way, I lifted my hand and poured coffee over Matt's head. It was satisfying, but only mildly so. Matt didn't move out of the way or try to stop me. I wanted him to catch my wrist, because that would have involved some sort of intimacy, but he just sat there. Coffee dripped down his face. He didn't even wipe it away.

'Yes,' he agreed. 'You have a point. I am a fuckwit.'

I looked at him and smiled. He looked funny with coffee all over him. He caught my eye and smiled back. I giggled. I was beginning to feel hysterical. He looked worried.

'You're not coming with me just yet, then,' I said.

'I'm not coming with you at all.'

I couldn't think of anything else to say. There was too much, so I said nothing. I tried to imagine what I would do when I left this flat. I could call Charlotte and let her update everyone. I would tell Christa and Geoff to fly to France. I would try to get a flight to Bordeaux that afternoon. I would be with my little girl, my sister, my friends later in the day.

I might have to try to live without Matt, because he was nothing but an illusion. My Matt had never existed. All along, my Matt had been somebody else's Hugh.

'I would never have had anything to do with you if I'd known you were married,' I told him.

'That's why I didn't tell you.'

'Does Jo know that? Does she hate me?'

Matt exhaled heavily. 'She went to France hating you. She expected to hate you. But she doesn't. She realised straight-away that you had no idea what was going on. She hates the fact of your existence all right.' He looked at me, and away. 'She doesn't want me to have any contact with you ever again.'

'And you've agreed to that?'

'We'll need to sort out maintenance and access to Alice once you two are back over here.'

'But essentially?'

'Yes. Essentially I've agreed to that.'

I walked to the door. I desperately wanted him to stop me, to change his mind, to proclaim his love for me and Alice. He could have made me feel better with a couple of words. He didn't say anything. Not even goodbye.

I slammed the door loudly behind me, as a meaningless gesture, and sat on his neighbour's step, and cried.

chapter twenty-four

Hugh paced the flat. He was going to have to wash the coffee out of his hair before Jo came home. He would have to use an unscented shampoo. She was suspicious of him and he knew that she would pick up on anything. He was not sure that there was an unscented shampoo in the bathroom. Or indeed if such a thing existed.

'That went well,' he said aloud. He had always enjoyed being Matt. Matt was kinder, stronger than Hugh. Matt was Emma's pillar. He had supported her in everything. Emma had needed Matt, while Jo and Hugh were not quite equals. Jo was an alpha female, without a doubt. Matt, he thought, could have been an alpha male. Hugh was decidedly beta.

He wandered from room to room, unsure what to do with himself. It was strange to think that Emma was not in his life any more. He could not think about how much he was going to miss her. If he did, he would find himself running after her.

I knew this would happen, he reminded himself. I took the easy path. I knew that was what I was doing. I always knew that I was storing up trouble for the future. When the year was up, if I'd still been getting away with it, I would have carried on. I was never going to drop myself into this situation voluntarily.

As he walked round the maisonette, he knew without a doubt that he would not be living there for much longer. This flat was his marital home. He and Jo had lived here since before they were married. Hugh remembered the first time they had come to look round, nine years before. He had still been amazed that this beautiful woman wanted to go out with him. He had been even more grateful when she had suggested living together.

He had always known that he had been lucky to get Jo. She was, when he met her, a slim 25-year-old, with long blonde hair and good clothes. Jo could have done anything she wanted, could have had anyone she wanted, and she had known it. Her ambition had always been to run her own gallery, and by the age of twenty-eight, she had achieved it.

They had looked at four flats, but this was the first one Jo had deemed suitable.

'It's perfect!' she told the estate agent crisply. 'We'll be in touch later this afternoon with an offer.'

Hugh had nodded in agreement. He would have been enthusiastic to move into a cowshed had Jo suggested it.

Hugh supposed his relationship with Jo had never been quite healthy. He had been desperately grateful for her attention from the moment she had first spoken to him. Knowing her as he now did, he imagined that she must have relished the challenge. He had been her project. She had met a slightly geeky young man, twenty-five but in many ways still fifteen, who was living in a scummy bedsit. She had transformed him into a man she was proud to call her husband. In fact, she had transformed him too well.

They had met at a party. It was a hot summer night, the sort that gave Londoners a new verve and allowed them to imagine themselves as Spaniards or Cubans. Hugh hadn't known whose party it was. He had been in the pub after work when someone who knew someone had suggested they all go along. Hugh had, of course, had nothing else planned. He was living in a bedsit in south London, sharing a bathroom with three invisible strangers while he saved up to buy a place of his own. There was a small, smeared window above his bed, which looked out onto the fire escape and the back of some other flats. There was no garden, not even a patch of concrete or a flat roof, and no view. Going home was not an enticing prospect. Going to someone's party would be more interesting than spending yet another evening in the pub.

Later, he was sitting on the grass in a parched garden, nursing a bottle of beer and watching some women. Hugh was frustrated. He had had girlfriends, and women had been interested in him, but he lacked the confidence to approach the women he really liked. The ones who approached him were not, he thought, mocking himself, his type. It did not take much analysis to realise why this was. His type was a slender blonde with big eyes and long legs. He had never been particularly imaginative. Whereas the women who thought he might like them tended to be flawed and human, and even if they were appealing sometimes, he didn't quite know how to talk to them. He drank from his bottle and wondered if he would ever work it out.

When he looked up, Jo was standing in front of him.

'Hi!' she said, and sat down next to him. She was his feminine ideal, brought to life.

'Oh,' he answered, looking at her and then down at his drink. 'Oh, hello.'

'I'm Jo.'

'I'm Hugh.'

'That's funny. You're called Hugh, and you look like Hugh Grant.'

He frowned at her. 'I don't look anything like Hugh Grant. My hair's the wrong colour.'

'Yeah, I know.' She smiled at him again. 'You don't look exactly like him, I mean I didn't think you *were* him when I saw you, or anything. But you've got that shy thing that he does.' She peered at him, her eyes laughing. 'You don't realise how cute that is, do you? It's not an act, is it?'

Hugh was baffled. 'What's not an act?'

'You sitting there like that, looking at me and looking away again. The way you keep running your fingers through your hair.'

He shook his head. 'No idea what you're talking about.' This was the summer of *Four Weddings*. It had never occurred to him that this might make his own brand of awkward ineptness suddenly attractive and charming. Panicking slightly, he wondered what he could do to consolidate his advantage.

Jo took his hand. 'I'm a little bit drunk,' she told him. 'Are you?'

Plan B

He felt the pressure of her hand on his and smiled. He wanted to squeeze it but wasn't sure if he ought to. 'Maybe. Just a little bit.'

She looked around. 'This is a nice party but I think we should go now. Um. I arrived by cab with a load of people. I wasn't paying attention. Do you know which part of London we're in? North, isn't it?'

'We could walk to Hampstead Heath from here,' he suggested. 'Easily.' He had been stunned at his own audacity.

She had leapt up. 'Come on then.'

He picked up a photograph of himself and Jo at their wedding. It had not taken her long to smarten him up, to buy him nice shirts and ties in interesting colours rather than the white and blue that had filled his wardrobe before. By the time they got married, when they were both twenty-seven, Hugh was confidently buying his own Armani and Ted Baker. He paid a lot more than seven pounds to have his hair cut. In the photo, Jo looked exquisite in an elegant thirties-style dress with flowers in her hair. He did not look too bad either. He was grinning so widely that it almost split his face. He had had it all, back then. He had hit the jackpot. He had married a beautiful woman who loved him. He had been able to talk to Jo. She was different from any other woman, because he could say anything to her, and if she laughed at him, it was in exactly the right sort of way.

He put the photo down and ambled up the stairs. He could barely say a word to her now. Anything he said would be seized on and dissected for evidence of further deceit. She despised him, with good reason.

Sometime after their first wedding anniversary, Hugh had

begun looking at women differently. Jo had moulded him into a confident and stylish art-world husband. He had been promoted at work. He started having to go away to work on projects all over the world. He realised that women took notice of him, that everyone from air hostesses to conference organisers to waitresses to economists looked at him with sparkling eyes. They flicked their hair and searched for eye contact. They smiled at him and brushed their hands against his. Sometimes they would see his wedding ring and make remarks about all the best ones being taken.

He had loved it. At first he would report every flirtatious woman back to Jo and they would laugh together, while she warned him not to let it go to his head and reminded him that the many men of the London art world were in a state of collective lust around her, which was true. He assured her he had no interest in any other woman. Jo was the only woman in the world for him. He meant it when he said it. Gradually, however, his interest was piqued. He told himself that he had only been twenty-five when he met his wife, and that that was extremely young these days. And although he hadn't been a virgin when he met her, he might as well have been because she had transformed his sexual ability completely. He had never been admired before.

He told himself that he was allowed to take a beautiful woman for a drink, as an experiment. He would not, he assured himself, dream of being unfaithful to Jo. The very idea made him indignant. He was simply allowing himself to enjoy the attention, to keep his spirits up while he was away from his wife.

He was at a meeting in Rome when a beautiful girl who

was serving coffee brushed her hand across the back of his neck in passing. He turned and gave her a brilliant smile. She returned it. He caught her hand and held it for a second. She let him. After the meeting, she came back in to collect the coffee cups. He walked over to her, amazed at his own audacity, and said hello. She was small but curvy, with long dark hair and deep brown eyes. She was the opposite of Jo and he liked that.

They had a drink that evening. They had dinner. He flirted with Delfina, lavished attention on her, kissed her. He spent the night being repeatedly, joyously, extravagantly unfaithful to his wife. They had breakfast in bed. She laughed and kissed him when he confessed to being married.

'I know!' she told him. 'Silly. You have a ring. And besides, these sorts of men are always married, more or less.'

He had liked the idea of being married more or less. Hugh didn't feel a twinge of guilt until he arrived at Heathrow, and even then, his main fear was that Jo would take one look at him and know what he had done. She didn't notice anything. She was perfectly normal and affectionate towards him, and he was wonderfully considerate to her.

It had become a habit. He reasoned that it hurt no one, since Jo was never going to find out. It was his hobby. Casual sex in foreign hotel rooms was what Hugh did to relax. He discovered interests that he had never imagined before. He could ask these compliant girls to do whatever he wanted, and they rarely refused. He made it a point of honour never to see the same girl twice. He had it under control. He was determined not to be caught, because he knew that Jo would leave him, and that he would be nothing without her.

Hugh went into Oliver's bedroom. It was filled with crap. When Olly was born, Jo had made a rule that he could only have wooden toys, no plastic, and no brand names. It had lasted until his first birthday, when he had been inundated with plastic toys, from both their families. Jo's parents were rather in awe of their daughter, so had half stuck to her rules and had at least bought non-branded plastic toys. Hugh's mum and dad, on the other hand, had gone overboard with Thomas the Tank Engine, Teletubbies, and Bob the Builder merchandise. Jo had hidden her fury behind tight smiles. Hugh had not dared confess that he had instigated it all with the words, 'Buy him whatever you like.'

Olly had loved Thomas the Tank Engine at first sight. He had worn his Teletubbies pyjamas day and night. The first time he put two words together was to sing 'Yes! Can!' in reply to Bob the Builder's query. He had discarded the wooden objects and played with the plastic. Eventually, Jo had conceded defeat. They got CBeebies soon afterwards.

Olly was out but this room was filled with his spirit. There was a pile of his clean clothes, folded on top of the chest of drawers. Posters of Nemo and Monsters, Inc. adorned the walls. His trucks were piled up in a corner. A giant marble run took up most of the floor. Hugh had built it with him yesterday afternoon. They had made it as high as they could and clattered all the marbles down it in a long line. Hugh had been super dad, horribly aware that although he was doing his best to persuade Jo that he would never dream of cheating on her or lying to her again, he was unlikely to be resident in Highcroft Road much longer. Of course she couldn't trust him. Every time he promised not to lie to her again, she just told him that he was lying. He could not win.

It was not going to work. He knew it, she knew it. He didn't even know if he wanted it to work any more. Each time he contemplated a lifetime of contrition and craven considerateness, he wanted it less. This had swayed their power balance completely. They would never have a functioning relationship now.

Jo could barely bring herself to speak to him. She had told him that, if they were to try again, he must never speak to Emma. He could, she had said, support Alice, and he must, of course, stay in touch with her, but he had to put money into Emma's account for Alice's maintenance without talking to her, and he must send presents and letters directly to Alice, and not to Emma. She had supervised the horrible letter he had written, and she had posted it. He had agreed to everything because he had felt desperate to salvage whatever he could. They had been living together for the past week, but her hatred had been tangible. He was approaching the point when he was going to be relieved to leave.

He hoped Emma had not realised how tempted he had been by her pleas. He had not imagined Emma's feelings through any of this. If anything, he had assumed she would turn away from him and never speak to him again. But she wanted him back. She seemed to know as well as he did that there was no future in his marriage. He knew he had to resist. A relationship built on the knowledge that he could do anything he wanted with impunity would not be good.

His days of shagging strangers in hotel rooms seemed a million light years behind him. He had stopped doing it when he met Emma, because he had been surprised at how much he had enjoyed himself when he was with her. He had spent all his spare time with her. He teleconferenced whenever he could, and because he was senior in his company by that point, he had largely got away with it. He managed to change his role slightly so he could work from home half the week and in the office the rest of the time. He avoided overseas travel altogether and spent half the week with Emma, working in her tiny third bedroom. In fact he spent so much time with her that after a while, he realised that she had assumed he had moved in.

He had never intended to hurt her. Although he had always told himself that Emma coped with everything, he knew, really, that she was fragile. He remembered that she had said something about her mother. He had barely heard her mention her mother before. She must have been in a state. He shuddered to think what he had done to her. Yes, Jo was extremely upset and angry, but she would get over it. He could imagine her now, calling him a bastard to all her friends. They would be rallying round. This was the kind of event Jo's friends lived for.

Emma, though, could be set up for a full-blown crisis. He had thought he was being cruel to be kind this morning, but perhaps he should have been gentler. Perhaps he could go back to France and work from home. Perhaps he and Emma could retreat from the world and try to have a real relationship.

That idea was scary. He had never had a real relationship.

He had fallen in love with Jo because she was blonde and beautiful and slender, but they had never been soul mates.

He thought of Emma, standing on the doorstep looking small and desperately hurt. Everything about her had been a bit different. She would never have dreamed of calling him a bastard before, would never have lost control and cried in front if him, would certainly never have poured her drink all over him. He was glad she had done that. It had shown spirit, and she was going to need spirit.

He would not be able to tell Jo that she had come to the house. So he would be lying again already.

Jo had been amazed at Emma.

'You cheat on me with *her*?' she had demanded, last Monday morning in the Aroma café on Piccadilly. 'You throw away everything we've got to set up an extra home with some mumsy little woman who wouldn't say boo to a goose? You only went after her because she was Pete's Emma and you wanted to get one over on him. You could at least have picked a nubile teenage model.'

Hugh had been tempted to assure Jo that he had cheated on her with plenty of other women too, not just with Emma, and that some of them had undoubtedly been teenagers and very nubile, but he had managed to censor himself.

'Don't you like her?' he'd asked, for want of anything else to say.

'Of course not. I hate her but it's not her fault. She's sweet. She has no fucking idea what she's got into, has she? She has not got a clue that you're married, that you're called Hugh, that you have a large and forceful family. I would say she's clearly stupid, but you fooled me too.'

Hugh had known this was his moment to try to salvage something. 'Josie,' he had said, 'I'm so sorry. I really am. More sorry than I can ever tell you. I got into this thing with Emma without meaning to, really. I suppose it flattered my ego that she was so keen. I was about to break it off when Alice came along and I just felt I couldn't.'

She had agreed, against all judgement, that they would stay in the house together for a month and see what happened. Hugh knew what was happening. He decided to save them all some pain, and bail out.

He took out his usual travelling bag from its place under the bed, and he filled it with as many of his clothes as he could squash in. He added a few toiletries, and took down a painting from Olly's wall and laid it flat on top of everything else.

Then he left.

chapter twenty-five

I drove through a thunderstorm to get home from Bordeaux airport. I was not a confident motorway driver at any time, and I had never had to drive for any distance in conditions like these. I slowed right down and concentrated on the road ahead. It was an effective distraction. Huge raindrops splashed heavily onto the motorway in front of me. Even with the wipers on full throttle, I could barely see past my windscreen.

I crawled along the ring road in the slow lane. Lorries passed by, driving too fast, and splashed the car with dirty water. I was blinded whenever this happened. I was barely moving when the thunder clapped directly overhead, and the road was suddenly brightly lit by electricity. At the same instant, the car started shaking. All four wheels seemed to come off the ground and crash back down. I knew at once that a truck had smashed into me. I knew I was seconds from death.

The impact never came. I did not find myself crushed in twisted metal. The accelerator responded to my foot. I inched over to the hard shoulder, put my hazard lights on, and rested my forehead on the steering wheel.

I thought that my car had been struck by lightning. I was all right, and the car was all right. I was shaken. I had been holding myself together by a thread and now I didn't think I could do it any more.

I had to keep going. I had to drive through this rain to get to Alice. It would pass soon. I guessed that the hard shoulder was a bad place to be in such poor visibility. The rain was coming down in torrents. All I could see of the lorries that were passing were blurry red tail lights. I knew that I was all but invisible.

I indicated and pulled tentatively back onto the road. When I came to the exit signed 'Villeneuve', I was relieved, because the traffic was much lighter, but it was still the motorway, and I was still miles and miles from Alice. After half an hour of inching along nervously, I was frustrated that the rain had not let up. A sign for petrol loomed up at me, and I pulled in gratefully, found a parking space beside the café, and phoned home.

Alice sounded fine. I had only been away overnight and she seemed barely to have noticed. She and Bella were sheltering from the rain, watching through the windows as sheets of pink lightning illuminated the valley. I had not been away for long, yet the world had changed. I felt that I was observing myself from a distance. I picked up my tatty handbag, and ran through the rain into the welcoming glow of the café. I was not the only one sheltering there. It was a small room, full of travellers. I looked round at the men and women, smoking, drinking, and passing the time. The windows had steamed up and the staff were busy stoking up the coffee machine.

I bought a large white coffee, which was much smaller than a small coffee from Starbucks, but at least as powerful, and found a high stool in a corner by the window. I looked out at the water that was sweeping down the window. I was stranded. The strange feeling overtook me again. Mummy, I whispered. I want Mummy. I tried to imagine myself making this journey with Sarah, my mother. She would be fifty-four, younger and more relaxed than Christa. She would probably have made fun of Christa for being so uptight. Sarah and I would have sat here and laughed at the rain. She would have put an arm round my shoulder and told me it was all going to be all right. I would be fine, because I had her to look after me.

In a practical sense, living without Matt was going to be easy. We were used to having a part-time husband and father. I was trying to absorb the fact that he had been doubling up as a part-time husband and father to another family. I had never known him at all. The gentle, caring soul mate I had adored had been a figment of my imagination. I tried to stop myself revisiting scenes from the past four years, but I could not help re-evaluating every missed plane, every unavoidable birthday absence and its accompanying mortified phone call, in the light of the truth.

I took Sarah's letter out of my handbag. I did not need to read it again. Touching it was enough. I tried to hold on to the fact that she had loved me. The one person who had really loved me had died.

Alice and I were accustomed to being a unit of two. We

would get on all right without him. It was the rejection that I could not bear. I was humiliated, discarded, second best. His words sounded in my head, far too often. *You've always been the other*. I had never been The One. Now I knew why I had only ever met one of his friends. I was sure I had only met Pete because he had introduced us and so it had been unavoidable. Now I knew why Matt had told me that he didn't have any family. I remembered Pete looking at me, a day ago, and telling me that he was sorry. He must have laughed at Matt's escapades over the years. He had probably enjoyed it all along, knowing that I was going to be hurt.

I was mortified by the knowledge that Pete, the former Po, had known about Matt's real identity. Whenever I had seen him, he had betrayed no unease at all. I imagined him laughing at my delusions of security. I wanted to curl up and die. I had never thought of myself as a bad judge of character. I had flattered myself by assuming that I was perceptive. I started to wonder what else had been going on beneath my nose without my realising it.

I wondered if I would ever be able to think of Matt as Hugh. I didn't think so. I wondered if one day I would go from one month to another without thinking of him at all.

I tried to see through the steamed-up, wet window. The car park outside was almost dark. Sheets of rain distorted my view. Cars pulled in, their lights illuminating the millions of raindrops that continued to pound down. The air indoors was hot and the window was almost opaque with condensation as more and more people hurried in to shelter from the storm. I drained the dregs of my coffee and asked for another. A dark-haired man took the stool next to mine. A skinny older woman in magenta lipstick stood on my other side. I forced a smile at each of them and we exchanged pleasantries. The man announced that, according to his car radio, the storm was destroying houses all over the south-west. We shook our heads and agreed that it was terrible.

I stared out of the window and hoped that I didn't have to talk any more.

I was not sure that I was strong enough. I didn't think I could manage to be on my own all the time. I had no partner and I had no mother. Both of them had chosen to leave me. No one loved me best except Alice, and that was only because she was two, and anyway she preferred her father. She would go to live with him as soon as she was old enough to make that decision.

I could not bear it. I didn't know whether to go back to England or whether to stay in France. Either way, I could barely see a future. I realised I was crying, silently.

The unisex toilet was basic but it looked clean enough. I locked the door and leaned back on it. The sobs came faster and stronger. I had always prided myself on self-control, and now I could do nothing but cry. I cried for my stupid mother, who had put her mania above everything else, including me. I cried for Matt, and for Alice. I cried for myself, and even for Jo and Oliver. The whole world was miserable. I felt desperate for some sort of comfort. There was nothing. I wanted to scream with pain, so I did. I did not care who heard me. I shook with the sobs, glad that there was a tempest outside. I could not control myself any more. I gasped for breath. I had only ever lost control like this once before, when I was in labour.

I slid onto the floor and curled up into a ball, hiccuping and trembling, all dignity gone.

I did not get home. Someone started knocking on the loo door, since it was the only one serving the establishment and I found myself having to unlock it and face the public. The man who had sat at the stool next to me was standing on the other side of the door. When he saw me he looked astonished, then sympathetic. He ushered me to the bar, propelling me by the elbow when I hesitated, and bought me an alcoholic drink. It was some sort of spirit. I didn't even notice what. It felt warm as it slid down my throat.

I looked at my rescuer. He was about forty, dark-haired, and he looked very French. He had a kind face, as a certain type of Frenchman invariably does. It was lined, but with gentle, happy lines, as if he had spent most of his life smiling. He put a gentle hand on my shoulder.

'*Madame*,' he said, '*Ça ira*.' It will be all right. It also translated as 'It will go'. I let him buy me another drink. I was not embarrassed. I was a long way beyond embarrassment. I had spent my whole life worrying about what other people thought of me. It had been a waste of time. I was, instead, mortified at the realisation that I should have been looking at this man as a potential partner, as a mate. I didn't want to be single. I didn't want to have to look at strangers in that way. It was horrible, animal, beyond me.

'*Merci*,' I told him. I summoned my strength and did my best to project self-control. I put down my empty glass, making a steady effort to stop my hand trembling. Matt, Alice and I had been an exclusive unit. Perhaps we had been a little too exclusive. We had had lots of acquaintances, but few people had made it to the inner circle. We had been all that we had needed. Apart, of course, from Matt's other family. He, apparently, had needed another wife and another child as well. We had been the spare ones. So it was just Alice and me who were cut off from the world. Our life was going to change radically in ways I could not imagine.

I put a smile on my face, pushed my stool back, and walked out of the café door, back into the rain. I walked slowly to the car, letting my hair fall into drenched rat's tails. My so-called raincoat proved unequal to the task. It was merely decorative, I decided, as my clothes were slowly soaked.

When I reached the car, I stood still for a moment. The rain was letting up a little, and the sky was clearing. There were so many cars in the car park that it was going to be hard to manoeuvre myself out. I could not drive anywhere. I would drive into a ditch. I opened the door and sat at the wheel for a while, watching the drops hitting the windscreen. I put the radio on and listened to Nostalgi. They were playing 'Pretty Woman'. I hummed along for a while, then I flipped down the sun shield and looked at myself in its mirror. I was anything but a pretty woman. My face was purple and blotchy. I looked terribly ill. My eyes were slits. Everything was puffed up and stained with crying. No wonder everyone had stared at me in there. Frenchwomen never looked like this.

I supposed some Frenchwomen must have done, from

time to time. It was too easy to see France and the French largely as stereotypes. Coco was, of course, well dressed and chic, but so was Bella and she was British. Many of the other mothers I saw at the school gates were dressed in any old thing, just like me. Frenchwomen were just women, and Frenchmen were just men. Many of them had mistresses, just like Matt. In fact, they were renowned for it. I hated the fact that I had been a long-term mistress. I wondered how stupid I must have been, not to have realised. How wilfully blind I had been. I wondered why.

The rain became heavier again. I took out my mobile. The network flickered on and off. I tried calling home anyway, but it rang once before reception disappeared. I looked at myself again. I had just enough presence of mind to see that I was in pieces. I could not drive home through the rain. I would probably die. I reversed out of my parking space and drove around the buildings to a sign saying 'Hotel'.

It was a chain hotel; cheap and efficient. My room was small, and it smelt of stale cigarette smoke. I sat on the bed and tried to pull myself together. First of all, I regulated my breathing.

Then I ran a deep, hot bath and tried to comfort myself with platitudes. It would be all right, I told myself, echoing the man in the café. I tried the concept out. It was going to end up all right. People went through the process all the time. Not, perhaps, exactly the same, not the discovery that their life partner was essentially a bigamist, but relationships that had been supposed to last for ever did go wrong, and they went wrong every day. People deceived each other.

Lots of people were divorced. They had all been through this heartache.

And lots of people lost their mothers. Many children grew up motherless. My situation was nothing special; it was just part of the human condition.

This may have been true, but it was not cheering. I had wanted to give Alice the perfect life, and now I was not going to manage it. I had always pitied those people who had to talk about *my dad's girlfriend*. I would now, sooner or later, have to explain to Alice that Jo was her stepmother, and that Oliver was her brother, and that we had not known anything about them until Daddy's wife had tracked us down. She would have to find a way of explaining that to her friends. *My dad's girlfriend* was nothing next to *my dad's secret wife*.

My half-brother is two months younger than me would also take some explaining. I wished Jo had told me the facts when she came calling. That is what she would have done in the Hollywood version, and we would have concocted a plan to get even with him, humiliated him horribly, and become best friends for life.

I knew that the situation was not her fault, but I hated the way she had handled it. She had tricked me. She had used me. She had insinuated herself into my house, armed with facts that I would never have suspected. I had liked her. She had manipulated me into liking her. In a detached way I admired her self-possession.

The worst thing about Jo was that, manipulative and sneaky though she clearly was, Matt had chosen her. He liked her better; loved her more.

The bath was small, but I lay back with my knees sticking up, and the water was hot and comforting. The TV was showing a terrible dubbed film, starring Gwyneth Paltrow in a fat suit. I washed my hair with some horrible two-in-one shampoo from a tiny plastic bottle. I scrubbed my body clean. Then I wrapped myself in a towel and ordered a cheese and ham sandwich on room service. I forced myself to eat it. I called Bella and explained that I had not been able to make it through the storm and would be back in the morning. I lay on the bed and drifted in and out of sleep. At five o'clock I got up, washed my puffed-up face, and checked out. It was a cool, silent morning. I watched the sun rising as I drove home on empty roads.

The house was dappled with the early morning sun shining through the cherry trees. The morning air was perfectly still. A few birds were singing and there was a distant rumbling of an early tractor. Bella had locked up too well. All the shutters were bolted from the inside, and I could not get in. I walked round to the back garden and wished the builders had got around to making the windows there. The door was bolted. I was locked out. I sat at the little table where the terrace was going to be, and looked at my garden.

The house lifted my spirits a little. It was a beautiful house. I was proud of it. It was slightly renovated, and that had been my doing. I had done everything. The garden was looking good. I made a mental note to cut the grass. It was almost overgrown, and dandelions and daisies were pushing through everywhere. I walked over to the dahlias and pulled off their dead heads. I decided that we should get some chickens. Everybody else had chickens. I could hear a cockerel crowing.

The storm had gone and the air was fresh and cool. The sky was a pale, eggshell blue. The leaves on the trees were not moving at all. I walked around my garden. I was happy there. I was happy at that moment. I did not think I could live there for long, not as a single mother. I could not imagine myself being that isolated. It would be impossible to live here with no other adult in the house. It would, however, be silly to sell the house with the building work half done. Alice was about to go back to school for the autumn term. We would, I decided, stay until Christmas. Then we would sell the house and go straight back to Brighton.

I was desperate to see Alice. I went back to the front door, and banged on it. After a couple of moments, I heard keys turning in locks. The hinges creaked, and there she was.

'Mummy!' Alice shouted, lifting her arms to be picked up. I looked beyond her, to Bella, who looked sleepy and anxious. 'Mummy! You're home! I love you too much, Mummy.'

I picked her up. But when I looked at her eager face, everything changed. I didn't see Alice. I saw Matt's child. She was half Matt. All I saw was him.

'I love you, too,' I told her, fighting the horror. She was smiling and nuzzling me.

'Where's Daddy?' she asked.

I didn't answer. I handed her abruptly to Bella, ran to the edge of the road, and was violently sick.

chapter twenty-six

Christa and Geoff arrived that afternoon with Bella's Jon and the twins. They brought presents for me – perfume, body lotion, bubble bath, alcohol – but I barely noticed. They brought half the Disney Store for Alice. She wanted me to play with her. I told her that Felix and Oscar would like to see her new toys. She gave me a disappointed look before she trotted off to find her cousins.

I was desperately trying to get over what I was not feeling for Alice. I reminded myself that I had loved her creamy cheeks, her long lashes, her eyes. I stared at those features, but I could only see duplicity. Alice was her father. Loving her was supposed to be the most natural thing in the world for me. I tried and I tried. I couldn't even join in an Incredibles game.

Christa hugged me. Geoff hugged me. They looked at each other. They looked at Bella.

'Stop looking at each other,' I told them. 'I can see you're doing it.'

Geoff laughed, too loudly. 'Stop looking at each other? Any other house rules we don't know about?'

Plan B

I frowned at him. 'Stop trying to talk about me without saying anything. I know what you're doing. You're making snap assessments of me and giving Bella meaningful glances. Just come out and say it.'

Bella rolled her eyes. 'Emma. We're all concerned about you. Mum and Dad are desperately worried. Nobody's victimising you. Look. It's very hot. Why don't we all sit out in the shade and relax. Or you could have a nap. You've had a hell of a couple of days.'

'I'll be upstairs,' I announced.

'We won't disturb you,' promised Christa.

'Disturb me if Matt phones,' I decreed, and went to lie down before they all started looking at each other again. I lay on the bed trying to hear what they were saying about me, but all I could hear was a general concerned murmur.

I stayed in my bedroom until Bella sent Alice to fetch me down for dinner. Alice was barefoot in red shorts and a dirty white T-shirt. Her hair was damp and she was giggling.

'Mummy,' she said, climbing up on the bed as she always did. 'We've been in the paddling pool. Oscar can kick the football into the top of the tree. Felix climbed up and throwed it down. Oscar can put his face in the water for a long time.'

She wriggled close to me, sweaty and happy. I closed my eyes and tried to capture my maternal instinct.

'Felix can jump right over the ditch,' she continued, as I lifted my arm and put it round her shoulders, as I normally did. 'I did try but I did fall in.' Alice lifted her leg into the air and showed me a livid red scratch down the side of her calf.

'Did you cry?' I asked her.

'Yes. I cried and then I was better.'

'Did someone kiss you better?'

'Felix fetched Bella. Bella kissed me better and then Christa kissed me better and then Geoff gave me a Kinder egg and it had a witch inside.'

I studied her face as I pretended to be concerned and interested. Alice looked like me, but she had more of Matt in her than I had ever realised. She had his eyes. Her top lip was exactly the same as his top lip. I thought their ears were similar. The worst things, though, were the mannerisms. She held her head on one side like Matt. She said 'It certainly is!' in exactly the way he used to say it. Suddenly, she was a little Matt, and that meant she was treacherous and it meant I wanted to take it all out on her.

I knew that I was failing her utterly, just as Sarah had failed me when I was Alice's age. I felt fatalistic, certain that the pattern had always been destined to be repeated. I now knew that, whatever she had tried to say, my mother had not loved me enough. I knew this because I did not love Alice enough.

Alice was curled up against me happily. I let her stay there because I knew I shouldn't push her away. She chatted on, idolising her cousins, until there was a knock on the door, and Christa stood there. She looked at us cuddled up together, and smiled.

'You two!' she said. 'It's dinner time. Geoff's made his special pasta for us. It's quite an event. And it's just about on the table.'

Alice sat up and bounced on the bed. 'Come on, Mummy.'

I shook my head. 'I'm not hungry. You go without me. Enjoy the pasta. Tell Geoff I'm sorry to miss it.'

Christa frowned. 'No, come on, Emma. You need to eat.'

'I don't. I'm fine.' I looked at my aunt and I hardened slightly. 'You have a nice family dinner. Alice will enjoy that. I'm still getting myself together here. Let me have a day or so to collect myself, hey?'

She sighed and nodded. 'Of course. Take all the time you need. Come on, Alice. I've put a place for you in between Oscar and Felix. How does that sound?'

chapter twenty-seven

Three weeks later

The beach was too busy. Even though it was September and the holiday period was officially over, this was a hot, sunny Saturday and Biarritz was packed. The *Grande Plage* was crammed with sunbathers, with topless women, small children, and surfers. Most of them looked happy, and those who didn't look actively joyful still seemed to be calm and serene. I looked at them curiously. Being happy seemed a strange, deluded state. As I stared, I began to see that every single person was on the edge of a crisis. They smiled, they stretched, they felt the sand running through their fingers, but their lives were fragile.

There were too many people here. Fear assaulted me, and I stopped walking. I looked to Bella for help.

'Sure this is a good idea?' I asked in a monotone. A day out with three small children was, according to my sister, guaranteed to bring my focus back to the present. Today was supposed to pull me out of myself. Naïvely, Bella was counting on me to look at Alice playing on the sand and realise that I had been gravely neglectful of my little girl.

Plan B

She was assuming that the outside world was going to flick a switch and bring 'the old Emma' back.

I was sick of hearing about the old Emma. I did not like her.

This was the first time I had agreed to go out in three weeks. Jon and Christa had gone back to England to work within a few days of each other, but Bella and Geoff had stayed behind, with the twins. I supposed they were missing work but I never asked because I didn't care. Every day, they tried to get me to snap out of myself. Every day, I disappointed them. I was rude to them constantly. When Alice had started back at school, I had gone with her, reluctantly, in the back of the car. At the school car park, I had refused to get out. For one thing, I was wearing my pyjamas, and my face was somehow at once both shiny and grey. For another, I knew that everyone would be gossiping about me. I sank down in the back seat so no one would see me, and I waited for Bella to take Alice in and hand her over to the capable hands of the teachers.

I had sunk into a pit. If I let myself think about where I was, it would have scared me, but because I simply existed from one moment to the next, I felt nothing. I saw no future. The past was ruptured and destroyed. Alice was a part of Matt and I could not bring myself to be her mother any more. Nothing mattered. I cared about nothing. The days passed by around me, and that was the only way I could exist. I identified with nobody apart from Sarah. I wondered if this was how her lows had been.

Selfishness was a revelation. I had divested myself of all responsibility, even for Alice. I kissed her when I had to, then pushed her away. I answered her questions in monosyllables, and let Bella chat with her. I had not fetched her milk or made her a meal in three weeks. I had not bathed her or washed her clothes or put her to bed. She was brought to me, each night, for a goodnight kiss, like a Victorian child. Then she was taken away and cared for. Bella told me she cried for me. Christa said she asked for Daddy. Geoff told me she was doing 'just fine'. Even I could see she was confused. I told Bella to tell Alice that Daddy was working in London for a while. She rolled her eyes, and said that 'obviously' she'd already done that.

I took no responsibility for the builders, who had started working in earnest. I did not care if they saw me in pyjamas, with baggy jowls and bird's nest hair. They managed to give me a wide berth.

I knew that Andy and Fiona had been coming round to see me. I knew that Coco had called. I had heard Bella speaking to her on the phone about me, in a mixture of English and French, several times a day. I refused to see anyone.

Bella and Geoff were torn between indulging me and trying to bring me back to my senses. Geoff was patient, probably because he was desperate to avoid confrontation. He buried himself in endless games with his grandchildren and left Bella to deal with me. Bella, I could tell, was itching for a fight. That week, she had marched into my room each morning, opened the shutters and said pointedly, 'I'll take Alice to school, shall I?'

I had rolled over and shut my eyes. I could not bring myself to give a fuck whether Alice went to school or not, beyond a vague feeling that it was better for me and for her if she was out of the house. I wasn't going to take her anywhere. I sometimes laughed in Bella's face at the idea that I might.

I generally levered myself out of bed later, when there was no one around. Sometimes I bothered to brush my teeth and wash myself. Sometimes I didn't. I drank a bit of water, and ate if Bella forced me. I was somewhere different, somewhere I had never been before. I was aware that I was behaving strangely, but my capable self – the old Emma – steadfastly refused to come to my rescue. I could not snap myself out of it. I swore at Bella, and even at Geoff, when they tried to jolly me along with platitudes. As the weeks went by, I found myself keeping further and further away from Alice. I was certain that if she began even one sentence with the word *why*, I would have told her to fuck off. I knew I could not do that. Sometimes I saw her looking at me with hurt bewilderment. I always looked away.

I did not care about my daughter, but I was obsessed with my mother. I thought about her all the time. I wanted her to be watching over me. I tried to see signs. I made little bargains with her. *If you're there*, I would whisper, *make that blackbird land on the window sill. If you're listening, make that fly buzz around the light*. She never did anything I asked, so I made the tasks easier and easier until I started to get results.

Bella mentioned antidepressants repeatedly, but the idea of going to the doctor, who was a capable but terrifying woman, appalled me. I had always quite liked Dr Moulin, because I knew she would be a pillar in a crisis, but she had made me feel stupid every time I had seen her, and I knew she would find my garbled explanations of my situation tiresome. She was an immaculate, slender Frenchwoman twenty years my senior, who already thought I was perverse because I preferred to give my daughter Calpol rather than put a paracetamol suppository up her bottom. I had no desire to admit to her that I had failed to notice that my partner had already got a wife.

That morning, Bella had given me an ultimatum. She marched into my bedroom, yanked open the shutters and flung them back. I closed my eyes tightly and rolled onto my front, hiding from her.

'Emma!' she said sharply.

'Go away.'

'Right.' She slammed a cup down on the bedside table. 'This is your last chance.'

'What last chance?' I pulled a pillow over my head. I didn't want to hear about last chances.

'It's Saturday,' she continued. 'No school. The boys are raring to get out to the beach. If you don't get up right now, get some clothes on, eat some breakfast and come to the seaside, I'm going to make an appointment with the doctor, and I'm going to take you there myself, and we're going to get you some happy pills.'

'Go away.'

'No.' She stood there for several minutes while I tried to lull myself back to sleep. 'Drink that tea,' she added. I looked at her through slits of eyes. Bella was efficiency incarnate. She was dressed in a white dress with turquoise flowers on it. It clung to her body, to midway down her shins. I glanced at the clock.

'It's quarter past eight!' I told her, outraged. 'I was still awake at six. That's not fair. You can't expect me to do anything on two hours' sleep.'

'Come to the beach. You might sleep if you're tired out.'

'I *am* tired out! You don't understand. I've never been so tired.' I was exhausted to the point of hallucination. I could see nothing clearly and I had no concept of time. I was in pieces. I thought I was having a breakdown, but Bella didn't take me seriously. She just told me I would get over it.

'I know you're tired,' she said, a bit more kindly, 'but it's mental exhaustion. You spend too much time dwelling on things. If you spend a day kicking a football on the beach with the kids, you'll sleep tonight and that will do you the world of good.'

I rolled my eyes. 'Bella, you have no idea,' I told her. I think I even laughed a bitter and mirthless laugh at the idea that chasing a ball on a beach might make me snap out of myself. Then I thought, with dread, of the doctor. I made a decision.

'I'm not driving,' I said sulkily.

'Bloody right you're not,' she told me as she stalked out. 'Breakfast's on the table. We're leaving in half an hour.'

Now I stared at the beach, frozen to the spot. There were too many people.

'Of course it's a good idea,' Bella said briskly. 'Look, there's a piece of sand over there.'

Geoff came and stood next to us, with an entourage of children. 'We can squeeze on,' he said. 'The boys and Alice will want to mess around in the sea anyway. Plus people will drift off for lunch, won't they?'

'Of course they will,' Bella said heartily.

I raised my eyebrows at her. 'I used to be the one who did that,' I remarked.

She frowned. 'What are you talking about?'

'Being all jolly. Keeping people's spirits up.'

She shook her head and dropped her sunglasses down over her eyes. 'No idea what you mean,' she said. 'Now, where's Alice. Alice? Come back, darling.' Alice obediently ran to us. I looked down at her and tried, yet again, to feel the old surge of love. Her fringe was cut straight and dark, just above her eyebrows. Her eyelashes curled upwards, soft and long. Her skin was peachy. I waited for the old rush of tenderness. It didn't come.

Alice was becoming part of Bella's family. She ran around with Felix and Oscar, and sat on Bella's knee. She adored Geoff who was far more a grandfather to her than a great-uncle by marriage. He was the only grandfather she would ever have, I was sure, because I would never bother to find my real father. I knew that she needed to live in London. I was never going to be able to look after her now, and if Bella took her in, Alice would have a ready-made family. She would have two big brothers who would dote on her, and a stable pair of parents. Every time this thought surfaced, I recognised, with detachment, that this was exactly how my own mother had felt about me.

Bella adored Alice. She had none of my ambivalence. She was a better mother to her than I would ever be. I was sure Bella would have liked a daughter. I needed her to take Alice off my hands so I could get on with drowning in this treacherous world.

Plan B

I silenced the voice that reminded me that Christa was not my mother, that she was unmistakably an aunt, and that I would have given anything in the world to have been brought up by my real parents, however flawed they were.

I should have been starting to feel better, now that the shock was wearing off, but I was getting worse. I watched my little daughter running down the steps to the beach. She was trying to catch up with Oscar. He stopped, turned, and waited for her. He was wearing a pair of long shorts, and his hair had already been bleached by the French sun. Felix looked exactly the same. They were beautiful boys. I had wanted our second baby to be a boy.

Alice and Oscar threaded through the bodies on the sand and sat down, triumphantly, when they reached the designated spot. I decided that I felt more for Oscar, in his physical beauty, than I did for Alice.

Bella, Felix and Geoff started walking across the beach, too. I held back.

'I'm just going to get a coffee,' I told them. Bella turned, as if to stop me. Geoff took her arm.

'Fine, Em,' he said, with forced nonchalance. I wanted to laugh at him. He looked so silly, with his paunch overhanging his long shorts. He touched Bella's arm. 'I might join her,' he said. I sighed ostentatiously. I probably sneered.

'I'll be over there,' I told him, pointing at the smart café tables on the wide promenade.

It was all I could manage to do to get myself to a table. I slumped on a chair, and pulled my sunglasses over my eyes.

If he came back now, I would take him gladly. I didn't

know whether I loved him or not. That was not relevant. He had been holding me together for years, and I needed him. Only Matt had the power to pull me out of my swamp.

Geoff sat down opposite me, with a big smile.

'Stop pretending,' I said rudely.

'Pretending what?' he asked, looking hurt. I looked at the top of his head, which was now completely bald.

'That everything's great.'

'I'll go in and get some drinks,' he said, huffing some air out through his mouth.

'They'll be out in a minute.'

'I'll get them anyway.'

'Coffee,' I said, looking away.

I stared out to sea. The waves were large and frightening. I knew that Bella would not let Alice be swept away by the fearsome current. There was a cluster of surfers out to sea, by the rocks to the left. I stared at them. The waves were enormous. Each time a wave approached, a few sleek black shapes disengaged themselves from the group, paddled frantically, then, as the wave carried them aloft, scrambled to their feet and stood triumphantly on their boards, carried towards the shore by the mass of water. Their arms were out to the sides, for balance. I watched and watched. I would have loved to have had the skill to do something as magical as riding on the sea. I thought back to Matt laughing at my ambition. He was right. I could never actually do it.

The sun scorched my face. I should have asked Geoff to get me some water. I looked at the bodies on the beach. The women depressed me. So many of them were slender and topless. After breastfeeding, I could not imagine that my breasts would ever be exposed to the gaze of the public. They never had been before, either. I was not a topless sort of girl. I was uptight, slightly overweight, and, I now realised, completely unstable. I had always been unstable. That was why I had exerted such a rigorous discipline on myself. It was the only way I had functioned.

The women of Biarritz were unfeasibly glamorous. I revised my earlier decision that people were just people, that stereotypes were lazy. Frenchwomen took much more care over their appearance than their British counterparts. That was a fact. They were not fat. They wore make-up every day. They dressed well. As a woman who looked like a retired ballerina slunk by with a fluffy dog on a pink leash, I noted that they had facelifts. That woman's face was smooth and tight. She was probably ninety, but she looked about forty-five.

Two teenage girls strutted by. My body had probably been like that once. I had never appreciated it like these girls appreciated their beautiful bodies. What a waste that was. I had been divine-looking, like these two, and I had kept it all hidden beneath drooping skirts and men's cardigans. The girls were tanned and sure of themselves. One wore a white bikini with a halter neck. Her dark hair was tied carelessly at the nape of her neck. The other was in bright blue, which set off her tan to perfection. Her blonde hair reached her shoulders. They both had clear eyes, firm skin, and only the right sort of curves. They walked with a slight wiggle, revelling in their beauty, laughing together. I watched them until they were out of sight, and then I looked at myself. My legs were white and chunky. I had spent the early part of the summer keeping

Alice in the shade, and when we had been unavoidably out in the sun, I had plastered myself in factor fifty as a good example. The latter part of the summer I had spent festering in bed. My thighs were bulging against the metal chair, and they were covered in broken veins. I was wearing an old pair of denim shorts, and a pink T-shirt which was not quite long enough, and which, therefore, displayed an unappealing slice of midriff. No man ever looked at me twice.

I had felt much better in my Gap clothes in London. If I was up to it, I mused, I ought to let Bella or Coco sort my wardrobe out. I knew that I wouldn't. I would carry on being messy and fat and ugly. It kept me invisible.

There were many things I should have been doing, yet I could not find the energy to brush my teeth in the morning. All I did was drink. I drank coffee all day and alcohol all evening. I forced food down when I had to, and felt slightly sick and trembly all the time, probably because of the caffeine. I knew I ought to visit the doctor, but I didn't want to. I was a mess, and I was almost proud of it.

'You do realise, Emma love, that Bella and I both have to go home?' Geoff said, as he put an espresso and a large glass of iced water in front of me.

I managed to smile. 'I thought you must,' I agreed, sipping the water, then gulping the coffee. 'Can you take Alice?'

Geoff raised his eyebrows and ran his hand over where his hair used to be. 'Can we *what*?'

I kept my voice light. 'Take Alice. I think she should live with Bella and Jon for a while. Or with you and Christa – whichever's easiest. Whoever wants her.'

Geoff was shaking his head. 'You want us to take Alice

to London and leave you knocking round your big house in the middle of nowhere, on your own?' I nodded, smiling. 'We can't do that, love. You know we can't.'

I felt the tears starting. 'You can.'

Geoff leaned forward. His face was red from the sun. 'But what we can do,' he said confidentially, 'is to take you both back with us. That's the plan. Come back to Holloway for a while. Get back on your feet. I know your aunt and I work, but we'll help you out whenever we're around. We'll take Alice all weekend if you like, every weekend. You can just take your time and when you feel ready, you can come back here, or get a flat of your own in London, or Brighton. Whatever you like.'

He stared expectantly. I realised that Geoff had just imparted the plan that had been born of all the telephone conversations and whispered conferences that ended whenever I entered a room. I shook my head and looked away.

'No,' I told him. 'I can't do that.'

'Love, it's the only thing you *can* do. Come on, Emma. We all hate to see you like this. Bella says she never had you down as the going-to-pieces type, but Christa and I have been waiting for this for years.' He shifted in his chair.

'You hate talking about this kind of stuff, don't you?' I asked, mocking him.

'It's not *me*. You know that. But you need support. And that's what we're here for. And you need to learn to stop pushing us away, and particularly to stop pushing Alice away.'

'I'm not,' I said listlessly.

'Alice needs you,' said Geoff, slapping his hand down on the table. 'She's a very upset little girl.'

'You said she's fine.'

'Well, she's not. She's lost her daddy and now she's losing her mummy, too. She wants you to take her to school. She wants you to be a mother again. You can do better for Alice, love, than Sarah did for you. You're not Sarah and you don't need to become her.'

I was briefly furious at this, and then I couldn't be bothered. I ordered another coffee, and Geoff ordered a demi pression for himself.

'Geoff?' I said. 'Tell me what Sarah was like.'

'I thought Christa already did.'

'What did you think of her?'

Geoff's eyes widened and he swallowed. 'What did I think of her? She was complicated. She was different. Good company some of the time. I don't know. It's hard to see someone objectively after an event like that.' He looked at me. 'But I do know that you meant the world to her.'

'Right.'

'Really.'

'She would have taken her medication properly if that was true. She didn't love me enough. I don't love Alice enough. She reminds me of Matt.'

'That is enough self-indulgent twaddle!' He was half shouting. People looked at us. I was surprised. He carried on. 'Come on, Emma. She's your little girl. She's nearly three. It's breaking our hearts to see what this is doing to her. Pick her up and hug her, for God's sake. She's your reason for keeping going. You have to come home with us.'

'I can't.' I blinked hard and looked down the promenade, at the dozens and dozens of holidaymakers. 'I can't because

Matt and his wife and his son live in north London and I know I'd see them everywhere. Even if it wasn't actually them, I'd think I saw them. I couldn't do it. It would drive me truly insane.'

Geoff stared at the horizon. After a while, he nodded.

'Well, you've got to do something,' he said. 'You're skinnier than a rake and you mope in bed all day. You were never like this as a teenager. Maybe you're having your teenage years late.'

I stared at the surfers. 'I'm not skinny.'

'Don't be ridiculous. There's nothing of you.'

'You're just saying that because you've got three daughters, two daughters and a niece rather, and you've been well trained.'

'I'm not. You have lost rather an alarming amount of weight, Emma.'

We both sat for a while. I poked my thighs. No doubt about it: they were fat. Geoff was talking bollocks.

Alice was running in the shallow water with her cousins. Bella was standing nearby, watching. People walked past the table where I sat with my uncle. They probably thought we were a couple. A group of three surfers strolled nonchalantly past, wearing board shorts and carrying surfboards under their arms.

'I'd like to learn to surf,' I said.

'So do it,' Geoff said immediately. 'That's the first time you've said anything positive. Greg's back from Asia soon. He'll come out and show you how it's done.'

I laughed. My cousin Greg was a brilliant surfer. 'Will he?'

'Not unless you've got your act together. I hear what

you're saying about London. We'll get together this evening, you and Bella and I, and we'll get Christa on the phone, and together we'll work out a plan B.' Geoff slumped in his chair. 'Bloody hell. It's hard work, this.'

I smiled at him. 'Tell me about it.'

chapter twenty-eight

Hugh lay in his single bed and watched the time change from 2.59 to 3.00. He had been feeling strange, incomplete, since leaving Jo. He was living with Pete and his girlfriend, Jane. They had both said that he was welcome to stay as long as he wanted, but he knew that the welcome was cautious on Jane's part.

If Pete had been single, the brothers could have found a flat together, but, for the first time ever, he was cohabiting. Hugh found this irritating. Pete had been perpetually single. He was the most screwed-up bloke Hugh had ever known, prone to huge passions and dysfunctional, short-lived affairs. He had always suspected that Pete had never got over Emma, his first grand passion.

He had often wondered how that had happened. The reason he, Hugh, had liked Emma so much was because she was so agreeable. She had no mystery about her, no feistiness, no unpredictability. Emma was nice. She seemed a mightily unlikely focus for Pete's angst.

Now, just as Hugh had broken Emma's heart and ended

283

his marriage to Jo, Pete had settled down. Jane brooked no nonsense. Hugh found her deeply annoying. She fussed around both of them, cooking, making cups of tea, placing their shoes side by side in the hall. She had long, limp hair and she liked to hold Pete's hand. He wished Jane away, and barely spoke to her. He wanted his brother for himself. He felt that Pete owed it to him to drop everything and spend time with him. That was what brothers did.

It was not, of course, something that Hugh had ever done for Pete. He sat up in bed and looked round the edge of the curtain. The street was silent and still. He was going to have to get his own flat soon. Jo wouldn't let him have Olly here overnight.

The last time he had lived alone was when he lived in that skanky bedsit. He had been defined through women for the past ten years. There was nothing wrong, he told himself, with an active love life. He considered the restorative effect that a couple of meaningless flings might have on him now. He knew that he could turn his two wives into an amusing story to illustrate his rakishness. He could become the sort of man who had children liberally sprinkled around Europe. There was a certain type of woman who would love that.

Somehow, though, he lacked the impetus to get out there and start again. He twisted on the bed, trying to relax. He could have gone to any bar and met a woman. He had been good at that. But he didn't want to. Casual sex was not alluring presently. He reminded himself that he had always known that he would be found out. He had known it, yet he had never thought about what would really happen. Part of him had enjoyed the risks he had taken, and the prospect of being exposed had been a heady motivator for covering his tracks. He had got into the mess because of weakness, because something had clicked between him and Emma. He had liked her a lot, so he had carried on seeing her, without ever mentioning his marriage. He had carried on deceiving Jo because he had seemed to be getting away with it. There had been a huge thrill in keeping all the balls in the air at once.

Now he was on his own. The balls had crashed to earth, and the thrill had gone. He was flat, bored, guilty. Now that he was morally free to do whatever he wanted, the excitement had vanished and there was nothing he wanted to do, no one he wanted to see.

He should have trusted his feelings for Emma, told her from the start that he was married, and left Jo. That was what he should have done, but he hadn't. By the time he had realised that he wanted to settle down with Emma, he had been lying for too long, and it was too late to tell her the truth. She would have run a mile.

Now the truth had seeped out. Everyone knew. Those whom Jo hadn't told straightaway were finding out. Only this afternoon, his mobile had rung, and an unfamiliar number had been displayed. He had answered warily, half hoping for Emma, half hoping for Jo.

'Hugh! It's Claire.' An old school friend of Jo's. Someone they used to see once or twice a year. Clearly, someone out of the loop. 'Listen,' Claire had said. 'This is a bit awkward but I've just heard on the grapevine that you and Jo have split up. Is that right?' She had paused, waiting for his confirmation, which he gave with a grunt. 'I'm so sorry to hear it. I just wanted to say, if there's anything Vic and I can do, just say. This is such a shock – we've always thought you were the perfect couple. I hope you manage to work things out.'

'Thanks, Claire. I doubt it.' He was annoyed with her; she was blatantly digging and he decided to get straight to the point. 'You want to know the details? I'm surprised the "grapevine" didn't furnish them.'

She sounded put out. 'No! No, that's not the case at all. Christ. I'm just trying to say that I'm sorry. We don't want to take sides and if there's anything we can do for either of you, just say the word and we'll be there.'

'Look, you may as well know. Everyone else does. You'll start calling me a bastard in about ten seconds from now.'

'I won't!'

'I've got another child who lives in France. I have another partner. Neither of them knew about each other. Now they both do. My daughter's the same age as Olly.'

There was a short pause. 'You're shitting me.'

'Really. Ring Jo and check.'

'I did ring her. She was out.' There was a pause. 'I'm amazed at you, Hugh. You fucking bastard.'

He had hung up before she could.

He remembered Emma begging him to come back to her. He knew he couldn't do it. The relationship could never work now. Briefly, he wondered how she was doing. She had few friends, just her family of cousins, and he hoped they were taking care of her. Then he pushed her from his mind.

Plan B

After a while, he crept out of the spare room and into the living room. He picked up the telephone handset and took it back into his bedroom. He sat on the bed and imagined Emma in bed in France. Was she, he wondered, asleep? Probably not. He had not heard from her for three weeks, not since the day she had turned up in Highgate. He wondered how she was coping, whether she was coping at all. He dialled 00 33, but pressed the disconnect button before going any further. Perhaps she was asleep. Perhaps she was getting over him.

He needed to get in touch with her soon about practical matters. He knew he needed to make arrangements. He had to support Alice, to help Emma sell the house, to pay off the builders. He hoped Emma would allow him to see his daughter. Perhaps, when they came back to Brighton, he would rent a small flat there, too, so he could see Alice on alternate weekends. The other weekends he would spend with Olly. Jo had flatly refused to have Olly sleeping at Pete's place, but she had informed him, in the new, stiff voice she now reserved for him, that when he was sorted with a flat of his own, Oliver could stay over with him on every other Saturday.

At least he had more money now. Pete and Jane weren't charging him rent. But he knew any spare cash would go on child support, and he didn't want money anyway.

Life as an absent father was going to be grim as fuck. It was strange that, just a couple of months ago, he had been complaining to Pete that he never had any time to himself, that both families quite reasonably expected more than half of him.

He looked at the telephone for a while, then took it back to the sitting room. He went into the galley kitchen and turned the light on. He thought about tea, coffee and alcohol, but settled for a glass of water. He checked the clock. It was ten to four. The street light outside was throwing a sickly orange light onto the ceiling.

Pete coughed, and Hugh turned quickly.

'Sorry, mate,' he said at once. 'Did I wake you? I thought I was being quiet.'

'You were,' Pete assured him. 'I was awake anyway. Heard you turn the tap on.'

'Right.'

The two men stood in the kitchen in silence.

chapter twenty-nine

Three weeks later

Alice woke up mad with excitement. At half past six, she climbed into bed with me, pulled my face round to look at her, and tugged at my hair.

'Mummy! Mummy! Happy birthday to me! Mummy, is it mine birthday?'

I forced myself awake. The sleeping pills I was taking made me extremely drowsy at the best of times. Normally our day started at about eight. Half past six was not the best of times.

But it was Alice's birthday. This was going to be a milestone. I had been watching the post for a gift from her father, but nothing had arrived, and today was Sunday. I wondered if he would ring. I suspected he wouldn't; and I wondered how the loving, indulgent father Alice had adored had detached himself from her life so completely. My heart broke for her and I knew that this was going to have to be a special day. I made an effort to pull myself out of the mire.

'Happy birthday, darling,' I said, rolling over and hugging her.

'You sing.'

I gave her my best rendition of Happy Birthday. She listened, beaming proudly. As soon as I finished, she demanded an encore, and joined in with me. I held her as tightly as she would let me, as we both sang, at the top of our voices: 'Happy birthday, dear Alice!' We were warm under my duvet, in the biggest bedroom in the house, shuttered away from the world in an obscure corner of Europe. I snuggled my face into her hair and smelt Alice's smell. My baby girl was three. I was still nowhere near as devoted a mother as I should be, but I had managed to inter my evil self, and we were getting through the days.

She smiled up at me. 'I'm three now. I think I need some presents.'

Everything I did was an effort. I was scraping by. I knew that Alice's third birthday was more important than anything, and I tried to force myself to be cheerful. Matt and I had planned an extravagant party for her. We had been determined to be properly settled by 20 October. We were going to have a clown and party food, and balloons everywhere and all the children in the class were going to come to tea.

It had been a stupid, deluded dream. I had invited no one. I knew I did not have the resources for socialising, for a house full of excitable three-year-olds and their parents. I could not have coped with it. My official excuse was that our central heating was not working yet, so the house was no place for children. Unfortunately, this was true. The builders were hard at work now, but so far there had been a lot more destruction than construction. We had five gaping holes in the back wall, and the windows were not due to be fitted for another three weeks. Heating seemed to be going to come last.

'Rosie will be here at eight,' I told Alice.

'Will she bring me a present?'

I rolled my eyes. 'Probably. But you mustn't ask her straightaway. She's coming to film your birthday.'

Rosie had been aghast and elated at the sudden change in my fortunes. She had passed an urgent request to talk to me through Andy and Fiona. As soon as I had started forcing myself to see people, Rosie had been there.

'I'm gutted for you,' she said smoothly. Her eyes were alight with the scent of a story. 'And you know what? The best revenge you could ever get on that creep would be if you let me make a little film all about you. Show the world what he's like. Just go about your normal life and I'll work around you. It'll be just me. I'm going to shoot it myself, edit it myself. It's going to be a one-woman show. Or a two-woman show: mine and yours. I'm excited about it. How about it?'

I opened my mouth to say no, but found the word 'yes' coming out instead. I just didn't care. So, while Plan B had involved a steady stream of family members coming to babysit me, my real companion had been Rosie. She was completely focused on her work, and since her work was me, I was becoming fond of her. I knew that I was using her as an emotional crutch and that this was completely inappropriate, but I could not bring myself to care. Rosie was in my house a lot. When she was there I had to make an effort with Alice. This was good.

The autumn had recently kicked in properly, and it had become cold. I was pleased. It was odd to be living here through a season that Matt had never seen, but I was glad I was doing it. I was glad it was not summer any more. The grass was green again now. The plants were stronger, getting ready for winter. Even the figs on the fig tree had all rotted away. The garden was carpeted with brown leaves. One day I was going to rake them all into a pile and burn them. Or perhaps I would build a leaf mulch bin. Or maybe I would simply leave them where they fell.

It was still dark outside, but I opened my bedroom shutters anyway, so we would see the sun rise. I left Alice muttering about presents and went downstairs to fetch her milk and my tea. These were the mechanical tasks that lent structure to my day. I had, as part of Plan B, been to see the doctor. I took my antidepressants when I was meant to. I wasn't even sure whether they had kicked in yet. I didn't particularly feel that they had, but, on the other hand, I was generally making it through the day, and that often felt like a big achievement.

'Here you are,' I said, handing Alice her milk, and retrieving a large parcel from under the bed. Alice nodded and concentrated all her energies on opening it. I leaned back and gulped my tea. I felt as if I were made from lead. Every action cost me a mammoth effort. I did not want Alice to have any idea how I was feeling. Beyond the window, I watched the sky turning pink and pale blue. It would, I thought, be a good day for our outing.

'Oh wow.' Alice was staring in wonder at her Playmobil airport. 'Oh wow, Mummy. You help me make it.'

Plan B

'Please,' I said wearily.

'You please help me make it.'

'OK. And then you can bring it in the car, because we're going to the real airport today.'

Before we went out, I allowed myself to rummage through the bin bags in the barn. I even let Rosie film me doing it.

'Do you think it's all getting too damp out here?' I asked, looking at the camera. 'Sorry. But do you? Should I take it back inside? I only threw it all out here because Bella made me. Otherwise she was going to take it to the dump.'

'What are you looking for?' Rosie asked, in the sepulchral voice that meant she thought her comments might feature in the finished product.

'A jumper. That's all. Just a sodding jumper. Matt had some great jumpers. I want to wear one to the mountains. I don't care if that's an unhealthy impulse. I'm cold and all my clothes are crap.' I found a green one, slightly bobbly and knitted through with ambiguous associations. I smelt it. It was just on the right side of musty. 'That's the one,' I said, holding it up for the camera.

I stood on the lawn for a moment. The maize had been harvested several weeks earlier, and I liked the fact that I had a view again. I liked the fact that I had watched it grow. All we could see was an expanse of wintry looking fields which extended to the horizon, but it felt good not to be enclosed any more. It felt good that things were changing.

Greg sauntered through arrivals, looking like someone arriving in Bangkok. He was wearing baggy cotton trousers that were too flimsy for Europe, and a long sleeved T-shirt that needed a wash. His light brown hair was long and he had a bit of a beard.

I had known Greg for ever, had lived with him since he was a baby, and he was the cousin who felt most like my sibling. Bella and Charlotte could both remember my mother. As far as Greg was concerned, I had always been his sister. I had seen him progress from dirty-faced toddler to dishevelled schoolboy, to withdrawn teenager. After taking a history degree, he had become a perpetual traveller. Greg had never had a career, nor professed any interest in one. He just worked to fund his travels. As a schoolboy he had told his careers adviser that he wanted to be a quantity surveyor. That had been specific enough to stop them bothering him, though he had never had any idea what kind of quantities a quantity surveyor was expected to survey, and had always held his breath and hoped for no follow-up questions. He had never had any ambitions with regard to status. All his ambitions concerned his lifestyle.

I had not seen Greg very often since he left home, but he had always kept in touch with postcards and emails. When Alice was born he had been teaching English in China, and he had surprised me by flying home a month early, just to see her.

Greg had flown to Pau airport, on the edge of the Pyrenees, rather than to Bordeaux, which was much closer, because he had managed to book a ticket that was almost free. I had been delighted. Bordeaux airport was the last place I wanted to visit, since it would forever be associated with Matt. Greg's arrival in Pau, on Alice's birthday, had neatly excused me from party duties. We were combining his arrival with a day out in the Pyrenees. I wanted to take Alice up in a cable car and see how she liked being up a mountain. Rosie was excited about the change of scene. She said it would be 'brilliant to bung in a bit of landscape'.

Alice barely remembered Greg, but when I pointed him out, she jumped up and down, shouting 'Greg! Greg! Here!' then ran towards him at full pelt. Surprise flickered across his face, then a smile. He gathered her into his arms and kissed her.

'Is that him?' asked Rosie. 'Mmm. Very Ewan McGregor.' She twiddled a stray blonde lock around her index finger.

'Happy birthday,' Greg said, very seriously, to Alice, and he handed her a small bag. She reached inside, beaming, and took out a little bronze Buddha. It was sitting down and had a fat tummy. Alice smiled at it, confused, and looked back at Greg.

'It's a lucky Buddha,' he explained. 'You rub his tummy and make a wish, and he looks after you. You need to keep him by your bed. He's been travelling with me and he's very lucky, so I thought he might help your mummy look after you.'

'Thank you,' she said, and rubbed the Buddha's stomach with great concentration. I unexpectedly found tears pricking my eyes at Greg's gesture. I quickly blinked them away.

'What are you wishing for?' I asked gently, certain that the answer would be 'Daddy'.

'A pink bicycle,' she replied, rapt.

'Thanks, Greg,' I said, and kissed him on the cheek. 'Thanks for coming. This is Rosie.'

A smile spread across his face as they shook hands politely. 'Delighted to meet you, Rosie. I wasn't so keen on the idea of Ems doing this telly thing, but now that we meet, I can imagine you're very persuasive.'

'I certainly can be.'

Greg tore his eyes away from her and turned back to me. 'Hey. Thanks for asking me out. Thanks for letting me be part of this Plan B business. And for coming all this way to get me, on the boss lady here's birthday as well. I can't believe the size of her. I was still expecting a baby.' He turned to Alice. 'Hey, guess what, I've got some more presents for you in here.' He tapped his rucksack. 'Christa and Greg have sent you shitloads of stuff. Sorry, shedloads. And Bella and Jon and the boys. Even scatty old Charlotte's managed to come up with the goods.'

Alice looked at me urgently. 'Mummy, can I open them? Can I open them *just right now*?'

'In the car,' I told her. 'Greg can't open his bag here.'

'Now!' she said. 'I said, now.'

'*And I said in the car.*' I said it too loudly. I found it hard to judge. Everything was a bit too hazy. The edge had been taken off my life, and while I was grateful for that, it saddened me, too.

To get to the mountains we needed to bypass the town of Lourdes. I had never been there, and neither had Greg. He was fascinated by the idea.

'A miracle place,' he said, several times. 'A miracle place that belongs to Catholics. I just know it's going to be wild. Can we go?'

'On the way back,' I said firmly. 'We don't know how long

it's going to take us to get up into the mountains. On the way back we'll know. So we can pace ourselves.'

Greg looked across at me and smiled. 'Sensible as ever, Ems. Nice to know some things haven't changed.'

I sensed that Greg was ill at ease with my emotional issues, and was particularly keen not to talk about them in front of Alice. He asked Rosie not to film him until he felt more comfortable. Instead, he told us all about his travels while Alice filled the back seat, and Rosie's lap, with paper as she ripped open her numerous presents and exclaimed loudly about each one.

' . . . I finally got off to sleep,' he concluded as I took a wrong turning and drove towards Lourdes town centre, 'despite having five of us wedged into a seat for two, and even though the bus was speeding over potholes as if they weren't there at all. A little while later I woke up because someone was in my lap. It must have been three in the morning, and at first I thought someone had gone to sleep with their head on my legs. So I reached out to shove them off and it started bloody bleating at me.'

'Bleating?'

'A goat had climbed onto my lap, curled up, and gone to sleep, and I hadn't even noticed. Can you believe that? I couldn't. So I shouted at it and the woman next to me woke up, snatched her goat away, and slapped me. An actual slap across the bloody face! I think she thought I had no business being so rude to her animal. In spite of the fact that it was obviously on the bus to certain death at the market.'

Despite myself, I laughed. 'So you really got her goat,' I remarked.

'I did indeed.'

'Mummy!' came a shout from the back. 'A Barbie doll!'

I sighed. 'Oh, great. Who from?'

Rosie looked at the card. 'Charlotte.'

'She couldn't help herself,' Greg added.

Greg was outgoing, but also strangely self-contained. As a little boy he had lived under the thumb of three older sisters and a mother who ruled the household, while his father padded around the house, and stayed late at work, and lurked in his study. Until the age of about four, he had submitted to what had appeared to be his destiny: to be dressed up elaborately by Bella and inserted into any imaginative game she was foisting upon us all. He played the baby Jesus, a fairy, a posh lady, a chimney sweep, and several trees. He had taken the place of the Girls' World that Christa had refused to let us have, and had borne the brunt of make-up experimentation. Then, one day, he had refused. He had not been dramatic about it. Greg had never had tantrums. He simply declined, went to his room, and shut the door. Eventually, Bella had given up.

'OK,' I announced. 'Not quite sure which way to go here.' I was idling at a red light, behind an old-fashioned blue bus with a red cross in the back window and the words '*Transport des Malades*'. 'Hey, look,' I said, pointing. 'That's a huge ambulance.'

Greg sat up. 'Taking people to get cured. Cool.' He nodded approvingly. 'So we're not taking the bypass?'

'Not through choice. I've buggered it up.'

'You shouldn't have taken that right back there.'

'Thanks, Rosie.' I caught her eye in the rear-view mirror

and she smiled and shrugged. She was the cornerstone of my life. I knew I might regret the total access I had granted her, but at the same time I did not give a fuck.

The streets were busy with pedestrians, and I was tense about driving through this place. The street signs were too local, and they all pointed to places, like the caves and the town centre, that I would have preferred not to visit. I followed the road straight on, at random. The ambulance turned right. The street seemed to close in on me. People were walking on the road, paying no attention to the traffic. I knew that this was not a pedestrian street, because there were cars in front of me and behind me, but nobody on foot seemed aware of the fact that normal highway rules should have applied. As I inched the car along, an elderly man stopped by the kerb, looked me in the eye, and stepped straight out in front of my car. I gasped and performed an emergency stop. He frowned, shouted something at me, and waved the stump of an arm aggressively at me. I fought back the urge to yell back at him, to tell him that I was driving at no more than ten kilometres per hour, on a road. *I am not doing anything wrong*, I screamed internally. Leave me alone. My fingers gripped the steering wheel so hard that my skin went white and papery. I was breathing too quickly. I waited for the man and the woman with him, who looked embarrassed, to reach the other pavement. He glared back over his shoulder.

'Nice place,' I said as lightly as I could. I was holding myself together because Greg was next to me. He laughed, but I was scared. One cantankerous old man, who was suffering and on a pilgrimage to seek some sort of respite, had brought me to the brink of furious tears. That did not fill me with confidence about my future.

I looked back at Alice. Rosie was pointing her camera at me.

'Sorry,' she said, not looking sorry. 'Caught it all. This place on a Sunday is just irresistible.'

I followed a Slovakian coach around the town centre, driving at a snail's pace and frequently stopping altogether to let serious-faced pilgrims amble across the road.

'Interesting,' said Greg, staring out of the window. 'It's just like all pilgrimage sites. They all fill up like this, and they all have shops selling religious paraphernalia.' He peered at a shop window as we passed. 'Jesus Christ, some of this stuff is amazing. Look at that: *Approved by the Vatican*. Five years ago I'd have nicked that sign.'

'You still would if there weren't so many witnesses.'

'True. Might even try it now if I wasn't on celluloid.'

'Have you been to Mecca?' I asked, to take my mind off the fact that we seemed fated to spend Alice's third birthday driving around Lourdes, trapped in some sort of twilight zone of aggressive Catholic pilgrims.

He snorted. 'No. Saudi Arabia hasn't enormously appealed. I don't think a tourist visa would be easy to come by. And I'm sure they wouldn't let me near Mecca at hajj time unless I pretended to be a Muslim, and frankly, although I've got nothing against a good adventure, going to Mecca as a fake Muslim would be a tad *too* adventurous.'

'Even for you.'

Plan B

'Even for me. But I've been to less glamorous pilgrimage spots in India and south-east Asia, and the atmosphere is just like this. The roads here are better, though.'

I was uneasily following the bus across a bridge and up a hill. Although we had left the town centre behind, I did not think the coach driver was leading me to the mountains. Sure enough, it soon became clear that we were on the road to the caves where St Bernadette had had her visions of the Virgin. A quick U-turn took us back to the centre, which seemed to have filled up even more. We drove up a narrow street lined with shops selling Virgin Mary statues with flashing haloes, and Jesus clocks, and plastic bottles in various holy shapes. People sauntered down the middle of the road, either pretending not to notice us or possibly genuinely deaf. I felt my sanity slipping away again. I held tight to the wheel and silently asked the car to find its way out of town. Another big blue ambulance disgorged its passengers, who were shepherded onto the pavement by nurses dressed in starchy white uniforms. I saw one with a name badge reading 'Bernadette' and another reading 'Marie'.

'Real names probably Sharon and Tracy,' commented Greg. 'Or whatever the French equivalents are.'

'I'm not sure there is a French equivalent,' I mused. 'Not particularly. Hey, look!'

A green sign indicated the way to Pau. Although we had come from Pau, I surmised that this must be the way to the bypass, and, indeed, this proved to be the case. As I pulled onto the dual carriageway that led to the mountains, I smiled with huge relief at the sign with the word Lourdes crossed through. The Pyrenees stood, proud and beautiful, in front of us.

The mountain air was clear and cold. It smelt fresh and crisp, with the scent of different, unfamiliar flowers and herbs. We were all grateful to get out of the car and stretch our legs. Alice ran around us in mad, energetic circles. Rosie stretched her arms above her head, and Greg and I both looked at her toned midriff. After the drive, my legs felt strange. The mountains loomed over us, high and clear, lit by the sunlight, with a small amount of snow on top. It was much colder up here.

The cable car left from the centre of town, right next to where we had parked, and we rushed up a long curving ramp to the booth, keen to buy tickets and head up to the top of a mountain as soon as we could.

The sign read '*Fermé*'. All the lights were off, the place was deserted, and a smaller sign stated that the lift had closed on 5 September. It did not say when it was going to reopen.

I began to panic. We had come to the mountains because I wanted to do something exciting. I wanted Alice to experience the cable car, and the glorious sensation of leaving the earth behind and heading high into the sky. I wanted to experience all that myself. I wanted to stand on a mountain top and look down at France, and to appreciate how small I was and how insignificant my problems were. But I couldn't. I tried not to see the thwarting of my wishes as meaningful.

I looked up. The mountains towered ahead of us. I craned

my neck back. Small whirls of cloud swirled around the summit of the nearest peak. I tried not to cry. I longed to be up there, lost in the sky.

'So,' I said, trying to prompt Greg to say something.

'Hmm. Shame. I'll carry Alice if you want. We can have a bit of a walk. But we won't get very high and it's not going to be the same.'

'I should have checked.' My eyes had filled with tears, despite myself. I had messed up our big day. I could not shake the feeling that this setback was portentous. I looked down at Alice. 'Sorry,' I told her.

'That's OK, Mummy.' She skipped around me. 'I don't mind. Can we go up the mountain now?'

Greg and I looked at each other and smiled. It was a poor substitute for the team spirit I used to feel I shared with Matt, but the camaraderie with Greg was, at least, genuine. And the mountains stood impassively above us, sheer and inaccessible, with the smallest glint of snow right up at the summit. The sun was about to disappear behind a peak, but for the moment it was shining in our eyes. I smiled, contented again, with the tears still hanging in my eyes.

My mood swings were curious. I had never had them before. Sometimes I could be objective enough to find them quite interesting. The most interesting thing was how much I got away with. I had always assumed that if I were myself, everybody would hate me. It was beginning to dawn on me that this might not be the case.

'There's no point trying to walk anywhere,' I decided. 'Let's have a look round the village.'

It was a funny little place, nestling between mountains

on one side and perched high above the valleys on the other. It was shady and cold, then sunny and open. We wandered around, taken aback by the off-season atmosphere. There was hardly anybody there. The people we passed said a polite *bonjour* but seemed to be asking under their breath what on earth we were doing there. We must have made an odd group.

No shops were open. It was nearly lunchtime.

'Back to Lourdes?' Greg asked, raising his eyebrows.

'Never,' I said, too fervently.

'Can we have pizza and chips?' Alice asked.

'I'm not sure,' I admitted. 'Depends if anywhere's open.' As I spoke, we rounded a corner and emerged in the main square. This was, thankfully, geared up for tourists, even out of season. There were two restaurants, both of them open, as well as a newsagent, and three souvenir shops standing next to each other. A few people were sitting on benches in the weak sunlight. A woman walked past with a huge dog, and Alice held tightly to my leg until they were gone.

'It's still mine birthday!' she suddenly remembered. 'Let's buy me a present.'

We took her into a shop to buy some trinkets, emerging with a luridly decorated Pyrenees cup and two snow shakers for Alice, and one each for Greg and Rosie.

'Can we give this one to Daddy?' she asked brightly, brandishing her spare one.

'Of course,' I said, trying to be pleased that she was, at last, talking about Matt, when she had barely mentioned him for the past six weeks. I was torn in half by the normality of her request. Of course a little girl on her birthday, in the mountains with her mother and her uncle (and a film-maker), would want to pick up a present for her daddy. I hoped she would get the chance to give it to him.

As we waited to cross the road, Alice started singing, loudly. She sang happy birthday to herself, then moved on to other numbers in her repertoire. By the time we were outside the restaurants, she was halfway through 'Twinkle Twinkle Little Star'. I knew she was being loud, and I was pleased. I was always pleased by things that suggested she had not been crushed by events, as I had been at her age.

An elderly couple walked past and looked at us with obvious disapproval. The woman's mouth was pinched, and she tutted and shook her head. Her hair was short and brittle, her face absurdly over made-up. The man was hunched inside a raincoat, and looked as if he hated the world.

I could not catch what she said to him, but he nodded, and they both stared back at us, frowning. Alice stopped singing and watched me running after them.

'Excuse me,' I said, in my best French. I consciously tried to make my accent as good as it could be. The woman turned round and looked at me, displeased. 'Excuse me,' I continued, 'but I think you have a problem with my daughter singing on her birthday. What exactly is your problem?'

She tutted. 'There used to be standards of behaviour for children,' she said drily. 'In public, children should be quiet. That is, in France. Perhaps things are different where you come from.'

I shook my head. 'It's her birthday. She has lost her father. But she's happy today. I'm not going to stop her singing and nor is anyone else. I feel sorry for you if that's what you want.' It wasn't very eloquent, but it was the best I could do in the heat of the moment. I waited for the woman's face to soften, but it didn't. They turned and stalked off, so I called, '*Trous de cul!*' after them. Arseholes. I knew I had proved their point, but it felt wonderful.

We had a large birthday lunch in a fondue restaurant. Rosie insisted on paying, to my relief. Alice drank Orangina, and the adults shared a bottle of good red wine, though I only had a couple of mouthfuls because I was both driving and taking antidepressants. Greg and Rosie finished the bottle easily, and ordered another. I was jealous of their instant intimacy.

Alice took to fondue as if she had been eating it all her life. She picked the fork with the blue spot on it, and carefully twisted it round and round to scoop up all the stringy cheese.

'I like this fondue a *lot*,' she said, every time she got a mouthful, and I resolved to buy a fondue set for the house. I knew we would probably move away from France before we used it, but I reasoned that we could always take it to England with us, put it at the back of a cupboard, and forget about it for fifteen years.

The restaurant rustled up three candles which stood, precariously upright, in the floating part of her *Ile Flottante* pudding. Some other diners even joined us in a round of '*Joyeux Anniversaire*'.

'I'm happy you're here,' she said to Greg, giving him a sticky kiss as she finished her pudding. 'Are you going to make Mummy happy again?'

I stared at her. 'Mummy's happy,' I said and I knew as I said it that I was being unconvincing. I sniffed heavily and blinked several times.

'Well,' said Greg, ignoring me and looking earnestly at Alice. 'I think between us we can make your mummy pretty happy. But it's quite complicated. Mummy's doing really well and she loves you very much, so she's all right really. Everything's all right.'

As we stood up from the table, he said, under his breath, 'The fucking bastard.' He looked at Rosie. 'And you can quote me on that.'

While I still felt dazed and half dead, Greg was a tonic. I knew it was good for me to have someone in the house, because I often wished he wasn't there. He stopped me wallowing, and made me get on with the routine things. Greg didn't notice if I forgot to brush my hair for a week, if I never bothered to shower or if I drank too much coffee. But he did frown if Alice was late for school or if I announced that we were all having toast and jam for dinner. With him around, we all ate three times a day, and I managed not to go out looking like a bag lady very often. Watching the development of his romance with Rosie took my mind off my own troubles, and I was constantly trying not to say anything cynical to either of them.

'You're much less bossy than Bella was,' I told him one day. He looked surprised.

'Good!' he said. 'I would be a little put out to be told I was more bossy than the woman known throughout north London as Gengha Khan.' Greg had called Bella Gengha throughout his teenage years, to her fury. He had sat back and smiled his lazy smile, knowing that with every protest, scream and threat she was reinforcing his point.

'I mean,' I told him, 'Bella was great. She pulled me out of myself just in time.'

'I know. But she's bossy as fuck. And annoying. And, I don't know, I'm on strange territory here because I know nothing, but maybe she, like, should have let you go to pieces. Maybe you might have needed it. I don't think that trying to be superwoman when you feel as crap as you obviously do is necessarily the thing.' He looked away, embarrassed.

I tried to think about what he had said. 'I don't know,' I told him. 'I was in pieces for a few weeks. It wasn't just Bella who kept me going. It was your mum and dad, too. Specially Geoff. He tried to take me to London. I wanted to stay here. I couldn't have gone to London.'

'Then they could have found you somewhere else to go with more support. Having a kid to look after is such a responsibility. It must make you internalise things because you've got so much to do to get through the day. I just don't think that internalising things like this is the way to deal with them.'

I shook my head. 'I'm not internalising,' I told him. 'I'm struggling through the days. You're right, I do feel like crap, but that's good. I've never felt like this before, so raw, because up till now I've bottled it all up. This is me in pieces, Greg. And it's all right.'

After eating, Greg would sometimes lean back and put his socked feet up on the table, to Alice's delighted horror.

'Greg!' she would squeal. 'It's *naughty* to put your feet on the table!' She would give me a sideways glance to check my reaction, then put her feet up too. Reluctantly, I would tell them both to sit up properly. I began to enjoy my role as the responsible adult. It made me feel like Bella, like a proper grown-up.

Rosie turned up extremely regularly while Greg was around. I kept expecting to find her in the bathroom in the morning, wearing one of Greg's big T-shirts. Rosie's camera was perpetually trained on him. He would turn and make faces, or roar at her, or flick her the finger. She loved it.

The builders, meanwhile, were aiming to finish by Christmas. Most weekdays, my house teemed with friendly men in overalls, and at the end of each day I would derive some level of satisfaction from the tangible changes that had taken place. One day they arrived at six and started putting the long-awaited windows into the back of the house. By the time I came back from dropping Alice at school, the downstairs two were in. By the time I picked her up, the whole back wall boasted five brand new wooden windows. We were finally airtight. I liked things like that, things I could see happening.

The masons worked, and made the house so dusty that I would change Alice from her pyjamas into her school clothes at the front door, to minimise the risk of her brushing against anything. If she did brush against a wall, I would have to grab something from the ironing pile and smooth it down against her body, telling myself she looked tidy enough. Nonetheless, the changes to the masonry were quick and satisfying. The fireplace was soon reworked; it lost its ugly stone cladding and was moved up to a foot off the ground, with a niche for logs underneath it.

'It would make the room smoky otherwise,' the mason explained. 'Now you have your new windows, there won't be any draughts.'

The new, improved fire heated the sitting room beautifully, and the three of us, or, often, the four of us, spent our evenings there, huddled round the fire, roasting chestnuts.

Then, just as suddenly as they had started, the builders stopped work. When they did turn up, they would mention waiting for materials, or the fact that the plasterer was behind schedule. Some of the upstairs floors had been replaced. The local pine floorboards were pale and new, with a certain MFI quality to them, and I knew that I needed to stain them. There was rubble everywhere. Some electric sockets worked, and others did not. Many walls were crisscrossed with snakes of blue plastic, which carried wires to the approximate positions of future light switches and sockets, and stopped abruptly. After the electrician's burst of autumn activity, I had two working sockets downstairs, and three upstairs. We managed surprisingly well with a tangle of extension leads that Greg and I worked out together. Occasionally, the electricity supply would give up, but we had torches waiting in all appropriate spots, and I was easily able to light my way around the house unplugging unnecessary appliances, then to the fuse box to flick the switch back up. In fact, I had previously had no idea that things like that were so easy. The builders stopped talking about finishing before Christmas.

Plan B

Rosie was so pleased with the access I was giving her that she told me I should think about getting more TV work.

'You're actually a bit of a natural,' she told me. 'You really know how to relax in front of the lens.'

'I'm not a natural,' I told her, 'I'm just too tired to give a fuck.'

'You swore again!' she said, with an admiring nod. 'You never seemed the type before.'

One morning, early in November, I dropped Alice at school. I always had a rush of wellbeing after taking her into the classroom. I loved the way she instantly switched to French when we arrived. Her teacher had told me that Alice's French was now so fluent that she treated her exactly like a French child.

After leaving her, I drove home, trying to ignore the gnawing emptiness. Only the fact that I knew that Greg was waiting for me with coffee stopped me from driving and driving, at random, until something happened.

I stepped over the threshold and called, 'Hi!' Greg's voice answered from upstairs. I heard his footsteps bounding down, louder and closer by the second, until he was standing in front of me.

'Hey, Ems,' he said cheerfully. 'Some guy just called for you.'

'French?'

'English. He said he'd ring back later.'

My heart was suddenly thumping. I clasped my hands together to stop them trembling.

'Was it Matt?' I asked, as steadily as I could. I had been waiting for him to get in touch about the practical things.

I felt I had been waiting forever. It seemed he had abandoned us entirely. Sometimes I wanted to ring him, but I could not bear the idea of speaking to Jo or, indeed, to him. I had no idea how I would feel if I heard his voice. He had left me in no doubt about the fact that I had never meant anything to him.

Greg smiled and shook his head. 'Definitely not. He wouldn't say who he was. Said he'd call back tonight. Anyway, I've made a plan. Let's go to the beach and hire surfboards.' He looked at me expectantly. I forced a little smile at him. Greg was scarcely more than two years younger than me, but usually I felt that he was eighteen and I was about fifty-five. Today, he was wearing a pair of yellow cotton trousers that flapped halfway down his shins, and a T-shirt with the Red Bull symbol on it and some Thai writing. It was unusually warm this particular morning, but still, he must have been freezing.

'Nice idea.' I was not really concentrating 'I've got so much on today. Tell you what, let's plan a beach day. We can take Alice again. Wednesday?'

Greg stepped closer. 'I think today's the day, actually. Alice is a great kid but I want you to have some fun without being a mummy. Geoff said you wanted to surf. You said you wanted to surf. You said Matt laughed at you for wanting to surf. So, hey? Alice is in school till half four. It's not even half nine. I'll drive. Rosie's in Bordeaux today so it's just us.'

'I . . .' I tried to think of a valid objection. 'I was going to rake the leaves,' I said, lamely. 'And the builders might need me.' I looked around. I could hear the masons hammering in the old kitchen, making it ready for the new one which was due two weeks ago.

'They don't need you. And I'll rake the leaves if you really think it's essential. Tomorrow. *Mañana*.' He took the car keys out of my hand and set off back towards the car. 'Got your handbag? I've sorted everything else.'

I started trying to put on my wetsuit awkwardly, under the cover of a towel. The beach was far less busy than it had ever been over the summer. There was really no point in being coy.

'Look away,' I instructed Greg, and I stripped off and stepped, naked, into the wetsuit. It was much easier that way.

I knew I was bony, now. Parts of my skeleton jutted out where they had never jutted before. Yet, somehow, I still had a wobbly, untoned stomach, and huge thighs and an enormous bottom that stayed cold long after the rest of me had warmed up.

I looked, again, out to sea. There were some clouds building on the horizon. Around twenty surfers were out beyond where the waves were breaking. The waves were big and splashy. They would knock me down instantly.

'I think I'd be better off watching,' I told Greg casually.

'Bollocks will you,' he answered equably. He picked up his board, held it under his arm, and walked towards the sea. I watched for a moment, then picked mine up and followed him. I felt self-conscious, pretending to be a surfer, but I also felt liberated. Look! I wanted to shout. Look at me! And the great thing was that nobody did look at me, because Mimizan beach was always full of surfers, and I was blending in with them. My stride became more purposeful.

There was a sprinkling of people on the beach. Some walked dogs. Others changed into wetsuits; and a few people just sat on the sand, wrapped up in fleeces and scarves, and looked at the sea. Nobody noticed Greg and me. If they were aware of us, it was just as another couple of surfers. I was always jealous when I saw people in wetsuits walking past, heading with purpose for the shore. Surfers looked careless. They never looked worried. They never seemed to be thinking about broken relationships built on lies, or single parenthood, or the fact that their money was running out. They never appeared to be missing mothers they had barely known. They just seemed to live in the moment.

I decided that, while I was in the water, I would do my best to live in the moment too. Looking at the size of the waves, I believed I would have no choice.

We stopped at the edge. Shallow water was lapping around my bare feet.

'Right,' I said, with a nervous laugh. 'What now?'

'OK. We'll take it slowly. First of all, let's get wet. Just for fun.'

Greg and I left our boards on the sand and walked into the sea together. When I reached the point where the water was past my knees, I began to feel extremely nervous. I could feel the current dragging at me and I remembered the scary exhilaration of the previous time this had happened. We stepped a little further and the waves were suddenly breaking on us. I jumped over them, laughing despite myself. When a huge wave was heading towards me, I leapt as high as I could, and felt myself being carried up, while my legs disappeared from underneath me. I flapped around, trying to regain balance, then gave up and let the water carry me in towards the shore. My head dipped underwater and I spun around, but before I could panic, my whole body scraped along sand, and I was thoroughly beached. It was less frightening than it had been the previous time. Laughing, I got up.

'OK,' I told Greg. 'Wet. Now what?'

'Now,' he said, 'we sit down.' We sat together on the sand. I was surprised at this development and watched my brother, my cousin, quizzically to see how he planned to teach me to surf sitting on the beach.

'Right. Look at these guys out there.' I followed the direction of his finger and gazed at the black figures beyond breaking point. One of them paddled furiously and was suddenly, miraculously, standing on his board. We watched him surfing in, halfway towards the shore, before he fell off. His board flew in one direction, and his head popped up next to it.

'I wish I could do that,' I sighed.

'You can. Now, let's watch them properly. You see them all sitting there, looking at the horizon? What are they looking at?'

'Waves.'

'Yes. There's a nice set coming through.'

'What's a set?'

'It's a group of waves. They come in sets. Right. These guys are all jockeying for position. They're trying to get to the best point, where the most obvious peak of the wave is going to be. There's a lot of unspoken rules about who gets to go when but don't worry about them for now. See? This guy's there.' Greg pointed. 'He's got it, the best place. He's going for it. See, he's turning, facing the beach, paddling away from the wave to pick up speed. Right. See that? He's got up on his feet.'

'How did he know when to do that?'

'When your board goes from flat to vertical. It's easy to jump up then. And there he is. Dropping down the face of the wave. And a tight bottom turn. Very nice. So he's bringing the board right the way round and now he's facing back up. See that? He stuck his hand in the water to give him a bit of support. Nice. And he's back up. There. He kicked off the top of the lip. And he's cruising back down. That's a nice wide bottom turn so the white water doesn't get too close. And a lovely finish. There you go.'

He was looking at me expectantly.

'Wow,' I said. 'OK. Can you do that?'

'On a good day, yeah.'

'Really?'

Greg smiled at me. 'It's the greatest feeling in the world. And I have to say, you live impressively close to the best surf in Europe.'

We went into the water, to waist depth. Greg left his board on the sand.

'OK,' he said. 'Here we go. Lie down on the board.'

I made a couple of false jumps, falling back into the water, but got up there in the end. I lay on my stomach, already feeling like a professional.

'Great stuff,' said Greg. 'There's some white water coming now. It'll be a bit bouncy.'

'Bouncy?' I was regretting this.

'Yes. But you'll feel the surge when the wave comes and you'll feel the power take you. Now when I say paddle, you need to paddle hard. Once you feel the board being taken along, taken by the wave power not by your arm power, then you need to jump to your feet.' I nodded. 'OK,' he said suddenly. 'Paddle!'

I started splashing around with my hands. The wave picked me up and left me behind. I frowned. This was not how it was supposed to be.

'That wasn't paddling,' Greg said sternly. 'Let's try again. Your arms are supposed to be working here. They're supposed to hurt like hell tomorrow. Give it a proper paddle this time. Right, go! Paddle!'

I paddled as hard as I could. This time I was carried along for half a second before the wave surged out from underneath me and left me staring after it. The next time I fell off as soon as it reached me. Then I managed a reasonable paddle. Then I tried standing up, and fell in. Then I did the same thing twenty more times. I was wet and my face was frozen, and I was completely failing to stand on my board, and I was happy.

'OK,' Greg announced. 'We're going down the beach. Over there, where they're breaking.'

I followed him down the sand, and paddled out to waist depth, again. Again, I paddled unsuccessfully for wave after wave. Again I fell in and got a face full of water. Again, I came up wanting to try again.

In the end, it came. I paddled as hard and fast as I could for a wave, and when the board surged forward and began to tip down, Greg yelled, 'Stand up!' I got to my feet and threw my arms out to the sides. I had scarcely had time to realise that I was standing when Greg shouted: 'Lean down on your front foot!'

I took my weight off my back foot, and felt the back of the board being swept round. I was almost parallel to the wave. For five long seconds, I felt myself gliding along, standing on the water. It was by far the best thing I had ever done.

I relived that moment on a loop for the rest of the day. I was too thrilled to mind that, while we were out, the builders had taken up the hall tiles and left the floor as bumpy earth. I barely noticed the mud that we trampled all over the new upstairs floorboards. As I read Alice her school library book, I was standing on my wave. I had never imagined that I would be able to do it, let alone on my first day. All my thoughts were focused on doing it again. I wanted to buy my own board. I wanted to surf several times a week. I wanted to get good. It had been a very long time since I had been excited by anything. In fact, I had never been unguardedly enthusiastic about anything in my life before, least of all a physical activity.

Alice's book was called *Belle la Coccinelle* and, on her orders, I was translating it from French to English as I went along. This made for a clunky and bizarre bedtime story but Alice didn't seem to care. She never let me read to her in French. I guessed it was because my accent wasn't acceptable. She was cuddled up against me, sucking her thumb.

Greg's head appeared round the door. 'Em! Phone. It's that same bloke again.'

Plan B

I looked at Alice. 'Can Greg finish the story?'

She nodded, and I passed him the book. Greg took one look at the page.

'This is in French! Can't I read you something else?'

'Yes. You can read *The Snail and the Whale*.'

'Sounds more my scene.'

I left them leaning back on Alice's *Toy Story* pillow and settling in to a new book. The cordless phone was on the floor outside the bedroom door, and I picked it up with trepidation.

'Hello?' I asked it, almost whispering.

'Emma. Pete.'

I padded downstairs and shut myself in the dining room, which was both cold and dark. It was currently doubling as a temporary kitchen, while we waited for the perpetually delayed arrival of the new one. It had a fridge, microwave and kettle, though no water supply. 'I thought it had to be you,' I said, nervous and angry and unsure how to handle myself. I told myself to stay in control of my feelings. The surf had made me confident, and I knew I could easily be very, very nasty to Pete.

'You weren't expecting Matt? I don't want to disappoint you.'

'No, Pete,' I told him crisply. 'It's gone a bit beyond disappointment.' I opened the fridge, the phone held between shoulder and ear, and took out the wine. I thought that a little bit could do me no harm.

'I'm just calling to say I'm sorry about what's happened. I really am.'

'Cheers for telling me what he was up to,' I said as I

poured myself a large glass, then tried to decant half of it back into the bottle. I stepped out of the front door and sat down at the outside table, shivering. 'Thanks for making me look so stupid.' My eyes filled with tears and I did everything I could to control my voice. I took a large gulp of wine. 'You obviously knew all along and you didn't say a word. You must have enjoyed it.'

'It was hard not to tell you but it wasn't up to me.'

'Right. Your mate acts, well, like Matt – Hugh – has acted, like a wanker, and you're the only one who knows – were you the only one?' He grunted affirmatively. 'And you decide it's not up to you to warn me. Pete, that speaks volumes about your character, and no justification you may invent after the event is going to change that.'

He paused for a moment. I wondered where he was, whether he still lived in Brighton. 'We have some history, don't we, you and I?' he said after a while. 'I didn't want either of you to think I had any agenda of my own going on. My best bet was to stand back and not get involved.'

'It's not really *history*, though, is it? You had a crush on me for a while because you thought it was cool that I was an orphan. You never actually knew me, you just projected stuff onto me. You made a dramatic gesture and got over it. That's not frankly something that should have stopped you doing the decent thing.' I stopped myself. Nothing I said now would change anything. I needed to do what was best for Alice, which was to extract information. 'Is Matt going to contact us?' I asked. 'Call me naïve but I had a crazy idea that he might like to keep in touch with his daughter.'

'He misses her. He doesn't want to bother you.'

'He's too thoughtful. So kind of him not to bother her with a present or a card or a phone call on her birthday.'

'Didn't he?'

'No.'

'You're right, that's crap. He's a wanker. He doesn't want to bother Jo either so he's only seeing Olly every other Saturday. I think he's assuming that when you and Alice move back to Brighton he'll be able to make some kind of arrangement then.'

I looked up at the bare branches of the cherry tree, silhouetted against the dark grey sky.

'Jo kicked him out?' I asked.

'He jumped before he was pushed.' Pete laughed briefly. 'Jo wasn't impressed with me either, actually, when she realised that I'd known. First she was outraged with Hugh on my behalf for having a thing with "Pete's Emma", as she kept calling you. She thought Hugh was lying when he told her I'd known all along. Then she realised that I really had. I don't think she's going to speak to me again.'

'Pete, Matt always told me that he didn't speak to his parents. He said he was estranged from them but he wouldn't tell me what had happened. Looking back at it all now, I guess that's a lie. He was stringing me along, wasn't he, telling me he had no family because he couldn't introduce me to them because they all loved his wife?'

Pete snorted. 'I'm sure they would be extremely surprised, and indeed rather confused, to hear that they were estranged from Hughie. He's the golden boy. There's a lot of them. He's got a younger sister as well as, well, his little brother. Emma, you've met his parents. You just never realised that was who they were.'

I put my glass down. 'What? When?'

'Just after university.'

'I didn't know Matt at university.'

'I know you didn't. But you knew his brother.'

'Did I?'

'Work with me here. I'm trying to tell you something. Do I have to spell it out? You knew me, back when I was Po. Obviously being Po is not something I ever shout about these days. Let's not go back over all of that. But when I did that stupid thing, at your house, you met my parents at the hospital, didn't you?'

I got up and stood by the gate. It was almost dark now. A green tractor passed, and I waved to Patrick. He didn't see me standing in the dusky shade. 'Your parents were really nice.' I thought about it. 'You had an older brother and you were annoyed about living in his shadow.'

'That's the one.'

'You're Matt's brother?'

'I generally call him Hugh.'

'You're Alice's uncle.'

'Yes.'

'And Olly's uncle.'

'Indeed. Hence I get it in the neck from you and from Jo.'

'Why the hell didn't you both tell me that before? Why was *that* a secret? God, you are one fuck of a twisted family.'

'Because Hugh asked me not to. And as the little brother with the inferiority complex, I did as I was told.'

'So you met me again in Brighton, and you introduced me to your married brother and stood back while he started an affair with me without telling me that he had a wife. At what point did he ask you not to mention that you were brothers?'

The outline of Greg appeared in the doorway. I drained my glass and held it out to him for a refill.

Pete sounded strained. 'Well, straightaway, obviously. Do you remember?' I did remember. I remembered that, after walking over to introduce himself, Matt had said he was visiting his friend Pete. Po had come over and we had said hello. I had not taken much notice of him. I never did.

'I moved to Brighton because you were there,' Pete said quickly. 'I knew you were there because I phoned your aunt and uncle and said I was a university friend. They said you were living in Brighton. So I went there too. Sorry about that. I just wanted to be close to you. I used to walk around town at weekends and look out for you. I knew you'd be walking by the sea. I would walk by the sea as well. We used to bump into each other, didn't we?'

'Yes. And you would be all chatty and happy. You'd tell me about your girlfriend.'

'Funny, isn't it? I had an imaginary girlfriend and Hugh had the opposite. He had a secret wife. I had no women and he had two. So yes, you're thinking I wasn't over you after all, and you'd be right. I didn't get over you for years.' He was speaking briskly, his tone businesslike. 'So one day Hugh was in town and I took him to the Boardwalk for a coffee because that's just where you take people, isn't it? And there you were. I remember saying to him, look, over there, that's Emma. And he said, *the* Emma? Heartbreak Emma? So I said yes, and straightaway he said, "She looks nice. I'm going to say hello." I felt sick because I knew what he was like.'

'Which was?'

'Persuasive. Immoral. Adulterous.' I shivered. My Matt was persuasive, but it made me cringe to hear that he had been immoral and adulterous even before he met me. 'So I said, *don't*, and he laughed and said he was just having fun, and that I wasn't to say he was my brother. He said he was going to use his middle name. And of course I went along with that, even though I hated it, because I've always done what Hugh said.'

'Pete?' The anger was bubbling inside me and I didn't think I could stop it coming up.

'Mmm?'

'Pete, you are one sad, pathetic fuck. You know that. Are you over me now?'

'Yep.'

'Really?'

'I'm living with my girlfriend. Jane. She's really nice.'

'But do you still have this twisted and just *weird* obsession with me? Do you?'

'What do you mean? I'm living with Jane.'

'So if I said, oh, Pete, but I need you to drop everything and come to France and comfort me, and maybe now that everything's out in the open we can see if a relationship between you and me might work out after all. If I said that, you'd turn me down?' He did not reply. 'I thought not.'

'Do you mean it?'

'Of course I don't mean it.' I was shouting. 'Pete, you *doormat*. You are the only person I know who's made more of a mess of their life than I have. Pete, *you* ruined my life. It was you. You went all weird at me at uni, and if anything was going to put me off having anything to do with blokes, it was you. *You* made me think I'd never attract anyone except nutters. You followed me to Brighton. You introduced me to your vile brother, you sad tosser. You stood by and watched everything he did. You are the saddest, most masochistic, most pathetic loser I've ever met.'

The pause stretched out. I watched the clouds rushing across the sky. Above my head, the few remaining leaves of the cherry tree rustled ominously. It was about to rain. I opened the door to the hall, picked my way carefully across the exposed earth and sat on the stairs. I was not sure what else to say, so I waited for Pete to respond. After a while I started to think he had hung up on me.

'I'm sorry,' he said at last. 'I'm really sorry. You're completely right. I've screwed up. I have no life. I'm only with Jane because she took pity on me. I don't love her. I don't even find her attractive.'

'I don't care,' I told him. 'Really, I couldn't care less.'

'Right. I am sorry, though. I do love you, so I should have done what was best for you. I suppose I was a bit hurt that nothing I did was ever going to make you interested in me, but you went off with my brother without looking back.'

'I wouldn't have done if I'd known the facts.'

'So I kept the facts from you. I suppose I was waiting for it all to go wrong in the hope that I might feel better then. I wanted you to hate Hugh more than you hated me, and I wanted you to regret ever talking to him.'

'At which point I would turn to you for comfort?'

'In my dreams.'

'So why are you ringing me?'

'I don't know. To see if we can cut my brother out of this loop, I think. My folks haven't heard any of it yet but they will. They're upset that Hugh and Jo split up. They're good people even if they did spawn two psychos. I know that if they knew about Alice, they'd want to be in her life. So I'm asking you if I can tell them, and if I do, whether I could bring them to see you so they can meet their granddaughter. We'll stay in a hotel,' he added quickly. 'You won't have to see me on my own. Or they could come without me if you prefer. I just thought it might be easier if I was there to introduce you.'

I could barely answer. I was tired and upset, and I wanted to go to bed.

'OK,' I told him without enthusiasm.

Alice was going to acquire some more grandparents. She already had Christa and Geoff. In a strange way, my mother was in our lives again, too. When I had put her picture up beside my bed, Alice had pounced on it.

'Who's that?' she had said.

'It's Granny Sarah,' I'd told her. 'My mummy. She's dead.'

I had spent so much time terrified of the day Alice found out about death. In fact, she had accepted it quite equably.

chapter thirty

Hugh sat on a stool by the bar and nursed his vodka and tonic while he watched the room. Christmas parties had always been good to him. He had enjoyed the chance to be out with colleagues, to get properly drunk, and to forget about the logistics of his life. Now his life had no logistics. He reminded himself that this was good, that he was free, now, to do exactly what he wanted.

The party was in a bar near the office. The room was already crowded, and it was hot and smoky. He took off his jacket and hung it awkwardly over the back of his stool. Then he loosened his tie. He scanned the dance floor. There were plenty of people here whom he had never seen before. He tried to dredge up some interest in talking to any of them.

After a while, he knocked back his drink, bought another one, and stepped down from his stool. Nobody had come to talk to him, so he was going to have to find someone to speak to. He was going to have to be proactive. He had no idea how many of his colleagues knew about his private life. Some of them did, so that probably meant all of them.

He took his tie off altogether. It was a purple tie, shiny, that Jo had got for him. He had always liked it. Now, he slid it into his pocket and ran his fingers through his hair. He headed straight for a girl he had noticed. She was little. A bit too little for him, really. She could only be five feet tall, if that. Her build was minuscule. What drew him to her was the waist-length blonde hair that she threw around with a toss of her head as she danced. She had huge blue eyes. As he got closer, he noted that, although she was small, she had breasts. She turned and smiled at him.

'Hello!' she said, in a little girl's voice.

'Hi,' he told her, feeling gruff and manly in comparison. 'I'm Hugh.'

'Hello, Hugh!' she almost squealed. 'I'm Sandy!'

He felt himself beginning to relax. Something told him that Sandy wouldn't be interested in settling him down and having his child.

'My real name's Alexandra,' she confided, after he bought her a drink. 'My family used to call me Alex but when I was about twelve I decided that Sandy was more me!' She looked at him expectantly.

'It suits you,' he told her. He laughed and she joined in, uncertainly. 'So, Sandy,' he continued. 'Do you work at Johnsons?'

She nodded. 'Mmmm-hmmm! I certainly do! I know you do because I've seen you. That sounds silly, doesn't it? Sorry. I've just noticed you about, that's all.'

'No,' he said, leading her to a quiet corner. 'It doesn't sound silly at all.'

He was making all the right moves, saying all the right

things. He wondered if he had to go through with this, now that he had started it. He wondered whether she could tell that his heart wasn't in it, that he would rather be anywhere but here.

chapter thirty-one

Jo took a deep breath and walked into the bar. She looked around. Every second of this was excruciating. The bar was packed with groups of people. They were laughing in her face, parading their stupid happiness.

She had not known what to wear this evening. She had settled on a black dress which almost reached her knees, with a plain black coat and medium heels. Now she felt frumpy. All the other women were in teeny tops, and they all had their thighs on show, whatever the state of them. But she could hardly have turned up on a blind date looking like that. It would have implied all sorts of things that weren't true.

She pushed through groups, towards the bar. 'Excuse me,' she said, in a small voice. 'Excuse me. Excuse me. Could I just . . . ?' People shifted resentfully. Nobody looked at her. Jo was used to having people looking at her. But she was not used to being single. Being a single 25-year-old with no baggage had been wonderful. Every encounter had been laden with possibilities. Now she was thirty-five and she had a son. And she wanted to turn round and walk out.

Plan B

He was sitting at the bar, as he had said he would be. She knew it was him because he was wearing a red rosebud in his lapel. She stood next to him and tapped his shoulder. He looked up at her. At least he had the decency to look like his internet profile picture.

'Jo?' He had to shout to be heard above the music. She nodded.

'You're Malcolm,' she yelled back.

'Shall we go somewhere quieter?'

She nodded and they pushed their way back through the crowd. The street outside was quiet, and cold. Malcolm motioned down the road with his head.

'There's a sports bar this way. Should be OK maybe?'

Her heart sank. 'I know a nice pub this way. Does good food.'

He shook his head. 'Nah. Let's do the sports bar. I wouldn't mind seeing a bit of the footy if they've got it on.'

Jo had decided in advance that she was not going to waste a single evening, that if there wasn't a flicker of a spark, she was going to walk away.

'Actually, Malcolm,' she said, 'why don't you go and see the footy. I might give it a miss. Nice to have met you, though.' She walked briskly towards the main road, hoping to hail a taxi, aware of his eyes following her.

'Crazy woman!' he yelled at her back.

chapter thirty-two

Christmas Day

The doorbell rang. Greg, Charlotte and I looked at each other and laughed. The doorbell had been in place for three weeks. Nobody had used it, apart from us. Alice had pressed it incessantly for five days and had then forgotten about it. Callers still tended to stand and shout, or just to walk in.

'It's Martine,' I said, smiling as I opened the door. 'Come in, please. Merry Christmas!' She stepped into the hall and looked around, raising her eyebrows and nodding at the improvements. I noticed the presents from Alice's stocking all over the floor, and pushed some aside with my foot. We exchanged kisses and Martine handed Alice a small parcel.

'Just a little present,' she said.

'*Merci*,' said Alice, with a shy smile. She took it off into the corner and opened it.

I looked at Martine. She had been delighted when I had invited her over on Christmas Day. Even though her son and his family were coming for lunch, she had managed to come for an aperitif once she got the meat in the oven. Martine was a widow, and she knew everybody. It had never occurred to me that she might be lonely, and I vowed to call in on her more often.

Greg fetched four glasses of champagne. Martine giggled and put her hand over her mouth. It was half past eleven in the morning. I noticed that she had dressed up. She was wearing a brown and red printed dress, shoes with small heels, and lipstick. She sipped her champagne and imparted village gossip, which was not extensive. Apparently, Patrick and Mathilde's younger son had just told them he was gay, but they were not heartbroken. There was going to be a new priest. Did I know whether the English woman in Aurillon was still seeing Didier? Valerie was very upset.

I wished I had made an effort to buy something smart to wear. Everyone else looked wonderful. Alice was beautiful in a pink dress that Charlotte had brought out for her. It was Armani and she claimed to have bought it on eBay for a pittance, though I didn't believe her. Charlotte, of course, was dressed to impress in a long corduroy skirt that followed the contours of her thighs before spreading out in what I thought might be called a fishtail style. This was pink, too, as was the tight knitted top she wore with it. Her hair was loose and sleek down her back. She and Alice looked like a mother and daughter from a clothing catalogue. Even Greg had managed to buy himself a pair of warm cords at the market, and he had teamed it with one of Matt's old shirts. He looked surprisingly presentable.

I, on the other hand, had managed to remember not to wear my jeans. The black trousers I had got from Gap were a bit bobbly now, and they were far too big, but I was wearing them anyway as I had nothing better. The smartest top I had been able to find was a red and white maternity shirt, which was quite pretty but unmistakably baggy. I knew I looked weird. The clothes drowned me, and made me look almost anorexic.

'A chocolate Santa!' cried Alice, smiling at us all.

'Father Christmas,' I corrected her. I didn't know where she had picked up 'Santa'. Probably from one of her numerous DVDs.

'*Merci beaucoup*,' she said to Martine. 'Can I eat him now?'

Charlotte and Greg turned expectantly to me for my pronouncement.

'You can eat a bit of him now,' I told her. 'But try not to get your dress all chocolatey, hey?'

Greg and I took Martine around the house. She had known the house since she was a girl, and so she was better placed than anyone to comment on the changes. It was not, of course, finished, but we now had more than half of it habitable. The electricity wires were embedded in the walls, and many of the walls were plastered. The new kitchen was in, and the dishwasher had been connected two days previously.

'*Mais . . . c'est super!*' she said, looking at the oak units, the granite worktop and the Smeg cooker. I was almost embarrassed. I started explaining about the British housing market and the spare cash it had given me, but she was not interested. And I was well aware that the spare cash was almost spent, so I put it from my mind.

Then I led her into the new dining room. The back of the house, which had been dark, windowless and uninhabitable, was now a huge, tiled room, with two wooden supports running from floor to ceiling, like pillars, to hold it up. The ceiling was low and wooden, and supported by oak beams. The warm terracotta tiles made me realise how dusty and dirty the old ones had been. We had dragged the dining table in there that morning, and Greg, who had plenty of experience as a waiter, had already laid seven places for lunch. He had folded paper napkins, put side plates on the correct sides, and had placed the large candlestick in the middle of the table. There were several wine glasses each, because Andy had announced that he would bring different wine for different courses.

Martine stood and stared. She let her breath out in a huge sigh. Then she looked at me and smiled.

'You have done very well,' she said. 'When you consider what has happened . . . I'm proud of you.'

'It's just a shame,' I told her, 'that now I have to sell it.'

Christa and Geoff had both tried their hardest to get Alice and me to come to Holloway for Christmas. I had refused to entertain the idea. I knew that Christmas was going to be difficult, but I was almost excited about it, too. At least this year no one was lying to me. I remembered Christmases past. Each of the previous four Christmases was tainted by the knowledge that, if Matt had been with us, he had been sneaking away to call Jo and Oliver. Last year, he had been with us in Brighton. I wondered where he had been pretending to be. I could imagine him, out in my back yard, leaning into the wall to avoid being overheard.

'Darling, it's me!' he would have said. 'Hot here in Hong Kong. And miserable. Sorry it didn't work out for you to come too. I'll make it up to you both when I come back.'

Then he would have slipped back into the house, and picked Alice up for a tickle.

The year before that, he had been unavoidably absent on a trip to Tel Aviv.

'They don't have Christmas there,' he'd told me. 'It's just another working day, and we need the contract. I'm so sorry. I'll make it up to you afterwards.' And he had called us from Tel Aviv, and he had even brought us back lots of duty free presents. No souvenirs of Israel, I recalled. He had bought me perfume and chocolates, and Alice a toy plane and some British Airways teddies. You could pick them up anywhere.

That Tel Aviv year, I had taken Alice to Christa and Geoff's for Christmas. Matt had suggested that I invite my family to Brighton instead. Now I knew why. He had been in Highgate. Alice and I had been in Holloway. That was far too close for safety. I imagined him refusing a Christmas walk on the Heath, and Jo asking him why. I remembered the first year we were together. He and I had spent New Year in Holloway. He had been jumpy and uncomfortable, and I had thought it was because he was shy at meeting my family. Perhaps he was, but it could not have helped that his wife was a few miles away.

Once I started thinking along these lines, the floodgates invariably opened. I made an effort to stop, and fetched the champagne to give everyone a refill.

Lunch was enormous, delicious, and lazy, just as Christmas lunch was supposed to be. Rosie turned up just before two, as instructed, and slipped her arms round Greg's waist.

'How's the chef?' she asked.

He stroked her hair. 'Wonderful. Even better now you're here.'

Andy coughed. 'You two! Some of us are trying to be jaded. Stop being in love.'

I looked at Andy. He looked at Fiona, and away. She frowned slightly.

'Is it ready?' I asked brightly.

Greg nodded. 'Mmm-hmm. Just doing the gravy. Why don't you guys all sit down. Rosie and I will bring it in.'

'Rosie?' asked Fiona. 'Are you filming today?'

Rosie shook her head. 'Probably should be, but I don't think an Xmas scene is essential. We've got Alice's birthday. No, I'm thoroughly off duty. Which means I'm drinking, and it means anyone can do or say anything they like.'

'Don't say that,' complained Andy. 'Christ knows what could happen.'

Later, we were drinking dessert wine, and Greg was single-handedly tackling the chocolate cake that Alice and I had made. The phone rang.

I jumped up to get it. I wobbled slightly.

'Not drunk, are we?' bellowed Andy.

'Not at all,' I told him, wondering why the room was swaying. '*Allo?*' I said, in my best French accent, into the phone. It kept ringing. I pressed the button to answer it, and tried again.

'Hello . . .' he said.

I knew that he was dithering between announcing himself as Matt or Hugh. My heart started thumping. This was the first time he had called in over four months. I backed out of the dining room, mouthing 'Matt' to everybody at the table.

I knew that if he wanted to come back, I was going to let him. I thought about him all the time, and I still loved him. It was the masochist in me; I could not help myself.

I shut myself in the sitting room.

'Hello, Matt,' I said, carefully. 'I can't ever call you Hugh.'

'I prefer Matt, anyway. He's a nicer guy.'

The comment hung in the air for a while.

'Is he?' I asked.

'That came out wrong. I preferred being Matt. Oh, crap. This is never going to sound right. I think I'll just stop. Merry Christmas, Emma.'

The sound of his voice, as familiar as if I had seen him yesterday, made me wince. I banned myself from thinking, or, worse, from talking about the babies I would never have, the wedding, the years we were going to spend growing old together in this house.

'Merry Christmas, Matt,' I said icily.

'Look,' he said. 'I know this isn't easy. I'm very embarrassed.'

'Oh?' I asked mildly. 'Poor thing.'

'Are you being sarcastic?'

I lay back on the sofa. 'What did you ring for?' I stared at the ceiling beams.

'Well, because it's Christmas Day. I thought you might let me wish my daughter a happy Christmas.'

'You can wish her a happy birthday while you're at it.'

'I know, I know. Sorry. I didn't want to bother you both.'

'Here's a pointer for next time: most three-year-olds don't

object to being bothered by their parents on their birthdays.'

'Misjudgement. Embarrassment. Sorry.'

'You can talk to Alice in a minute. What else?'

'Money,' he said. 'I need to support you and Alice. How much do you need to tide you over till you get back to England?'

'Nothing,' I said firmly. Then I remembered how little was left in the bank. 'Perhaps something for Alice,' I said quickly. 'Not me. I'm an adult and I don't need anything from you.'

'But the least I can do is help you,' he said. 'I made you move out there and then all this happened.'

'Oh, it *happened*, did it?' I asked. 'It just happened? What was it, an act of God?'

'No. It was me. I did it.' He sounded sheepish and lost. I imagined that the silly-me act was a time-honoured way of winning over distraught women.

'I spent all my time trying to keep you happy,' I said. 'I wish I hadn't. You were a moody fuck most of the time. I think I must have known, in some way, that you weren't committed to me, that you were never going to commit to me. That was why I went for you. Because subconsciously I knew you weren't available. There was Pete committing to me like crazy, and I couldn't bear to look at him. Then you come along and you're a bastard and unavailable, so I fall for you wholeheartedly and have your baby two years later. And now I know that Pete's your brother and you *have* got a family. It was just lies and lies and lies. It makes me sick to think about it. Do your parents even know they've got a granddaughter yet?'

'Mmm. Unfortunately, they heard it from Jo. Go on then. Why was it that you were waiting for a bastard to come along and ruin your life?'

'Probably because I didn't think I was worthy of anything more. I hated Pete because he treated me like a goddess and I knew I wasn't one. You were what I wanted because you reinforced my lack of self-esteem. You didn't think I was worth a proper relationship either. Christ. Your parents heard about Alice from Jo. That says it all.'

'Pete was right, though. You *are* a goddess.' He sounded matter-of-fact as he said it.

'What?' I wavered for a moment, then pressed the button to cut him off. He had called me a goddess, and I was in danger of losing my composure. I sat and stared at the phone, waiting for it to ring. When he did, I took it through to the dining room, still ringing, and handed it to Alice.

'Darling,' I said, as she took it, looking bemused. 'I think there's someone on the phone for you.' She pressed the button carefully.

'Hello?' she said. Her face lit up. 'It's Daddy!' she shrieked, looking at us all in wonderment. 'Daddy, where are you *gone*?'

Greg's Christmas present to me was waiting in the garden. After coffee and chocolates, we trooped out, full of food and wine, to see what it was. It was bitingly cold, and the sky was filled with snow clouds. Charlotte, Rosie and Fiona were all wearing unsuitable footwear. They stepped delicately over my back lawn, which had been dug up for the replacement of the septic tank. The grass that I had tended so carefully had all vanished, every last blade of it. The hillocks of mud had been frozen solid by the morning's frost.

'I hope you like them,' Greg said, as he led us over the strange terrain towards the smallest outbuilding.

'What are they?' I was suspicious.

'You'll see.'

Charlotte kept looking at me and smiling knowingly. Rosie was holding Greg's hand. Andy and Fiona walked apart from each other. Greg opened the door, and three red hens ambled happily out of the shed.

'Chickens!' I gasped. I watched them grouping together, trying to decide which way to walk. 'Greg, that is the most brilliant present anyone's ever given me! Thank you!' I hugged him and kissed each cheek. Charlotte had given me a winter wetsuit, and now Greg had got me chickens.

The chickens started to explore the garden, pecking at the cold, hard ground. Alice ran after them.

'Thought you needed them,' said Greg, a hand on my shoulder. 'Everyone else has got them. Martine got these ladies for me. Are you going to name them?'

I smiled. 'You'd better name one, for starters,' I told him.

'Lenin,' he said at once. 'I was hoping you were going to ask me.'

I laughed. 'Lenin? Lenin's a man.'

He shrugged. I saw Rosie looking dewy-eyed at him. I wished I had someone to look at me like that.

'It's a good name for a chicken,' he said. I agreed. I called Alice back and asked her to name another.

'Emperor Zurg,' she said instantly. 'This one here. The purple one.'

One chicken had dark tail feathers. It took an imaginative leap to see her as purple, but I knew what Alice meant.

'And I'm calling the third one Sarah,' I said firmly. 'One of them has to have a normal name. A girl's name, at least. A slightly bizarre memorial to my mother, but it is one, nonetheless.'

'Are you sure you're putting the house on the market?' Fiona asked, sidling over. She had been quiet during lunch. I led her out of earshot.

'Of course I am. I've got no money and there's no work round here, is there? Fi, is everything all right? You're so quiet.'

She sighed, and smiled at me. She looked strained, and even through all her make-up, I could see she was pale.

'It's been eventful,' she said quietly. 'Not all bad.' I followed the line of her gaze. She was staring at Alice, who was holding Charlotte's hand and running at the chickens, trying to jump over them, and sending them running, wings flapping, in a squawking panic. Charlotte's high pink shoes were being ruined, but she was being extremely game about it.

'Alice is a pet,' Fiona said. 'I'd like to have a little girl just like that.'

'Do you mean you and Andy are going to try for a baby?'

She giggled. 'No. I mean the deed is done.'

'Really?'

'Really!'

I bit back the first question that sprang to mind. 'Fi!' I said, instead. 'That's amazing. Congratulations! When's it due?'

'June. It's still quite early days so we're keeping it quiet.'

'Of course. Is Andy pleased?'

She grimaced. 'On days when he believes it's his, he's over the moon.'

I shook my head. 'He'll come round. How wonderful. A baby.' A new baby always made the world look better, fresher, full of possibilities.

Alice came bouncing up and took both of us by the hand. 'Charlotte says I can have some more of my Santa. Auntie Fi, will you help me with my tights so I can do a wee?'

'Of course I will, darling.'

We walked to the back door. I took Alice's boots off and helped her into her slippers. 'You're honoured,' I said to Fi. 'Plus, consider it practice.'

'Come on then,' Fiona told Alice. 'Do you use the potty or the toilet?'

'Normally the potty. At school we have little loos.' They disappeared indoors. I could hear Alice talking earnestly about wees. I went in to light the fire.

'I'll come in too,' said Andy, making me jump. He had crept up behind me. 'I could use a good strong cup of tea.'

While he made the tea, Andy spoke, without looking at me. His words rushed out, one on top of another. 'Emma,' he said, 'I know you knew all along about Fiona's thing. I know that everyone knows. It was back in August when Alice told me about Auntie Fi's dirty weekend with the gardener. You explained it away and I believed you. I wish you'd told me the truth.'

I looked over my shoulder. The fire was refusing to get going. 'Sorry,' I said. 'It's over now, isn't it? And congratulations about the baby.'

He shrugged. 'Is it over? You tell me. Is it my baby? She says so, but she would, wouldn't she? I don't like being taken for a mug. And watching my wife giving birth to the gardener's kiddy spells M-U-G to me.'

I added another log and stood back to see if it caught. 'What are you saying? You're not leaving her?' I could see why Andy felt humiliated. Everybody knew about Fiona and Didier. In the market the previous Saturday, a woman I had never met before had planted herself in front of me and had demanded to know, in an extremely hostile manner, whether I was the English lady who was messing around with Valerie's husband. I had denied it hotly. I had accidentally defended myself by saying, *'C'est l'autre Anglaise.'*

The woman had nodded and her face had softened. 'So,' she said, 'it's you who are all alone. With the little girl. Your husband had another wife and another daughter.'

'A son,' I told her, with a nod. She smiled and stroked my arm.

'These things are hard,' she said, with what had sounded like the voice of experience.

'No,' Andy said now. 'I'm sticking with her for the moment. But I feel like the last to bloody know. I trusted her, Emma. Everyone's laughing at me.'

'I am sorry,' I told him. 'That was the weekend that Matt vanished. I didn't really care about anything. And anyway, it's hard to know what to do. If I'd told you, Fi would have been mad at me. We couldn't have been friends any more. And for all I knew, you might not have wanted to know. It's hard to know how other people's relationships work. Fi said you had, well, done similar things yourself.'

He laughed quietly. 'I'm sure she did. She's thrown that back at me often enough. Yes, I have had affairs. Twice. So yes, I know this doesn't put me in a good position. I'm a hypocrite. Acknowledged. Still, if I'd had an inkling what Matt was up to, I'd like to think I'd have tipped you off.'

'The scale of that was a bit different. As he pointed out to me, he was having an affair, and it was with me. I had no idea I was the other woman. He told me I was. He said, you've always been the other.' I shuddered as, once again, I heard him saying those awful words.

Andy handed me a cup of tea. 'Anyways, no hard feelings. She should never have dragged you into it. Fuck knows, you're going through worse than me. No arguments there.'

'Andy?' called Rosie, from the doorway. 'Could you say that last bit again but without saying fuck? It's so much better when we don't have to beep it.'

He raised his voice. 'Rosie! This is a fucking private conversation! Fuck off!'

Rosie looked at me, eyebrows raised.

'You said you weren't filming,' I reminded her. I was annoyed. 'I didn't even know you had your camera. Please don't use that footage.'

She slumped down in an armchair. 'Sorry. Sorry, both of you.' Rosie looked exhausted. 'Habit. And, well, if I'm behind a camera it means I don't have to participate. I'm trying to take my mind off things.'

I left the kitchen and joined Rosie. 'What things?' I asked. Rosie seemed efficiency incarnate. She and Greg appeared to be in the idyllic first stages of what could be a lasting relationship. She was devoted to her work, she looked good, and everyone liked her. 'What on earth are you taking your mind off?'

Andy appeared with amber liquid in three glasses. 'Here we are. Everyone needs it.'

We clinked glasses.

'Oh, just some stuff that I need to sort out,' Rosie said airily.

chapter thirty-three

Boxing Day

The beach was bleak and almost empty. I struggled, freezing, into my brand-new wetsuit, and my boots, gloves, hood and something called a rash vest, all of which had come from Bella. Greg had told my sisters exactly what to buy me. He changed next to me, quickly and efficiently. He had shaved off his beard since he had been with Rosie.

We ran down to the water and straight in, before my courage failed me. I paddled out as quickly as I could. I was not good, but I was getting better, and I was intent on becoming a real surfer.

Suddenly, after twenty minutes, I caught my biggest ever wave. As I paddled for it, I realised how huge it actually was. My legs almost gave way under me. I forced myself to my feet, and I surfed it. I was shaking with excitement when I fell off, and when I popped up I was unable to stop grinning. I splashed to the shore.

'Did you get it?' I asked. Rosie nodded. 'Promise you'll put that on telly?' I badgered.

'You bet.'

I was desperate for Matt to see me surf. I wanted him to regret the day he scoffed at my surfing ambitions, and I wanted him to respect me for doing it.

When I had money, I was going to buy myself a board. It was depressing to realise how many things, these days, came under the heading of 'when I've got money'. I was a single mother, and the handsome profit I had made on the house in Brighton had evaporated. I was glad that the builders were taking so long to finish the house. The longer I could put off their final bill, the better. The longer I could delay putting my beautiful, troublesome house on the market, the better.

After our surf, when we were dressed again, Greg suddenly turned to me.

'Emma,' he said. 'Can we maybe go and get a coffee? I need to talk to you.'

'Course.'

I noticed Greg and Rosie exchanging glances.

'I'm going to make some calls,' Rosie said, getting into the front seat of her car and taking out her mobile phone. 'I'll see you when you're done.'

'This is intriguing,' I told Greg, as we took a seat in a beachfront café that should not have been open. We were the only customers. The plate-glass windows opened out onto a panoramic view of the bleak beach. A man walked past with a dog, a scarf pulled up over his face to keep the cold wind at bay.

'There's something I need to talk to you about,' Greg said, pulling off his knitted hat.

'Is it to do with Rosie?'

He laughed briefly and shook his head. 'No. Rosie's fine. It's to do with you.'

'I'm listening.'

'Um,' said Greg, then started to speak quickly, as if he needed the momentum. 'It's about your father. I know he's a mystery, you don't know who he is, and you think my mum knows. Well, she does. I do, too. I have done for a few years. He got drunk at New Year a while back and told me. He said he'd promised my mum he'd never tell you but he wants to. He said I can now.'

The waiter came. I ordered my coffee without taking my eyes off Greg.

'Who?' I demanded, as soon as the waiter had gone.

Greg swallowed. 'Who? My dad, of course. Your dad. Our dad. Apparently Sarah and him had a thing once. He was married to my mum at the time, obviously, and Charlotte was just born. I didn't really want to hear it, I can tell you. It's not the kind of confession you want to hear from your own father. But once he started he couldn't stop talking. Sarah was very happy, very keen and excited about everything at the time and she kind of seduced him and he was caught up in the moment and went along with it and afterwards he felt terrible.' Greg looked at me and looked away again. 'I mean, of course he did – what kind of man sleeps with his wife's little sister? Particularly when she has mental health issues. A right bastard. So, Sarah got pregnant. She told Mum who the father was, Mum went mad, as you can imagine, and it was all hushed up. Dad gave Sarah money for you. So.' He put his hands, palms up, on the table. 'There you go. I really am your brother. And now I've told you.'

I tried to think of something to say. 'OK,' I said in the end. The coffee arrived. It was so strong it took the inside off my mouth. I was grateful. I tried out the concept in my head. I was not an orphan. I had a parent. Geoff was my dad. 'Bloody hell,' I said suddenly. 'Christa must hate me.'

Greg leaned back. 'I think you'd know if Christa hated you.'

'But she must. Her husband shagged her sister. I'm the evidence. And she brought me up. The woman is a saint.' I thought about it. 'She must hate me as much as I hate Jo. I bet she can't even bear to look at me.'

'It's not like you and Jo. It's like you and Oliver. You don't hate him, do you?'

I considered this. 'Of course I don't.'

'How do you feel about him?'

'Sorry for him.'

'Because?'

'Because his life's been fucked around by adults and he's so innocent that it's heartbreaking. Like Alice.'

'And there you have it. And if by some weird quirk of fate you were ever called upon to take him in and bring him up, you wouldn't hold anything against him, would you?'

I tried to imagine it. 'I suppose not. Have you spoken to Christa about any of this, or just Geoff? Why didn't he tell me himself?' Questions were falling over each other as they occurred to me. 'Do Bella and Charlotte know?'

Greg sipped his drink. 'No, I've never spoken to Mum, though she knows I know. Just Geoff. He said he nearly told you in September at Biarritz, but he was worried that you were so fragile, he thought it might do more harm than good. He asked me on the phone yesterday if I'd tell you before I left. He's going to be hanging by the phone now waiting for a reaction.'

'Oh, bloody hell. What's my reaction?'

'You tell me.'

'Immediately it's about Christa. But then . . .' A smile grew across my face. 'Then, after that, it's all fantastic. If Christa hasn't been secretly hating me all these years, then . . . My God.'

After half an hour's discussion, I remembered what Greg had said earlier.

'You said you had to tell me before you left. You're not leaving, are you?'

'Mmm. That was kind of my way of telling you – by presenting you with a killer fact straight afterwards so you wouldn't mind.'

'Don't go! You've only just got here.'

'I've been here two and a half months. And the thing is, I love it here, but I can't stay for ever. You're not even staying for ever. I've got a few plans, and I need to go back to London and find some godawful job in a restaurant so I can smile unctuously at rude rich people and save up all the tips they give me. So I can go away again. A friend of mine's planning a trip to Cuba and I'm just dying to go along.'

I looked at him closely. 'This friend wouldn't be called Rosie, would she?'

Greg laughed bitterly, and shook his head slowly. 'No, Emma. This friend would be called Danny. Rosie can't go hotfooting it off to Cuba. She's got two films to edit, for one thing.'

'So wait for her.'

'How can I wait for her if she doesn't want me to?'

I looked at him. He wouldn't catch my eye. He was looking, instead, out of the window, at the waves that were crashing onto the sand, sending white water high into the air.

'But surely she wants you to?' I asked gently.

He shook his head. 'She says nice things. She says them all the time. But she's got complicated stuff going on with an ex, and I don't want to be in the middle of it. And she doesn't want me to be, either. I need to leave her alone for a bit to get her head together. Then she might or might not want to give it a proper go with me. And I might or might not want to take her back. So, I guess this is what you've all been waiting for. A love affair crashes to earth.'

'Jesus, Greg. How can she have a complicated thing with an ex when she's been out here for so long? She's been making these films for ever and she's never had a bloke with her, except for you. And you and her are so great together.'

'I know. I think it's over with the ex, really, but she still, you know . . .' he made quote marks in the air with his fingers, '"loves him". Which is kind of crushing for me because I thought this thing with her could go somewhere. I mean I've never had a relationship that I thought was so good. I was really, seriously keen to make a go of it with Rosie.'

I shook my head and mimed for the bill. Then I looked at Greg 'Sounds like she's got cold feet to me. But I do see that you can't hang around waiting. When are you off?'

'Rosie's doing another few weeks here, isn't she? I think I'll go sooner. You know, be the one doing the leaving.'

'You can see her in London. Will you be living at Christa and Geoff's?'

'Christa and Dad's, you mean.'

'Yes.' I tried out the concept again. 'Christa and Dad's.' I laughed at the thought. 'I suppose we'd better ring him, hadn't we?'

We sat in the car and called Holloway on my mobile. Christa answered.

'Hello, Christa,' I said. I was bubbling with excitement. I had desperately wanted Geoff to answer the phone. I didn't even know whether Christa knew that Greg was going to tell me. I jigged my foot up and down on the accelerator as I waited for her to say something.

'Oh, Emma,' she said. 'How are you?'

I looked at Greg and shook my head. She didn't know.

'Fine, Christa,' I said. 'More than fine, actually. We're at the beach, me and Greg.'

'Where's Alice?'

'At home with Charlotte. She's fine.'

'OK. Good.'

She paused politely, waiting for me to say why I had called. Outside, the waves were splashing, too big to surf. I raised my eyebrows at Greg. He nodded frantically, motioning for me to tell her.

'Greg's just told me something,' I said, hoping that she would guess.

'Oh, that he's leaving? Will you be all right?'

'Yes, but I didn't mean that. He's told me that Geoff's my father.' I said the last three words quickly, knowing that I had to get them out before I thought better of it.

'Oh,' said Christa. 'Oh, I see.' She said nothing for several seconds. I held my breath, waiting for her reaction. Geoff's my father. I said it again and again in my head. I have a dad. Geoff's my father. 'OK,' she said. 'You were always going to find out. We should have told you sooner. Geoff's been champing at the bit to be your daddy. I had a feeling that Greg might tell you.' I heard her shouting, away from the receiver, for Geoff. 'Sorry, Emma. I suppose it was my fault. I felt that some things were better kept secret.'

'No, Christa. I'm sorry. All I care about is whether or not you hate me. You don't, do you?'

My aunt actually laughed. 'You ridiculous girl. No, I don't hate you. The only person truly at fault was Geoff. He knew that Sarah was ill. I forgave them both a long time ago. Here he is.'

I gave Greg a thumbs up. Then Geoff came to the phone.

'Emma,' he said. His voice was hopeful. 'Emma, is this all right?'

I laughed loudly. 'Of course it is, you great idiot.'

chapter thirty-four

Coco met me in Villeneuve one day, when the children were at school. She insisted. According to Coco, according to Bella, according to both Rosie and Fiona, I was going to feel better if I looked better. I was willing to try anything, and besides, I was sick of always being the scruffy one. I had more energy, all of a sudden, and I wanted to try out being different. I wasn't a sad and lonely orphan any more. I was a sad and lonely woman with a father, a half-brother and two half-sisters, doubling up as cousins. That had to be an improvement.

It was a cold day. The trees were bare and the puddles were thick with ice. I parked in the centre of town, opposite the imposing DVD and stationery shop that bore the curious name of Madison Nuggets. It always made me think of a computer-generated password. Perhaps, I thought, the shop was trying to convey a sense of Americana: Madison Avenue crossed with Chicken McNuggets. I put a few euros in the parking ticket machine and locked my car. If that was the case, it was not really succeeding, but I liked the eccentricity of Madison Nuggets. I smelt the smell of France in the air. Even though I had been here for nearly a year, it still seemed exotic. I never worked out what it was that made France smell different from England.

There were a few people around. A woman walked past with a wicker basket full of paper bags of vegetables. She was wrapped up in so many layers that she was spherical, yet she was still shivering. A man hobbled painfully by, helped by a walking stick. I dropped the car keys into my handbag, and strode ahead to meet Coco. I was glad to have a focus.

I knew that Rosie would be meeting us at the café, because she was getting increasingly excited about the idea of my makeover.

'This will be perfect,' she had said, when I mentioned it to her. 'It's exactly what you need. And what I need. You go for it.'

I looked at her. 'It's easy for you to say.' Rosie was, as ever, dressed in expensive black, with dark glasses balanced on top of her head despite the season. She had become slightly withdrawn since Greg had left, but her chicness hadn't faltered. She could be bothered. I couldn't. That particular divide had never looked so great. The women who could be bothered were frighteningly keen to bring me over to their side.

I didn't care enough. I owned nail files but rarely troubled to find one when I could bite instead. I got my hair cut about a month after I decided it needed it, and that was just to keep it out of my eyes. Sometimes I did it myself, with the kitchen scissors. I wore T-shirts and shorts in the summer and jumpers and jeans in winter. I was still in Matt's jumpers. I had muddled along without bothering anybody for years. Now, suddenly, everyone was telling me to stop being a woman and become a lady.

I knew I was going to be scrutinised by skinny women today, so I had done my best to dress up. I was wearing my Levi's, which fell around my hips, and a brown jumper which was slightly more flattering than Matt's green one. I had put on a little lipgloss and a lick of mascara. This, I knew, clumped my eyelashes together and made me look like a nine-year-old girl messing around with her mother's make-up for the first time. Every time I blinked I could feel my top lashes sticking to the bottom ones.

Coco was already there. She was sitting inside the café, and when she saw me come in, she beamed.

'Hello, you,' she said, jumping up and kissing me on each cheek. Perfume wafted towards me. I had no idea what perfume it was, but it smelt expensive.

'Hello,' I returned nervously, and ordered a large white coffee. I took the opportunity of analysing her clothes. She was wearing jeans, too, but hers were tight-fitting and showed off her tiny body. She wore a white long-sleeved T-shirt and a thick cardigan, belted at the waist. Coco's hair was loose down her back, but styled away from her face. She was wearing bright pink lipstick. I wondered if she was going to try to make me wear make-up, too. I had rarely worn more than a little mascara and some brown lipstick, and that was only for special occasions.

'I don't want to wear pink lipstick,' I blurted out. Then

I felt rude. 'It looks nice on you,' I added hastily, 'but I would look like a child playing with Mummy's things.'

I looked at her expectantly. She frowned for a few seconds. 'You think I'm going to make you wear pink lipstick?' She understood, and laughed. 'No, Emma. You don't have to make yourself up to look like me. I want to help you to look like yourself.'

I was not sure about this. 'I already look like myself.'

She shrugged. 'Then it will be easy.'

Rosie joined us five minutes later, looking businesslike in a long black coat and black high-heeled boots. 'Cheers for this, you two,' she said briskly. 'I appreciate being invited along. Where are we going first?' I knew Rosie well enough, by this point, to understand that she was being businesslike to ensure that I had no window for backing out and sending her away. I also knew that she was missing Greg and that she was trying not to talk about it.

Rosie spoke resolutely in English. She did have school-girl French, but she used it only when necessary, and when she did, her confidence was far greater than her capability. She saw no reason to attempt a French accent, so she would use a French word as if she were annexing it into English. Coco was baffled by her, but in an amiable way. She saw her as an extreme eccentric and often had to check with me whether Rosie was speaking in English or in French.

'Hello?' Rosie shouted across the café, immediately draining her espresso. A waiter looked at us from the far side of the room, eyebrows raised. He was thin and spectral. 'Can we have the *addition s'il vous plaît*?'

'It's on the table!' I told her, with urgent embarrassment.

'Right. *D'accord!*' she called to the young man, who was smiling with good-tempered incomprehension. '*Nous avons l'addition ici, après tout.* So, Coco. Where are we taking her?'

Coco understood. 'Nouvelles Galeries,' she said. '*Et puis, après ça, j'ai beaucoup d'idées. On verra.*'

'In English?'

I translated. 'After that she has lots of other ideas.'

'Right. Off you go, girls. Forget about me. As ever.'

I soon forgot Rosie altogether, as I was entirely absorbed in the horror of my makeover. Nouvelles Galeries was not too bad because, as it was a department store, the assistants left us alone. Coco picked up outfits for which I would never have spared more than a glance, and made me put them on.

'You're a thirty-eight,' she said, handing me a shiny green shirt and a pair of skinny black trousers.

'Forty,' I corrected her. 'Maybe forty-two. You're not seriously telling me to put these on? They won't fit, they're tiny, and they also happen to be horrible.'

She shook her head. 'Just do it.'

She stood in the corner of the cubicle as I changed, and smiled at me. 'We need to get you a lot of new lingerie, Emma,' she observed cheerfully.

'Stop! This is my best underwear.' She laughed. She thought I was joking, but unfortunately I was serious. There was, I felt, nothing wrong with my black Marks and Spencer's bra and matching knickers from a five-pack. I made sure it matched this morning, on purpose. If she thought this was bad, she should have seen the grey range.

The trousers fitted over my thighs and, to my surprise, they even fastened round my waist without any trouble. The green shirt hung down nicely from my shoulders. I had thought green was a horrible colour for me. That was why I had worn the green jumper so much. I had been making myself look terrible on purpose. All the same, I had to admit that the shirt looked reasonable.

I twisted in front of the mirror. My body was completely different from the way I had expected it to be.

'Is this a trick mirror?' I asked suspiciously.

She laughed. 'No. I promise.'

'So when did I get all . . . thin?'

'When you were depressed and didn't eat,' she told me. I nodded. Everyone had told me I had lost weight, but I had never really appreciated the difference it made. I had thought I had a pot belly and a huge bottom, and all of a sudden it seemed I didn't. The shirt looked quite nice with my new body inside it. I pulled back my shaggy hair and studied my face. I was pale and drawn, with bags under my eyes so pronounced that I looked as though I had applied grey eyeshadow upside down. The mascara had already smeared my face. But although I looked as buffeted as I felt, I noticed now that I had cheekbones, that my cheeks were hollow under them, and that the double chin that always shocked me when I saw photographs of myself had gone. I was skinny. My body was small, and my waist curved in instead of out. The shirt clung to my ribcage and made me look fragile and little.

'OK,' I said, trying to assimilate my new self. 'Let's buy these. What else?'

Plan B

That was when the horror began. Coco took me from shop to shop, stood me in front of assistants and explained her mission. Rosie often put her camera down to offer advice, or to scour the rails for the perfect item. Bossy women I had never met before and never wanted to see again parked me in changing cubicles and prodded me, commented unfavourably on my underwear, and made me try on garment after garment. They stood in front of me as I tried on bras, even going so far as to lift each breast and make sure it was properly in the cup. I was mortified by the whole process, and ended up spending money I doubted I would ever have, on my credit card, just to be allowed to leave.

It was a huge relief when everything closed at midday. I had five shopping bags, containing my new wardrobe. They contained what amounted, apparently, to all the basics I would need until summer, including one pair of shoes, one pair of knee-high boots, several pairs of trousers, skirts and tops, a long expensive coat, and a lot of sexy underwear.

'I don't really think anyone's going to be seeing it,' I objected as Coco added expensive scraps of silk to my lingerie purchases whenever anything caught her eye.

She giggled. 'I bet they will. And even if not, you'll feel better. You will walk differently. It will make you wiggle.'

I shrugged. 'If you say so.'

She nodded. 'I say so. I'm single, aren't I? I am the expert.'

'You're only single because you want to be,' I told her dismissively. 'You could marry again in a second if you wanted to.'

She looked at me, indignant. 'Who could I marry?'

'Coco! You could marry anybody. You're perfect.' I looked

at her clean, silky hair. She washed and dried it every morning while Louis was still asleep. Then she put on her make-up. Then she got dressed in clothes she had ironed the night before. Then she woke Louis up for school and dressed him immaculately, too. All through the summer he had worn shorts with creases ironed down the front and short-sleeved linen shirts. 'You're beautiful. Your only problem is that most people aren't good enough for you. That's all.'

'Emma,' she said, with a sad smile. 'You're sweet. But it's not true. I live in St Paul. I need to move somewhere if I'm going to meet anyone. You don't get eligible bachelors around where we live. I've known every man since crèche. The ones who are single, by and large there's a reason for it, and I know that reason. And I'm thirty-three, divorced, with a child. I am no great catch. Most of the interesting men have moved away.'

'Yes.' I thought about myself. If Coco couldn't meet anyone, I had no chance. I didn't want to, but perhaps one day I would. I saw, again, that moving back to Brighton was my only option. 'So will you move away?'

'Yes. Probably. One day soon. It will be hard to start again somewhere new. I'm looking for jobs. Perhaps we won't go too far away. Perhaps I'll go away, meet someone and bring him back here. This is very much my home. I don't want to leave it all behind.'

'I don't either.'

She looked quizzical. 'What? You don't want to leave your home? Or this home?'

I wasn't quite sure what I had meant. 'This home.'

'I thought you were going back to England.'

I nodded. 'I am. When the house is finished. I'll miss my life here, though. I'll miss it terribly. I can't think too hard about what sort of poky apartment I'll be able to afford to rent. I'll miss the garden and the chickens and you and Andy and Fiona and Martine and Patrick and Mathilde and everyone. I'll miss the market. Alice will miss her friends and her school. Going back to England is the only thing we can do, but it'll be sad.'

'Maybe I'll move to England,' said Coco. 'Louis and I could come with you. His turn to learn another language. And mine.'

Rosie interrupted us. 'Look, darlings,' she said. 'This is all lovely, but I don't understand most of it.' She looked at me. 'What's she saying?'

I translated. Rosie nodded. 'Fabulous idea, Coco. I can film you making the opposite journey from Emma. A twist in the genre. Nice.' She looked at me. 'That might give me consolation for dying alone and unloved.'

Coco frowned. 'I think I understand,' she said in English. 'You film me? No.'

Rosie shrugged. 'Think it over. Now, in honour of Emma's decision to show the world that there is a gorgeous lady lurking under those grotesque jumpers, let's go somewhere special and drink champagne.'

'OK,' I agreed, 'but we can't get drunk. I need you to get me to a hairdresser's this afternoon, and kit me out with cosmetics. And then show me how to put them on. And Rosie,' I added. 'I need you to tell me what the hell is going on with your love life.'

'Yeah, right,' she said.

*   *   *

363

I found I enjoyed looking after my appearance. It gave me something to think about, so I quickly adopted it as my crutch, and thought about it almost constantly. It replaced Greg. It occupied the empty moments, the times when I was not with Alice, or surfing, or gardening. If ten empty minutes opened up before me, I would usually have sighed and fumed about Matt, or cried about my mother; now I would go upstairs and touch up my make-up. I would re-pin my hair, hand-wash my stockings and bras and lacy knickers. I felt different as a woman with a parent. I knew it was illogical.

I was role playing. Alice liked my new hobby, and we would sit at the kitchen table together while she advised me on shades of lipstick and asked me to make her up, too. I painted her fingernails pink and let her wear a tiny bit of make-up for an hour or so if it wasn't a school day. She started asking to have her ears pierced.

'Of course you can't,' I told her with a laugh. 'You're three years old.'

'There's a girl at school with earrings in her ears.'

'Well, you can't have them.'

She scowled, folded her arms, and withdrew. I wondered what I was doing wrong to be encountering this conversation so early on. I hadn't been expecting to have it until she was at least seven.

I was pleased to note, almost immediately, that men were looking at me in a way they had never looked at me before. The transformation had, however, cost a frightening amount of money, and money was something that was very close to running out. I was living off my credit card, and I knew I had no chance of paying it off. Even when he had been with us, Matt had contributed little towards our daily expenses, nothing towards the house or the renovation. I hadn't minded: he had explained that he spent most of his salary on commuting and the rent on his London flat, so I had always bought the food and paid the bills.

Now, however, the costs were escalating and I knew I could not ignore the situation any longer. The builders were billing us regularly, and Alice and I were in urgent need of some funds. We had just about enough cash left to pay for the rest of the building work. I did not want to contact Matt, who was making small and irregular payments into my French bank account. I wanted him to contact me again and take care of his responsibilities properly. He did not.

Because I knew I needed some work, I made enquiries about teaching English. To my surprise, I was instantly offered an interview by the local Chamber of Commerce, who ran a comprehensive range of language classes. I laughed at the idea of myself as the language assistant. Coco and Fiona laughed at the idea of me meeting businessmen who needed to speak English for work. The Chamber of Commerce was, they agreed, the very best place in Villeneuve for me to meet a new husband; a real one, this time.

'You'll meet someone,' Rosie told me, when I got the call offering me two afternoons' work a week. 'I know you will.'

The day before I taught my first class, Rosie put down her camera and asked if she could come and stay with me.

I blinked. 'Of course you can. This house is way too big

for Alice and me. You could have stayed here all along. But only if you tell me about the sticky ex.'

Rosie sat at the dining table and shook her head. She looked exhausted.

'There is no sticky ex,' she admitted. 'I just needed to say something to make Greg believe it was over.' She ran her fingers through her thick hair. 'It's not an ex. It's a tumour.'

Rosie had found a lump in her breast, back in November.

I hardly dared breathe. 'And?'

She put her shades down on the table. 'And I ignored it. I had my Elll but I didn't dare go to the doctor on my own. My French is crap. And I was scared.'

'I'd have gone with you.'

'You had enough going on. I mean, we had a professional relationship. Imagine how unprofessional it would have been if I'd put the camera down and asked you to help me.'

'That's not true.'

'Anyway, I went in the end. Fiona told me that her GP spoke some English, so I snuck off to see him, on my own. And he sent me straight to a specialist at the hospital for a biopsy. So I had it, and the outcome is that it's malignant. I found out two days ago.'

'When did you have the biopsy?'

'Last week. When you didn't see me for a couple of days. I needed Greg to go before I did it because he'd have noticed. I'm going back to England for chemo and surgery. I've got private health insurance because my parents are Tories, and they keep insuring me, too. So I'm going straight in to Bupa.'

I wanted to shake her. 'Why the hell didn't you say

anything? Rosie! You could have told me. And what the fuck were you thinking of, not saying anything to Greg? Are you insane?'

She shook her head and put her shades back on. 'Greg's perfect,' she said. 'I knew he was too good to be true. He's a free spirit. I met him in between Cambodia and Cuba, for God's sake. He likes me because I'm independent. He doesn't want to be tied down to some whining woman with no eyebrows.'

I sighed. 'Rosie. I'm going to tell him. He loves you. Believe me, loads of women have fancied Greg over the years and he's never been one-tenth as into them as he is with you. You two are brilliant together. He'll support you through anything. You have to let him. And eyebrows grow back. You can pencil them in. You know he won't notice.'

'Look, it's too much pressure on Greg. I don't want to put him in that position. He can hardly say, "No, I won't be there for you because you've got cancer." Can he? If I tell him, he'll have to drop everything and hold my hand. And I don't want to make him do that.'

'I'm going to tell him.' I held up a hand to stop her protests. 'Don't. Nothing you could say would stop me. I'll tell him that you don't know I'm talking to him. And I'll leave it up to him what he does. He's my brother and he has a right to know.'

Rosie sighed and nodded. Then, suddenly, she burst into tears.

'I'm going to make the best programme ever about you,' she said.

*   *   *

Rosie moved into the room I had once allocated for my second child. We cheered each other along. Alice adored having her about, particularly since Rosie let her use the camera, under strict supervision, from time to time.

The builders were used to dealing with me, and by and large I left them to get on with it. Suddenly, they were making the final touches. The interior walls were painted white. The new bathrooms were put in. Everything was, suddenly, nearly finished.

Monsieur Dumas, the head builder, dropped by to check up on the progress of it all. He walked around humming to himself and nodding in approval at his men's work.

'And how is Monsieur Smith?' he asked, sipping his coffee and smoothing his hand against the kitchen wall tiles, which were small and white. 'You really did order the best of everything,' he added, sizing up the tiles, and he looked at me for an answer to his question.

'Monsieur Smith?' I echoed. He nodded, eyebrows raised. 'You haven't heard?'

He shook his head. 'Heard what?'

'Oh, he left.'

'Left?'

'He doesn't live here any more. He lives in London now. He has a child there.' I looked straight at him, as bravely as I could. I tried to imagine whether he was single. He was tall and bald and thickset. I could not force myself to be attracted to him. I knew that I was a long way away from wanting to date. I doubted I would ever do it.

'He is mad,' said Monsieur Dumas kindly, and he lit a cigarette and told me a long story about his wife's brother's ex-wife, her multiple lovers and her credit card debts. Rosie joined us, accepted one of his cigarettes, and leaned back on the walls, half understanding. We were delighted to hear about someone else's misfortunes for once.

chapter thirty-five

Jo sat in Lara's kitchen. She kicked off her work shoes and leaned back in her chair. She could hear the distant cheerful noise of CBeebies, and she knew that Olly and Trixie were sprawled on the sofa staring at the screen. Olly probably had his hands down his pants. He generally did when he was concentrating.

'. . . and then she said, well, we were actually planning on making the wedding adults only,' Lara was saying. 'Which is fine, of course it's fine, it's their decision. But she could have told me sooner! So now we have to find someone to take Trixie for the day, and then I've got to rethink the accommodation thing . . .'

'I'll have Trixie,' Jo said.

'Oh! No, I wasn't hinting,' said Lara. 'Really I wasn't. I was just offloading.'

'I know. I didn't think you were hinting. But I'd be happy to have her. She can stay overnight. She's no trouble and Olly will love it. What date is it?'

'May the fourteenth. Saturday.'

Plan B

Jo took out her diary. 'That's fine,' she said. 'Olly's meant to be with Hugh but I'll swap things around so he's home. And it's not as if I have anything to do on a Saturday night, is it? It'll be fine.'

'Jo. Thanks. But you're so down these days. Is there anything I can do?'

Jo shook her head. 'I wish there was. I wish there was something I could do. If only I could jack it all in and go away somewhere. But I can't leave the gallery. I'd never dare sell it. And Olly's starting pre-school this year. So I'm utterly tied down. And there are no fucking decent men anywhere.'

The doorbell rang. Lara laughed.

'Bang on cue. Sorry to do this to you, Jo. I'm sure you'll hate me. He's moved in next door and I invited him over for a glass of wine.'

Jo was aghast. 'How could you? Lara!'

'Look,' said Lara, moving to answer the door. 'He has no idea about this. You just happen to be over for supper with Olly. I'm just being neighbourly. It's nothing. He's divorced, by the way. Couple of kids. Older than ours. Worth checking over.'

Mike was the same height as Jo, with dark hair and eyes. He smiled at the two women as he handed Lara a bunch of gerberas. Jo thought he looked open. She thought he looked interesting. The gerberas were exquisite. It was the best first impression she had had for a very long time.

chapter thirty-six

Rosie filmed me as I filled my biggest wheelbarrow with the bags of Matt's clothes, and wheeled them to the communal bins. I was not feigning my smile when I threw them in. There were so many of them that I couldn't close the lid afterwards. The only memento of Matt, now, in the whole house, garden and outbuildings, was the photo in Alice's room. I longed to throw it away. He kept catching me off guard.

'Right, gorgeous,' Rosie said, putting her camera away. 'Off you go to work. Off I go to the hospital.'

I squeezed her hand. 'Good luck.'

'I'll be fine,' she said firmly. 'It's not as if I'm actually doing anything.' Rosie was collecting all her notes, referral letters, and paperwork, ready for her return to England in two days' time.

I kissed her and she got into the car.

I picked up my bag and set off for work. I thought of the twenty-minute drive to the Chamber of Commerce as my transition time. By the time I arrived there, I was a teacher.

I was outgoing, firm and enthusiastic, qualities I still often lacked at home. I was getting better, however. I could sometimes wake up, now, without the thud of realisation hitting me. Now that the pain was becoming more manageable, I was discovering that Alice and I really had been a single parent family all along. There was nothing for me to do, now that Matt had left, that I had not done before. Some mornings I woke up and enjoyed a few moments of brief solitude before Alice climbed in with me. I would stretch out, luxuriating in the expanse of sheets. Other times I would still find myself curling in to where Matt ought to be, reaching for him, half asleep, and waiting for him to push the hair off my face as he used to do when he was with me.

Alice had almost stopped asking about her daddy. She would only mention him when she saw somebody else's father, or when Louis' dad came from Geneva to take him out for the weekend. Her eyebrows would knit together and she would turn her face up to me. Her puzzled expression broke my heart.

'Where's mine own daddy gone?' she would ask.

I always had an answer ready. 'He's working very hard,' I told her. 'He's going to come to see you soon.'

I pulled into the staff parking area. This still thrilled me. It was strange to feel that somebody valued me enough to pay me for my time. I reapplied my lipstick and checked my nails before I got out of the car.

The building had a self-consciously modern pillared edifice with an indecipherable sculpture in the middle of its grassy front garden. The corridors inside smelt of polish. People clicked efficiently along, holding files under their arms. I liked joining them, carrying my own files of class notes and my big dictionary. I liked the sound my new small heels made as I descended the stairs to the language teaching corridor. I liked everything about being a teacher.

There were six students in each of my classes, and as they were adults, they all wanted to learn. The youngest was Chloe, who was about twenty and highly ambitious in her management job for a telephone company. I predicted that she would shortly be moving to Bordeaux and then on to Paris. Her ambition was to work in America, and she gave my English classes everything that she had to further this goal. Chloe had creamy skin, rosy cheeks, and black hair. Sometimes I looked at her and imagined Alice at her age, looking just as beautiful. The oldest was Bernard, in his late fifties, who had been sent by his company to learn English and was slightly grumpy about it. He failed to see, as he often told me, what was wrong with speaking French.

They all went to grammar classes with a qualified teacher. My job was simply to sit with them around a table in a tiny room for two hours, and to get them talking, to speak to them only in English, and to make sure they used a wide variety of vocabulary. I had been nervous the first time, but had covered it up by being stroppy and strict, and by refusing to countenance a single word of French.

Today I stood in front of the class and asked them to tell us about their families.

'Chloe,' I said. 'You start us off.'

'OK,' she said, pleased. 'I have a sister, Béatrice, who is seventeen. She lives with our parents, near Villeneuve. My father is a teacher. My mother is a nurse. One day I will have my own family. I have three boyfriends but now I am single. I think this is OK.'

'Very good,' I told her. 'But you should say, I have *had* three boyfriends. Otherwise it gives the wrong impression. Bernard?'

'My name is Bernard,' he said carefully. 'My family is my wife. My boys are old. Twenty-eight year and thirty year. They live Bordeaux and Lyon. I do not speak English good. I like the French. I have visit England. I do not like to eat in England. Have you eat English food? Is terrible. I ask for chicken and it comes . . .' He slipped into French to share his horror with the other students, and, intrigued, I didn't interrupt. 'It said chicken something on the menu, so I thought, *poulet*, good, *poulet* must be good, but when it arrived, the chicken was covered with orange breadcrumbs, and it tasted like rubber, and . . .' He drew breath to announce his punchline. 'There was cream cheese in the middle!'

'In English,' I told him sternly. 'Bernard, I think you ordered Chicken Kiev. That was a mistake. The food in England is not always terrible.'

'*Si.*'

'*Non*. I mean, no. OK, let's talk about food. Because British cities are so multicultural, you can find any cuisine there. French, Japanese, Ethiopian, lots of Indian. Curry is the national dish. Has anyone been to the Indian restaurant here in Villeneuve?' They shook their heads. 'It's supposed to be good. We'll all go at the end of term.'

It was a revelation to me to realise that responsible adults with good jobs respected me as a teacher. I knew that I would never have got this job without my good haircut and my new clothes. I generally wore black trousers and my green shirt to teach in, since I could not afford to expand my wardrobe, and I felt both smart and funky. Sometimes Rosie lent me skinny black clothes, and I loved myself in them. I began to see the glimmer of a future. I started to suspect that if I could maintain a positive mindset, I might have potential.

'What about you?' Chloe asked suddenly. 'Emma, tell us about your family.'

I drew a breath. For a moment I contemplated lying, creating the family I thought I had, months ago. Then I decided that I had nothing to lose by being honest.

'You might regret this,' I told the room, 'but I'll tell you if you like.' They all nodded, intrigued. I caught a whiff of the relief that hits any classroom when a teacher decides to go off at a tangent and the pupils are required to do nothing more than sit back and nod.

'Right,' I announced, determined to tell them my story. 'From the beginning. I never knew my father. My mother was ill with manic depression.' I noticed some frowns and quickly looked it up. 'She was *maniaco-dépressive*. Come on, guys! You should have worked that one out. I lived with her until I was three, and then she committed suicide.' I watched them, checking they understood.

A handsome man in his forties, called Alain, whispered, '*Elle s'est suicidée?*'

I nodded, and eyebrows were raised, sympathetic looks and murmurs extended. 'I lived with my aunt and uncle and my cousins after that. But I didn't know until last month that my uncle is also my father. No, not incest. He's my mother's sister's husband. So my cousins are my brother and my sisters, too. I have one brother and two sisters.' I scanned the faces, surprised at how liberating it was to tell this story. This is me, I thought. This is who I am. And it's all right. 'It goes on,' I warned them, laughing. 'In fact, it gets worse. I have a daughter, Alice. She's three. I moved to France with her and my partner, her father, but he was still working in London. He travelled back and forth every week. Then I discovered that he had another family, another child, in London. He had been married to someone else all the time I had known him, and I never realised. You can call me stupid if you like. Believe me, I have called myself stupid. So now, it's just Alice and me, and many different friends and relations who stay with us.' I looked at them and grinned broadly.

They looked wary. Alain, who was a classic example of a beautiful, well-worn Frenchman, asked Chloe if he had understood correctly. I assured him that he had. I was sick of being sad. It felt good to be able to tell strangers about my life. For as long as I could remember, people had gossiped about me. Now I was gossiping about myself.

'I'm sorry,' said Chloe, eventually. The others nodded and joined in. Bernard pronounced, in French, that such a beautiful woman should be cherished like a rose. I masked my delight by telling him sternly to speak in English. Then we got on with the class.

The only catch with my new venture was the fact that the money came nowhere close to what we needed. It covered our food and petrol, but it did not touch the builders' bills, the mortgage, or anything extra. Geoff offered a loan, but I refused it. I knew I could fall back on him if necessary, but it would have felt shabby to have discovered my father, and immediately bailed myself out with his cash.

'It wouldn't be bailing out,' he said grumpily. 'It would be a just redistribution of resources. A nice Old Labour gesture. You should approve.'

I banned myself from little treats. I wouldn't meet someone for coffee if I could invite them to the house instead. Better still, I would go to their house. I stopped buying Alice her favourite cake bars, shaped like teddies, and started baking biscuits. I saved up money for her school lunches, and bought fifty canteen tickets at a time so I would not run out. At weekends, we would walk through the fields, or stay at home. We did nothing that cost any money.

I had promised myself a surfboard, but now I knew I could not pay for one. I could not even afford the petrol for outings to the beach. Surfing, like everything else, was filed under 'when I've got cash'. Which was a shame, since surfing was free.

On the night that Rosie flew, terrified, to London, I sat in front of the fire. The family liaison committee, comprising Geoff, Christa and Bella, had decided that none of them needed to take time off work to babysit for me. They declared me to be all right. I was responsible. I loved Alice. I was coming back to London anyway. I was officially trustworthy again.

I curled into an armchair, with a blank sheet of paper and Matt's old laptop in front of me. I stared at the screen. All the shutters were closed, the doors were bolted and

Plan B

Alice was asleep upstairs. The building work was almost completed now, and this sitting room, where the three of us had lived on a lilo for our first five days, was cosy and warm. A lamp in the corner provided a low light, and the flames of the fire made shadows on the oak beams of the ceiling. The terracotta tiles glowed. There was no dust in the air, no piles of rubble, no more drilling to be done. They were fiddling with the electricity and doing the last details. My house was my home at last. Paradoxically, this meant it could be my home no longer. I knew I was going to have to put it on the market. It broke my heart.

Those first few nights seemed a lifetime ago. A year had passed since Matt had shifted Alice and me out here, to keep us away from his other family. I looked back on my preoccupations then with fond sorrow. I had been terrified of the move, of leaving my home and having to start again somewhere new, but I had known I would be all right because I had Matt. I had been naïve and stupid. In the event, the move had been all right. Matt, not France, had been the problem, and I had not expected that for a moment.

Everything had changed. I desperately missed his companionship. I never admitted it to anybody any more, because Bella and Charlotte and Greg, and Fiona and Andy, and Coco, and Rosie – everybody in my life – all believed that I was getting over him, that I despised him. But I had been waiting for his calls. He'd not phoned me since Christmas.

I wrote a large heading on the sheet of paper. MONEY, it said. Then I copied down the contents of the bank account

379

from the internet banking screen: €5,439.39. This was all the money I possessed. The proceeds of the house sale had withered away. I had just paid a builders' bill, and there was only one more to come. I doubted I had the funds for it. The mortgage was €755 per month.

I wrote down my earnings. They were insignificant.

I turned the paper over and wrote down the word OPTIONS. I could think of only two, and the second one was a dream. In the morning I would ring the estate agent.

Rosie called me from London. She sounded as if she was crying.

'You knew, didn't you?' she said, accusingly.

I pretended I didn't. 'What?'

'That Greg was meeting me at the airport.'

'How else would he have known what flight you were on? Are you all right?'

'Mmm. Scared.'

'Is he with you now?'

'He's barely left my side. I'm dragging him down. I feel terrible. I can't believe you did that to me.'

'Don't be so stupid. Just get yourself well again. When are you going to hospital?'

'Tomorrow. God, Emma. I'm going to die.'

I sighed and tried to say the right thing. 'We're all going to die one day. And I'm certain that your day isn't now. You're young and strong. Just look after yourself, let Greg look after you, and for God's sake, stop feeling guilty.'

Winter dragged on and on. Everyone said it had been a particularly cold one, and indeed it had been frosty since November. I felt that I was emerging from hibernation, and impatiently awaited the weather emerging with me. The fields behind my house were solid with frost, and twice we had had a sprinkling of snow.

'What can I do?' I asked Fiona. She had asked me to meet her in St Paul for a manicure. I had managed to turn the invitation around and go to her house instead. I was drinking coffee, and she was sipping herbal tea, in an unfeasibly warm living room. Its ceiling was so high it must have been extortionate to heat. 'I literally haven't got any money,' I told her. 'We can manage to live here for a couple more months. After that I'm bankrupt.'

She put down her teacup. It was a delicate, hand-painted cup from an expensive shop in Bordeaux. I wondered whether, now that I had smartened up my appearance, I was supposed to throw out my chipped random cups and replace them with chic, expensive ones. I knew it could not happen.

'What should you do?' she asked incredulously. 'What do you think you should do? Squeeze Matt for every last *centime*, darling. What else?'

'I haven't heard from him since Christmas,' I reminded her. 'We've had one conversation, on Christmas Day, and that was crap. He hasn't written or even emailed. I kind of thought he'd email. It's the coward's medium.' I looked at her, trying to work out from her expression whether she knew anything about his present circumstances. I had a strong suspicion that Andy stayed in touch with him. Fiona gave nothing away. She looked permanently queasy these days, and that was all.

'Emma,' she said, widening her eyes. 'You have to get

in touch with him yourself. Duh. You *have to* demand money. He owes it to you. You cannot possibly be expected to pay a mortgage, for a house you bought with him, and look after his child, all on your own in a foreign country when you only have four hours a week of paid work. The man has already proved himself to be a bastard. Don't you dare sit around waiting for him to do the decent thing. He's charming, granted, but he's not a decent man. He's relying on you not to push him. He knows how nice you are and he's taking advantage of you. As he always has done.'

'I don't want to get in touch with him. I can't nag for money. I want to be more independent than that.'

'Did he say he'd support Alice?'

'Several times.'

'And does he?'

I put my head on one side and tried to be fair. 'He has made payments into our bank account.'

'How much?'

'A couple of hundred euros. But it wasn't regular. And it didn't go very far.'

Fiona shook her head and stood up. 'Top-up?' She took my cup. 'Emma Meadows,' she called over her shoulder, as she went to the kitchen. 'Two hundred euros is nothing. We both know that. It's a token. More insulting than nothing, in my opinion. I understand why you don't want to contact him. No one wants to be in a position where they're demanding money from someone who's screwed them over.' She came back and handed me my cup back. It was filled to the brim with coffee. 'But, love,' she said, 'you're not doing it for you. You're doing it for little Alice. You know that Andy and I have had our rocky patches. If I was in your position, with this little baby in here to think of . . .' She patted her stomach. 'I tell you I wouldn't hesitate.'

I looked at my lap. I felt like a failure for the fact that I couldn't support my daughter. 'I know,' I admitted. 'You're much stronger than me. I know that I need his help. Even if he was helping out, I'd still put the house on the market. I need to move away for my own sanity as much as anything. I can't stay out here with next to no work. London's fine for children really. There are parks and stuff, and good schools, and galleries, and the London Eye and the Aquarium. I'll be close to Geoff and Christa, and I'd love that. And Bella and Charlotte are in London, and so's Rosie for the moment. Alice can go to the French Lycée when she's bigger. I could get a proper job and support us both. We'll come back here on holiday to see everyone. The estate agent's coming over tomorrow.'

Fiona leaned back on the absurdly comfortable sofa.

'Are you sure?' she asked. 'Could we offer you a loan?'

I shook my head. 'Geoff offers me a loan every day. It's not the answer. I can't live off borrowed money. I need a longer term solution.'

'We'll miss you.'

I forced a smile. 'Don't.'

I picked Alice up from school at half past four feeling nervous. As usual, she came across the playground holding hands with her current best friend, a doll-like child called Melanie. When she saw me she rushed into my arms. I scooped her up. She turned round and waved to Melanie. '*Au revoir*,' she called.

She looked just like the other children. She was wrapped up in a big coat, with her scarf knotted round her neck. She was wearing clumpy winter shoes and cream woolly tights which were splattered with mud from the playground puddles. Her skin was edibly perfect, and she glowed with happiness and health. Alice loved school. Since she had been able to understand what was going on, and now that she was increasingly able to join in with games in French, she had blossomed. She often ate school lunches without complaint, and she no longer dismissed it to me, afterwards, as 'funny food'. She had a nap on a camp bed on the floor with the other children. She asked me every week when she could start using the school bus.

'Alice,' I said, after I had strapped her into her car seat. 'Do you remember our old house in England?'

'And the teacher said, you mustn't go outside because it's time for singing,' she told me brightly. 'She told us off.'

'I don't expect she was really telling you off,' I said, as I started the car. 'She was probably just telling you it was singing time. What did you sing?'

After Alice's confident rendition of a song which, as far as I could understand, was about fingers and thumbs hiding and jumping out, I tried again.

'You remember our old house?' I looked at her in the rear-view mirror to check that she was concentrating.

'Yes,' she said. 'In English.'

'In England. Would you like to go back to England?'

'Daddy's there?'

'Yes. You can see Daddy a lot if we go there.'

'Why?'

'Because Daddy's work is there.'

'Why's Daddy's work's not here?'

'Because Daddy doesn't speak French.' I decided against detailing the other reasons.

'Why doesn't Daddy speak French?'

I sighed. 'The issue is, darling, that we will probably go and live in England again.' And you will have to go to a nursery that, while perfectly pleasant, will not be a patch on the village school. And you will live in a busy city, where we will only just manage to afford to rent a tiny flat. And we will have no garden, no playroom, no log fire, no cows nearby, no tractors trundling past, no chickens. And I will work full time so we can manage without your wayward father. You and I will only really see each other at week-ends. And it will probably be alternate weekends, at that.

I looked at Alice in the rear-view mirror. Her attention had wandered.

'Did you bring me a biscuit?' she demanded.

I passed one back to her. 'You know I always bring you a biscuit.' Children are adaptable, I told myself for the thousandth time. The upheaval to Alice is the least of my worries. It seemed heartbreaking to me, but she would take it in her stride.

That evening I phoned Matt. There was no reply at Pete's flat, and I was relieved. On the spur of the moment, I punched in Jo's number. I didn't need to look it up. I knew it by heart, even though I'd never called it.

I hoped that she, too, would be out, but she answered after three rings.

'Hello, Jo,' I said quietly, and left a brief pause for the woman to tell me that she wasn't Jo, she was the babysitter. Sadly, she didn't. 'It's Emma,' I told her.

There was a short laugh. 'Hello, Emma,' she said. 'I've been wondering how you were doing.' I heard the glug glug glug of wine being poured, and I remembered how much we had drunk on our evening together.

'I'm doing OK,' I said lightly. I decided not to allude to her visit, which still rankled enormously. Our situation was beyond absurd and neither of us was the villain. I reminded myself that the fact that she had fooled me reflected worse on her than it did on me. 'How are you?' I added.

'Oh. You know. Single mother and all that. We're getting by. You?'

'Same.'

'You're still in France?'

'For the moment. I'm putting the house on the market tomorrow. Then we'll be back.'

'Do you hear from Hugh?'

I was pained to hear him called by his real name. 'Pretty much never. Do you?'

'He takes Olly every other weekend. I don't say a word to him. We make arrangements by email. I still can't believe he did it. To all of us, I mean. I thought he was one of the good guys. That was why I married him. I don't know about you but I'm kind of stuck at the outrage stage. I'm getting over it though. I've been on a couple of dates. It's going to be OK.' Her voice faltered and I knew that Jo was struggling. I pictured her on the other end of the phone, her blonde hair framing a sad face. Jo's life, carefully constructed for safety and happiness, had crashed down, just as mine had. We had thought we were safe, but we weren't. The day-to-day happiness had been an illusion.

'I wish you'd told me,' I said suddenly. 'When you came. I mean, Jesus, I felt stupid.'

'God, yes,' she said immediately. 'Sorry I was so manipulative. I know you must hate me for it. I couldn't help myself.'

'It just makes me see how naïve I was,' I said. 'I wish I could say now that I'd started suspecting something was wrong back then, but I didn't have an inkling. I liked you. I didn't doubt for an instant that you were a lost tourist. It's humiliating.' I took a deep breath. 'But it doesn't matter any more.'

'I wish I had told you. I was a bit possessed. I had just about worked out what was going on, but I didn't want to confront him because I knew he would deny it. And part of me was certain there would be a rational explanation. God knows what I was thinking, dragging Olly over there. It could have been disastrous. It was disastrous. I was expecting you to know everything. I assumed Hugh had a willing mistress. I was going to make a huge scene. Then I could see straightaway that you knew less than I did. I thought about telling you, but I was so caught up in the horror of it, and the fact that your little girl was the same fucking age as Olly, and everything that that implied. And I could barely imagine what you'd have said if I'd told you that your Matt and my Hugh were the same person. You'd have had me sectioned.'

I sighed. 'I suppose I would. I flipped out afterwards too. You can't predict how you'll react when something like that happens.'

We talked, in a stilted way, for a while, and agreed that when I was back in England, we would meet up. Alice and Olly were going to have to know that they were brother and sister. They needed a relationship with each other. We could cut their father out of it.

We were being too mature. I would never like Jo. She would never like me. That was a friendship that could never get started. I wanted to stay in touch with her, though, purely because it would annoy Matt. I was certain that she felt the same way.

After I put down the phone, I wailed for half an hour. I was outraged for Alice. He spent every other weekend with his son. He had no contact whatsoever with his daughter. She missed him. I missed him. I hated him, hated him, hated him.

chapter thirty-seven

The house went back onto the market. I put it on for a vast amount more than I paid for it, at the estate agent's suggestion. I was dealing with Ella, the same woman who had handled our purchase. She was small and kind and she was amazed to hear that Matt and I had parted. I spared her all the details.

'It didn't work out,' I told her in what I hoped was a dignified manner, and I looked away as I felt her watching me.

'I'm sorry to hear that,' she said.

'Thank you.'

Ella was a little formal and self-conscious, because she was not at all comfortable with the camera. Rosie had handed over the end of the documentary to a colleague called Jim, who was dishevelled and who didn't converse. That suited me. He hung around me, sizing situations up wordlessly. His job was simply to get the sale of the house on celluloid, to wrap things up. I had offered to do it myself, but Rosie had laughed.

Ella had only agreed to be filmed out of politeness, and after securing Jim's agreement that her agency's name would be shown. I wondered if she would see the finished programme. Then she would certainly find out, in graphic detail, what, exactly, 'not working out' involved.

She didn't put up a For Sale board because I didn't want Alice to know what was going on, if a board had gone up she would have demanded to know why it was there. We had so little passing traffic that it was hardly worth it anyway. Ella did, however, come over one crisp sunny day with a digital camera, and take endless photos for her website. Three days later, I looked it up and easily located my house. She had made it look pretty and desirable, and I was torn between pride and dread. I wanted to sell it easily because I needed to move away, but I half hoped no one would be interested.

Spring was arriving. This year, the weather was perfect: crisp, clear and warm. My house was almost perfect. One morning, I walked around the garden by myself. The electrician was indoors, fitting sockets and switches so that all the lights would work and the power would no longer fuse every day or two. I walked slowly, despite the chill. It was a bright day, and, far in the distance, I could see the hills that marked the very beginning of the Pyrenees, silhouetted against the sky. At the end of the garden were the bare fields. There were no leaves on the trees, just the tiny beginnings of buds. The barns were full of crates of walnuts and hazelnuts from our trees, and the freezer was full of apples and pears and plums and figs. I would need to cut the grass, soon, because it was beginning to grow again.

Plan B

The chickens wandered around, pecking at the hard ground. I took the lid off the Tupperware container I was carrying, and emptied its contents onto the earth. Lenin came running and began pecking furiously at the limp lettuce leaves and leftover potatoes. Sarah came to join her, and though Lenin tried to fend her off, she failed. Finally, Emperor Zurg, always the last, ambled over, picked up a lettuce leaf, and carried it away to peck in peace. I liked the fact that my chickens had personalities. Lenin was always the leader, and Zurg always came last. I loved the fact that Sarah, the one I thought of as *my* chicken, was the balanced one. She was in the middle. She was named after my mother, yet she was normal.

My mother had seduced Geoff. I was constantly trying to imagine it. The idea made me laugh.

My wellies were glistening with the melting frost. I was wearing my black trousers. It was frustrating that I couldn't afford to spend any more money on clothes. I would have loved a good pair of well-fitting jeans. If I had had such a thing, I would have worn them every day. As it was, my black trousers, black T-shirt and tight red cardigan made me look like a parody of a chic country woman.

The back of the house was unrecognisable. I wished Matt were here to admire it with me. Last winter it had looked bleak. The wall had been blank but for the back door and a dead creeper. Now five newly fitted windows, with pale blue shutters, looked out onto the garden. This was a welcoming, friendly house. The wall had been re-rendered, with the big stones at the corners and around the door left exposed. This was my dream home. I had created it, and now it was being snatched away. I vowed to enjoy it while I still had it.

Inevitably, a buyer appeared far too quickly. Ten days after the house went on the market, Ella received an email from some English clients, describing what they were looking for. An old house, preferably in a small village, that they could use as a holiday home. They wanted at least four bedrooms and two bathrooms, and a big garden either with a pool or with potential for one. They wanted it to be already renovated as they did not want to spend time or money smartening it up. Then they described their taste: 'terracotta floor tiles, white walls, exposed beams and an open fireplace'. Ella was so excited that she forwarded me the email.

'Your house is so much to the English sensibility,' she wrote at the end. 'I know these are your buyers.'

I waited nervously for their arrival. There were vases of early daffodils on the mantelpiece and the table. Everything was tidy and clean. I felt that these people were coming to pass judgement on every aspect of my life. It was all tied up in this house.

The first thing that struck me was the fact that they dripped with money. Jim, who was filming their visit, gave me a cynical thumbs-up behind their backs. It pained me to watch them eyeing up my house critically. The adults were in their late thirties, and their two children were, I estimated, about seven and ten. They were a boy and a girl, both blonde. Alice jumped and danced around them, desperate to play. It was the school holidays in France, though not in England, and Alice was missing her social life.

I saw the children looking at the garden with interest,

and, remembering the day Matt and I had first looked round, I told them to go outside, if they wanted, while their parents checked out the interior. Alice skipped after them, delighted. I had to drag her back to force her into her coat and boots.

'This is my garden,' she said grandly, entering into the spirit of the occasion. 'These are my chickens. I'll show you my swing.' The girl took her hand and Alice basked in the attention.

The man was tall and broad. 'Good tiles,' he said approvingly as we walked slowly around. 'Good sized dining room, too. So you've done the renovation yourselves, have you? Hard finding builders, I hear.'

'I've done it myself. I'm on my own. It's been quite a process, but worth it.'

'I'd say.' He nodded. 'Smeg kitchen. Black granite. We like that.'

I laughed. The Smeg kitchen had been entirely Matt's idea. I had, naturally, paid for it, but I would have been quite happy with something far more ordinary.

'I think that's a male thing,' I said. 'My partner liked it. The kitchen was his project.'

The woman, who was bright and tidy, with a tinkling laugh, looked at me with sincere curiosity. 'He's not on the scene any more? Sorry if it's a personal question.'

I was very aware of the camera, for once, so I made my voice as resolute as possible. 'He's not on the scene any more because I discovered that he had another child, and indeed a wife, in London.' I smiled, watching her trying to mask her excitement as sympathy. 'That's why I'm selling.'

'No place for a lady to be alone,' boomed the man.

'It seems not,' I agreed. 'Unfortunately, because Alice and I both love it here.'

'Well, you've done a stunning job with the house.' He looked at his wife. 'We could spend the hols here, couldn't we, darling? Put in a pool?'

'I'd say so.'

'Good neighbours?'

'Lovely.'

'It's nice to see a place that's been done up to the English taste. The French prefer modern houses, by and large. Need to rip it all out and start again. This is exactly our style.'

I frowned. I knew plenty of tasteful French houses, and many French people who preferred old houses. Many had been priced out of that market. I didn't say anything. I knew for certain that this family were going to buy my house, and that it was going to stand empty for forty-eight weeks of the year. Selling a house was not supposed to be easy. It was sod's law that it was going to happen smoothly this time.

I accepted their offer, which was not far below the asking price. When I called Bella she was delighted.

'Well done, Emma,' she said, several times. 'We can't wait to have you back. You sound like you've really got yourself together.'

'I have my moments.'

'You're OK though, aren't you?'

I thought about it. 'I really am, actually. I'm OK. I'm doing what I have to do, and we'll start all over again in London, and maybe one day I'll meet someone new. I hope so.' This was a new hope of mine. I was beginning to feel ready to try again, and not with Matt this time.

'Of course you will. You couldn't fail to. How's Alice?'

Christa called me, too. 'Don't bother househunting in London before you get back,' she advised. 'You and Alice can come and live here while you get things sorted out. Geoff's dying to see you. He's got a new lease of life since you and he got things out into the open.'

I was still nervous of Christa. 'Are you sure you're all right with it all?'

She snorted. 'I've already told you I am. It was a long, long time ago. Sarah's misdeeds were completely overshadowed by her death, and you weren't exactly an accomplice. It only concerns Geoff and me, and we came to terms with it years ago. For God's sake, just stop asking.'

'OK. Sorry. We'd love to come and stay with you. Thanks. It'll make it all a lot easier.'

I spoke to Greg, too. 'I'm moving back to London,' I told him, trying out the idea.

He took a few seconds to respond. 'Seriously?' he said in the end. 'Sure?'

'Not really, but I need a plan, and all of you guys, my family, are in London. When are you off to Cuba?'

He answered at once. 'When Rosie's got the all-clear. She's doing well. We're just going to see how she goes.'

I walked down to Martine's house to tell her that the house was under offer.

'More English?' she asked.

I nodded. 'I'm afraid it's going to be a holiday home,' I confessed. 'I'm really sorry.'

'You don't need to go,' Martine said doggedly. 'It's OK to be alone here. I am.'

'I wish I could stay,' I told her, and I meant it. It was an enormous wrench.

Alice's school were surprised and disappointed that I was withdrawing her.

'She's doing so well,' her teacher told me. 'She is one of the easiest pupils. She understands French, and she speaks beautifully, and she plays and eats and sleeps. If only they were all like that. We will all miss Alice.'

Half our boxes had never even been unpacked. I taped them up again and looked for the number of the international removals company, so that I could ask them to take it all back across the Channel. When I made that phone call I felt, for the first time, that I was admitting defeat.

'I remember you,' said the man who answered the phone in the Brighton office. 'Coming back?' He laughed. 'Not all it was cracked up to be?'

I almost forced myself to laugh along and agree with him. At the last minute, I decided to embarrass him with the truth.

'Oh, it was more than it was cracked up to be,' I assured him. 'It's just that Matt, you remember him?' He grunted in affirmation. 'Matt turned out to have a wife and child in London, so he's not living here any more and this is all a bit rural for me on my own.' I seemed unable to stop telling strangers. It did me good every time I said it.

The man surprised me. 'I'm really sorry to hear that, love,' he said. 'The bastard, eh? Plenty more pebbles on the beach, as they say here. I'm sure you won't be alone for long.'

I smiled. 'Thanks,' I told him.

That night, I told my conversation class that I was leaving at Easter.

'Why?' asked Chloe.

'Because my family and friends are mostly in London,' I said. 'Because there isn't enough work for me here. Because Alice needs to be near her father.'

Bernard frowned. 'Her father should come to her. Not her go to him.'

'I know. But—'

'There is always work for a teacher of English,' Alain butted in. 'There are many language schools nearby.'

'I suppose so, but—'

'You don't like it here because it's too rural,' Chloe said confidently. 'Especially around St Paul. You want to get back to London because you miss the city and the vibrantness.'

'Vibrancy. No, that's not it. I love it being rural.'

Alain looked at me. 'Then why do you go?'

After the class, he waited behind for me. I looked at him with a bright, teacherish smile.

'Alain,' I said. Normally if students hung around to talk to me alone, they were either going to an English-speaking country on a work trip, or they needed me to translate something.

Alain was about forty, dark-haired, and I had always admired his looks. He took care of himself. He dressed well, groomed himself well, and his face was at ease with itself. He always made me think of French film actors.

'I am sorry to disturb you,' he said, in English. 'I wonder, will you have dinner with me next Saturday?'

chapter thirty-eight

It was Saturday, the day of my date, and I was getting ready to go to market. I had just received the deposit on the house sale, and had used it to write a cheque which paid the builders off completely and finally. I was feeling strange, mixed up. The house was finished, and we were leaving in three weeks, and I was going out with a man I hardly knew that evening. Alice was going to stay overnight with Coco and Louis. This was a proper date. I didn't think I'd ever been on one of them in my life.

I was considering going on to Villeneuve after doing the vegetable shop. I could not afford to, but I was nonetheless keen to buy myself a new outfit. Alain was taking me to a restaurant I'd heard of but never been to. There were, it seemed, many good restaurants around, and now I was about to leave without ever having visited any except the pizzeria and the crêperie in St Paul. Both of them were favourite haunts of Alice's. At least, I told myself sternly, I would get to try out this one. It had a Michelin star. Celine liked to take Coco there, and Coco had raved to me about the open fire, the ambience, and the rustic chic.

'Actually,' she had said, pensively, 'it's quite like your house.'

I knew Alain was divorced, because he had talked about it in class. If I had had to choose anybody I had met in France to take me out, I would have chosen Alain. Yet the idea petrified me and I did not want to go at all.

'Shall we go to Villeneuve after the market?' I asked Alice as I put two wicker shopping baskets into the car.

'It's *Villeneuve*,' she corrected me. She pronounced it exactly like a French person. My daughter's French was now officially better than mine.

'Sorry. So, shall we go there?'

I looked at her. She was busily climbing onto her booster seat and arranging her animals on her lap.

'If you like, Mum. Can we go to a café?' She looked at me eagerly and, perceiving something unusual in my mood, adjusted her request upwards. 'Can we have pizza for lunch?'

'OK. Just this once. As a special treat. You know we don't really have any money for that sort of thing. But what the hell. Sold the house. We may as well.'

She beamed. 'Thank you, Mummy. Thank you thank you.'

It was a gloomy day, with thick grey clouds and the threat of rain. Drizzle seemed to hang in the air, ready to drop at the slightest provocation. I had blow-dried my hair and put on some pale lipstick for the market, as I usually did these days. I knew there wasn't an umbrella in the boot, because I remembered Alice and me sheltering under it a week ago, running screaming from car to house in the middle of a sudden drenching downpour. My glossy hair would get wet, my make-up would suffer, and I would have to blow-dry it all over again for my date. It did not matter.

When I reached the top of the road, I waited while another car drove up, then turned into our road. It had a non-local registration, with 60 at the end of the number plate. I was mildly curious, because Pounchet on a rainy day in March was not a magnet for tourists.

I was even more curious when the car stopped next to my house.

'Look, Alice,' I said. 'That car's stopped at our house. We'd better go back and see who it is.'

She barely looked up. ''Kay.'

I reversed down the road and stopped next to the car. I got out into the moist air, pulled my long coat tightly round me, and walked over to the green car.

Matt and I stared at each other. I tried to think of something to say, but nothing came to mind, so I decided to let him speak first. I looked at him closely while I waited. He looked pretty much exactly the same as he had always looked. His face was tight and closed, but his hair fell in the same way, and he was as tall and strong as ever. I thought I even recognised his clothes.

'Hello, Emma,' he said, eventually.

'Hello,' I replied. I listened to my voice as I said it, and hoped I sounded normal. I went back to my car and opened Alice's door and unclicked her seatbelt. 'Look who's come to see you, Alice,' I said, holding her hand as she jumped down. I regulated my breathing, made myself stay calm.

She looked. Then she hid behind my legs.

'Alice,' I said, pulling her out. 'Look. It's Daddy.'

She shook her head and hid her face in my skirt. I picked her up.

'Alice,' I said again. 'Daddy's come to see you. You've missed Daddy, and he's missed you. Give him a kiss.'

She looked at him, and he smiled at her. Suddenly, she wriggled down.

'My daddy!' she shouted, breaking into a run. Her face was alight with joy. 'My daddy, my daddy, my daddy!' Matt caught her in his arms and picked her up, squeezing her tightly. He pushed his face into her hair and shut his eyes.

'Alice,' he said softly. 'I've missed you so much.' He looked at me over her head. 'Can I come in? Were you going somewhere important?'

I drew a deep breath. 'No. Just to market. Come on.' I took my keys out. 'You must still have keys of your own, haven't you?'

'I'll give them back.'

I didn't reply. When I'd opened the shutter over the kitchen door, I looked at him. He was still carrying Alice. He looked serious. He did not look as if he had spent the past seven months being happy. He was wearing a brown jumper that I knew well, his old jeans, and a new waterproof jacket. His blond hair was, I thought, slightly longer than it used to be, and I could tell instantly that he had shaved that morning, because his skin was still pink with the shock.

I was surprised by how normal he looked, how normal it felt to have him here.

'Come in,' I said carefully. 'What can we do for you?'

chapter thirty-nine

Hugh was surprised by Emma. For one thing, she had always been pretty, but she had never bothered to tart herself up. He had liked that about her. He had loved the fact that she was completely natural. Emma's world had always been different from Jo's world. Emma was, he had always thought, still a little girl. She had never been sophisticated. She had been lovely and unspoilt.

Yet here she was, living in a stunningly renovated country house – a house he had made her buy but which he no longer recognised – looking as if she had stepped from the pages of a magazine. His funny little Emma had lost all the baby weight, got herself some nice new clothes, and he suspected she was even wearing make-up. Her hair was glossy and cut so it just brushed her shoulders. The haircut, the weight loss and the extra confidence were, according to Pete's Jane, classic post-break-up behaviour. Jo had done the same.

'You look nice,' he said, as she shrugged her coat off and hung it on a peg by the bottom of the staircase. 'And the house looks amazing.'

She looked at him with a smile. 'Right. I look nice but the house looks amazing?'

'Sorry. You look amazing and the house looks nice.'

'Better. Thanks.'

He wasn't sure whether she was flirting with him or laughing at his ineptness, and he had no idea what to say next. He was scared to launch into what he had come to say, so he stalled.

'Are these floor tiles the ones we chose? They look great, don't they?'

'Yes. We chose them. Yes, they look great. The whole house looks great. Why don't you look round while I make the coffee? I'm assuming you want coffee?'

'I always want coffee.'

'I know,' she said. 'Alice, can you show Daddy round the house? Show him all the things the builders did. And the garden. Daddy hasn't seen any of it. I'm afraid most of your stuff's long gone,' she added to him quietly, 'so I hope that's not why you've come.'

'Of course not.'

He wanted to stay in the kitchen with Emma, to try to work out what she was thinking and feeling. She appeared to be calm, but he hoped she wasn't. He hoped she had not got over him to the extent that she felt no emotion when he turned up out of the blue. Emma had always been nice, but now she was being enigmatic. He was not sure what to do about that.

Alice took him by the hand and led him into the sitting room.

'Hey, Alice,' he said. He could hear himself using the same

too-jolly voice he used with Olly on alternate Friday nights. When they were used to each other again they chatted perfectly naturally, but for the first few hours, Hugh knew he acted the weekend father, and he hated himself for it. 'Hey, I've got something for you.'

She beamed up at him. 'What is it?'

He handed her the small parcel and watched her rip the wrapping off.

'Oh,' she said, in a small voice. 'Dinosaurs.'

'Yes, dinosaurs!'

'But Daddy, I don't like dinosaurs any more.'

'Don't you?'

'No.'

He took the bag of dinosaurs back and crammed it into his pocket. 'That's OK. You can choose something else. We'll go to the shops later, shall we?'

'I like other animals and I like Toy Story and Monsters, Inc. Here is our sitting room,' she said. 'Here is Mummy's chair. Here is my chair. This used to be Greg's chair and sometimes Rosie's chair. Here are the tiles the builders put on the floor.'

There was ash in the grate, the remains of the previous night's fire. The chairs and the sofa were covered in comfy cushions. The walls had been replastered and painted white. He pressed the light switch, and two wall lamps cast a soft glow. It was a cosy room, unrecognisable from the cold, unwelcoming box they had slept in when they had arrived.

'Now I'll show you my bedroom,' said Alice, and he let her pull him around the house, showing him everything that Emma had achieved without him.

'So,' she said, looking at him across the table.

'I can't get over this room,' he said quickly. The huge dining room had been his idea. It incorporated a former corridor and a former shed. It was magnificent. It had come to fruition exactly as he had imagined it. There were three windows looking out to the back garden. In the garden, he could see daffodils and crocuses. There were small pale leaves on the trees. The whole garden was being soaked by the rain.

'Are those hens?' he added. They were definitely hens. He was playing for time because he was certain of what he wanted, and he was terrified of asking.

'Of course they're hens. Why are you here, Matt?'

He smiled, despite himself. 'It's good to be Matt again. I'm here . . .' He drew a deep breath and made his speech. 'I'm here, Emma, because I've realised that I made a huge mistake. I'm here to apologise to you for everything. I was weak and cruel and I had no right to treat you and Alice like I did. Um, this is going to sound cheeky, this next bit. Emma, I haven't been able to stop thinking about you. I've missed you both so much that I haven't really known what to do with myself. I stayed out of touch because I didn't want to mess you around any more, I wanted to give you a chance to start again without me. But I couldn't stay away. I had to see you. So I wondered if you would consider, even for a moment, giving us another go. Starting all over again but with me getting it right this time. There'll be no one else, ever. I could easily work from home. It would involve a sideways move or even a demotion but I'd happily do that. Or I'll leave work and do freelance consulting from home. Or something completely different. I could come back here and we could all live together and just see how it went. I would love to be back in the centre of Alice's life. Could we try it? Try a blank slate and see what happened? Obviously Jo and I are getting divorced, and if you would have me and if things went well for us, I would be honoured if you would marry me, one day.'

Emma was watching him. He clenched his fists and hoped that he didn't look as scared as he felt. Everything hung on her reaction. There was nothing more he wanted in the world than to take his place back here, in France, with this woman who, he now realised, was the woman he wanted. They had a house and a daughter. He thought of offering another baby, but stopped himself.

'Why have you stayed out of Alice's life since the summer? It's March. You left us in August. And you haven't set eyes on her since. You're lucky she even recognised you.' Her voice was devoid of emotion.

He floundered. 'I didn't want to make things harder for you. I thought I'd give you a bit of time. I was getting my head together, too. Staying at Pete's was no good, because he, well, he has a lot of unresolved issues of various sorts as you undoubtedly know, plus his girlfriend hates me. Does Pete ring you, by the way?'

Emma nodded. 'He has done. Not often.'

'Thought so. Anyway, I got a place on my own and I tried to put my screw-up behind me and get on with life, but I couldn't. I only wanted to be with you.'

'You think you can stroll in and everything can be how it used to be? Except presumably without the double life?'

'I know it's a lot to ask. I'm throwing myself on your mercy. I'm in love with you, Emma. I'm begging you to give me a chance. I might surprise you.'

'You surprised me last time.'

'Give me a chance for Alice's sake.'

'I've got a date tonight.'

Matt was surprised. Then he was surprised that he was surprised.

'I'm not surprised,' he lied. 'You look stunning. Is this . . .' His voice was small. 'Do you have a boyfriend?'

'Not a boyfriend. Just someone I've met through work who's asked me to dinner.' She looked at him levelly. 'And I'm going to go. And by the way I've sold the house.'

Matt nodded. 'Right.' He had known this was a long shot. Pete would be furious with him for coming out here to try to get back with Emma. He still claimed to be happy with Jane. Hugh did not believe him. Particularly not if he had been calling Emma. 'Who to?'

'A British family. They love it. They're going to put a pool in. They made a great offer.'

'OK.' He wanted to ask how much, but he didn't. Emma had paid for the house and he knew that her profit margin had nothing to do with him. 'I expected you to sell it. So, where do you work?'

'I teach English conversation at the Chamber of Commerce. I've had a few enquiries about private tuition lately, but I've turned them down because Alice and I are leaving here the week before Easter. We're going to stay with Christa and Geoff for a bit and then we'll find a place to rent. Maybe in Brighton. Probably in London.' She gestured around. 'Sadly a French country house, in perfect nick with enormous garden, doesn't get you much of a London pad.'

They sat in silence for a while. Hugh tried to work out how it was going. He knew he was being colossally cheeky. He was relieved when Alice ran back into the room.

She looked at him shrewdly. 'Have you seen my school, Daddy?' she asked.

'Yes. Remember? I used to take you to school sometimes.' He felt wretched. 'Do you like school?'

'Yes I do. I play with Melanie. She's my *best* friend.'

'I bet you speak perfect French by now.'

'I speak French at school.'

Emma interjected. 'She's bilingual. It's awful that she's going to have to lose it.'

From the way she was looking at him, Hugh realised that this, too, was his fault.

'She doesn't have to,' he said, on impulse. 'Cancel the sale. Let me live with you both for a bit. See how it goes.'

Emma shook her head. 'You can't waltz in and throw that at me. I'm off to do the shopping. You and Alice stay here for a bit. Spend some quality time together.'

Hugh nodded, bemused to see her breezing away. 'See you later. Think about it.'

Emma kissed Alice, and left.

Hugh looked at his daughter. 'Right, Alice,' he said, with too much enthusiasm. 'What would you like to do?'

Her reply was instant. 'Pizza for lunch.'

chapter forty

I drove into St Paul and did my vegetable shopping quickly at the market, pausing only to exchange the briefest of pleasantries with acquaintances. I saw Fiona in the distance, looking at pot plants, but hid from her, because I did not know what to say about Matt's return.

I chatted to the women I saw every week, and kept my demeanour studiedly casual. Then I drove for another twenty minutes, to Villeneuve, parked illegally in the middle of town and rushed into Nouvelles Galeries at ten to twelve. I picked up a tight black dress. It fitted me perfectly. It clung in all the right places, and its hemline was uneven. I had never felt as glamorous as I did with that dress on. It cost one hundred and fifty euros, but I told myself that, at the very least, Matt was now going to have to support Alice properly, so I could afford to get myself something to wear. I bought some high, sexy shoes. I would wear my long coat and make-up and I would look fine for my date.

The last thing I felt like doing was going out with Alain. I hated Matt. I hated everything he had done to me. I hated the months of misery he put me through. In many ways, for much of most days, I was still miserable. I was functioning now, doing all the things I had to do, being brave, but I still ached all over when I thought of him. He had given me a life that had been nothing but an illusion. Seven months later, I was still reeling. These days I was able to put on a show, that was all.

My self-control was rigorous. I never let myself drink more than a glass and a half of alcohol. I never let my fingernails grow, my eyebrows take their natural shape. Some days I was so busy not breaking down that I could not allow myself so much as a deep breath. This was my way of managing. It was the only way I could look after Alice, and the chickens, and the garden and the house and myself.

And now he was back. As I walked to the car, swinging my shopping bag, a surge of excitement overwhelmed me, and I stood still on the bridge and looked to the future for the first time. The river was high. It swirled around in little eddies and rapids, all the way to the next bridge. Water covered the riverside walkway. The sun came out from behind a cloud and shone, suddenly, into my eyes. Matt wanted to come back. He said we could start again with no secrets this time. I could cancel the house sale, give back the deposit. I might have to give back double the deposit – I thought that was the penalty for pulling out on a whim – but Matt could help with that. We could be the ones to put in a pool. We could live as a family. Alice would have her daddy, and I would have my Matt, and I wouldn't be lonely, and together we would find a way to be happy in spite of everything.

If I were stronger, I would be throwing him out. I knew I ought to be outraged that he had even dared to suggest coming back. But I was not that strong. I loved him and I needed someone to lean on. I knew what my answer was going to be.

I walked the last few yards to the car with a spring in my step. Coco and Fiona would be disappointed in me. Rosie would be disappointed in me. Bella and Greg and Christa and Geoff would be disappointed in me. None of that mattered. This was my decision and mine alone. I was going to spend the afternoon talking to him, and then I would decide whether or not to cancel Alain. I quite liked the idea of going on a date, because it had clearly made me more desirable in Matt's eyes. I was not going to be silly, timid Emma, desperately trying to please everybody and being trampled underfoot. I was going to be strong, this time. We would be equals.

The journey home was exciting. I bounced in my seat as I drove, imagining our future. For the first time in seven months I allowed myself to picture a future which involved marriage and babies. The sun had broken through the clouds now, and I screwed up my eyes to see the road ahead. I had never loved anyone but Matt. I was never going to meet anyone I could talk to like that. He had betrayed me, but he was sorry. It was going to be different this time, better this time.

When I got home, the house was silent. Matt's hire car had gone. All the shutters were open, and the doors weren't locked. I walked into every room, calling, 'Alice!' although I knew I wouldn't find her. Matt would not have driven off and left her at home on her own. He must have taken her out somewhere.

I hung up my new dress on the outside of my wardrobe door. I placed my new shoes under it, and stood back to admire the ensemble. Matt might have taken Alice to the toy shop. But the shops were shut now. And if Matt was trying so hard to win us back, he would have left me a note. I went downstairs two steps at a time, and looked on the dining table, the kitchen worktops, and the coffee table in the sitting room. There was nothing.

They had probably gone out visiting. Matt would have wanted to see Andy. I dialled their number. I would pop over to Aurillon, if they were there, and maybe we would all stay for lunch.

Andy answered.

'Hello, Andy,' I said expectantly.

'Emma! All set for this evening?'

'Are they there?'

'Who?'

'Clearly not. I'll call you back.'

I had a creeping feeling of dread. Matt had lied to me so much that I could not believe anything he said now. He had probably been lying today. What if he'd had a completely different reason for coming back to France? What if he had come to take Alice away?

I felt sick as I began searching for evidence.

Alice's clothes were still in place. Her passport was still there. Her coat and her hat were missing. Whatever he had done with her, I was glad about that. At least she was warm. My big umbrella was missing too.

Plan B

He could not have taken her out of the country without a passport, unless he had magicked up another one from somewhere. I told myself I was being silly. Then I told myself that anything was possible. Matt was desperate to be a full-time father. I had seen it in his eyes. And desperate people were capable of many things. Matt, in particular, was capable of anything.

They could be at Bordeaux. They could be waiting to board the lunchtime flight to Gatwick. I went cold. He could not have taken her. I had never done anything bad to him, and no court in the world would give him custody.

I felt stupid for imagining that our relationship could ever have worked. He had never wanted it. He had lied to me again. He had taken our daughter.

The idea of living without her took hold of me. It was impossible. Alice was my life, my world, the reason I was functioning. My duty was to cherish her, and she had gone. This was punishment for the way I had rejected her in the autumn. I had always known that punishment would come one day.

I picked up the phone and dialled.

'Coco? Emma. Have you seen them?' I remembered that Coco was French and asked again, in French, 'Have you seen Alice and Matt?'

'Alice and Matt?'

'Are you busy? Can you go to the cafés and look for them?'

'Of course, but—'

I didn't explain. I hung up, and opened my phone book, and dialled again.

A woman answered. 'Hello?'

413

'Is Pete there?' I asked abruptly.

'Well, hello to you, too,' she said sarcastically. 'Who should I say is calling?'

'Emma.'

'*The* Emma? I'm honoured.'

'Oh shut up,' I told her. 'I need Pete.'

'I'm sure the feeling's mutual.' I heard the phone being put down, and some scuffling at the other end. Then Pete came on.

'Emma?' he asked cautiously. 'Emma, were you just rude to my girlfriend?' He sounded impressed.

'Mmm. Where's Matt? Hugh? Whoever he is. Where has your brother gone with my daughter? I went out and left her with him and when I came back . . .' I heard my voice rising, felt hysteria threatening. I filled my lungs with air, exhaled from the diaphragm, and enunciated the words as calmly as I could. 'When I came back he had taken her away.'

Pete was silent for a couple of minutes. 'Last time I saw Hugh was yesterday,' he said. 'He said he was away for the weekend. He didn't say where. I didn't know he was heading to France.'

'He asked me to have him back.'

'And you said . . . ?'

'I didn't give him an answer.'

'And he's gone walkabout?'

'Yes.'

'I'll call his mobile. You home? I'll ring you back.'

I sat and stared at the phone. The house was silent. I picked up the cordless phone and held it in my hand, waiting for it to ring. I wanted to call Bella but I needed to wait for

Pete to ring back first. I tried to fill my mind with trivia. I wondered what Pete's girlfriend was like. I wondered whether she knew that he had once slashed his wrists in front of me. She must have had an idea that he had feelings for me, or she wouldn't have been so affronted. He had only called me once since I had rashly agreed to let his parents meet Alice. I was glad. I could never love Pete. I didn't like him, either. Everything about him was repulsive. I wanted Alice to know her grandparents, but I could not imagine the couple that had produced a bigamist and an obsessive. I planned to keep them at arm's length, whatever happened.

The ring shattered the stillness. I snatched up the phone.

'Can't reach him,' Pete said. 'His phone's off, or he's out of reception. Now, don't worry about it. If he did bring Alice back here, we'd send him straight back to you. He won't get away with it.'

I heard a car door slam outside, so I ran out, and saw Jim approaching with his camera.

'Bugger,' I told him. 'I thought you were Matt.'

'What?' asked Pete. The phone was still clamped to my ear.

'May I?' Jim asked.

'Whatever.' I stood by the gate, looking up and down the road, not caring about the camera. 'Sorry, Pete, thought they were back,' I said into the phone. 'If they don't turn up soon I'm coming to London.'

'I'll meet you at the airport.'

'Thanks. Keep trying him for me, hey?'

'Touch base soon.'

I paced around, trying to formulate a plan. I wondered whether Matt had hired a car seat with his car. I hoped so. I told myself that he could not have had a bigger plan, that he must have taken her on impulse. He could not be rushing off, say, to Australia, to start a new life with her. Could he?

I swept some crumbs off the table into my hand, and tipped them into the bin. I bent to pick up a piece of paper from the kitchen floor, to throw it, too, into the bin.

It was an envelope. On the back, a message was scrawled in green felt tip. I recognised Matt's handwriting. 'We've gone to the pizzeria for lunch. Come and join us if you like. M & A xxx'

I clutched my head. There was no mobile reception inside the pizzeria.

I turned to the camera. 'OK,' I said. 'I feel silly.' I called Pete, Andy and Coco, and told them that it had been a false alarm. I couldn't get hold of Coco. I wondered whether she had got as far as the pizzeria yet. Then I leapt in my car, let Jim into the passenger seat, and drove off. I wondered, uneasily, how long it would be before I would trust Matt again.

chapter forty-one

I stepped out of the cold evening into a warm, bustling dining room which smelt deliciously of good food. A huge fire burned in the enormous stone fireplace. A suckling pig was roasting in front of it. There was a display of fresh vegetables beside the fire which made me think, incongruously, of the Harvest Festival at school, even though it lacked the tins of baked beans and corned beef that had always been the staples of a Harvest Festival in north London.

Alain was sitting at a table in the corner, sipping his drink. He looked relieved when I walked over to him. Wearing my new dress and my high shoes, I walked carefully, aware of my posture. Coco had been right about the way that luxurious underwear would make me feel.

The waiter held my chair out, and I sat down. I managed to co-ordinate my sitting on it with the waiter's pushing it in, which pleased me.

'Sorry,' I told Alain. I had decided to start the evening in English. I was the teacher, so I was allowed to make decisions like that. 'I'm really late.' I grimaced. 'Family problems.'

'That is nothing,' he said, gallantly. 'It's OK. I am happy you are here.' He dropped into French. 'Emma, you look beautiful. I'm proud to be seen with you.'

I grinned at him. His eyes had smile lines around them. He was wearing a well-cut suit without a tie. I felt far more comfortable than I had expected. I had always felt there was something about Alain. 'Thank you,' I told him, and looked around, at the other diners. The women were chic in shawls and heels, and the men all looked comfortable, as Alain did, in good suits. 'This place is wonderful.'

Alain had already ordered me an aperitif; a champagne-based cocktail. I clinked glasses with him and took a sip. It was exquisite. I had come here intending to cut the evening short and get back to Matt. Now I began to revise my plans.

'My daughter's father turned up today,' I told him.

He raised his eyebrows. 'Hence the family problems?'

'He wants to come back.'

Alain nodded. 'Of course he does. You told him no.'

'I very nearly told him yes. At the moment I haven't told him anything.'

He frowned. 'This man deceived you? He had a wife and child?'

I sighed. 'I know.' I dropped back into English. 'I've just been thinking I'd be better off with the devil I know.' I looked around me. 'I don't want to spoil the evening. This is perfect. I don't know, Alain. I'm not sure I'm strong enough to resist trying again with Matt. You're right, I should tell him to bugger off. I should never have let him in the house. I'm sorry. Here we are, out to dinner, and the first thing I talk about is my ex-partner. Not very stylish of me.'

'*Si, si*. I'm concerned. I like you. Of course I do: you are a beautiful and intelligent woman. And I speak just as a friend, nothing more. And not just as a friend, but as a divorced friend. With the voice of experience. Once a relationship has failed, it's easy to want to go back to it, but the cruel fact is, it will have failed for a reason, and that reason will reappear. I know. My former wife and I tried to reconcile on three separate occasions, but it was doomed. And in fact, it was worse each time we tried. It hurt just as much each time we failed.'

'Why did it fail?'

'Originally? Because she didn't love me enough. There were many manifestations, but that was the underlying reason. She married me for the wrong reasons, too young.'

'And did you love her enough?'

'I think I did.' He laughed. 'I don't any more. I don't even like her. That, I think, is inevitable when you've shared your life with someone. We are forever speaking through clenched teeth in front of the children, in a pretence of civility. And this intrigues me, Emma. This man has treated you worse than any story of any marriage I have ever heard. Mostly, separations don't happen in black and white, but in this case there is no grey. He was wrong. Your only fault was that you trusted him and so you must have overlooked warning signs. But you're willing to consider taking him back?'

I looked at Alain, and then up at the waitress, who was young and happy looking, and who was standing a few discreet paces back, ready to take our order.

'You're right,' I told him. 'I am being a bit hasty. I've been lonely. Anyway. Let's order.'

To my great surprise, I had a wonderful evening. It was a treat to be out in the evening at all, and the restaurant was exquisite. I ate a salad followed by monkfish with vegetables and potato gratin, and finished with a raspberry meringue, and, each time, I finished everything on my plate. Alain and I left the subject of Matt alone, and talked, in both languages, about the differences between France and Britain. I was only just beginning to see how profound these differences were. I knew that I had dismissed the stereotypes, and told myself that everyone was just a person, that nationality didn't matter. Now, partly as a result of seeing the difference in the way the two countries treated three-year-olds, I was changing my mind again. In nature, we might all be the same, but nurture produced enormous cultural differences.

'It intrigues me,' I told him. 'In Britain, children take packed lunches to school. Alice took a packed lunch to nursery when she was two. So there's no emphasis on eating good food, no responsibility by the establishment to teach the children about food. It's just something you get out of the way, just fuel. The nursery would happily feed the children any old crap the parents put in the box. Whereas here, the school canteen provides a three-course meal every lunchtime, heavily subsidised, and Alice has the menu stuck in her school book every single day, and the twice-a-day *goûter* menu stuck in once a month.'

'Of course she does. Because the French are obsessed with good food. And with eating. You think that's good?'

'I think it's wonderful. It has done wonders for Alice. And shopping at the market and the fishmongers and the butchers means you cook proper food, not just supermarket junk. And I was reading that school vending machines have been refitted to sell apples, not chocolate. It's brilliant. But I do think France is closed to outside influences. Britain's the opposite. It's stuffed with Indian restaurants and sushi bars. In London it seems like every other pub offers Thai food. Because the national cuisine really isn't that special.'

'So I have heard.' He smiled. I smiled back.

'It's a cliché to say that French people aren't fat and Anglo-Saxons are, but it's true, too. You just don't see fat people in France like you do in Britain.'

He shook his head. 'I see plenty of fat people in France.'

'You don't. Not compared to Britain. America's far worse, even. Have you been to America?'

'No. Perhaps one day. Now I have such a charming English teacher.'

'Shut up.'

'But really, I think I'll go. My children are always telling me to take them to Disneyland. They don't want to go to Disneyland, Paris. Apparently it has to be Florida.'

I laughed. 'You will get a massive culture shock if you go to Florida. You should start with New York. You'd love it. There's no Disneyland.'

'Perhaps, one day. Maybe you could come with me, one day. Be my translator.'

I smiled at him. 'Who knows?'

At the end of the meal, we came back to the subject of Matt.

'But I think I still love him,' I told him. Then the wine loosened my tongue, and I spoke to him in a way I would never normally have done. 'I know he messed me around,' I said, staring at my new friend imploringly, 'but there's a part of me that feels that that's OK. That I wasn't worth any more. Part of me feels like an unwanted little girl and that if Matt won't have me back on whatever terms he wants, no one else will.'

Alain was frowning at me. Oh shit, I thought. I have to teach him next week. I will never be able to look him in the eye. I seemed, however, to be unable to stop looking him in the eye. He carried on looking at me. Then he reached out and touched my hand, lightly.

'You know you are worth more than he could ever give you,' he said. 'There will be plenty of men out there who are worthy of you. This one is not.'

We were the last to leave the restaurant. I was pleasantly drunk, and glowing. I let Alain put a hand on the small of my back to guide me to the car. He had offered to drop me off at home. I would retrieve my car from the restaurant in the morning, with the help of Matt and his hire car.

We drove back to Pounchet in near silence. I was not used to being out in the evening, and stared out of the window at the total darkness. When we were on a particularly dark stretch of road, with tall trees on either side and barely enough room to pass an oncoming car, an owl flew directly in front of the headlights. For a second it was illuminated perfectly, and I could see every feather, every crease on its talons. It stared at us with unreadable glassy eyes, then flew up and away with a screech. I smiled at Alain.

'I've never seen an owl close up before,' I told him.

'But you live in the countryside!' he marvelled.

'And I don't often go out in the night. I've seen them at a distance, seen their outlines on electricity lines, but I've never ever seen one like that. It's wonderful to see. I'll have to start taking Alice out with a torch in the evenings to look for more.'

'That has made you happy,' he commented.

'Yes,' I readily agreed.

'Are you sure you want to go back to England?'

I was deflated. 'I'm not sure about anything. You know that.'

When we got back, Alain stopped outside the front gate, and kissed me gallantly on each cheek, with the engine still running.

'Thank you for a wonderful evening,' I said. 'I'll see you on Thursday.'

'Thank you for your company. I hope you make the right choice. Remember that you are worthy of everything.' He swept his hand around, encompassing the stars, the house, the countryside and the owls.

I was still smiling as I walked through the front door. Matt was standing in the hall, looking at me.

'Hello,' I told him, with a slightly drunken smirk. 'Everything all right? Alice all right?'

'Alice is fine. She didn't go to bed till nearly ten, but she's fine. She's sound asleep now.'

I looked at him, trying to read his face. 'Good.'

He said nothing, so I walked into the kitchen and put the kettle on. 'Tea?' I asked, politely. 'Coffee? Herbal tea? I'm going to have a green and mint one. Because green tea's so good for you but I hate the taste of it. And these tea bags just taste of mint which is nice. So you get all the benefits of green tea without the nastiness.'

'Yeah,' he said. 'Sure, why not, I'll have one of them.'

He watched me pour boiling water into the two cups. I felt self-conscious as I bashed the tea bags around a bit with a teaspoon, and put them in the compost bin. He took the cup as I passed it to him, and we sat in the armchairs by the fire.

'Good evening?' he asked. It almost sounded casual.

'Yes,' I said. 'Lovely.' I was still glowing. 'That was the first date I've been on, by the way,' I added.

'Perfect timing on my part, then,' he said.

'It doesn't make any difference. I hardly know Alain. He knows all about our situation. I'm not in the least bit romantically involved with him. But he does seem to be a good friend.'

'He'd like to be more, I'm sure.'

'Maybe he would.' I put another log on the fire, and waited a couple of seconds for the flames to leap up. I kicked off my uncomfortable shoes and pulled my legs up under me. 'How does it feel, being back?' I asked him.

'Weird,' he said at once. 'You and Alice have done so much. I've missed it all. And it's unbelievably odd to be your babysitter.'

'I'm sure.'

'Have you been thinking about my suggestion?'

'I've been thinking about little else.'

'You must have been a fun date.'

'He didn't mind. I don't know, Matt.' I looked at him. His eyes made me melt slightly, but I wanted to be honest with him and with myself, so I said what I thought. 'At first I decided to accept your proposal. To see what happened. But when I came back from shopping and you and Alice weren't here, I thought you'd kidnapped her. I don't know how long it would take before I trusted you again. I don't want to live on a knife edge, waiting for something terrible to happen.'

'It won't.'

'And you've lied to me so much that I can't believe you. You have no idea what I went through. I fell apart. I'm all right now, just about, but that's recent. I hated you for what you did. I still do. It was the worst sort of betrayal, because I don't even have any happy times to look back on. They're all tainted by what I now know, by me imagining you sneaking off to phone Jo all the time. I never really knew you.' I looked at him, waiting for a reaction, but he didn't say anything. He was staring into the fire, so I carried on talking. 'I don't think you did it out of malice,' I said. 'I think you were very, very weak. I think that if we did try to create a proper life together, it would take a few years before we would know if it was working. But if we tried, I would only be doing it because I didn't think I was worth any more. And I'm starting to think that that might not be true.'

'Emma,' he said slowly, 'I can't tell you how impressed I am by you. You look stunning. The house is . . .' He paused, looking at me with a smile. 'Nice. Alice is a well-balanced and lovely little girl, in spite of her crap father. I'm humble before you. I won't leave your side for years, if you like. You'll know where I am the whole time. I will never ever do anything to hurt you, ever again. I'll help you with everything. You're worthy of everything. We'll be real partners.'

'It's tempting,' I told him. I did not try to hide the tears in my eyes. 'It really is. I just don't know, and I'm not going to decide tonight. I'm going to bed.'

He stood up. 'Can I come?' He laughed at his own cheek. 'I don't know what the future holds. But please, Emma, let me sleep next to you, for old time's sake. I've missed you so much.'

I opened my mouth to say no. Then I changed my mind. My evening with Alain had left me feeling deeply attractive, and I still loved Matt. I felt stirrings that had not troubled me for many months. I knew exactly what would happen if I let Matt sleep in my bed.

I stood up, in my stockinged feet, and held out my hand. Why the fuck not?

'Come on then,' I said, smiling at him.

epilogue

October

'It's nearly time,' called Fiona. 'Five minutes. Get yourselves in here, quick.'

I picked up my kir royale and went into the sitting room. Fi was sitting on the sofa with baby Maxime on her breast. He was a hungry baby. She seemed to have spent the four months since the birth sitting in front of a TV, with him clamped to her nipple.

Andy followed me in. 'Oi,' he said. 'Max. Your days are numbered. I'm reclaiming Mummy's boobies one day, OK, mate?'

Fiona spoke in Max's voice. 'All right, Daddy. But I need to be breastfed for six months so you have to wait a bit.'

'I'm counting, little sod.'

Alice adored Max. In her eyes, he fell somewhere between a doll and a pet. She was staying with Coco that night, because I had no idea how the programme would look and there were certain to be many things on it that I did not want her to see. She had become too French, rarely going to bed before nine, and I knew that, had she caught wind of the excitement – had she realised that she and I were on television – she would have been stationed in front of the screen for the duration. I could not have her in the house.

I was desperate to watch it myself. I had had satellite installed especially. At the moment, the adverts were on. *Moving On* was 'next up after the break'. It was eight o'clock in England. Prime time. And this programme was all about me.

I was overwhelmingly relieved to be watching it in my house in France. Geoff had finally succeeded in lending me the money I needed to stay, and I was surprised at how much work I was getting as a private tutor. My finances were precarious – satellite TV was a luxury I could not really afford – but I was managing.

Alain came in and sat next to me. I moved up to let him in, and pulled down my microskirt for decency's sake. Coco had made me buy it. Now that I went running most days, she said I had the legs for it. It was a magnificent garment: red velvet and barely there. Alain adored it.

He draped an arm round my shoulder. 'I hope I will understand enough of this,' he said in English. I frowned. I hoped he wouldn't. I hadn't wanted Alain to see it. After seven months of increasingly intimate dates, I was still getting used to thinking of him as 'my boyfriend'. I preferred talking about him in French, when I could just call him '*mon ami*' which was nice and enigmatic.

Alain and I were happy together. He seemed to adore me. I was comfortable with him, and I trusted him. Gradually, I was beginning to see that we could very well have a bright future together. After Max's birth, Alain had hinted that he would not mind having a fourth child, one day. I was on the brink of asking him to move in with me. The house was too big for just Alice and me. I basked in his whole-hearted appreciation of me.

Sending Hugh away had been the best thing I had done, and I thanked my lucky stars every day that Alain had come along in time to stop me prolonging the pit of mistrust and recrimination that would have been my renewed relationship with Alice's father. I had stopped calling him Matt, now. He had always been Hugh.

I knew that Rosie's camera had captured me at my absolute worst. I was steeling myself to remember those days. I knew I was going to see myself when I was fat, shiny-faced, and desperately, horrendously miserable. Alain had insisted on coming to watch. He was massively excited on my behalf and he had assured me that *of course* he would not be shocked by anything I said or did before I met him. He was terribly proud of me. But he had never seen me badly dressed. He had never seen me raw.

I tried to regulate my breathing. My hands were shaking and I felt sick. I was dreading the next hour, but at the same time I was compelled to watch every second of it. I wanted to know what film Rosie had made about me. I wanted to see my crisis through someone else's eyes. I was agitated and almost tearful. Alain pressed his hand against my shoulder.

'*Ça ira,*' he kept saying, as if to a child. I knew I was stiff beneath his touch and made a conscious effort to relax. I was completely myself with Alain, because I had no appetite at all for being anyone else. I made no pretences, and he seemed to like me all the same.

Andy nodded to me. 'Rosie won't have screwed you over, will she, Ems? Course she won't. She's practically family now.'

The programme began with a shot of me surfing. I was standing up on the board, wobbling slightly, but on my feet and grinning insanely. I came to the shore and almost screamed, 'That is the best thing I've done in my whole life!'

The voiceover, a woman's voice but not Rosie's, intoned, 'Emma Meadows moved to the south of France last year with her partner Matt and their young daughter Alice. Matt commuted to work in London, Alice started at the village school, and Emma set about renovating the house. At first everything went smoothly.'

'It did not,' I said, under my breath.

'In the summer, however, Emma was to discover that something was very, very wrong. She found out that the father of her child was, in fact, married to someone else, and that he had a young son in London. Matt had been leading a double life and Emma faced a momentous decision. This is her story.'

The theme music kicked in, and the words 'Moving on' appeared in a cursive script across the bottom of the screen.

'Fuck,' I said, racking my brains, again, in a further attempt to remember all the time I had spent with Rosie. I had never cared whether her camera had been on or not. The camera had become a piece of furniture. I had seen it as an irrelevance. Now, everyone I knew, and millions of strangers, were sitting down to watch my most intimate moments. 'Can I back out at this point, do you think?'

Fiona smiled beatifically and shook her head. Motherhood suited her. She was dazed and tired, but she seemed extraordinarily contented. Max was sweet-natured and sleepy, which helped. Andy had made her life hell for the last couple of months of the pregnancy, insisting that he was going to have a DNA test performed the moment the baby was born, but as soon as he had seen Max, he changed his mind. He said now that he knew Max was his son, that he did not need science to confirm it for him. I sensed that he did not want to know if he wasn't.

They had featured on *Moving On* the previous week. I had been excited for them, and embarrassed by my own brief appearance in their programme. Rosie had obligingly edited out all but the most cryptic references to the Didier episode, and they had both come across well. Fiona had been enormously relieved.

The programme began with Matt pushing open Andy and Fiona's front door. He stared straight into the camera, and turned and ran away, his arms over his head. He looked ridiculous, and, indeed, everyone except for me laughed as the camera stayed focused on him as he ran past me and Alice, who were crouched down playing with dinosaurs next to a plant. He flung open the wrought-iron gate and ran away. The camera focused on me. I was frowning, staring after him. I was heavier, with my double chin greatly in evidence, but I didn't look as bad as I had expected. I pulled Alice, who looked tiny, close to me, and told her not to worry.

'When we first met Matt, he was slightly camera shy,' smirked the voiceover. 'The reasons soon became clear.'

I shut my eyes and gathered my strength. This was going to be a long hour.

Hugh had not intended to watch it. He had strongly intended not to watch it. All day long, he had worked hard, creating projects where there weren't any, sorting out all of his personal filing, filling in his expenses. Anything to keep his mind occupied. He knew that everyone he knew would be watching this programme. His parents knew about Alice – indeed, they had met her briefly, in the summer, when she had come to stay with him – but he had tried to keep all the details of his behaviour from them. He knew they knew it all already, but he was humiliated beyond belief that it was being televised.

By ten to eight, however, he was home. He stepped into his cramped flat and sighed. The hall needed sweeping. There were bills all over the doormat, and he was about to be exposed as the world's biggest bastard on national television. He phoned for a pizza and tried to stay away from the television. He resolutely surfed the net for the first couple of minutes, then shut down the computer and switched on to Channel Four in time to watch himself running away down the main road in Aurrillon. At the time, they had assured him that they couldn't show his image without permission. Unfortunately he had buggered that up completely by signing a form that that Jim bloke had given him at the pizzeria, when he was trying to get Emma back. He had agreed to be in the film because Emma had wanted him to be in it. Then, with the cameras rolling, she had taken two days to decide to send him packing. He felt thoroughly fucked over.

The phone rang. It was probably Eleanor. Eleanor was twenty-two, blonde, sexy and vacuous. He had no desire to speak to her. She would be annoyed. She would probably give him the elbow. It didn't matter. London's bars were full of Eleanors, Sandys, Katies, and Leannes, to name just four of his recent companions. He pulled the phone line out of the wall. Then he fetched a bottle of Scotch from the corner cupboard, filled a large glass, and shifted his chair round for a better view of the screen.

In Brighton, Anne brought her dinner into the sitting room, and flicked through the television channels idly, searching for something mindless.

'Ooooh,' she said to herself when she found *Moving On*. 'Just the thing.' She loved programmes about people moving abroad. She watched the titles, then stared in disbelief.

'That's Matt,' she said. 'And that's Emma.' She put her fork down and watched the story unfold, open-mouthed. 'But what about the baby?' she muttered to herself, puzzled.

Jo had invited her best friends to watch it with her. She needed other people with her, because she knew that, in company, she would make a supreme effort to appear amused by the whole sorry tale.

'I'm over him,' she explained to them, as they waited for it to start. 'I just don't much fancy watching this on my own.'

'Of course you don't, honey,' said Lara immediately, and hugged her. 'Olly's in bed, yes?' Jo nodded. 'Where's Mike?'

Jo grimaced. 'I told Mike I didn't want him to see it. So I don't know where he is.'

'You do. He's watching it at home.'

'I know.'

Mike was officially Jo's partner. She was taking things extremely slowly this time, but it seemed to be going well. He knew all about Hugh's behaviour, but she still didn't want him to see it in technicolour.

'Jo, this programme's not about you. You know that.'

'Yeah. It's kind of strange that I'm sitting down to watch a documentary about my ex-husband's other partner. But no, I'm hoping this will all be about Emma. I wouldn't touch a thing like that with a bargepole. God knows what she was thinking of. I imagine she just didn't care.'

Her other friend Sheila spoke up. 'You don't mind Emma though, do you?'

'No. I don't mind her. Good luck to her and all that. I hate her. And I really really hope she doesn't tell all the people at home how I turned up and pretended to be lost.'

They settled back, with white wine and crisps and choco-late. The programme was, indeed, all about Emma. She appeared to have had a total breakdown. It was raw. Jo had never seen anything so raw on television, and she wanted to avert her gaze. She was embarrassed to see any woman being exposed in such a manner. She was angry that the television people had taken advantage of Emma's mental state to steal her private moments. Emma's grief looked frighteningly familiar. She was heartily thankful that no camera crew had captured her own worst moments during that first year of separation.

The breakdown, however, was followed by a striking recovery. All the women, including Jo, cheered Emma on. Then, when she was about to leave France, with her fabulous clothes and a nice haircut, Hugh turned up again. The voiceover was sniffy about his reappearance.

Jo was devastated. The bastard ex-husband had gone to France last spring and told Emma that he had realised that he had loved her all along. She bit her knuckles. Sheila touched her arm.

'Bastard,' she said. 'You knew he was a bastard.'

'But look at him,' Jo whispered. 'He means it.'

Lara stroked her arm. 'He's a liar,' she reminded her. 'That's what he does. He lies. He was just scared of being alone.'

'But he never tried that with me. He never came back to me like that.'

'Because he knew you'd tell him to fuck right off. Just like she's about to.'

They held their collective breath, all of them willing Emma to kick Hugh out. Jo tried to work out whether they could have got back together without her knowledge, whether they could be a happy family unit to this day. She was sure Emma would have told her. Emma, unlike Hugh, was decent.

But Emma might have been trying to spare her feelings, or she might have been worried that she would be angry.

It looked for a tantalising few moments as if Emma was going to agree to his request that they give it their best shot for Alice's sake. Jo thought she was going to be sick. When she did the right thing, the room erupted into cheers, and Lara quickly refilled the glasses. They happily toasted Emma's future.

Jo drank an enormous amount of alcohol that night. The next morning Mike proposed, and she accepted him.

As it finished, Pete looked nervously at Jane. She had not reacted at all during the documentary and he had no idea what she was thinking.

'Your brother came out of that well,' Jane said mildly. Pete frowned. He had not seen it that way. 'NOT!' she added loudly, and burst out laughing. 'What a wanker!'

Pete laughed too, relieved. 'Indeed.'

'That film shouldn't have been called *Moving On*. It should have been called *Emma's Revenge*.'

'She's done all right, hasn't she?'

'Yes.' Jane snuggled up to him. 'You know, I used to worry that you were going to rush off to France and leave me so you could declare your eternal love for Emma.'

'I know. That's all behind me.'

She looked him in the eyes. 'Promise?'

He looked at her. Jane had grown on him. Emma had always been a fantasy. For the first time, he felt ready to let her go, to commit himself wholeheartedly to reality.

'Promise,' he said.

When it ended, I had my head in my hands and tears running down my cheeks. Alain pulled me in close, and I allowed myself to cry on his shoulder. I bitterly regretted being in the film. I wished I had kept it all private. It was undignified to parade that sort of experience in front of the public. It was none of their business, but I had allowed it to become their business.

'Fuck,' I said. Alain certainly understood this.

'It was good,' he said. 'You did fabulously. Everyone who sees it will like you. I'm so proud of you. You can't imagine.'

'We're all proud of you, Ems,' said Andy, in a tight voice.

I looked to Fiona for confirmation. She was stroking Max's cheek and avoiding everyone's gaze. There had been far too much about her affair in the film, and I could see she was mortified and scared. 'You were great,' she said, looking at her baby.

I closed my eyes. I desperately wished I could go back and change it.

The phone rang, and the atmosphere lightened. It was Greg. He, Rosie, Bella and Charlotte had watched the programme at Christa and Geoff's house.

'Hey, famous girl,' he said.

'Hey, famous boy,' I replied. 'The camera loves you. And your fiancée makes a damn good movie.'

'Doesn't she just? Hang on, she's snatching the phone.'

'Emma!' said Rosie, intensely. 'Emma, what did you think? If you hated it I'm sure Greg won't marry me.'

'I didn't hate it,' I said. Then I said it again, more forcefully. 'I thought you did a great job,' I added. 'I don't imagine Hugh agrees and that has to be good. How are you feeling?'

'Oh,' she said. 'You know. Fine. Feeling fine. Looking forward to getting away.'

Greg took the phone back. 'Good surfing,' he said.

'Cheers. I'm much better than that now. Alain looks after

Alice while I practise. His kids think it's great that I can surf. They think I'm cool. You two off tomorrow?'

'Tomorrow afternoon. Gatwick-Madrid. Madrid-Havana. Can't wait. I think a bit of sun will do Rosie a power of good, too. Hey, and you really were great. We were all yelling you on.'

'Don't tell Rosie, but I hated it.'

'My lips are sealed.'

He passed the phone round. I spoke to Bella, and Charlotte, and Christa. Then Geoff came on.

'Hello, Emma,' he said. Geoff had opened up enormously. He was a different person from the uptight uncle who must have been perpetually tormented by guilt. 'Emma, I'm extremely proud of you,' he said. 'Well done. Sarah would be thrilled with you. And I want to stop strangers on the street and tell them I'm your father. In fact I might go out there right now.'

'Don't,' I told him. 'The streets are full of dog shit. But thanks.' I thought about it. I tried out a name I had never called him before. 'Thank you, Dad,' I said.

EMILY BARR

Baggage

Bestselling, award-winning author of *Backpack* and *Atlantic Shift* – 'believable characters that are variously biting, insightful and sympathetic' *The Times*

At twenty-nine, you're backpacking in the Australian outback when you see her. She has a husband. She has a ten-year-old son. She has a baby on the way.

She claims to be someone else. But you'd recognise her anywhere.

Back in England you tell your journalist boyfriend. While he never knew her, he always knew of her – her name is Daisy Fraser and she was awaiting trial over the death of four people when she jumped off the Severn Bridge.

He says: Happy Christmas – I'm taking you to Australia to find Daisy.

He thinks: This could be the scoop of the century.

Praise for *Baggage*

'It's impossible to dislike Barr's chatty, infectious prose style. The plot is compelling and the book is invested with a strong sense of place' *List*

'Mixing girly infighting with insightful travellers' observations and the joys of motherhood, Barr certainly knows how to spin a yarn' *Guardian*

'Barr has a great premise and an engaging cast' *Publishers Weekly*

0 7472 6677 8

review

You can buy any of these other **Headline Review** titles from your bookshop or *direct from the publisher.*

FREE P&P AND UK DELIVERY
(Overseas and Ireland £3.50 per book)

Atlantic Shift	Emily Barr	£7.99
Cuban Heels	Emily Barr	£7.99
Baggage	Emily Barr	£7.99
Backpack	Emily Barr	£7.99
The Wedding Day	Catherine Alliott	£6.99
A Married Man	Catherine Alliott	£6.99
Secrets of a Family Album	Isla Dewar	£6.99
Dancing in a Distant Place	Isla Dewar	£7.99
Sleeping Around	Julie Highmore	£6.99
Play It Again	Julie Highmore	£6.99
The Wives of Bath	Wendy Holden	£6.99
Azur Like It	Wendy Holden	£6.99
The Distance Between Us	Maggie O'Farrell	£7.99
My Lover's Lover	Maggie O'Farrell	£7.99

TO ORDER SIMPLY CALL THIS NUMBER

01235 400 414

or visit our website: www.madaboutbooks.com

Prices and availability subject to change without notice.